Undeniably Yours

Undeniably Yours

a novel

BECKY WADE

BETHANYHOUSE
a division of Baker Publishing Group
Minneapolis, Minnesota

Published by Bethany House Publishers
11400 Hampshire Avenue South
Bloomington, Minnesota 55438
www.bethanyhouse.com

Bethany House Publishers is a division of
Baker Publishing Group, Grand Rapids, Michigan

Printed in the United States of America

Library of Congress Cataloging-in-Publication Data is on file at the Library of Congress, Washington, DC.

ISBN 978-0-7642-0975-8 (pbk.)

Scripture taken from the HOLY BIBLE, NEW INTERNATIONAL VERSION®. Copyright © 1973, 1978, 1984 Biblica. Used by permission of Zondervan. All rights reserved.

This is a work of fiction. Names, characters, incidents, and dialogues are products of the author's imagination and are not to be construed as real. Any resemblance to actual events or persons, living or dead, is entirely coincidental.

The internet addresses, email addresses, and phone numbers in this book are accurate at the time of publication. They are provided as a resource. Baker Publishing Group does not endorse them or vouch for their content or permanence.

Cover design by Jennifer Parker

Cover photography by Mike Habermann Photography, LLC

13 14 15 16 17 18 19   7 6 5 4 3 2 1

For Jim and Terry

*You are two of the most compassionate,
hard working, and generous people I know.
I'm blessed to have married into your family.*

*Thank you for everything,
especially for being Granny and Grandad
to three kids who love you dearly.*

Chapter One

She was too softhearted to be an oil tycoon.

Meg had always known it, but she'd never worried about it much because while her father was lousy at being a father, he'd always been very, very good at being rich.

William Cole had shouldered the responsibilities of the family company for twenty years, and if the pressures and stresses of his position had ever been difficult for him to handle, he hadn't shown it. He was an old-school oilman who sometimes wore Stetsons with his suits and could be ruthless, arrogant, or demanding if the situation called for it.

William Cole was also, unfortunately, dead.

Which was why Meg herself was about to have to fire this Mr.—she consulted the file sitting on the surface of the desk—Mr. Porter. He'd be arriving here at her father's home office at Whispering Creek any second for their scheduled meeting. At which time she'd have to look him in the face, turn his world upside down, and crush his dreams.

A deep sense of panic rose within her. It swirled and clawed, causing her chest to tighten.

In an effort to counter it, Meg jerked her worn sudoku book from the desk drawer. Almost desperately, she ran her gaze over the columns of numbers, trying to concentrate, praying the puzzle would help her settle her mind.

She'd spent the last two weeks holed up at the Ritz with Cole Oil advisors, undergoing a crash course on the family holdings. Among many other things, they'd counseled her on Whispering Creek Ranch—a huge plot of land situated thirty miles northeast of Dallas, near J. R. Ewing's beloved Southfork. Whispering Creek included their family home and her father's horse farm.

The advisors had unanimously urged her to release the Whispering Creek employees who'd fit into her father's life-style but couldn't possibly fit into her own. Thus, she'd already terminated three people on this Monday morning, her first official day in her new capacity as her father's successor.

She'd fired her father's driver (she didn't want a chauffer), the man who had kept his kennel of hunting dogs (she'd didn't hunt), and the man who had managed his weapons and shooting range (she definitely didn't do guns).

Next on the guillotine list? Mr. Porter, who ran her father's Thoroughbred horse farm. While all of her father's hobbies had been costly, none were nearly as expensive as the Thoroughbreds and none further from her own interests.

Even so, she didn't want to deliver this sad news to Mr. Porter or take away the jobs of the people who worked for him. More than that, she didn't want to face *any* of this. She didn't want to be in this predicament at all, smothering under the weight of overwhelming responsibilities.

She'd faced some hard knocks in life—one really hard one five years ago—and had managed to cultivate a protective shell for herself. But like a Godiva truffle, she was only hard in a thin outer layer. Her insides were still as tender as ever.

Her disobedient heartbeat started thumping like a bass drum as her stomach burned and knotted. Meg popped open her container of antacids, chewed two, and tried to think harder about sudoku.

Dratted anxiousness. Years ago she'd gone twelve rounds with it and bested it. But three months ago, when she'd heard the dreadful news about her father, it had come rushing back for a grudge match. She'd been trying to white-knuckle it through the grief, the shock, the difficulty sleeping, and the stress. She'd been hoping like crazy to escape any full-fledged panic attacks.

But at the moment, it felt like a *very* full-fledged panic attack was chasing her, gaining, right on her heels. If it caught her, it would mean a trip to the ER on this, her first day back at Whispering Creek. The thought sent her anxiety rising, fast and jagged. *No no no no no.*

Meg gave up on sudoku, gripped the armrests of the leather chair, and screwed her eyes shut. She should breathe. Wasn't her doctor always touting the calming benefits of deep breathing? Something about breathe in for a count of six, hold for six, breathe out for a count of seven?

She worked to follow his instructions but soon simply stuck her head between her knees to keep herself from hyperventilating. *God, come*, she pleaded. *Help me.* Where could she find a paper bag?

A knock sounded on the office door.

Meg reared upright, her gaze jerking to the platinum-edged clock on the edge of her father's desk. Mr. Porter had arrived right on time. "J-just a moment, please."

She stashed her antacids and sudoku, then pushed to her feet and paced once around the perimeter of the office, shaking out her wrists and trying to determine whether she could hold herself together well enough to meet with Mr. Porter or whether she'd be needing a straitjacket.

With trembling fingers, she smoothed her black Fendi suit. "Come in."

The man who let himself into the office was young. Maybe thirty? Thirty-three? Much younger than she'd expected. Tall and powerfully built, with dark hair shaved close to his skull. Such short hair would have made an average-looking man look worse. But he was handsome, she realized, as their eyes met. The close-cropped hair suited his rugged features.

"Bo Porter," he said.

She introduced herself, shook his hand, and took her seat. He lowered into one of the two chocolate-colored leather chairs that faced her father's desk. In his jeans, beige henley-style shirt, and weathered boots, he looked every inch like a man who made his living working with horses.

"My father . . ." She cleared her throat.

"I'm sorry for your loss."

"Thank you." Her stomach clenched horribly. "My father loved the Thoroughbred horse farm that the two of you built here together. If he'd lived, I'm sure that he'd have continued working with you toward your goals for the farm for years to come."

He regarded her with an even expression, just a hint of tension around the mouth. Slowly, he nodded.

"But as it is, it falls to me now to decide what to do with Whispering Creek Horses. I regret to inform you that I've decided to close down the farm."

He frowned, concern clouding his eyes.

"I'm sorry."

Silence stretched between them, heavy with the weight of the disappointment she knew he must be feeling.

"May I ask why you've decided to close it down?"

Meg shifted a little. "My father loved horses and horse racing, but I do not. There's no logical reason for me to continue supporting the farm financially now that my father's gone."

"We're very close to breaking even," he said calmly, his words accented with the mellow north Texas accent she'd grown up hearing. "Once we do, you'll begin to earn a profit."

She flipped open the file before her and consulted the column that listed the horse farm's net earnings and losses since it had begun, four years prior. "Yes, I'd noticed that."

"It cost us a lot to get the farm started. Your father and I decided to pay down all those expenses in these early years. That's why we're not in the black already."

"Be that as it may, my decision stands." Suffocating in remorse and trying hard not to show it, Meg extracted a professional-looking report from a desk drawer and handed it over. "This is the severance package we're offering you. I hope you'll find it adequate."

She knew the package reached far beyond adequate. She'd insisted on triple the amount of money recommended by her father's advisors so this gentleman, and all of the other terminated employees, would have plenty of time to find new jobs. She'd even guaranteed anyone unable to find work a position at the downtown headquarters of Cole Oil.

The three men she'd met with prior to Mr. Porter had all accepted the bad news with disappointment mixed through with good manners. In every case, the severance package had softened the blow. But Mr. Porter didn't even open the report. "Ma'am, more than twenty people work for me at the farm."

"I'm offering severance packages to each of them, depending on their position and how long they've been working at the

11

farm. You'll find all of that information in the report. I can . . .
go over it with you if you'd like."

He let her offer slide, watching her, his expression troubled.
"We have ninety horses."

"I'd like to sell the horses as quickly as possible. I'm not interested in making a profit on them, so much as I'm interested
in speed. Perhaps an auction?"

He stared at her with light gray eyes, rimmed with darker gray.

"I give you," she said, "my . . . ah, permission . . . to go ahead
and take whatever steps necessary to sell the horses. You can
keep as many staff members as you'll need to complete the
task. And I'll send over someone from Cole Oil to oversee the
process and help you with accounting or any other financial
service you may need."

"We've already made plans for the next several months. We
have commitments."

"I have attorneys who can help with the contractual side of
your obligations." She'd rehearsed most of these lines last night
and practiced them today on the three previous victims. Still,
that she sounded like a somewhat intelligent business person
astounded her. Five minutes ago, she'd had her head between
her knees.

Meg laid her palms on the glossy desktop. "Well. I believe
that's all then."

"It's a good farm," he said. "We've all worked hard for its
success, and I'd hate to see it shut down."

His honest, plainspoken words twisted her heart, but Meg
knew if she let herself fold in any way, she'd cave. "I'm sure
that's true, Mr. Porter. I'm sorry that my father's passing has
led to this, I truly am." After a beat, she pushed to her feet.
"Thank you."

She offered her hand. He shook it, hesitated, then turned and left.

Once the door shut behind him, she sank back into her father's chair, her muscles quivering.

The cool air of the office and the almost inaudible whir of the electronic equipment in the space slid around her. Bookshelves lined three sides of the room. A wildly expensive Remington statue of a bronze cowboy riding a bucking bronco stood on a stand in front of one of the windows. Her father's desk sat before her in the center of it all, a birchwood monument that practically shouted, "SIZE MATTERS!" with a megaphone.

This room, just like every other room in the house, had been done up by someone who'd graduated with honors from the "Opulent Texas Lodge" school of design. Everything in the place was either costly, a shade of brown, or lifted off a dead animal. She didn't like the big house. She'd grown up here. But she'd *never* liked it. This was her father's house, and her father should be the one sitting in this chair.

Meg had always expected him to face death across a negotiating table and haggle out a favorable bargain for himself. Instead, he'd died on the floor of his penthouse office in downtown Dallas in early January, three months ago. Catastrophic heart attack at just sixty years of age.

In that one moment Meg had inherited his controlling share in Cole Oil, his diverse and far-flung investments, hundreds of employees, three properties, six luxury cars, and a plane. She, his only child. She, who'd insisted on living on her own meager salary for the last five years and had found contentment in the simplicity and independence and accomplishment of it. She, whose knowledge of high finance consisted of her checking account at Bank of America. She, who was nothing like her father.

The office door swung open, and Bo Porter strode back in. She jerked upright.

He stopped about three feet in front of the desk, facing her squarely. "Ma'am."

She stared at him with round eyes. "Yes?"

"I'm sorry, but no."

"No?"

"No, I'm not going to close down the farm. I'm not going to sell the horses." She didn't hear any anger or threat in his tone, only an abundance—oceans—of implacable resolve.

Meg's thoughts all dashed in different directions and then vanished. She feared her jaw had locked into place. Um . . .

"I know I don't have the right to make that decision, but I want to try to persuade you to give me that right. I want a say in what happens to the farm." He held his body still and under perfect control, but his gray eyes blazed with intensity. "I've earned it."

Her courage began to unfurl in a long strip, like an ace bandage held out a car window. "Would you care to have a seat?"

"No, thank you. I'll stand."

She released a long breath, measuring the determined cowboy in front of her, longing for her old job as assistant-to-the-assistant-of-the-curator at the museum in Tulsa. "I'm sure you've worked very hard," she said carefully, "and I'm sure that you *have* earned better than this situation. But the attorneys have assured me that the only one with a say about the future of Whispering Creek Horses . . . is me."

"Then change your mind."

Her brows lifted.

"It's a matter of pride. I can't let you inherit a debt from the farm."

"If that's what you're worried about, I can assure you that the horse farm's debts don't concern me."

"I know you don't need the money. But that farm is *my* business. And my business is going to pay for itself."

"The auction . . ."

"No, ma'am. Even that won't be enough to make back what we've spent. I need time."

Meg caught herself spinning the back of her earring with her fingers, something she did when nervous. She dropped her hand and walked to one of the floor-to-ceiling windows, taking in the second-story view of the front yard and the drive, lined with mesquite trees, that led away from the house. Beyond, acres of rolling Texas land stretched toward the horizon, the tips of the trees feathery against the blue of the sky.

Horses? Not her thing. She didn't want a horse farm on her property; all those animals, all those strangers coming and going. She had no interest in this particular passion of her father's and no need of the money it might one day generate. The advisors had all counseled her to dump it. Meg couldn't reverse her decision now just because an honest, good-looking cowboy had asked it of her.

Except that her hard outer shell, already thin, was melting fast. Her gentle heart wanted to help him. "How much time?"

"Six months."

She chewed the inside of her cheek. Six months was a long time, but not unbearably long in the scheme of things.

"That'll give me enough time to break even," he said.

"What if you break even before then?"

"I still get six months to wrap things up."

"What if you still haven't broken even in six months?"

"Then the farm stays open until I do."

"No. That'll just give you an incentive to lose money."

"Ma'am." He waited until she looked at him. "I've never done anything in my life with the goal of failing."

Quiet crackled through the room. Bo Porter stood at his full height, impressive, radiating purpose.

The decision hung in the balance in her mind, both sides evenly weighted. Meg measured him, trying to think, to be tough and impartial, to decide—

"Please," he said.

And with that single word, the scales tipped with a ringing clatter in his direction. She nodded. "I'll give you six months, but that's it. Regardless of whether you have or haven't made back the cost of the farm by then."

"Thank you."

"You're welcome." She'd honored his request, but they both knew she'd presented him with a stay of execution, not a pardon.

He made his way to the door, pausing on the threshold. "There's one more thing."

"Yes?"

"I'd like for you to come out and visit the farm."

"It's not necessary."

"To check on your investment?"

Meg regarded him with skepticism. He must know she had employees far better qualified for that.

"Then come so that you can see what your father built," he amended. "I'd like the chance to show it to you."

Still, she hesitated.

"Sometime this week?" he asked.

"If you'd like."

"You'll let me know when you're coming?"

"Sure."

"Thank you again." He dipped his chin and left.

Meg called herself every synonym she knew of for *cream puff*. She no longer had a driver, a kennel of hunting dogs, or an employee who specialized in guns. But she *did* still have a Thoroughbred racehorse farm, of all things. She released a gasp of a laugh. She hated horses!

A moment later one of the women who cleaned the house stuck her head into the office. "Ms. Cole?" She held aloft the severance package Meg had given Mr. Porter. "Did you want me to dispose of this? I found it in the hallway trash can."

"No, I'd better keep it." She sighed. "I'm going to need it again in six months."

Chapter Two

After his meeting with Megan Cole, Bo drove away
from the mansion and along Whispering Creek's
paved back roads. When the horse farm came into
view, he pulled his truck to the shoulder and sat motionless, his
hands gripping the steering wheel, his attention traveling over
the buildings and land.

A redbrick barn, one of the farm's five. A few cars. White
fences that followed the land. A groom hand-walking a yearling. Texas prairie covered in places with pink wildflowers and
bluebonnets. Trees.

The scene as a whole was simple. Plain. There was nothing
about it that should have made him love it as much as he did.
But he *did* love the farm.

Kids he'd grown up with had been into cars or rodeos or
sports. It had always been Thoroughbreds for him. He'd started
studying them at the age of ten. Back then he'd watched every
race he'd been able to find on TV, subscribed to magazines, pored
over library books, and just about memorized the studbook and
auction catalogues.

In the years between then and now, many things had changed.

He'd grown up. Served overseas. Lived in various places. But Bo's passion for horses had never wavered.

As farm manager at Whispering Creek, he got paid well. But the reward—the reason why he put in twelve-hour days, woke at the crack of dawn, and thought about horses 24/7—was the work itself.

This job was his dream job. This ranch his dream ranch. As good as it would ever get for him.

His memory ran back over all the hours, effort, and sweat that had gone into building this place. He thought of the horses, each one carefully handpicked. He thought of the people who worked here. He knew them all well, and he understood just how much they relied on the farm for their income and how much pride they took in their work here.

Megan Cole had given him the worst possible news just now when she'd told him she planned to shut it all down. Ever since William Cole had died, he'd worried this would happen, but he'd hoped . . . he'd been hoping with everything in him that William Cole's daughter would decide to keep the horse farm running.

Scowling, he drove to the hay barn located at the back of the ranch's property, near the place where they stored equipment. He turned up the truck's radio so that he'd be able to hear the music within the barn. George Strait's "Troubadour" filled the air.

Bo pulled on his work gloves as he walked into the barn. He cut a glance across the space, then got busy stacking hay bales. Did the bales need to be reorganized? No. Was the boss expected to stack hay? No. But he needed to get his thoughts in order before telling his employees the bad news. When upset, he'd never been able to sit still—he'd always been driven to do something physical. He blew out his breath and heaved a bale up to shoulder height, then set it on top of a pile on his right.

He'd expected to dislike Megan Cole. He'd even kind of worked himself up for it, in the event that she told him she wanted to close down his farm. Dislike would have been the rational response, so it surprised him that his own reaction had been so different.

In the past, when he'd heard people gossiping about her, he'd pictured her as a Paris Hilton type of person. She did look rich. That, she did. She must have spent two hours getting ready this morning. Her makeup could have come straight out of a magazine ad. She'd put up her long blond hair in a twisted style that reminded him of bridesmaids. Her black suit probably cost more than a normal person's monthly salary. She'd worn earrings made out of yellow gems surrounded by diamonds. And she'd had on a pair of little black glasses.

The whole effect had reminded him of a hot teacher out of an '80s rock video. Blond hair, curvy build, ultra feminine—exactly his type. When he'd walked into the office to meet her, the whole room had smelled like her, like roses.

Bo paused, his breath coming hard with exertion. As much as Megan Cole had looked the part, though, there had been something about her that had struck him as strange for a rich girl, something he'd sensed more than seen. Over a lifetime of working with horses, he'd come to trust his senses.

Beneath her appearance he'd recognized a . . . What should he even call it? An uncertainty in her. A vulnerability.

Which was bad news for him, because he'd always been a sucker for vulnerability. Megan Cole had pretty features. Not gorgeous. Pretty. But that hidden vulnerability of hers—combined with the kindness in her eyes—had fascinated him more than beauty would have. Worse, it had made him want to protect her.

Which was laughable. *She* was the one with all the money and power. *She* was the one firing him from his job. And yet he'd stood there in the mansion's office, fighting the urge to help and comfort *her*.

He wondered what her life had been like, growing up in the mansion with no mother and a father like William Cole. Had her childhood made her fragile? Or had something else happened to her?

He wiped sweat from his forehead with his wrist.

She'd given him six months and the opportunity to pay back her father's investment in the farm. It was a start, but it was also the minimum he could live with. What he wanted? To keep the farm running for good. He was going to have to do his all-out, absolute best to change her mind.

He'd asked her to visit the ranch because he had a small hope that she might soften if she could see the place for herself, meet the staff, and spend time with the horses. Over the next few months he could take her out on rides, escort her to the owner's box at the track for races, tell her stories about the history of racing, explain to her why her father had liked it so much, show her the farm's earning projections over the next decade.

If he couldn't change her mind, he couldn't.

But for the sake of the people who worked at the farm, and for his own sake, he had to try.

Whispering Creek's housekeeper might wear Birkenstocks, but she had the brain of a CEO and the work ethic of an Olympic triathlete. Meg found Lynn in the cavernous kitchen of the big house preparing a lunch of egg salad sandwiches, baby carrots, chips, and fruit salad.

"Mind if I join you?" Meg asked.

"'Course not." Lynn had on her standard uniform of leggings and an oversized T-shirt. Today's tee had a picture of a fading desert sunset, a howling coyote, and the words *Santa Fe* scrawled across the front.

Meg washed her hands, toed off her black high heels, and went to work slicing watermelon. Early April sunshine fell through the windows and illuminated her hands, the tan granite countertop, top-of-the-line stainless steel appliances, and the mahogany cabinetry. The beauty of it all should have calmed her. Instead, her surroundings only reminded her of how peaceful she *ought* to feel, how peaceful everyone else around her seemed to feel. They: normal. She: not.

After meeting with Bo Porter, she'd spent the remainder of the morning trying to reply to the numerous calls and emails she'd received from people at Cole Oil asking her for direction. Challenging work, since she didn't know how to answer a single one of their questions. She sighed and moved on to cantaloupe.

"Rough morning?" Lynn asked.

"Yeah. You?"

"No, hon." She gave a mellow smile. "It's just been the usual." Lynn dropped a handful of chopped pickle into the mixing bowl that held the egg salad, then went to work seasoning it. "So what's going on? I only got to talk to you for a second this morning."

"I know, I'm sorry." Meg had arrived at Whispering Creek late last night and greeted Lynn in a rush this morning before her first appointment. She set down her knife and propped her hip against the edge of the countertop. "What's happening is that Uncle Michael came to Tulsa two weeks ago."

"Huh."

"And he demanded that I come home. He feels strongly that Cole Oil needs me."

Lynn sampled the egg salad with a fresh spoon. "Well, after your father's funeral you were able to return to Tulsa and go on with your regular life longer than I expected."

"I was hoping I could go on with my regular life forever."

"Bad case of denial?"

"I guess so."

Lynn regarded her with sympathy. "You must have known you'd have to come back."

"I did, I just . . . I honestly hoped it wouldn't be so soon. I quit taking Uncle Michael's calls, thinking that might buy me more time."

"Voice mail has never stopped Michael Cole."

"No. He was pretty hard to ignore once he showed up on my doorstep in the flesh."

"I'll bet he was."

"Since he brought me back to Dallas, he's had me at the Ritz with a team of men who've been trying their best to teach me the family business." She released a wobbly laugh. "I was an art history major, for goodness' sake!"

Lynn tilted her head. Her short Julie-Andrews-in-the-*Sound-of-Music* hairstyle framed a rectangular, fifty-ish face without a wisp of makeup. "My advice?"

"Yes, please."

"Fake it until you know what you're doing."

"I've been trying, but I'm a bad faker."

"A bad faker is better than a sissy. You're the majority share-holder of the company now, so you'll have to do." Lynn scooped egg salad onto slices of brown bread. "I heard you've been busy firing people this morning."

"Yes, and I don't recommend it. You do know, of course, that you and your staff and Mr. Son will always have jobs here."

"I never worried about it for a minute."

She told Lynn about the first three gentlemen she'd met with. "Then I tried to fire Mr. Porter, but he sort of refused to be fired. We agreed that he could keep the farm running for another six months."

"I'm glad. I like Bo, and I like his brother Jake. I like a lot of the people who work out at the horse farm, actually."

Together, they set the kitchen table, which stood in a nook ringed with windows. For as long as Meg could remember, lunch had been served seven days a week at noon sharp for the employees of the big house.

Just as they were finishing, Mr. Son entered, wearing his usual mechanic's jumpsuit and slip-on canvas shoes. He and Lynn were around the same age and had both been working at Whispering Creek for more than twenty years. As their landscaper, every tree, shrub, blade of grass, and flower came under Mr. Son's meticulous care. "Meg."

She'd known him most of her life, and so she knew better than to try to hug him. She smiled and shook his hand. "Mr. Son."

His Korean features firmed into stern lines. "You been firing people today?"

"I was just telling Lynn that her job—and yours—will be here for you as long as you want them."

"You going to sell the house?"

"No."

"Then why *would* you fire me?" His words turned heated. "You need someone to care for the grounds."

"Exactly."

He grunted angrily and moved toward the table.

Two of the women who worked for Lynn cleaning the house drifted in, welcomed Meg home, and made their way to the table.

"Sadie Jo's coming, right, Lynn?" Meg asked.

"I'm here!" Sadie Jo called from the hallway.

Meg rushed to her and fell into her embrace. They hugged for a minute straight. Relief and comfort caught in Meg's chest, causing tears to brim in her eyes.

Meg's mother had hired Sadie Jo Greene as her nanny shortly after Meg's birth. It turned out that Sadie Jo would become the best gift Patricia Cole would ever have the chance to give her daughter, because a blood disease had taken her life just two years later. If Sadie Jo hadn't been there every day of every year to raise and love her, Meg would have been consigned to a life of utter loneliness. There's no telling what would have become of her. She didn't even like to think about it.

Twenty-eight years had passed since Sadie Jo had started working for their family, and in that time Sadie Jo had turned into a plump eighty-year-old who resembled nothing so much as one of Sleeping Beauty's good fairies.

"It's so nice to have you home," Sadie Jo whispered. "I've been waiting and waiting for you to move back. Oh, Meg." She cupped her cheek. "I love you so."

"I love you, too. It's wonderful to see you. You doing okay?"

"Very well. My, you look beautiful in that suit." She scanned her from head to toe. "Where are your shoes?"

"In the kitchen."

"Aren't your feet cold?"

"Nope, perfectly fine."

"Come." Sadie Jo took hold of Meg's hand with her knobby one and led her to the kitchen table, where the others were already passing the food. Once everyone had been served, Sadie Jo spoke a blessing over them, then talk and easy companionship circled the table.

Meg stilled, struck by her love for Sadie Jo, Lynn, and Mr. Son. She didn't know the other two women well at all, but in this moment—why not?—she loved them, too. She might not have a mother, a father, a sibling, a husband, or a boyfriend, but she did have these people. At this precipice-like point in her life, they were blessedly familiar. They were hers.

"Eat something, dear," Sadie Jo coaxed. "You must be hungry." Since toddlerhood, there'd been nothing Sadie Jo liked better than to see Meg stuff herself.

"Have you decided which bedroom you'll be moving into?" Lynn asked her. "There's the master suite."

"No thanks." Meg couldn't even contemplate moving into her father's room.

"Your old room, then?"

She'd stayed there last night, but she had no desire to move into it again permanently. It was full of kid memories. "I don't think so."

"There are a total of ten bedrooms to choose from," Mr. Son pointed out.

"Actually, I've decided that I'm going to use the guesthouse while I'm here."

Every face at the table regarded her with arrested surprise.

All self-respecting tycoons had free-standing guesthouses adjacent to their mansions. A person could reach the guesthouse at Whispering Creek via a short walk from the big house across the garden and along the length of the pool. "I'm going to have the furniture that's in there now moved out and my own furniture moved in."

They all continued to stare at her.

Welcome to the Reign of Meg, she thought. *All of you know good and well that I'm an oddball of an heiress.* "Would that be all right, Lynn?"

"You can do anything you'd like, hon," Lynn answered. "You own the place."

Two days later Bo was walking along the central first floor hallway of the mansion when Megan Cole rounded a corner ahead of him, bringing them face to face.

After thinking of little but her and his farm, his farm and her since their first meeting, the reality of seeing her again came as a shock. All his senses sharpened in a rush.

"Hello." She looked slightly confused.

"Hi."

"Is there something I can do for you?" she asked. "Something you need?"

He realized that she didn't know what he was doing in her house. "No, I . . . my office is just over there. I stopped in to do some paper work, and now I'm on my way to the farm."

"Oh, I didn't realize you had an office in the house."

"Right next to Lynn's and Mr. Son's."

"I see."

The little black glasses had disappeared, but she'd dressed in another expensive-looking suit and still smelled like roses. Even in high heels, she stood a good five inches shorter than him. *Man,* she was pretty. He hadn't forgotten, but as he looked into her light brown eyes, the power of it hit him afresh. "Do you have time to come out and visit the horse farm today, ma'am?"

"You can call me Meg."

"Thanks. You can call me Bo."

"All right."

He watched her closely.

"I'm afraid I can't make it out to the farm today." He could tell by her face that she regretted that she'd agreed to visit at all. "I'm headed to the office downtown. Maybe—sorry, I'm just trying to remember my schedule—maybe Friday?"

"Sure. What time?"

"Late afternoon? 4:30?"

"That'd be good."

"I'll have someone call you if I have to reschedule."

"Okay."

They said their good-byes, and she moved past him. He forbid himself to glance back.

For the entire rest of the day, hour after hour, he could not get her out of his mind. It was a reaction way out of proportion, and one that concerned him. He liked most people and usually felt the same level of lazy interest in everyone who came across his path, even the nice-looking ones.

But her.

Her. Something about her had taken hold of something inside him. And try as he might, he couldn't shake it loose.

It was only Thursday of Meg's first week at Cole Oil, and she already wanted to fling herself out a window.

She'd woken this morning to formless, inexplicable fear. It had been percolating inside her all day, constricting her lungs with an imaginary iron belt that kept notching tighter, tighter, tighter. *Go away, stress,* she thought frantically. *Please. Let me breathe, eat something, relax, sleep. Function.*

"You're doing fine, Meg." Her uncle regarded her from behind his desk. He'd just spent thirty minutes explaining an oil and gas exploration deal that Cole Oil was in the middle of negotiating.

"I'm trying."

Uncle Michael, her father's younger brother, strongly resembled her father. He had a head full of impeccably cut gray hair, a lean build, a closet filled with dark gray power suits, and a squirm-inducing stare. Meg had read articles by reporters who'd used words like *powerful*, *brutally smart*, and *distinguished* to describe the Cole brothers. All accurate.

"I know it's difficult for you to take all this on." His eyes missed little. "I'd spare you from it if I could."

"I know."

"But we're all bound by the way Cole Oil is structured. We all have our roles. I've had more practice at mine than you have, that's all."

She nodded.

His cell phone vibrated, and he glanced at it. "Excuse me for a second?"

"Sure."

He went to work typing a text message. Behind him, through a long bank of windows, the skyscrapers of downtown Dallas shimmered in the afternoon light.

When her great-great-grandfather, Jedediah Cole, had been thirty-five years old, he'd struck oil in East Texas. Endless barrels of black gold, untold riches, and ceaseless hard work had flowed from that original lucky hit.

Jedediah had been determined that his legacy, the Cole Oil empire, would withstand the test of time. He'd not wanted the decision-making power that would drive Cole Oil forward to be fractured more and more with every subsequent generation as one man's shares were passed down and split among that man's children. So he'd decreed that 51 percent of his company would always be passed down intact to the oldest child. The one who held that 51 percent also served as chairman of the board and president. The other 49 percent of the company belonged to the remaining shareholders, who were still to this day Cole family members.

Since every previous generation of Cole men from Jedediah on down had had oil-loving oldest sons, the responsibilities had passed along in happy fashion.

Until now.

Thankfully, they weren't about to appoint her as either chairman of the board or president. But her uncle and her other relatives certainly *did* expect her to spend the next twenty or thirty years working to earn the right to attain those positions.

Meg caught herself nervously twirling her earring back and returned her hand to her lap. She glanced at her uncle's profile. Clicking sounds filled the silence as he continued to tap out letters on his phone.

Michael had followed a parallel path to her father's. Both had gone to the University of Texas, both had been trained up in the ways of the company, both understood the innermost cogs of the oil business. They'd spent their lives working in this towering building side by side. But because Michael had been born second, he and his two sons had always known that while they would be important men, indescribably wealthy, well respected—they would never inherit the controlling share of Cole Oil.

That fact had always blanketed Meg with guilt, more so since Michael had brought her here to Dallas. She could believe that he'd made his peace with her father as the head of Cole Oil. But she knew it must be difficult for him to have to accept her—a woman far his junior in years, knowledge, and experience—as the company's majority shareholder.

What a joke! She didn't even accept herself as the majority shareholder. She'd done nothing to earn that kind of power.

Her uncle set aside his phone and returned his attention to her.

"I want you to know," she said, "that I'd give all this to you if I were able."

"Not going to happen. You're my only brother's only child, Meg." Determination marked his tone and expression. "I'll help you. I'm going to look out for you and your best interests, no matter what."

She didn't have anything to say to that. In the whole of her life, she'd never had anything to say in the face of her uncle's will.

"It's quite a birthright. You'll see that soon enough. I only wish you'd come to work with us years ago, so that this process could have gone more smoothly."

"My father and I had a deal." That she'd had to fight very hard for. "He agreed that for the first ten years after college I could choose my own career—"

"And when those ten years were up, then you'd come to work here."

"Yes." She'd always suffered from a lack of interest in Cole Oil, a sense that she was meant for something more and different, and a longing to live her own life. Meg could see now that she'd been impractical and selfish to bargain with her father for the right to follow her heart. Following her heart had only ever led her down steep and icy pathways that she bitterly regretted later. "The . . . the ten years still aren't up."

"The deal no longer stands, Meg. He died, and because he died, we need you here now."

"I know."

He flicked his fingers. "I never liked that deal." She could see a twinge of condemnation in his eyes.

31

The iron around her chest drew tighter, and her pulse picked up speed. She needed to escape. Quickly, she made her excuses and let herself out, her uncle's attention pursuing her.

As she approached her father's office, her two executive assistants rose to their feet. They watched her with the intensity of well-trained dogs waiting for a treat, clearly hungry for her to give them something to do. They were extremely qualified, organized, and fabulous in every way.

Meg was having difficulty liking them.

"I need some time alone," she murmured, then slipped inside before they could begin firing questions.

Within her father's office, Panic—capital *P*—swooped down and seized her from head to toe. She released the buttons on the front of her suit jacket and kicked off her shoes. She went to the desk, rummaging through it with shaking hands in search of her sudoku.

She couldn't do this. How did they, any of them, think that in her inexperience and ignorance she could do her father's job? She didn't deserve the money she'd inherited or the position here. She'd been born, as simple as that. And her birth had sealed her fate. Her heartbeat thundered. *I don't know what I'm doing. I can't pretend—*

Quit it, Meg! Think about something else before you lose it.

She shuffled to her current puzzle and forced herself to sit quietly and concentrate. "God, come. Help me. Please, come."

For long minutes, she tried very hard to do nothing but take deep breaths and think about numbers and squares. It helped a little, but not enough. Her breathing grew shallow, and she started to feel like she couldn't get enough air. Pins and needles pricked the ends of her fingers, and her whole body began to quake as if she had chills.

Stubbornly, she wrestled against the anxiety. She kept working the puzzle and making her muscles soften until eventually, her symptoms began to relax their grip on her.

As soon as she'd reached a rudimentary level of calm, she pulled her little book of Bible verses out of her purse. The verses were grouped together based on theme. She'd not had a lot of cause for the chapters on marriage or parenting, but she'd just about memorized the section on worry.

She read through several of the familiar verses, some of them over and over, letting them sink into her mind. Then she went into the adjoining private bathroom and dangled her wrists and hands under a stream of cold water. Feet planted on hard tile, she stared at herself in the mirror.

Her face looked white and bleak.

With sudden, aching intensity, she missed her father.

Gripping the edge of the sink, she started to cry. Sobs wracked her body and tears streamed down her face, falling off her chin into the basin. Her relationship with her father had always been distant and difficult. He'd been an infrequent visitor to her childhood, and when they had been together they'd mixed like oil and water—the bullheaded man obsessed with his career and his quiet, sensitive daughter. She'd last seen him over Christmas, and even then they'd stuck to their roles: him, unable to stop himself from bossing her around; her, simmering in resentment and feeling like she'd disappointed him because she wasn't (and never wanted to be) the person he'd hoped for.

Regardless of all that, he'd still been her father, the only parent she'd had, and she'd loved him. Meg wasn't certain if he'd loved her back, but at the very least he'd protected her. According to their deal, he'd even sheltered her from Cole Oil.

My father's gone.

In response, she could almost sense the presence of the Holy Spirit drawing near, comforting, reminding her that even though she'd lost William Cole, God remained.

I don't know what to do, Lord. I can't see my way forward. Please show me.

She'd been a lukewarm Christian for most of her life. But after the devastation she'd gone through five years ago, she'd thrown herself on God's mercy and discovered that He had a lot of grace to offer. Enough even for her. Meg understood with absolute certainty that whatever strength she possessed came from Him. On the days when she hadn't wanted to get out of bed in the morning, He'd rescued her.

She'd been doing so much better, feeling so much stronger and more sure of herself in recent years. Then her father had died, and now she was falling again.

A worried Christian. That defined her current state. Worried. Christian. Two words that shouldn't have gone together. An oxymoron.

She knew very well that God was holding out His hands to her through this situation, asking her to trust Him completely. She was trying! But she must not be doing it right. He hadn't given her a spirit of fear. This wasn't how He intended her to be. And yet here she was anyway: a worried Christian overcome with anxiety.

"I'm so sorry," she breathed, then mopped at her face with a paper towel.

Her cell phone rang. When she saw Sadie Jo's name on the screen, she answered immediately. Sadie Jo's sweet and reassuring voice flowed through the line. She'd called to check on Meg and offer support.

Meg squeezed the phone, thankful. God had led her through

rough patches exactly this way countless times in the past. Just when she was about to have a meltdown, a neighbor would knock on her door, a friend would invite her out for dinner, a loved one would call.

Then and now she recognized these small interventions for exactly what they were: God throwing her a lifeline through the words and hands of His people.

Chapter Three

Just what she didn't need to cap off her first week as Mistress of Whispering Creek and Head Know-Nothing at Cole Oil: a visit to the horse farm she'd vowed to shut down.

Yippee!

Meg arrived at the farm on Friday afternoon ten minutes early. Even so, she found Bo waiting outside for her, standing alone in the little car park area wearing jeans, boots, and a pale blue cowboy-cut shirt. The interlocking initials *WCH* for Whispering Creek Horses had been embroidered in tan thread on his shirt's pocket.

Meg winced inwardly. Apparently the people out here even had their own shirts.

He held her door open for her as she got out. "How are you?"

Nutty. "Fine."

"I'm glad you made it. Thanks for coming."

"Sure." The nervousness and pressures of the week had frazzled her badly. She longed to sink into a hot bubble bath, chomp antacids, and drown her sorrows in the biography of Claude Monet she was reading. She'd seriously toyed with the idea of having her assistant call Bo and cancel. But in the end, she hadn't gone that route because, very plainly, she'd told him she'd come. "So this is the horse farm."

"This is it. One of our barns, anyway."

Meg paused, shielding her eyes so that she could take in the details of the place. There'd always been a barn on this site, and her father had always kept horses here for him and his buddies to ride. But the structure that stretched across the land in front of her—redbrick with white trim and a gabled gray metal roof—was entirely new. A short wing that held the front double doors protruded toward them from the center. Otherwise, the structure formed a long east-west rectangle. "How many barns are there?"

"Five."

She glanced at him with surprise. "All this large?"

"Yeah. They're spread out around the property so we can keep the horses separate."

Dutch doors evenly marked the front of the barn. The upper sections of some of them hung open. Three horses had stuck their heads through and were regarding them with interest.

As they approached the entry, tall-reaching trees shaded their progress. Blue pansies lined the base of the barn and also surrounded the two posts that supported a white sign that read *Whispering Creek Horses* in tan letters. Like everything her father had touched, the horse farm oozed quality.

"This barn here," Bo stated, "holds broodmares."

"I see," she said, though she wasn't precisely certain what that meant. "How many acres does the entire farm take up?"

"Over four hundred."

Another surprise. She hadn't realized that her father had given up a third of his ranch to the farm.

Bo held open one of the front doors for her. She passed

through, grateful that she'd stopped at the house to change. She'd decided on an ivory wraparound sweater and a pair of skinny jeans that tucked into her wedge-heeled suede boots. She'd have felt laughably overdressed touring this place in her suit and heels.

The interior of the building welcomed her with the smell of hay, horses, and leather. When they arrived at the main corridor that ran the length of the building, she glanced to her right and came to a halt, startled.

At least twenty people stood quietly in a semicircle, all looking at her, all wearing light blue shirts that matched the one Bo had on. Her emotions veered downhill. These were the people she'd fired. *Would fire* in six months.

"Everyone," Bo said, "this is Megan Cole."

They answered with murmured greetings.

"Hello." Meg pasted on a smile and tried not to fidget over being the center of so much attention and, worse, the person who'd axed their jobs.

"Do you mind if I take you around and introduce you?" Bo asked.

She wanted to say "Yes!" and book it out the nearest door. "Not at all."

Bo led her to the closest person. "This is my brother Jake. He's the trainer here."

Jake took off his cowboy hat and shook Meg's hand with a firm, muscled grip. "Nice to meet you."

"You too." Jake and Bo shared similarities. Same height, same work-hardened body, same shade of brown hair, though Jake's was longer. But they also shared a glaring difference. Jake's face held a prominent scar that started at the slope of his nose, ran along his cheekbone, then curled under his jaw. Meg made an effort to look him in the eye while pretending not to notice it.

Bo guided her along, telling her each person's job title. He used terms like *rotating man*, *groom*, *yearling manager*, and *night man*. His employees, four women and the rest men, ranged from a sweet elderly gentleman who looked like he ought to be spending his days in a convalescent home, to a teenage boy who must have come straight over in his mom's car after sixth period.

She hadn't felt good about firing these people to begin with. She felt considerably less good about it now that she could attach faces and names to each of them. These people had real lives, and she knew that they counted on real paychecks.

Despite that they must be harboring caution, disappointment, or downright hostility toward her, every one of them welcomed her with courtesy.

When Meg had met the final person, the room fell silent. They watched her, waiting, as if they expected her to say something.

Why had she agreed to visit? Goodness, what a mistake. "Ah, thank you for having me for a visit this afternoon. I appreciate you taking the time out of your schedule to come and meet me. This is a beautiful facility, and it's clear that you all take a lot of pride in it, which you should."

The air writhed with hidden resentments.

Meg's stomach gnawed. "I . . . I know my father would want me to express gratitude to you on his behalf. As all of you know, he was very passionate about his horses. So thank you . . . for all you've done."

More painful silence.

"That's it," Bo said to the group. "Thanks. Y'all can return to work."

As his employees moved off, Bo drew Meg over to one of the stalls.

"Are the shirts some kind of uniform?" she asked in a low voice.

His lips quirked. "No, we only wear them on special occasions. Like when a potential buyer comes to look at a horse."

"You wore them for me today?"

"Of course."

"Why?"

"Because having you visit is a special occasion for us."

Her forehead furrowed. Surely not so special that it merited assembling all the employees in their matching shirts? He must have known that meeting the staff would tug at her heartstrings and fill her with guilt. "Did . . ." She re-cinched the tie of her sweater and straightened to her full height. "Did you ask me to come out here today so that you could try to change my mind about closing the farm? Because I'm planning to close it down, exactly as we agreed."

"I know you are."

"I don't want to give you any false hopes."

"You're not giving me false hopes. All you've agreed to is a tour."

"Exactly."

"So right now, I'm just glad for the chance to give you a tour."

For a long moment, she considered him, trying hard to discern his motives.

Bo looked back at her squarely, kindly. His lips curved up a little on one side.

Was he manipulating her? Meg couldn't tell. Her intuition read honesty and genuine goodness in him. But she'd been wrong about people in the past, and it would be naïve of her to think Bo had anything but his own self-interests at heart.

"Ready to see some horses?"

After a brief hesitation, she nodded.

Just as he'd done with his staff, Bo introduced her to the horses, sharing information and a story about each one. Even Meg could recognize how exquisite they were. Finely boned, shining clean, muscled, and well proportioned.

When they came to the far end of the building, Bo grabbed a straw Stetson off a peg, then ushered her through the door. Outside, several white-painted fences surrounded grass fields. "How large are these?" Meg asked.

"These paddocks are about two and a half acres each."

"And beyond them?" She gestured to another fenced area that followed the contours of the land into the distance.

"That's a thirty-acre pasture." He donned his hat one-handed, settling it easily into place.

She followed him to a section of fence. They stood next to each other, separated by a respectful amount of space.

Inside the paddock, two mother horses grazed, their babies moving closely alongside. "Oh," Meg whispered. The babies were so small and sweet, with their overlong legs, dainty little faces, and manes and tails made up of more fluff than substance. Just looking at them caused tears to lodge in her throat. She'd always been sentimental, even at the best of times.

"You okay?" Bo asked.

"Thank you, yes. They're adorable. That's all." She sniffed and ran her fingers under her eyes. "How old are they?"

"About two months."

She could feel his gaze. She glanced at him and found him watching her with concern from beneath the brim of his hat.

"I'm all right," she assured him. One more sniff and she had herself back in order. "I do this a lot. Really, nothing to worry about."

"Maybe I ought to start carrying tissues."

"That'd be convenient." She smiled at him, and he smiled back, looking as if he belonged in these surroundings every bit as much as the hills and the wildflowers. "If I had to guess, I'd say you're from around here."

"What makes you think so?"

She looked at him dubiously. Every inch of him, from the style of his Stetson to his roper boots, read "Texas Cowboy" to her. "I can just tell."

He glanced down at himself, then back at her.

"Am I right?" she asked. "Were you raised in Holley?"

"Yes."

"Have you lived here your whole life?"

"Before coming to Whispering Creek I worked at a horse farm in Kentucky for four years."

"My father stole you from the competition?"

"Something like that."

"Sounds like him." One of the baby horses executed a frolicking jump. "And before Kentucky?"

"I was in the Marines."

"Okay, sure." Meg tried to look natural, as if she knew lots of people in the military, when in fact she knew zero. "Where were you stationed?"

"In California when I was in the States."

"And overseas?"

"I did tours in Iraq and Afghanistan."

She could easily believe it. Bo emanated confidence and capability. It didn't stretch her imagination at all to envision him as a soldier dressed in camouflage, serving the United States in far away and dangerous places. "How long did you serve?"

"Six years."

"And before that?"

"I was in high school."

"Did you go to Plano East?"

He nodded. "What about you?"

"I went to Hockaday in Dallas. Have you ever heard of it?"

"No."

"It's a private girls' school." Which, no doubt, would strike him as snobby.

"You commuted there and back every day?"

"I did." Her father's driver had ferried her to Hockaday every morning, kindergarten through twelfth grade, crossing over the invisible boundary line between horse country and city suburbs. Sadie Jo had picked her up every afternoon. Meg could still remember how Sadie Jo's car had smelled—like Wrigley's gum.

"I don't recall ever seeing you around Holley," he said, "when you were younger. Did you spend much time in town?"

"Not much. Sadie Jo, my nanny when I was a child"—something else for him to find snobby— "has a little Victorian house near the square. I spent some time there growing up. And to this day she and I like to eat at that antique store that serves lunch. What's it called?"

If he was put off by her expensive childhood, he didn't show it. "Mrs. Tiggy-Winkle's?"

"Yes. And I go to the barbecue place now and then."

"Taste of Texas?"

"Right."

One of the horses neared, and Bo reached out and rested his hand on the horse's nose. He absently rubbed his palm up and down, then fiddled with a strand of mane.

"Oh," Meg remembered. "And my dad liked that diner near the edge of town."

"Wayne's."

"He had breakfast there a lot."

Bo waited for a few beats. "Is that it?" He gave her a lazy smile, with just a hint of good-natured challenge in it. "Is that all the experience you've got with Holley?"

"That's about it."

"What about Sonic, Catfish King, Deep in the Heart?"

"No."

"Sally's Snowcones?"

"No."

"DQ?" he asked hopefully. "Tell me you've been there."

"I've never been to the one in Holley. I've stopped at other Dairy Queens, though and, no offense, but I don't think I'm missing much."

"C'mon," he chided. "Their chocolate milk shake?"

"I'm not a big ice cream fan."

"That's sorry."

She laughed.

Smile lines crinkled around his eyes, making his handsome face even more handsome.

He was surprisingly easy to talk to, this man she'd tried and failed to fire. "It's strange to think that we grew up in the same town but that our experiences were so different, isn't it?"

"It is." Bo gave the horse a pat on the side of its neck, and it ambled off.

Of course, hardly anyone had grown up like she had. Still, it surprised Meg that she could have been raised in this county and have had *so* little interaction with men like Bo. She was much more familiar with your average wealthy, private-school-educated Dallas man. That breed wore expensive designer clothes, drove Porsches, and could carry their end of a long conversation about wine.

Bo's breed? Unapologetically masculine. Too practical for designer clothes. Drove American-made trucks. Drank beer.

A breeze combed through the trees, lifting Meg's hair. As she glanced up to watch the clouds creep across the dusky blue sky, a faint sense that she'd misplaced something needled the back of her mind.

She'd stashed her glasses in one of her sweater's deep pockets. That must be it. When she fished them out and put them on, her view of the horizon turned from slightly fuzzy to clear.

Yet . . . no. That wasn't it. Something definitely *was* missing, though. What? She could feel her car keys still in her pocket. She'd left her purse at the big house.

And then it hit her. The thing that had disappeared?

Her anxiety.

Gone, like a wisp of smoke that had vanished into the air.

Her stomach? Easy. Nerves? Steady. Heartbeat, respiration, blood pressure? Normal. It had been months since her body or mind had experienced this peaceful, untangled, lightweight state.

Astonished, she moved her gaze to Bo. He'd stretched his arm over the fence, his fingers extended toward one of the baby horses. He spoke quietly to the young animal, encouraging it to come closer for a visit.

He'd done this, she realized. Bo Porter had stilled the roiling inside of her. Or maybe some mysterious combination of the outdoors, the horses, and his nearness had done it.

She couldn't believe it! What therapy, antacids, breathing techniques, sudoku, and hours of self-talk had not been able to do for her, he'd done. This person she scarcely knew.

It mystified rationality, and yet she didn't want to overanalyze it. She only wanted to stand next to him and gratefully drink in the calm.

They chatted while the shadows lengthened and the sky turned bronze. When Meg heard the sound of a car starting, she turned to see it drive away and realized that hardly any cars remained. Almost everyone had gone home for the day.

"Well." Reluctantly, she pushed away from the fence. "I'm sorry to have kept you so late. I'm sure you're eager to head home."

"Not at all. We can stay as long as you'd like."

Tempting. "I'd best be going. Thank you for giving me the tour and for talking with me."

"You're welcome." He escorted her around the side of the barn toward her car. "Would you like to come out to ride sometime?"

"Me?" Meg gave a soft laugh. "No, I don't ride."

"I'd be happy to teach you."

"My father tried to teach me when I was a kid. I was terrified and ended up falling off. Predictable story." She shook her head, self-deprecating. "I haven't ridden since. I'd rather, I don't know, go to the dentist for a root canal."

"In that case, you're welcome to visit the foals anytime you'd like."

"That, I'd enjoy." He had no idea how much. It couldn't hurt to return here from time to time, to chat with Bo and admire his horses . . . could it? Not if it had the same relaxing effect on her the next time as it had today.

Who'd have guessed it? She still couldn't get over it. The company of this even-tempered cowboy had the power to quiet the tumult of her spirit.

Once Meg had gone, Bo shut himself inside the barn's warm room. Instead of getting started on the work that waited for him, he simply sat, his attention passing over the double sink, the shelves, the small fridge they used for employee lunches and horse medicines. Wooden table and wooden chairs. How could he be sitting here in such a normal way in this normal place? He looked down at himself, his chest, hands, legs. How could he appear the same when everything inside of him suddenly felt completely different?

He'd stood next to Meg at the paddock fence just now and shared a conversation with her. One conversation. They'd been together an hour and a half at most.

But it had been long enough. Long enough to shift everything within him, like a clock that had always run on one time zone and had just been reset to another.

The hold she had on him had grown in strength with every minute that he'd spent looking at her, hearing her voice, taking in her nearness. She was impossibly fine, like something that belonged behind ropes and glass at a museum. Fair and gentle. Refined, smart, and yet somehow desperately in need of an ally.

She drew at him so much that his attraction toward her felt like a physical pull. He'd been flooded with protectiveness, tenderness, desire. So much so that in her presence, he'd lost his grip on his goals for the farm. Which stunned and shamed him. The people who worked here were depending on him to do his best to keep the place running. He'd spent a lifetime working toward building a farm like this . . . it had been his everything.

Had been.

Because, Lord help him, he was afraid he'd just come face to face with the one thing—*one person*—on earth he believed he could care about more.

He set his elbows on the table and dropped his head into

his hands. Why her? Megan Cole? Of all the women on earth, why had he reacted to Megan Cole this way? He could drive to Holley right now and point to any unmarried woman walking down the street or shopping for groceries or pumping gas—any woman at all. And no matter whom he pointed to, that stranger would make a more logical choice for him than Meg Cole.

She was the one shutting down his farm, for pete's sake. And she was his employer, which meant that no matter how he felt about her, the requirement of a respectful professional relationship between them would prevent him from ever asking her out, from touching so much as the back of her hand, from giving his emotions voice.

As if that weren't enough, he and Meg lived in two different worlds that didn't overlap at all. No matter what he did, he could never be good enough for her. Her family would be furious if they even suspected the direction of his thoughts.

His cell phone rang. He checked its screen. "Hey."

"So?" Jake asked. "I heard you stayed out there talking with her for a long time. What do you think? Any chance she'll change her mind about closing the farm?"

"I'm not sure. As of today she's still planning to shut us down."

"I don't think she's as stubborn or as strong as her father. She seems like someone who might be . . . I don't know . . . easier to sway if you give her enough incentive."

Bo set his jaw.

"Well?" Jake asked.

"I just don't know."

"We've got to keep the farm open, Bo. She has to change her mind." What Jake had been through had nearly destroyed him, and Bo knew that Jake's job at Whispering Creek gave him the only sanity, security, and purpose he had left. His brother needed Whispering Creek Horses. It terrified Bo to think what would happen to Jake without it.

"You're not saying much," Jake said.

"I've got a lot on my mind."

"We'll talk later."

The brothers disconnected. Bo pushed to his feet, crossed his arms, and stared sightlessly at the floor. Even before meeting Meg for the first time, he'd thought up a hundred ways to convince her to keep the farm open if she decided to shut it down. Since their meeting, he'd thought up a hundred more.

But it turned out that Meg was more than William Cole's daughter. More than the person who held the power to decide whether Whispering Creek Horses lived or died. She was a person in her own right. A person who'd managed today to stop his heart dead in its tracks.

Guilt twisted Bo's insides, sickening him, because he'd do just about anything in the world for his brother and rest of his staff. But he already knew he wouldn't manipulate Meg. Not for the horses, not for those who worked for him, not for his own dreams, not even for Jake.

He still planned to work his hardest to earn back the money the farm owed. That, he could honorably allow himself. Maybe once Meg saw how profitable Whispering Creek Horses could be, she'd reconsider.

Beyond that, his conscience had whittled down his goals until only one remained: He would step into the breach for Meg and become, until someone better qualified than him took his place, the ally she desperately needed.

That night Meg enjoyed a restful dinner, a bubble bath, and a session with her Monet biography. Then she slipped into bed, flipped the covers over herself, and settled her head on her pillow.

When she closed her eyes, her mind pulled out and lingered over a pleasant memory of how Bo Porter had looked in his Stetson. Strong and relaxed, his hand on his horse's nose, his gray gaze reassuring.

For the first time in weeks and weeks, she fell right to sleep and slept soundly all the way through until morning.

Bo hardly slept at all.

Chapter Four

oney could buy lots of things. Based on the evidence in front of Meg—she and Lynn were standing side by side in the living room of Whispering Creek's guesthouse—money had just bought her a completely inconvenience-free move from Tulsa to Dallas. She hadn't so much as lifted a finger to help with the transition, and yet it had been beautifully accomplished. "Wow, it's perfect."

"I'm glad you like it."

It was just past sunset on Saturday evening, twenty-four hours after Meg's therapeutic visit to the horse farm. As she'd gone about her day, her anxiety had come creeping back. Not as bad as it'd been before her time with Bo, but returning nonetheless and escalating every hour.

Apparently, the cowboy wasn't so much a one-time miracle cure as he was a medicine that needed to be taken in regular doses.

"How 'bout I show you around?" Lynn asked.

"Sounds good." Carefully, Meg set down the animal carrier she'd brought with her and opened its little metal door. "We're home."

Her cat, Cashew, didn't look as if she had any intention of disembarking.

"You want to come see the house with Lynn and me?"

Cashew averted her gaze and stared disdainfully at the wall of the carrier.

"Grumpy about all the change lately?" Meg tested an empathetic smile on the animal.

Cashew continued to give her the feline version of "talk to the hand," so Meg and Lynn set off sans cat, moving through the guesthouse slowly, surveying all the changes.

Lynn had arranged for someone to remove the old furniture and someone else to paint. The color combo of warm ivory walls and bright white trim on the crown moldings and baseboards reminded Meg of a hot vanilla drink topped with whipped cream.

The moving company had packed every item in Meg's old condo, driven it to Holley, and unpacked it all. A Dallas interior designer had come earlier in the day. She'd positioned Meg's furniture, hung all the artwork, and placed each book, pot of greenery, lamp, and candle. She'd even set out vases filled with fresh-cut flowers and draped Meg's pink cashmere throw blanket over the edge of the sofa.

Meg's shabby chic furniture, all of it old and weathered, looked right at home in its new environment. Her fabrics—the pink floral on half the throw pillows, the green stripe on the other half, and the checked fabric on the armchair—soothed and charmed her the way that they always had. Her old-fashioned hooked rug with the pink peonies and pale green leaves warmed the floor.

Even her antique crystal chandeliers had made the trip. Someone had already installed them over the dining table, in each of the two small bedrooms, and the one bathroom.

"What do you think?" Lynn asked when they'd finished the circuit.

"I think that a girl can never have too many chandeliers."

"Words to live by," Lynn said dryly. "Is there anything you'd like to have done?"

"No, it's just right. I'm really happy with it." From earliest memory, the guesthouse had felt to her like an oversized, cozy dollhouse. During her childhood, she and Sadie Jo had sometimes come here for tea parties and sleepovers. On special occasions, she'd been allowed to bring friends here to play.

All these years later, it still suited her well. Certainly far better than the big house ever had or would. "Well, what do you think, Cashew?"

The cat, who hadn't budged from the rear of the carrier, emitted a contemptuous yowl.

The intercom system beeped. "This is George," came a voice, "with Britton Security. Can Lynn Adley please respond?"

Lynn frowned at Meg.

"What do you think that's about?" Meg asked.

"I don't know."

Britton, a private security company, protected everything inside the great brick wall that ran around the boundary of Whispering Creek. They staffed the guard station next to the main entrance gate around the clock.

Both women made their way to the intercom. Lynn pushed a button. "This is Lynn Adley."

"Ms. Adley, we have a visitor at the gate. A young woman. I've checked her ID, and her name is Amber Richardson. She's traveling with a child."

"Do you know her?" Lynn asked Meg.

"No."

"She's not expected," Lynn said. "You can send her on her way."

"There's just one other thing. She says that she knows Stephen McIntyre. She's asking to speak to Ms. Cole about him."

That name. *Stephen McIntyre.* It struck Meg with disastrous force, like the tail of a whip straight to her chest, an awful shock. Weakly, she moved to the nearest dining room chair and lowered into it.

Lynn, who'd known Stephen, regarded Meg with a grave expression.

Stephen.

Meg tried never to think about him, let alone say his name out loud or hear it spoken. What could this Amber Richardson want? Surely nothing good. If she was a friend of Stephen's, she was no friend of Meg's.

"Give us a moment," Lynn said into the intercom.

"Yes, ma'am."

In the background behind the guard, Meg could hear muffled wailing. "Is that a child crying?" she asked.

"What's that noise behind you?" Lynn asked the guard.

"The woman's baby is crying."

Meg's stomach, already shaky these past weeks, clenched into a tight·ball. She grew very aware of her breathing. In. Out. In. Out.

If she sent the woman away, she'd have to wonder about her, the crying baby, and why they'd come. She'd have to push all those concerns into a trunk in her heart marked *Stephen*, a trunk already full to bursting with stuffed-down memories, scars, and furies.

She met Lynn's gaze and recognized that once again, right at the moment when she needed someone, God had placed His person beside her. Meg drew on Lynn's sturdiness, using it to help her gather her nerve.

"I'll meet with her," Meg decided. "Have him frisk her and search the car for weapons." If Amber Richardson meant to hurt her, the wounds would only be emotional. "If she's clean, ask him to accompany her to the front door. While I'm speaking with her, I'd like him to run a background check."

Meg waited on the threshold of the big house, the light from inside spilling out onto the flagstone landing and the pots full of ivy topiaries and flowers. Gas-lit flames from the two decorative lanterns flanking the front doors danced and whipped inside their glass cages.

For privacy's sake, she'd asked Lynn to wait in the nearest of the indoor sitting rooms. Close by, if Meg needed her. But not so close that she'd overhear.

The guard's car pulled up first; a plain white unmarked vehicle. Then came a maroon Sentra that looked to be on the downhill side of its life expectancy.

The woman driving the Sentra parked and hurried around to open one of the car's rear doors. As soon as she did, the sound of angry sobbing filled the air. The woman lifted a little boy—more of a toddler than a baby, really—out of the car and into her arms. Blessedly, his weeping began to calm.

The guard escorted Meg's visitors up the walkway toward Meg, who waited at the top of a bank of shallow stone steps. "Thank you, George," Meg said to him.

"You're welcome, ma'am." He moved off as the woman and baby closed the remainder of the distance.

Meg held her body still, her face expressionless, and struggled to brace herself emotionally.

The woman—medium height, pretty face, perfect body—couldn't have been more than twenty-three. She had on a tight white cotton shirt, pink hipster sweat pants, and flip-flops. Her long dark hair, currently pulled back into a jumbled ponytail, had been striated with several big strips of blond. "I'm Amber, Amber Richardson." Her mascara had smeared. It looked like the baby hadn't been the only one in the car who'd been crying. "Are you Megan Cole?"

"Yes, I am."

"I'm real sorry to show up out of the blue like this and disturb you." She released a shuddering breath. "Real sorry."

"It's all right." Though, of course, it wasn't.

The little boy clutched at his mother's shirt, his expression apprehensive as he took in the night sky, the house, and then Meg. He had a broad forehead, big eyes, cheeks slick with tears, and a gently curling cap of light brown hair. His navy T-shirt and mini jean shorts looked faded, his chubby feet bare.

"Wow, what a house," Amber said weakly, glancing at the facade.

The ranch house had been built to impress even the most jaded millionaire, with beige stonework and brickwork, darkly stained wooden beams that soared to tremendous heights and stretched from the eaves, and iron double doors complete with hand-forged scrollwork.

"I've never seen anything like it." Amber bit her bottom lip. "I had no idea when I set out to find you that I was coming to a place like this, that there'd be a guard and all. . . ."

"How can I help you?"

Amber swallowed hard. "I need to find Stephen McIntyre. Were . . . were you married to him once?"

The answer stuck in Meg's throat. Hard to voice. Hard to admit. "Yes, I was."

"I only know because I've been online searching for him, and I came across the information there."

Meg nodded.

"Stephen was my boyfriend, and this is his son, Jayden."

Meg stood still, thinking everything and nothing at the same time. A sound, like a rushing north wind, filled her ears.

"Not that Stephen's been a daddy to Jayden, because he hasn't. He took off as soon as he found out Jayden was on the way, which makes me so angry every time I think about that I could just—" She frowned, jerked a chunk of hair behind her ear. A thousand despairs raged in her eyes, and Meg knew them all well. "Sorry about that."

"It's okay. I understand."

"Well, Jayden and I were doing fine without him, really fine. I was working a couple of jobs and managing to pay for day care. But then my roommate moved out and I lost one of my jobs, and I couldn't hold on to the apartment by myself. So, see, I need to find Stephen now. He has to help me support Jayden."

The rushing wind in Meg's ears howled louder.

"I've been looking and looking for him, but no luck. I'm kind of about to lose it, you know? I can't think who else to ask, so I decided to come to you because I've been hoping that—that maybe you know where he is."

"I'm sorry. I haven't known Stephen's whereabouts for five years."

Meg could sense Amber's hope escaping like air hissing from a balloon.

Jayden started whining. Amber rocked him, but in her agitation the motion looked more like a jostle than a rock. His little lips started to tremble.

Compassion turned within Meg. "Have you had dinner?"

"Not yet."

"Come inside and let me get you something to eat."

"You don't have to do that—"

"I insist. Come on in." Meg ushered them into the house and introduced them to Lynn. Lynn guided them toward the kitchen, murmuring about whipping together a meal of bread, salad, and leftover spaghetti.

Meg made her way past the sunken den with its three-story-tall stone fireplace, seating areas, cowhide ottomans, and massive antler chandelier. She shut herself inside the library and called George at the guard station. He'd already run a background check and was able to tell Meg that Amber had a few minor parking violations and speeding tickets, but nothing more sinister on her record. He'd pulled up a list of her past residences and employers.

"Can you call her most recent employer for me?" Meg explained the details Amber had given to her, about Stephen's abandonment before Jayden's birth and how she'd worked to support them both. "I'd like to know if her boss can confirm her story."

"Yes, ma'am."

"And is it possible to get a look at her son's birth certificate to see who's listed as the father?"

"Absolutely."

"I'd like to know that information, too."

"You bet."

"I appreciate it." Meg disconnected. She didn't think Amber had lied to her, but she'd feel better once she had proof. She recognized her own tenderheartedness for what it was: her best quality and also her greatest weakness.

While she waited to hear back, Meg clicked on one of the

room's lamps, perched on the edge of an aged leather chair, and stared at the nap of the carpet. The shock of Amber's unexpected arrival had sent her anxiety skyrocketing. Why didn't she carry Tums with her wherever she went? She should carry Tums.

Her father had paid Britton Security to be fast and thorough, so it didn't surprise her when George called back just minutes later. He reported that Amber's employer at the restaurant where she'd been waitressing had known Amber since before Jayden's birth and been able to confirm every detail of her story. And the individual listed as Jayden's father on his birth certificate? Stephen McIntyre.

It appeared that Amber had indeed been telling the truth.

Meg's emotions tangled together like vines, writhing and difficult to pull apart. There was the tension of having to think about Stephen. Concern for a mother and a little boy, both so young and in need of protection. Anger at Stephen. Guilt, because if Meg had done what she should have done five years ago, then Amber might not have met Stephen in the first place.

A soft knock sounded, and Meg looked up to see Lynn lean into the room. "Can I come in?"

"Of course."

Lynn shut the door behind her and handed Meg a steaming mug. "I thought you could use this."

"Thank you." Meg recognized the beverage by its smell. Sleepytime tea, her old friend. She blew on it and took a sip that tasted like chamomile, spearmint, and relaxation. Flavors in absolute contrast to the turmoil within her.

Lynn took a seat on the sofa across from Meg. "Amber and Jayden are squared away for the moment. I got a meal in front of them, and they're in the kitchen working on it."

"I'm sorry that I've put you to work on a Saturday night."

When Lynn had come to Whispering Creek, she and her bookish English teacher husband had moved into their own private semi-attached wing of the big house. Even though she lived on-site, Lynn strictly divided her work schedule from her private life.

"This isn't work. This is me helping a friend. So fill me in. What's going on?"

Meg outlined everything that Amber had told her. "She's driven all this way with her little boy, and it's getting late. I don't think she has a lot of money to spare for a hotel. I'm thinking I might ask them to . . . to stay here for the night. Is that crazy?"

"Why would that be crazy?"

"Well, my father would never have done something like that."

"No, he wouldn't have."

As a young man, her father had been burned a few times when he'd loaned money to friends and family members who'd never paid him back. From then on, no matter how close or distant the relationship, when people had come to him asking for help, he'd always responded by offering them jobs at Cole Oil. The hundreds of charities who courted him were always promptly referred to a company employee who handled his sizable charitable giving budget.

Her father had cautioned her numerous times not to be swayed by the sob stories of others. She'd always agreed privately and vocally, promising him that she wouldn't get sucked into other people's dramas.

Easily done in theory. Over the past five years, when she'd been living on nothing more than her own income, she certainly hadn't been confronted with dilemmas like Amber's. Maybe some people could look into the face of a young mother worried about providing for her child and turn her away, but Meg Cole wasn't one of them.

On the other hand, she *had* to be sensible! She'd been on the job for less than a week, and she'd already agreed to continue hosting ninety racehorses and their keepers. Now she was considering taking in her ex-husband's discarded child and ex-girlfriend. Who'd she be saving next week? A family of arctic seals?

She was either generous or the most massively gullible pushover alive. She honestly didn't know which.

She took a few more sips of tea, hoping to drink in some clarity right along with it. "I let Bo Porter keep his horse farm open. Now I'd like to invite Amber and Jayden to stay here, even though they're complete strangers, and even though they're going to need a lot more than a place to spend one night."

"That's true."

"I'm worried that I'm making bad decisions, that I'm letting myself get drawn into things I shouldn't."

Lynn regarded her with a knowing expression. "And?"

"And I'm worried that I'm letting people take advantage of me." There it was, out loud: the epicenter of the issue.

For a long moment, Lynn seemed to roll the situation around in her mind. "What would be so wrong with that? With letting people take advantage of you?"

Meg's brows lifted. "Wrong with it? Well, I . . . I don't want to be taken advantage of." *Ever again.* "It would make me feel weak, to let people walk all over me and manipulate me."

"Huh."

"Well?"

Lynn shrugged. "Well, what?"

"This is when you're supposed to give me wise advice."

"You want my advice?"

"Of course I do."

"Your father was totally different than you are, Meg. He

couldn't forgive or forget when people took from him without giving back. But you're not that way, I don't think. You have the ability to forgive people some hurts."

"I don't know," Meg said doubtfully.

"You do. So give yourself permission to help anyone and everyone you want. If a few of them take advantage of you, then so be it. Forgive them and move on. But don't let worry or mistrust stop you from helping people. You can afford to be generous. In fact, if anyone on earth can afford to be generous, it's you."

Meg nodded. Her thoughts and all those vines of emotion began to settle.

They walked to the kitchen and found that Amber had cleared the table and was rinsing off the dishes at the sink. Jayden stood at her feet, hugging one of her legs. She glanced back at them and smiled. "Thank y'all for dinner. It was delicious."

"Good, I'm glad." Lynn moved to the sink and opened the dishwasher to lend a hand.

Meg watched them from further back, struck by the scene and the Bible verse that it brought to the front of her mind.

For I was hungry and you gave me something to eat, I was thirsty and you gave me something to drink, I was a stranger and you invited me in. . . .

For better or for worse, her father's fortune belonged to her now. She didn't have to manage it the way he'd taught her because his ways and opinions no longer bound her. The only Father she had left was of the heavenly variety. And *that* Father? She knew the counsel He'd give.

I tell you the truth, whatever you did for one of the least of these brothers of mine, you did for me.

"Amber," she said. "Let's go get your suitcases. You guys are going to stay here with us tonight."

Chapter Five

In the feeble morning light filtering through the bathroom window shade, Stephen McIntyre studied his reflection. He brushed his dark blond hair into place until every strand fell exactly as his last hair stylist had intended. With a crisp tug, he straightened the sleeves of his pale blue Brooks Brothers shirt. Critically, he brushed a nearly invisible piece of lint from his dress pants.

As soon as he was satisfied, he let himself out of the bathroom and into the bedroom of the girl's second-rate condo. The room smelled of perfume and stale sheets.

He swept his change off the top of the dresser and slid it into his pocket. The girl in the bed roused at the sound. He collected his wallet and keys and made for the door.

"Aren't you going to say good-bye?" she asked sleepily.

He turned and regarded her, hesitating for a split second while he considered his options. Was what she'd given him last night all that she was worth? Or could he play her for more?

He'd met her last night at a bar. Based on her clothing, shoes, and handbag, he'd classified her as richer than her condo proved her to be. Still, he could run some kind of a simple scam on her. He'd told her he was a stockbroker. Without too much effort he could likely convince her to write him a check for a few thousand dollars, so he could invest it for her on a supposed "sure thing." "I didn't want to wake you, honey. I was doing my best to be quiet so you could get some rest."

"You're so sweet." Her lips curved.

He crossed to her, took her chin in his hand, and kissed her. "You're sweeter."

"No, you."

"You."

"Can't you stay?" She blinked up at him, her young face gullible, fresh, and free of wrinkles. "I'll make you breakfast."

"I wish I could. I've got to get to work. Call you later, all right?"

"All right."

"Get some more sleep." He gave her one of his patented smiles. The sexy, admiring one. Then he left, closing the door softly behind him.

In the kitchen, he opened her purse, extracted her wallet, and flipped to her driver's license. He jotted down the info from it on a magnetic pad stuck to her refrigerator. He tore the top sheet free, folded it neatly, and stuck it in his shirt pocket.

He'd check her out fully on his Mac later.

He cracked open the portion of her wallet that contained cash. Forty-three dollars. He'd do a heck of a lot better off her before he was done. Smoothly, he closed the wallet and returned it to her purse.

In the foyer he caught a glimpse of a framed family photo of the girl with her adult siblings and her parents. Probably last year's Christmas card shot.

He grunted and made his way into the cool, clear morning. He'd met this girl just hours ago, but he already knew everything pertinent about her, because he'd known a hundred others like her. She was a slutty, well-meaning, harmless girl-next-door. She saw herself as unique, which she wasn't, and brave, which she wasn't. In actuality, she was a pathetic rule follower, exactly like the rest of them.

Rule followers deserved to get taken by those smarter and those willing to break, bend, and twist the rules.

He slid into his BMW M5 and steered along the streets of Phoenix. He'd chosen this city because casinos, like desert cactus, flourished in these parts. And casinos offered him easy access to the excitement and risk he required.

He couldn't do monotony. Monotony made him twitch.

He pulled up smoothly to a stoplight. A woman in a black Mustang convertible came up next to him, caught his eye, and grinned. Stephen grinned back, while assessing her with a complete lack of emotion.

In this world you were either a victim or a conqueror.

Stephen McIntyre was no victim.

The morning after Amber's arrival, Meg attended Sunday morning worship, then returned to the solitude of the guesthouse to find acid reflux and worry waiting to greet her. It didn't make sense. She'd just been to church, and after all the songs, the encouragement, and the prayers, she ought to feel steady. But she'd discovered through the years that her panic came when it wanted, regardless of cause, and never listened to logic.

Supposedly, exercise reduced stress.

Apparently, in her case, so did proximity to Bo Porter.

If she'd had a choice between medicating herself with exercise and medicating herself with the cowboy, she'd have chosen calm-via-Bo hands down. But he had Sundays off. And when sudoku and breathing techniques proved useless, she dressed resolutely in a pale gray sweat suit, crunched more antacids, and headed to her father's home gym. Within, cardio machines stood like soldiers in straight formation. Several racks of weights lined one wall. Benches, balls, and stretchy bands took up a corner. Mirrors glared at her from every angle.

Okay . . . hmm. She immediately rejected the idea of using the weights, the balls, or the bands. She had no idea what to do with any of them. She supposed she could hire a personal trainer for next time. Except she didn't particularly want some uber-fit person demanding that she work harder than she wanted to, leading her around, and staring at her during her workout agony.

So maybe not.

After grabbing a clean towel from the stack and turning the TV to the History Channel, she climbed aboard the elliptical machine. Unsure of the settings, she chose a small incline and a small amount of resistance.

First and foremost, she craved exercise's anxiety-killing benefits. But it wouldn't hurt her to lose five pounds, either. Since her father's death she'd been so overworked emotionally that she'd been inactive physically. One would have thought that all her fretting and her dodgy stomach would have kept the weight off. But alas, no.

Almost immediately Meg started to puff. She tried valiantly to focus her attention on the large wall-mounted TV screen. But the general torture of cardio proved a slight distraction to her viewing pleasure.

Her heart rate must be impressively high! She gripped the metal pads, then checked the digital heart-rate display.

It read *130*.

130?! Not possible. She was *dying*. She didn't know much about target heart rates, except that a twenty-eight-year-old's rate should be a lot higher than 130 in order to achieve maximum benefits.

She didn't think she could push her heart rate higher without passing out.

She thought of her nine female cousins on her mother's side of the family and tried to use them as motivation. She'd see them all on Easter, and it would be *so* nice to look slim in the face of their gorgeous and stylish skinniness. Her cousins had all been born naturally fabulous, while Meg had to spend ages on her hair and makeup and carefully monitor her intake of Oreos.

Maybe she should give up Oreos.

Her heart gave a protesting *twang*. Was life worth living without Oreos?

While her gaze clung to the TV, she thought about Bo and the ranch. Her overwhelming responsibilities at Cole Oil. Amber and Jayden.

After Amber had agreed to stay last night, Meg and Lynn had given her an abbreviated tour of the big house. Since every bedroom stood empty, Meg had assured her she could stay in any one of them. Amber, who preferred to sleep in the same room as Jayden, had chosen a second-floor bedroom in shades of sage green located close to the central staircase. They'd carried in her small suitcase, Jayden's diaper bag, and a portable folding crib. And that had been that.

Meg didn't know what to do about Amber and Jayden next, which step to take, what kind of help to offer. An idea had been circling inside of her since late yesterday evening, but it scared her as much as it appealed. *What do you want me to do about them, Lord? If you'll show me, I'll do my very best to follow through.*

She wiped at the sweat on her forehead and cheeks with her towel. Her heart thundered with effort, her breathing labored in and out of her parted lips.

Panic attacks might be preferable to this.

She considered stopping.

But in the end, her desire to make herself stronger trumped her desire to quit. She needed, really needed, to prove to herself that she could be tough, that beneath all the trembling and fear she still had courage and she still had willpower. She blew a blond tendril of hair out of her face and kept on going.

After surviving thirty minutes on the elliptical, Meg treated herself to ten minutes of stretching, pounded back a bottle of water, grabbed a second bottle from the mini-fridge in the gym, and went in search of Amber.

She found her standing at the edge of the big house's manicured back lawn, watching Jayden run and explore.

Amber turned, her expression warming when she saw Meg. "Hi." She had on her flip-flops, a snug pair of jeans, and a turquoise scoop-neck T. Her shiny hair hung down her back.

"How did y'all sleep?" Meg asked.

"We had the best night's sleep we've had in forever."

"I'm glad."

"That bed . . . oh my gosh. Is it a pillow-top?"

"I don't know."

"It's so awesome that it must be a pillow-top."

Meg accepted the pronouncement with a nod and watched Jayden bend over to sniff a blazing white azalea bush.

"We woke up this morning," Amber said, "and one of the ladies who works here had breakfast waiting for us, and coffee, and offered to do our laundry. I didn't know what to say, so I let her feed us and gave her our dirty clothes. I hope that was okay."

"More than okay."

"Well, thank you. And sorry again about arriving like that last night. Jayden and I aren't half so mental today."

Meg smiled. "I'm mental now and then, too, so I completely understand."

"If it's all right with you, I thought I'd let Jayden have his nap here. Then we'll pack up and head out this afternoon."

"I'd like to talk to you about that, actually."

"Oh?" Amber slanted her a look of surprise.

"How about we sit down?"

"Sure."

Meg led her to one of the tables positioned along the back patio. They each took a chair shaded by a wood and canvas umbrella. A vase brimming with flowers cut from Whispering Creek's garden decorated the tabletop.

Both women kept an eye on Jayden as he moved to the steps leading from lawn to patio and practiced climbing.

Meg caught herself fidgeting with her water bottle and brought both hands to her lap. "I'd really like to know what happened with Stephen. That is, if you don't mind telling me."

"I don't mind—careful, Jayden!" Amber pushed to the front of her seat, but it appeared that Jayden could navigate the four wide steps safely, so she scooted back a few inches. "I met Stephen at one of the restaurants where I was waitressing. I fell for him right away. I mean hard, you know? He moved in with me after a couple of months and, like, two months after that I found out I was pregnant. Total surprise. It sure wasn't like I'd planned it. I told him the news, and the next morning he left for work and never came back."

"You never saw him or heard from him again?"

"No, nothing. He just . . . disappeared." Amber's gaze remained mostly trained on her son as she spoke, her fingers nervously picking at the peeling blue nail polish on her thumb. "At first I thought something had happened, that he'd been in an accident. I kept checking with the police and the hospitals. Then I thought maybe he'd needed to leave for a while, but that he'd have a good reason and he'd come back. He didn't come back. He left me on purpose."

"He did the exact same thing to me," Meg said. "Vanished."

"And you couldn't find him either?"

"I didn't try. I didn't want to find him."

Amber searched Meg's face until a squeal from Jayden drew their attention. He'd returned to the grass and appeared to be attempting toddler yoga—his head plunked down and one leg pointing high in the air.

"Stephen is such a jerk." Amber shook her head, scowling. "Such a jerk."

"Yes." Wild understatement.

"But unlike you, I *do* want to find him. Badly."

"Because you need help with Jayden."

"Yes. Also, I just . . . well, I'd like to find him for my sake, too. I want to look him in the face and tell him off. I'm *mad.* You know?"

"Yeah."

"I'm not sure where to look for him next. Can you think of anyone who might know where he is?"

"No, I never met his family. He told me he'd grown up in foster care."

"He told me his family lived overseas."

"That figures." Stephen's lies had turned out to be the only consistent thing about him. Meg could almost taste her resentment toward him, rising and filling her mouth with a bitter, metallic tang. "He's smart, moves around a lot, and always covers his tracks. I'm afraid that it's going to be hard for anyone to find him if he doesn't want to be found."

"I *have* to find him. I don't have a choice."

Jayden zipped across the patio and pulled himself onto a lounge chair. He tried to stand up on it, his arms outstretched as if riding a surfboard.

Amber raced over, scooped him up, and placed him back on the grass before returning to her chair.

"Do you have any family?" Meg asked carefully. "Could you turn to them for help?"

Amber's lips tightened. "Not an option. My parents and I don't speak anymore. We had a big fight after I graduated from high school, and I haven't seen them since."

"I'm sorry." Meg tried to imagine what it would have been like to strike out into the world alone at eighteen without money or education.

God? Internally, she asked Him several questions at once, seeking confirmation even though she sensed that she already knew what He wanted.

Yes, a voice within her seemed to answer.

A feeling of rightness expanded through Meg. "I'd like to help you."

"You already have."

"I'd like to do more."

Meg's words caught Amber's full attention.

"I'd like for you and Jayden to stay here until you get back on your feet. I'd like to help you find a job and child care."

Amber gaped at her, face blank, dark eyeliner framing wide eyes.

"Do you have any college credits?" Meg asked.

"Like, um . . . fifteen hours. From before Jayden was born."

"Are you interested in getting a college degree?"

"Yes."

"What kind?"

"I'd like to be a nurse one day. I've always wanted to be a nurse." Jayden ran up, and Amber swept him into her lap. He deposited a handful of pebbles, two twigs, and a leaf onto the top of the table, then went to work examining his treasures.

"Then you should be a nurse," Meg said. "I'll look into the possibility of getting you enrolled for the summer session at Collin County Community College."

Amber bit her lip, released it. "I want to take classes, but I don't have time. I work, and when I'm done working, I take care of Jayden."

"Then you'll work part time and go to school part time and take care of Jayden the rest of the time."

"I can't afford to pay for day care and college on a part-time salary."

"But I can." For the first time since hearing the news of her father's death, a ray of warm bright joy burst open within Meg. Her lips bowed, and she could feel her dimples digging into her cheeks. She'd done the right thing just now. She hardly knew Amber, and yet inviting her to stay at Whispering Creek felt more right to Meg than anything had in months.

From his mother's lap, Jayden peered at Meg warily, his baby eyebrows low. He looked nothing like Stephen. If he had, he'd have been blond and gorgeous. Instead, with his large head and widely spaced eyes, Jayden didn't even quite classify as cute—a fact that only endeared him to Meg's soft heart.

Amber smoothed a strand of hair behind her ear. "I'll never be able to pay you back."

"It's not a loan, Amber. It's a gift." She thought immediately of the grace that God had given to her. "I've received plenty in my life that I didn't earn. All this, for example." She gestured toward the big house. "So do me a favor and let me give you something. All right?"

Amber's blue eyes filled with doubt and tears. "I've made so many mistakes. I don't deserve your help."

"This isn't about what you deserve."

"I can't believe you'd do this for us. We're, like, strangers to you."

"Even so, it would make me happy for you to stay." Meg found that it was true. Maybe because she and Amber had both been mistreated by the same man, or maybe because she felt partially to blame for what Stephen had done to them. Or maybe because the Spirit inside of her had a capacity for compassion and affection bigger than her own.

"I . . ." A droplet spilled over Amber's lashes.

Meg had always found it physically impossible to witness someone else's tears and not cry, too. Her own chest tightened with emotion. "This place might look shabby," she joked, "but it's actually not too bad of a place to live. I think you and Jayden might be able to manage."

Amber burst out laughing, and Meg joined her. Jayden laughed, too, banging his tiny fists on the table and causing the pebbles to jump.

"Are you *sure*?" Amber asked.

"Yes. If you're willing to do your part—to work hard at school and at your job—then I promise I'll keep up my end of the bargain." It was time to take her father's money out for a test drive to see how it performed. "Okay?"

Amber looked at her for a long moment. "Okay."

Bo had been on his way to his parents' house after church when he'd made a sudden U-turn, a U-turn that had brought him here, to the mansion at Whispering Creek for lunch.

He'd bailed on the meal his mom hosted every Sunday for the family, which would cost him.

He was showing up unannounced for a meal, which wasn't polite.

And after he finished eating, he was going to have to work on his one day off, to justify showing up for lunch.

All of which would be worth it if Meg was there.

He wanted to see her.

Just that. See her.

He wanted it enough, had thought about it enough since her visit to the farm, that he'd taken that U-turn. The sane part of him knew that nothing good could come of spending time with Meg above and beyond what his job required. It would only fuel his fascination with her and cause him—the guy who could never be more to her than her horse farm manager—pointless pain.

However, the insane part of him insisted that, the situation being what it was, one little lunch together couldn't do much harm.

The insane part of him had beaten the sane part of him to a pulp. So here he was.

He rounded the corner from the hallway into the kitchen and found the space empty except for an unfamiliar maid pulling a pot roast out of the oven. She didn't speak much English, but she smiled and set him a place at the table and waved off his apology for arriving without prior notice.

When he'd come to work at Whispering Creek, Lynn had invited him to join her and the other employees in the kitchen for their daily lunches. Over the years, he'd only taken her up on her offer a couple of times. It had almost always been easier to eat with his brother in one of the warm rooms in the barns.

He walked over to the table and stood with his hands pushed into the pockets of his jeans. Six adult plates waited. He could only hope one belonged to Meg, since he had no idea whether she ate with her staff. One plastic blue plate also sat on the table, in front of a high chair and next to a cup with a screw-on lid.

Strange. In the four years he'd worked here, he'd almost never seen a child at Whispering Creek.

He heard someone approaching and turned, hoping—

A short elderly woman with glasses and white hair in a classic puffy old-lady style entered. She came to a stop at the sight of him, her expression pleasant. "Hello."

"Hi. I'm Bo Porter."

"The gentleman who runs the Thoroughbred farm?"

"Yes, ma'am."

"Ah! I'm Sadie Jo Greene." After they shook, she kept hold of his hand and patted it a few times before releasing it. "I was Meg's nanny when she was little. Now I'm just a friend of the family."

"It's nice to meet you. Meg mentioned you to me."

"She did?"

"Yes, ma'am."

"I never had any children of my own, so thank goodness for Meg. She's mine for keeps."

Another of the maids arrived, and they all helped to move bowls of food to the table and pour iced tea. The whole time, Sadie Jo asked Bo questions about himself, his family, his work.

"I find you so impressive," she said, gazing up—way up—at him with clear affection.

Had Sadie Jo taken a shine to him in particular, or did everyone have this effect on her? What a sweet lady. Meg's nanny was every kid's idea of the perfect grandma.

"To have accomplished all that you have with the horses," she continued. "My goodness. Just wonderful."

"Well, thanks."

"Outstanding. How many of your horses will be racing this season?"

"We have—"

Meg walked into the room and all words and thoughts dropped out of his mind.

She spotted him right away and stilled, her brows lifting a fraction.

Bo was deeply glad all at once—stupidly foolishly glad—that he'd taken that U-turn.

"Are you joining us for lunch today?" she asked.

"I thought I would, if you don't mind . . . before I head to my office."

"I don't mind at all."

"I'm not imposing?"

"Not in the least. Do you typically work on Sundays?"

"Not typically."

"Well, you're welcome to join us anytime for lunch." She turned to hug Sadie Jo. "Hello."

"Hello, dear. You look darling."

"Thanks." Meg greeted the maids, asked them how they were and how their kids were doing. Just as one of them finished telling Meg about her child's nut allergy, a young woman holding a baby entered the kitchen. Meg drew them forward. "Everyone, this is Amber Richardson and her son, Jayden. They're going to be staying with us."

She didn't offer any more explanation, which left Bo wondering what connection the two of them had to Meg.

"Sorry to keep y'all waiting," Amber said. "I had to change his diaper real quick."

Bo introduced himself to Amber. As the others did the same and took turns murmuring over the baby, Meg eased near him. "I worked out earlier," she said. "That's why I look like this. I don't usually dress this way in public."

"Well, you should."

She peered up at him for a moment, seeming to weigh his sincerity. He stared back, letting her read his honesty, feeling the power of their eye contact all the way down to his bones.

She had on a sweat suit that fit her the way it'd fit a Nike model. She'd done her makeup as perfectly as always, and her hair had been pulled into a ponytail, but it looked like she'd curled the ends. He guessed this outfit was as casual as it got for Meg Cole. Enough so that she felt embarrassed to be seen in it?

Those sweat bottoms. Shoot. He'd never been into skinny women. He liked women to look like women. Meg did, and then some. He was going to be chasing away thoughts about those sweat bottoms.

When they settled around the table, Bo managed to snag the seat next to Meg. Sadie Jo blessed the food, and they started in.

"Oh, he's just adorable," Sadie Jo said to Amber. "How old is he?"

"He's eighteen months."

"Is he saying much yet?"

"Just *mama* and *ball*." Amber cut the pot roast and vegetables into tiny pieces and placed them on Jayden's plate. "I think he's supposed to be saying more by now, so I'm a little worried."

"No need to worry," Sadie Jo said. "I'm sure he'll talk more when he's ready. Sweet angel." She stared at Jayden with a love-struck gaze and softly ran a hand over the kid's head. "Sweetest angel."

He'd wondered earlier if Sadie Jo had taken a shine to him in particular. He had his answer.

"I just remembered." Sadie Jo reached into her purse and brought out a small stuffed dog. "I brought this for him. Is it all right if I give it to him after he's done eating?"

"Sure," Amber answered. "Thank you."

"As soon as I told Sadie Jo about Jayden, she had to meet him," Meg said to everyone at the table. "She loves children, obviously."

Sadie Jo continued to croon to Jayden, clearly far more in-trigued with him than with the meal.

"Where are you from?" one of the maids asked Amber.

"I'm from Sanderson, Texas. Have y'all heard of it?"

They all shook their heads.

"It's a small west Texas town. I've been living in Lubbock, though, for several years."

"What brought you to Lubbock?" the maid asked.

Amber dabbed at her lips with her napkin. She seemed to find it hard to look anyone directly in the face. "I followed my high school boyfriend there when he went to Texas Tech. We broke up, but I stayed anyway."

He'd just met Amber, but based on her appearance, her accent, and the information she'd already given, Bo felt like he knew her. He'd grown up in Holley with a bunch of girls just like her. Poor small-town girls without much education who'd had babies too early. A lot of them were good-hearted. But a lot of them would take the shirt off your back, drink all your beer, and leave you for your best friend if he got a better-paying job.

It concerned him some that Meg had taken Amber in. He didn't want to see Meg taken advantage of or hurt.

"Did you bring all your things with you from Lubbock when you arrived last night?" Sadie Jo asked Amber.

"No, I didn't. I wasn't planning to stay."

"Well, you're going to need to go and get the rest of your clothing and Jayden's things."

The kid started fussing.

"Oh dear." Sadie Jo frowned with worry. "Do you think he has a wet diaper?"

"I don't think so," Amber answered. "I mean, he might, but I just changed him. Maybe he wants his sippy." She handed him his cup, and Jayden grabbed it with both hands and tilted his face to the ceiling to take some deep sips.

"I can rent you a U-Haul truck," Meg said. "So that you can drive to Lubbock to get your things. How large of a truck do you think you'll need?"

"Not big at all. Most of the stuff isn't worth keeping."

"I can send Mr. Son with you, or maybe Bo has someone on staff who could help. . . ."

"You bet," he said.

"No, no. There's really not much," Amber answered. "My friend Tammy and her boyfriend can, like, help me load up my stuff."

"How long is the drive to Lubbock?" Sadie Jo asked.

"About five and a half hours."

"Too long for this darling one here." Sadie Jo clucked her

tongue. "Meg, you've hardly touched your pot roast! C'mon now, dear. You'll waste away. Eat something."

Meg leaned toward Amber. "If you're comfortable leaving Jayden at Whispering Creek, I can watch him for you while you drive to Lubbock."

"What a lovely idea!" Sadie Jo said.

The women went back and forth over it for a while—Amber seeming uncertain, Meg and Sadie Jo reassuring her. Bo didn't guess that any single mother managed to raise a child without sometimes leaving that child in the care of trustworthy people. Meg and Sadie Jo were, at least to him, clearly trustworthy.

Amber looked back and forth between the two women. "Well, if you really wouldn't mind, I guess I'll take you up on it. Jayden hates car trips. I think he'd be much happier here."

"Then it's settled!" Sadie Jo gave Jayden a smooch on his cheek.

"I have to be at work all day tomorrow," Meg said, "but I could get off early on Tuesday afternoon to take care of Jayden. Maybe you could drive to Lubbock then, spend the night, and drive home on Wednesday."

"Works for me," Amber said.

"Lynn and I will keep him for you on Wednesday," Sadie Jo said. "To tell the truth, I wish I could help Meg baby-sit him on Tuesday afternoon, too, but I'm hosting bridge at my house that day."

"I'll help Meg on Tuesday," Bo heard himself say.

The five women at the table looked at him with surprise.

He shrugged. "Tuesday afternoons are usually slow out at the farm." Big lie. Tuesday afternoons were just as busy as the rest of the week. What was he doing? He'd only planned to allow himself this one lunch with Meg.

"Do you have children of your own?" Amber asked him.

"No, I don't."

"Have you spent time around kids?"

"Not much."

Amber smiled. "You're brave, then. He can be a handful."

Bo glanced at Meg, who was peering up at him. Spending an entire afternoon with her—very bad idea. And yet, he'd have dug ditches for the chance to do just that. He looked at Jayden, who was smearing potato into his hair. "How hard can it be?"

Chapter Six

hey say that cats deign to let their humans care for them. It was kind of like that between Meg and Mr. Son. He deigned to let her employ him.

On Monday morning before work, Meg introduced Amber and Jayden to the weekday indoor staff, then took them to Mr. Son's gardening room, a climate-controlled greenhouse connected to the six-car garage.

When they entered the moist, mulchy-smelling space, Mr. Son straightened from one of his long tables of plants. "Meg."

"Mr. Son."

He took off his gardening gloves.

"This is Amber Richardson and her son, Jayden. They'll be staying here at Whispering Creek, and I wanted them to meet you."

"Hmm." His dark eyes surveyed Amber and Jayden.

"Amber, this is Mr. Son. He's our landscaping genius."

"No, not genius."

"Yes, you are."

"No."

Meg's lips twitched. "All right."

"Are you surprised," he asked Amber, "that I'm a landscaper and not a computer guy or doctor or scientist?"

"Um," Amber said, "no, sir."

"Because Asians are supposed to be computer guys or doctors or scientists, right?"

Amber's expression looked like that of a raccoon about to be run over by a semi. "I . . . I don't think that."

"No?" Mr. Son asked her.

"No," she vowed.

Seemingly mollified, Mr. Son released Amber from his scrutiny and moved it over to Jayden. "Who do we have here?"

"This is my son."

"How old?"

"He's eighteen months."

Mr. Son gazed down the length of his nose at Jayden.

Jayden returned his regard with interest while sucking on several of his fingers.

"Young man," Mr. Son said, "it's time to get to work."

Amber just stood, fish-mouthed, frozen. Jayden extracted his fingers from his mouth with a wet popping sound.

"Mr. Son often let me help him with the plants when I was a kid." Meg hadn't forgotten those afternoons after school, and the comfort that the shy, introverted girl she'd been had found in gardening and in Mr. Son's stoic, dependable presence.

"Come." Mr. Son led them to a ruthlessly organized cupboard and brought out a small apron, a pair of little gloves, and a kid-sized spade. He handed them to Amber. "We work," he said to Jayden in an authoritative tone of voice.

By the time Meg left, Mr. Son had Jayden standing on a tall step stool next to him at the table of plants, garbed in the apron and gloves, using his spade to fill pots with soil. Amber kept trying to help Jayden, and Jayden kept pushing her hand away.

Jayden spilled more than he managed to get into the pots,

but Mr. Son didn't appear to notice. He treated Jayden with dignity and expectation, as if the kid were eighteen years old instead of eighteen months.

Meg smiled. Mr. Son might not look like a traditional baby whisperer. But he had a way —a stiff, prickly, and unusual way— with children.

Just like with his acres of flowers, he could coax them to bloom.

On Tuesday afternoon, Meg left the Cole Oil building in time to drive home, change, and prepare herself to spend the afternoon doing something highly unusual for her: baby-sitting a little male with the help of a big one.

She waded into her walk-in closet and flicked through her clothes, looking for an outfit that would strike the right tone. On her museum salary, she wouldn't have been able to afford this wardrobe. But her father, never interested in actually taking the time to shop for something unique for her, had given her jewelry chosen by a store employee every Christmas and a hefty gift card to Neiman's every birthday. Almost every item of clothing she'd bought in the last five years, she'd purchased with one of those gift cards.

She chose a long and breezy pink top and black leggings, then moved on to her shoe collection.

Running into Bo on Sunday at lunch had been a very lucky co-incidence, because his presence had once again—amazingly!— settled her anxiety. During the hour she'd sat next to him, she'd felt like someone who could cope with life. Calm. Normal. She'd been able to enjoy her meal, the company, the conversation. And again, when she'd gone to bed that night after seeing him, she'd slept straight through until morning without so much as a twitch.

Good sleep equals a closer approximation of sanity.

She considered Bo a newfound . . . friend. Maybe? He treated her kindly, had even volunteered to help her today with Jayden, despite the sad fate she'd guaranteed his farm. It could be, couldn't it, that he might simply be what he appeared to be: good? Safe? I mean, there had to be *a few* decent men left in the world.

Meg slipped on a pair of silver sandals studded with clunky gray, black, and white gems, then made a bathroom stop to brush her hair and fix her makeup.

When the doorbell sounded, she answered the door to find Bo standing a few steps below. On this eighty-plus-degree day, he'd chosen a plain white T-shirt untucked over jeans and boots. He smiled at her, the shade from his straw Stetson casting his eyes in shadow. The peace he brought with him unfurled into Meg, settling her spirit, relaxing her shoulder muscles.

"Come on in," she said.

"Thanks." He followed her inside, doffing his hat as he moved over the threshold. As he did so, his shirt rode up his bicep, giving her an intriguing glimpse of a tattoo that ringed his upper arm. Linear and perhaps Celtic. She'd never thought of herself as a tattoo-loving girl. But on him . . .

She wished she'd gotten a better look.

"Where's Jayden?" he asked.

"He's not here yet, but Amber should be dropping him off any minute." Meg crossed into the kitchen, putting the short strip of bar between them, trying to hold on to her Bo-buzz while shoving flustering thoughts of that hot-looking tattoo out of her mind. "Can I get you something to drink?"

"I'm fine. Just confused."

"About what?"

"I guess I was under the impression that you lived there." He motioned his thumb toward the big house. "But when I showed up there, Lynn sent me here."

"I see."

"You *are* William Cole's daughter." Humor laced his words.

"Yes."

"And you did grow up over there."

"I did."

"And you do own that house."

"I do."

He looked at her, waiting for her to elaborate.

"I don't really like the big house," she said.

"How come?"

"I . . ." *was unbearably lonely there.* "It's too big for me."

"Hmm," he said, as if he knew she'd dodged his question. "Mind if I look around your place?"

"Go ahead." While he walked into her bedroom, bathroom, and guest bedroom, she busied her hands making a tall glass of iced tea that she had no intention of drinking.

He eventually came to a stop at the living room bookshelves, hands in his back pockets. "You have a big collection of biographies."

"I do."

"About half of them look like they're about artists."

"I've always been interested in art. I worked at a museum before moving back here."

He left the bookshelves behind and returned to her. "Your house reminds me a little bit of my own."

"Is that right?"

86

"I also have two bedrooms and one bathroom. So I guess that means we have one thing in common, you and me."

"It's official, then. We have exactly one thing in common."

"One thing," he agreed. "That's more than I was hoping for, so I'm pretty happy."

She laughed.

"I can see why you like it here." He fingered the edge of a lamp that dripped pink tassels. "It suits you. It's really girly."

"Yeah. I'm girly."

"Who's this?" He indicated Cashew, who'd curled into a loop in the exact center of her only sofa.

"That would be Cashew." The cat raised her face, lowered her brow over her eyes, and scowled at Bo.

"Friendly," Bo said.

"Territorial of that sofa." Sadly, Cashew didn't even have beauty to recommend her. She'd been a stray Meg had been too tenderhearted not to take in. "You're welcome to sit in the chair."

"I'm good."

"Okay."

Those perceptive gray eyes focused on her with concentrated attention, which made the room, all at once, seem overly quiet. She could hear the *whoosh* of the dishwasher and smell the gardenia-scented candle she'd lit. "I was thinking maybe we could make some cookies for Jayden." She'd actually been thinking they could make cookies with Jayden once he arrived, but now it seemed like a good idea to have an activity to focus on while they were alone together in her house. "They're just slice and bake."

"Sure."

He joined her in the tiny kitchen and the space evaporated to nothing. She told him where he could find the cookie sheets, then she spun the dial to set the oven temperature, retrieved the package of sugar cookies, and snipped off the end.

They took turns washing their hands.

"So how do you know Amber and Jayden?" Bo asked.

Inwardly, Meg groaned. She could sidestep the truth, except he'd find out anyway. People loved to gossip about her, and any new tidbit—like the news of Amber and Jayden—would travel fast. She peeled open the cookie wrapper. "Did . . . did you know I was married once?"

His hands stilled beneath the towel he'd been using to dry them. Carefully, he folded it and set it over the edge of the sink. "I'd heard that."

"His name was Stephen McIntyre." She started slicing the sugar cookie loaf. She handed him the cookie circles, and he placed them on the sheet. "Amber is an ex-girlfriend of Stephen's."

She could sense him bracing himself. "And Jayden?"

"Is Stephen's son."

He was too well mannered to ask more, but the question hovered silently between them anyway. "Stephen left them a couple years ago, and Amber's going through a difficult time. I had an opportunity to help them, so I took it."

He nodded, outwardly composed. And yet her intuition told her that the news had ruffled him, which upset her. She'd never made peace with the fact that she was divorced and probably never would. She wore her past like a big red stain on a white shirt, always aware of it, but hating it most, embarrassed by it most, ashamed of it most, when she had to acknowledge it to other people.

DIVORCED. It's not what she'd ever imagined or wanted for herself. She handed Bo the last sliced cookie right as the doorbell rang.

"I'll stick them in the oven," Bo said.

Meg answered the door, and Amber bustled inside like a spring storm. "I know I'm late. So sorry!" She kept Jayden on her hip while she set down a bulging diaper bag and rattled off all kinds of information about what they could expect from Jayden, how his schedule was supposed to play out, and how best to put him down at night. Way more information than Bo and Meg could process or comprehend. "Got all that?" Amber asked.

"I think so," Meg replied bravely, wanting to appear to be a competent baby watcher.

"You wrote down the important stuff for us, right?" Bo asked.

"Right." Amber pulled a slip of paper out of the diaper bag and set it on the table. "And you can call me. My cell number's written at the top. Hopefully, he'll do fine for y'all, even though he woke up early this morning and took a short nap."

Meg didn't exactly like the sound of that.

"Thank you *so much*." Amber looked back and forth between them. "This is such a big help. Oh my gosh, I really appreciate it."

"You're welcome," Meg said.

"I guess I best be getting on the road."

Jayden was clinging to Amber like a spider monkey. When she tried to set him on the carpet, he started crying and gripped her around the waist with his feet. She had to peel him off.

As soon as she handed him to Meg, Jayden's sobs turned tremendously loud, his little mouth stretched open as wide as it would go.

Meg tried to comfort him, awkwardly patting his back while he lunged toward Amber with both arms outstretched.

Amber winced and scooted toward the door. "Sorry. He should quiet down in a minute or two."

"No problem," Meg said, then almost laughed out loud. Anyone could see that the screaming toddler she was wrestling was A. Very. Big. Problem.

"Thank you again. Love you, Jay. Mommy see you soon." Amber blew him a kiss, then slipped out the front door.

Jayden howled.

"Ah," Meg said, turning to Bo. "Any suggestions?"

"Maybe there's something in here." He went to the diaper bag and started extracting things. Baggies of food.

Jayden shook his head. Screamed.

Bo pulled out a flat green frog, pilling with wear and slightly stained. Jayden accepted it with the mistrust of a general accepting a gift from a sworn enemy. He fisted it against his chest and kept crying.

"Drink?" Bo asked him, extending a juice box.

Jayden pushed it away.

"Diaper?"

Jayden swiped the diaper from Bo's hand and threw it on the floor emphatically.

"Wipes?"

Those, too, he hurled to the floor.

"Change of clothes?"

Cashew skittered under the sofa.

"Strange maze toy?"

Jayden turned his face away.

"Weird knobby ball toy I don't understand?"

Jayden's skin darkened to the color of a tomato.

"Well," Bo said, "that's all the diaper bag has to offer."

Meg walked Jayden around her living room, rocking and bouncing, trying to talk to him. Huge tears rolled down his cheeks in steady tracks.

Sympathy swelled inside her. Poor little guy. He hadn't exactly been born into the easiest lot in life. His young, single, working mother had been doing her best to simply scrape by. Now he'd been taken from everything he'd known in Lubbock, brought to Whispering Creek, and left in the care of people he viewed as frightening strangers. He had no way of understanding that his mommy had only left temporarily, or comprehending when she'd come back.

Meg clicked on her TV and found a children's channel playing a cartoon.

Still didn't help. He kept right on sobbing his heart out with no sign of slowing down. "Bo? I'm running out of ideas." *And beginning to feel slightly frantic.*

He came out of the kitchen carrying two sugar cookies on a napkin. "Here, let me give it a try."

Gratefully, she handed Jayden over. The little boy blinked up at Bo with worry and fascination.

"Look, dude. If I had to eat the food that's in your bag and watch this on TV, I'd be mad, too. Cookie?" He lifted the napkin. Jayden took a long moment to decide. He glanced at the cookie, at Bo, and back at the cookie before finally quieting enough to take the cookie and give it a tentative bite. Bo settled into a chair with Jayden on his lap and used the remote to change the channel to sports. "Basketball good with you?"

Jayden watched the screen and chewed.

"Cool. It's good with me, too. What do you say us guys just sit and relax awhile?" Bo leaned back in the chair, and Jayden nestled against Bo's chest. Jayden's tantrum hiccuped its way into silence.

Bo glanced at Meg, who'd frozen in place, almost too afraid to move lest Jayden start back in on the screaming.

"I'm winging it," Bo said to her.

"You're a magician. Thank God you're here."

Bo winked at her.

Saint Bo, a man christened with the miraculous ability to gentle horses, nervous women, and one-year-olds.

Jayden spent the next fifteen minutes watching basketball, then took a sharp turn from calm couch potato into Tasmanian devil. He tried to pull things off Meg's shelves, climb on her chairs and tables, open every drawer and cupboard door on the property, and seek and destroy anything breakable.

Meg brought out the coloring books and crayons she'd purchased for his visit. He spared them ninety seconds of interest. She brought out a brand-new set of Play-Doh. Ninety-five seconds of interest.

Meg and Bo took Jayden outside, and spent an hour and a half chasing him around the lawn, repeatedly detouring his desire to run headlong into the deep end of the pool, and averting his tendency to stick anything under the subheading of "nature" into his mouth.

They baby-wrangled him through just about every room and closet of the big house for another hour, before finally imprisoning him in his highchair for dinner. Per Amber's instructions, Meg made quesadillas and carefully cut them into bite-size squares before serving them to Jayden.

"Bo?" They were sitting on either side of Jayden at the table in the big house kitchen while he ate.

"Yes?"

"I have a new goal in life."

"What's that?"

"To hire child care for Jayden."

He chuckled. "As fun as this has been and all, I think that might be wise."

"Best money I'll ever spend."

Jayden started pitching quesadilla pieces over the side of his chair.

"I think he's done already," Meg said with a trace of despair. She'd only been sitting down for what felt like five minutes and hadn't had a chance to drink even half of her bottled water.

"Don't see how that's possible," Bo answered.

Jayden shoved away his plate and tried to heft himself out of his high chair. Then suddenly he stilled.

"Oh good. Maybe he's changed his mind."

Jayden's gaze fixed on the middle of nowhere. He gave a muffled grunt. His face squeezed with strain.

"Oh, no you don't," Bo threatened.

Meg started to laugh. A poopy diaper. The cherry on top of the sundae of challenge and exhaustion that was the job of baby-sitting Jayden Richardson. And she'd imagined running Cole Oil to be difficult! She didn't know how in the world Amber did this work—alone—on a daily basis. Over the past few hours her respect and awe for the woman had skyrocketed. Forget Superman and Batman. Single mothers were the real superheroes. If she hadn't already pledged her support to Amber, this gig watching Jayden would have motivated her to do so ten times over.

Jayden finished doing his business and tried to hoist himself out of the chair again.

"I guess," Meg said, "a dirty diaper was inevitable."

"Actually, it's a bullet I'd been hoping to dodge."

"Any interest in changing him?"

"None."

"Me neither."

Bo tilted his head. "Want to flip a coin?"

"I'd rather you just do it." She tested a cajoling smile on him.

"You're not going to like my terms."

"Lay 'em on me."

"If I change him, then you have to go horseback riding with me."

He was right; she didn't like his terms. Toddler poop. Or horse phobia. Choices, choices. Toddler poop offered torture of much shorter duration. Maybe she'd go with that. . . . But then the smell hit her. Rank beyond belief. "I'll take you up on your offer," Meg said.

"You'll come out and ride."

"Yes." She'd brought Jayden's diaper bag with them when they'd come to the big house and now fished out the wipes and a diaper and handed them over. Bo tucked them in the waistband of his jeans. With a pained expression, he extracted Jayden from the high chair.

Meg fought to hide her grin. Bo's expression alone was almost worth the price of the horseback riding.

Bo held Jayden extended out in front of him, his big hands under Jayden's little arm pits. He paused in the doorway of the kitchen, the toddler dangling. "Should I just lay him down on the floor of the bathroom and change him there?"

"I guess."

They left and were gone for what seemed like an unusually long time. Meg finished her water and straightened the kitchen.

When they returned, Jayden was riding on the palm of Bo's hand and smiling widely.

"How'd it go?" Meg asked.

"I managed to come through Iraq and Afghanistan okay, but I'm going to need therapy after that."

"I'll foot the bill."

"I'm not sure if I got the diaper on forwards or backwards."

"Hopefully it'll work either way."

"Since you don't have a hazmat bin, I tied the bag from the bathroom trash can around the diaper and walked it to the outside trash."

"Very wise. Thank you."

"Then I washed my hands three times in burning hot water. I'm surprised there's still skin on them."

"Am I going to have to pay for therapy *and* worker's comp?" Meg accepted Jayden from Bo with a smile.

"Yes, and the bill's going to be more than you can afford."

"I don't know about that."

The two of them took Jayden upstairs for his bath. They hadn't yet started to undress him when he went through the whole grunting, straining, stinky thing again.

"No way," Bo said. "Not possible."

But it was.

Bo looked Meg straight in the eyes. "Two horseback riding lessons," he growled.

"Two lessons," she agreed.

He toted the boy into the bedroom Jayden shared with Amber. A few moments went by. "There's only one wipe left!" Panic and revulsion tinged his voice. "Gee, thanks, Amber."

Meg hurried in, trying to ignore both the stench and the sight of Bo holding Jayden's legs in the air while the kid did his best to perform a twist. She opened drawers until she located a fresh supply of wipes, tore some free, and placed them where Bo could reach them. Fighting not to burst into impolite laughter, she fled the room.

Once Bo had cleaned Jayden up, Meg plopped him in the tub and Bo made his second trip to the outside trash. It turned out that the bath contained Jayden and made him happy, so Meg and Bo let him play in the sudsy water until he finally grew irritable.

"I better start rounding up all of his bedtime stuff," Bo said.

"Sounds good. I'll get him dressed."

Toweling him off proved to be no problem, but forcing him into his jammies carried a medium-high level of difficulty. Meg kept trying to capture squirming limbs, and Jayden kept trying to roll off the top of the chest of drawers, which was serving as a temporary changing table.

When she finally succeeded, sweating, she checked her watch. Was it really possible for time to move so slowly? She felt like they'd been taking care of Jayden for decades, but they *still* had thirty minutes before the bedtime Amber had suggested. He seemed sleepy, though, and Bo had already warmed up a sippy cup of milk for him. So Meg decided to send up a hope and prayer and attempt to put Jayden down anyway.

"You got this?" Bo asked her.

"I think so. Did we do everything Amber said?"

"Yep, I put the sound machine on 'waterfall,' pulled the curtains, turned on the night-light, and checked to make sure his monitor was working. Just to be on the safe side."

"Then I should be good."

He stepped out, closing the door to Amber's room behind him. She clicked off the overhead fixture, then settled them both into the rocking chair Lynn had found in the big house's attic.

Amber had written on her page of instructions that Meg was now supposed to sing.

Single adult women weren't typically lullaby specialists.

She handed Jayden his green frog and his sippy cup, then rocked, searching her memory for anything that might suffice.

"Hush little baby," she sang softly, "don't say a word. Meggie's gonna buy you a mockingbird. If that mockingbird don't sing, Meggie's gonna buy you a diamond ring. If that diamond ring don't fit, Meggie's gonna buy you . . ." She couldn't remember any more of the lyrics, so she made something up. "A catcher's mitt. If that catcher's mitt don't catch, Meggie's gonna buy you a . . . doorway latch." She racked her brain for more rhymes. "If that doorway latch don't hold, Meggie's gonna buy you some ice cream cold. If that ice cream don't taste sweet, Meggie's gonna buy you a phone that tweets."

Fresh out of creativity, she stopped singing and simply hummed the melody. She gazed down into Jayden's little face, and he gazed up at her in the dimness, his eyes large and shiny. Trusting.

A silent communication passed between them in that moment, deep and heartfelt.

She understood, suddenly, why everything that mothers went through—the work, the weariness, the sacrifice—was worth it to them. Her throat swelled and tears rushed to her eyes. Her humming choked out, but she kept up the smooth motion. Back and forth. Faint creaking. Back and forth.

"I'm going to help you," she whispered to him, her words almost inaudible in the hushed, waterfall white noise of the room. "You and your mom came to the right place because I'm going to help you. You're safe here. I'm going to make sure that you both have every opportunity. Okay?"

His eyes held innocence and a sort of uncanny wisdom. His little fingers gathered his frog snug under his chin, next to the yellow duck pattern on his jammies, and he went to work sucking his thumb.

"I promise you," she whispered.

They continued to look at each other for a long stretch.

Tears blurring her vision, she finally carried him to his small portable crib and leaned way down to place him inside. She braced for screams, but stunningly, he simply turned onto his side and cozied down into the softness of his crib sheet.

She tiptoed out and closed the door soundlessly behind her. Bo stood leaning against the wall in the hallway, watching her.

"You waited," she said.

"I did."

She'd spent ages putting Jayden down. "Thank you."

His eyes narrowed. "You crying?"

"Just a little."

He reached into a front pocket of his jeans, brought out a couple of neatly folded travel-sized tissues, and handed them to her. "I told you I'd have them ready." He grinned crookedly.

In response, her insides gave a hot, insistent tug.

Wh—what?! It had been so long since she'd experienced physical desire that she hardly recognized it. So very, very long. Years. But the tug turned into an aching pull, unmistakable to her even after all this time. Dazedly, she took the tissues from him and dabbed under her eyes.

"You okay?" he asked.

"Yes."

She led him along the hall and down the central staircase. She'd noticed his handsomeness the first day they'd met, of course. But it had been more of a scholarly notation. Like the way she'd assess a painting: "Hmm. Handsome." It hadn't affected her . . . until now. Huge uh-oh.

In the great room, she checked the baby monitor. She could hear waterfall, but nothing else.

"Sadie Jo's going to take over for you soon, right?" Bo asked.

"Yes. She insisted on doing something, so she's going to sleep in the room with him tonight, and then she and Lynn are going to watch him in the morning until Amber gets back. She wanted to do even more, but she's eighty years old. He's too much work for her."

"I'm thirty-two and I feel like I need to sleep for a week."

"Exactly. Me too."

"If you want to head back to your place, I'll wait here for Sadie Jo."

"It's all right. Go ahead and take off. I don't mind waiting."

They faced one another across a pause of quiet. While Jayden had been in the mix, and before she'd felt that fateful tug, things had been easy between them. Now, though, that friendliness had changed. The intensity in his eyes had darkened to something much more personal.

The skin between her shoulder blades tingled in answer. She couldn't stop herself from making a very unscholarly assessment of him. In this instant, she found Bo Porter to be ruggedly, real man, take-your-breath-away gorgeous. And she had a wild whim to throw herself into his arms.

Impossible!

"I'll be going, then," he said.

"Thank you so much for helping me today."

"It was nothing."

"It meant a lot to me."

He retrieved his hat from a nearby table and settled it on his head, giving her another peek at his tattoo. *Goodness.* Could he . . . might he . . . have more tattoos somewhere? A blush burgeoned on her chest and expanded up her neck to her face.

They walked through the foyer to the huge front doors, and she opened the right one.

"G'night."

"Good night, Bo."

He moved past her toward his truck. When he reached it, she closed herself in and leaned against the inside of the door. Her hands, which had been overtaken with fine trembles, raked into her hair.

She couldn't. She couldn't like him in any way except the politically correct way that bosses liked the managers beneath them.

Her mind turned over slowly, its gears mired in tar. In recent years she'd had male colleagues she'd called friends. And that's how she'd been thinking of Bo. Calming cowboy; colleague. But her thinking had shifted, uninvited, to calming cowboy; *sexy* colleague.

Was it even legal for her to think like that? Didn't it constitute sexual harassment? She signed his paychecks, for goodness' sake.

Earlier today she'd been attaching words like *safe* and *friend* to Bo. At this point in her life, she dearly needed a safe friend. But thanks to those flashes of bone-melting chemistry just now, *safe* and *friend* both seemed questionable. She welcomed the peacefulness she felt around him. She didn't welcome, didn't want to feel, the whole he-makes-my-toes-clench bit.

And yet, at the same time, she *did* want to examine that tattoo.

If Meg had been anything all of her life, she'd been a rule follower. She respected the way of things, tried with all her might to do the appropriate. It made her comfortable and secure to do the right thing. To skate by without drawing undue attention to herself. To walk within the boundaries.

Harboring romantic feelings for Bo Porter? Outside the boundaries. Very inappropriate.

She'd probably have died of fatigue if she'd had to care for Jayden solo today. Even so, she'd overstepped when she'd agreed to let Bo baby-sit alongside her. Because no matter how willing Bo had been to help her with Jayden, no matter how thankful she'd been for his help, the situation had proven too intimate.

She was his boss.

Ooh, but he was hunky—

Meg Cole! You're. His. Boss.

Chapter Seven

*H*e was her employee. But Bo's feelings toward Meg
had just about nothing to do with employment.
They should have. But they didn't.

After they finished baby-sitting Jayden, Bo took himself to
Whispering Creek Horses and threw himself into work because he couldn't bear to sit still with either his thoughts or his
emotions.

He measured out the nutritionist's recommendation of feed
for the mares, adding his own adjustments based on his knowledge of each one. He mucked out already clean stalls.

When the night man came on duty, he gave Bo a look and
apparently decided, based on Bo's expression alone, to hold his
tongue and cut a wide path around him.

Bo drove to the yearling barn and examined his yearlings
with care, one by one. Then on to the stallion barn. He escorted
some of the horses inside and some out. He swept the asphalt
surface of the shed row.

By midnight, he'd visited each of his five barns, and with
nowhere left to go, he drove home. He paced his living room,
stared into the refrigerator without eating, and finally spent an
hour lying in his bed in a tangle of sheets thinking about Meg.

The whole time since the moment they'd parted company, he'd been trying to talk himself out of caring about her. Not caring would make his life a heck of a lot easier, would help him keep his priorities focused on the farm. Guilt twisted within him. It wasn't right for his thoughts to be consumed with Meg when his farm was dying.

Unfortunately, though, not thinking about her, not caring about her, wasn't an option for him. And hadn't been, almost since their first meeting.

He cared. He cared about her with a burning heat that filled his entire chest, mind, and heart.

The next morning Bo arrived at the warm room of the yearling barn and had just opened his laptop when Jake shouldered in, bringing with him a wave of chilly air.

Jake raised one eyebrow at the sight of Bo. "You look terrible."

"Thanks."

"Been up all night?"

"Something like that."

Jake shrugged off his jacket and settled into the chair across from Bo. Bo had picked up two black coffees from McDonald's on his way in. He nudged Jake's cup across to him.

"Appreciate it," Jake said.

They sat together for a few minutes, working on their coffee.

Even after four years of looking at the scar on Jake's face, it still hurt Bo to see it. They were both grown men, but Bo would always be the older brother. He'd never stop wanting to defend his siblings from harm and never stop regretting the times he'd been unable to. Ty, Jake, and their baby sister, Dru, all came after him, and he felt protective toward each of them.

"What're you looking at?" Jake asked.

"Your mug."

"Real pretty, huh?"

Girls had always taken an interest in all three of the Porter brothers. But they'd been the most interested in Jake because he'd been the best looking. Bo wished that were still the case.

Like Bo, Ty, their father, John, and their grandfather, Jake had gone into the Marines after high school and become an infantry rifleman. Bo, Ty, and Jake had gone on several tours of duty, survived countless combat operations, and lived through firefights to write home about. But only Jake had had an IED explode under his Humvee. Only Jake had seen three of his men mangled to death, had his face sliced open by shrapnel, and been plunged into post-traumatic stress disorder.

When the Porters had first heard about Jake's accident and been told that Jake would recover, they'd been filled with gratitude and relief. But when Jake returned home a grim, numb shadow, they realized that Jake himself didn't share their enthusiasm.

Thank God that Jake's gift with horses, at least, had been spared. He had an uncanny way with the animals: gentle and knowledgeable. He could communicate with them through body language and read them the way most people read books.

Jake had come back from the war right around the time that construction of Whispering Creek's stables had been completed. Bo had hired Jake as the farm's trainer before the first of the Thoroughbreds had arrived.

Four years later Jake still struggled with PTSD nightmares, memories, and survivor's guilt. He still lived as if protected behind a sheet of Plexiglas that none of them could break. Bo no longer held out hope that Jake would ever return to the man

BECKY WADE

he'd been before. Instead, Bo had to be satisfied with the fact that Jake had improved over the years and was, at least, better than he'd been when he'd first come home. Bo knew that most of that improvement had come because of Jake's work. Training horses gave Jake a reason to put one foot in front of the other.

"Were you up all night because Meg Cole's planning to close the farm?" Jake asked.

"Yeah." That had been part of it.

"Do you think she's starting to bend on that at all?"

Jake asked him this question at least every third day. "I'm not sure."

"You spent time with her yesterday afternoon, didn't you?"

"Yes."

"And? We've already burned ten days off that six-month deadline. What're you doing to change her mind?"

"Not much." He'd bribed her into a few riding lessons. But he'd been thinking mostly of himself and very little about the ranch when he'd made that bargain.

"Well, talk to her, man. Try to persuade her."

Bo didn't want Meg to think—not ever—that he was trying to capitalize on their friendship. And if he had a conversation like that with her at this point, or at any point in the future, how could she not? "Here's the thing, Jake. I don't feel right about trying to persuade her."

"What?" Worry lit his brother's eyes.

"I don't. I've thought about it a lot."

"Then why in the world were you over at her house for half the day yesterday?"

"She needed help baby-sitting the little boy that's staying with her."

"Help baby-sitting?" Jake repeated with disbelief.

105

In the pause that followed, Jake stared hard at Bo. A horse whinnied and muted voices passed by the warm room's door.

"You don't have a thing for her," Jake said. "Do you?"

Bo thumbed the lid of his coffee.

Jake released a whistling breath. "You do have a thing for her. What exactly is going on between you two?"

"Nothing. I work for her. We're friends."

"That's it?"

"That's it."

"But you like her."

"I like her." Such a huge understatement that it was almost a lie.

"It's impossible, Bo. A relationship between you two can't happen."

Bo held his brother's gaze. "I know."

"Say you two start dating and then three months from now, or five months from now, or fifteen months from now she gets mad at you for some reason. She could shut down the farm anytime she wants, just out of spite."

"I don't need convincing, Jake. I already told you that I know it can't happen."

"The livelihood of all the people who work here is at stake—"

"Enough," Bo warned, his anger rising.

Jake set his mouth in a line. "If you're not going to do anything to change her mind, then what can I do to change it? What can any of us do?"

"Nothing. She's a businesswoman. She can make an educated decision all by herself."

"She's already made a decision, and it's the wrong one."

"It seems wrong to us because we like horses. She doesn't, at least not yet. With any luck, she'll start coming out to the farm. And if that happens, maybe she'll get to know the place and the people."

"That's your strategy? Sit back and hope she visits?"

"No, my strategy is to focus on paying off the farm's debt. That, and pray."

Jake made a scoffing sound.

Bo had decided, back on the day when Meg had visited the broodmare barn, not to put the farm's interests above hers. The future of his staff might prove to ride on that decision. Jake's sanity might prove to ride on it. And yet still, for better or worse, Bo wouldn't choose differently. He only hoped he'd chosen correctly.

"Are you going to start selling horses?" Jake asked.

"I'm going to wait and see how we do at the track first, and how our yearling sales go. Selling off horses is my last resort."

"You'll not sell Silver Leaf."

"No," Bo answered automatically. "Not Silver Leaf." He wouldn't consider selling that particular horse, not even when the farm ran out of time and hope. He'd scrape together his life savings and buy Silver Leaf from Meg himself first.

Jake pressed to his feet and tossed his coffee cup in the trash. "I'm going back to work."

"I'll join you." The brothers walked together down the length of the barn, similar in height, size, and pace. They passed a groom hand-walking a horse in the other direction.

Jake led one of their yearlings from his stall to the round pen. Bo followed, coming to stand inside the pen, leaning back against it with his arms crossed over his chest.

Jake unhooked the shank from the colt's halter and chirped to him, urging him from a jog to a lope, around and around the pen.

Bo watched the animal's gait with a practiced eye, judged the colt's conformation, weighed his muscle development. All promising.

He'd meant what he'd said to Jake earlier, about praying. His parents had raised him right, with his butt in the church pew every Sunday morning. He was a praying man, and he believed that God could change Meg's heart in ways that he couldn't.

His brother might not believe it at this moment, but Bo loved this place. He loved it even more than Jake did.

Amber's return from Lubbock officially increased Whispering Creek's I-survived-a-connection-to-Stephen-McIntyre population by two.

Meg toyed with the idea of putting Amber to work at Cole Oil, but she decided not to go that route because the commute to Dallas and back would cut at least an hour out of Amber's time with Jayden every day. Instead, Meg made a call to Holley's mayor, a longtime friend of her father's, in search of a job opening for Amber. As it turned out, the mayor himself offered Amber a position as a part-time office assistant at his law firm.

Thus, Amber's employment began just a day and a half later. Meg and Lynn determined that Whispering Creek's maids would care for Jayden during the hours that Amber worked until a nanny could be found.

As the work week progressed and Easter Sunday drew near, Meg and Amber met each evening to sort through nanny résumés and references. After their meetings, Meg returned to the guesthouse and studied Cole Oil reports and manuals until her eyes crossed and her lids refused to stay open.

Faithfully, she read her Bible, prayed, and pored over her book of verses. She tried her best to accept His peace. Tried and mostly failed. Her job continued to overwhelm, and her panic continued to hover.

Every morning when she parked in the underground lot beneath the Cole Oil building, Meg wanted to throw up at the thought of the people above—her assistants, Uncle Michael, and all the smart executives—who would be waiting for her and expecting her to display the famous Cole confidence, intelligence, and business acumen.

She *longed* to take a trip to the horse farm to see Bo, but refrained. In the hours after their baby-sitting gig together, she'd talked herself into the idea that the crackle between them hadn't been all one-sided, that he might feel a little stirring of something for her, too.

She even prepared herself to rebuff him if needed. But the weekend came without him making any effort to contact her, which kind of took the wind out of her sails.

Maybe she'd gotten it wrong. Her man radar had always been haywire. Like a faulty sonar machine on a submarine, it had never been trustworthy. It was possible that she'd misread him. He might not like her romantically at all. Or, possibly, he did like her, but would rather go to the grave than violate the whole employer-employee thing.

Uninvited thoughts of him came to Meg at the oddest moments. She'd be washing her hair and would remember him at the paddock, his fingers twining with easy familiarity through his horse's mane. She'd be sitting in her father's office downtown looking at a document, and she'd remember the way he'd quieted little Jayden's separation anxiety. She'd fill her coffee cup in the morning and remember the way he'd extended those confounded tissues to her at the top of the stairs. *"I told you I'd have them ready,"* he'd said.

Who did that? Who carried around tissues for a woman they hardly knew, just in case she got teary? The tissues were to blame, she'd decided, for the turn her heart had taken. It was all, *all*, ALL the tissues' fault!

Meg enjoyed so many things about Easter.

She loved the boxes of Godiva truffles that she and Sadie Jo exchanged every year when they sat down to share a big breakfast of pancakes, bacon, orange juice served in crystal glasses, and coffee served in china teacups. She loved the praise, triumph, and hope of Easter morning worship service. She loved singing "Up From the Grave He Arose." She loved the foil-covered bunnies, wicker baskets, and jelly beans that overran the store shelves. She loved buying a new dress and matching high heels. She loved the dogwood trees with their bright new blossoms, and flower arrangements of daffodils and tulips.

However, she did not love the big formal lunch her mother's side of the family held every Easter Sunday. Her overriding emotion whenever she had to deal with her grandmother Lake, her mother's three older sisters, and her nine female cousins?

Intimidation.

This year the Lake family decided to gather at Aunt Pamela's newest McMansion in the ritzy Dallas neighborhood of Highland Park. Since Amber and Jayden had nowhere else to go to celebrate the holiday, Meg brought them along for lunch, and thank goodness. Because of them, Meg wasn't *the only* normal human at Pamela's mile-long table, a table otherwise filled with a convention of the most stunning and fashionable people the state of Texas had to offer.

All through the meal, Meg listened to her beautiful cousin Heather talk to her beautiful cousin Erin about their children's chic private schools, the merits of a personal shopper versus a stylist, the amazing career accomplishments of their husbands, and their own involvements with local charities. Meg made it through without needing to excuse herself to have a panic attack in one of the marble bathrooms, but only by a hair.

As soon as everyone finished lunch, the children clamored for the start of the annual Easter egg hunt. It was decided that Meg, along with an assortment of fathers and grandfathers, would watch the passel of children in the front yard, while the mothers went to work hiding eggs in the backyard. So Meg made her way outdoors and stood beneath a pearl gray overcast sky while the wind tossed the hem of her dress against her knees. The enormous edifice of Aunt Pamela's house stood next to her, gamely endeavoring to impersonate a French country manor despite the fact that it had been rooted in Texas soil.

One of the kids squealed, and Meg's attention swept over the girls, who wore bobbed haircuts, giant bows, smocked dresses, and shining sandals. The boys were dressed either in jumpers with knee socks and saddle shoes or in full seersucker suits.

In the midst of that impressive group, Jayden looked like a gargoyle.

Meg's heart tweaked for him. Unfortunate kid. Today he reminded her more than ever of a drooly-mouthed bobblehead doll. Amber hadn't helped matters by dressing him in a slightly too-small striped one-piece that looked like it had been through the wash a zillion times.

Still. Out of all the children in the yard, the lion's share of

Meg's affection centered on him. She herself had always felt like a gargoyle when surrounded by this branch of her family. Without a mother, she'd been like a puzzle piece set off to the side, unable to attach to the Lake family because she'd had no connecting piece. A sibling or two would have made all the difference, because then, even without her connecting piece, she'd have had allies.

How many times, she wondered, had she mourned the lack of a sibling over the course of her lifetime? Thousands.

She held her hair out of her face and watched Jayden careen around a cluster of boys, trip over a tree root, and fall forward onto his hands. Meg rushed over and set him back on his feet. "You okay?"

He glanced up at her, grinning.

"Time for the hunt, everyone!" Aunt Pamela held open the front door and beckoned them in.

As Meg led Jayden indoors, Aunt Pamela pulled her aside. "I haven't heard back from you, but you *are* coming to Tara's engagement party, right?"

"Ah . . ." She'd received the invitation to the party a few weeks back. But it had ranked lowest on her list of worries, and she hadn't given it a thought since.

"We're holding it at the Crescent, and you have to come. Tara would be crushed if you couldn't make it."

Meg didn't think Tara, the youngest of Pamela's four daughters, would bat a single fake eyelash if Meg didn't show.

Jayden tugged on her hand, and Meg swept him into her arms.

"Say you'll come." Pamela speared Meg with an unblinking stare.

Meg chewed the inside of her cheek, racking her brain for

a way to beg off. Aunt Pamela had benefited from some excellent plastic surgery. She didn't look tight or weird; just fresh, smooth, and impossibly young for her age. Her hair fell, glistening brown highlighted with cinnamon, in perfect layers to her shoulders. The oldest of Meg's mother's sisters, she'd always been bossy, and she'd always been able to apply pressure with a glance.

"Say you'll come," Pamela repeated.

"I'll come."

"Excellent! And you'll bring someone." More with the unblinking stare.

"Maybe."

"You have to. Everyone will be bringing a date. You don't want to be the only one there alone."

"Actually, I wouldn't mind—"

"You're *not* going to be the only one there alone. I'll count on you, plus one. All right?"

"Mmm . . ." Jayden stretched both hands out, leaning in the direction the other kids had gone.

"You plus one. All right, Meg?"

"Yes."

Appeased, Aunt Pamela preceded her into a sitting room at the back of the house. The parents passed out Easter baskets, then let the kids loose on the rolling backyard dotted here and there with partially hidden pastel plastic eggs.

Meg and Amber followed Jayden as he dragged around his basket and ignored all the eggs. After Amber showed him repeatedly how to pick up the eggs, Jayden picked up three in a row and placed them in his basket.

Amber and Meg clapped excitedly.

Then he tossed them out and stepped on them.

Amber groaned, and Meg laughed.

"Thank you for inviting us to come today," Amber said, sticking the eggs back in Jayden's basket.

"You're welcome. I'm glad you're here."

"Your aunts and your cousins are beautiful."

"Yes, they are."

"I mean, like wow. And their husbands and their kids and this house. The whole deal."

"I know."

"Are you the youngest cousin?"

"Close to it. There are a couple a few years younger than me."

"Is everyone married?"

"All but two."

"And does everyone in the family live in Dallas?"

"Yes."

"In houses like this?"

"Almost everyone." Meg's mother and her three older sisters had all been beauty-pageant worthy back in the day, and they'd all leveraged their looks into handsome, wealthy husbands. The handsome, wealthy husbands had given them gorgeous offspring, who in turn grew up to marry brilliantly. Her grandmother Lake, who had an Elizabeth Taylor–like proclivity for gems and furs, presided over them all with a combination of shrewdness, senility, and vanity. "I only have one male cousin on this side of the family. He lives in a regular house."

"Which one is he?"

"His name's Brimm. He's the one sitting on the patio, ignoring the Easter egg hunt so he can play on his smartphone." Unlike her, Brimm—the lucky duck—had managed to dodge lunch and arrive late.

Amber glanced over her shoulder. "I see him."

"He's great. He's the same age as I am, and we've always hung out together at family gatherings."

"What's he do?"

"He's a professor."

Amber's brows rose. "He doesn't look old enough to be a professor."

"He's a math and computer genius, so he graduated early from everything." Meg tried to extract her heels from the soft grass. "He teaches applied mathematics, though I'm not even sure what that means."

Amber opened a few of Jayden's eggs for him, revealing two foil-wrapped chocolate eggs, a bunny-shaped eraser, and a yellow marshmallow Peep. He ignored the eraser, plopped onto the grass, and went to work on the Peep.

Amber and Meg stood next to one another, watching him. "If your cousin Brimm is good with computers," Amber said slowly, "do you think there's any chance he might be willing to help me find Stephen?"

Meg's attention swung to Amber. She'd assumed that she'd set aside her search for Stephen now that she'd found security. "You . . . still want to try to find Stephen?"

"I do."

"Even though you're stable now, financially?"

Her expression turned apologetic. "Yes."

"Why?"

"There's just something in me that needs to find him." She exhaled and started picking at her nail polish. "I still don't feel . . . I don't know . . . *peaceful* about him. I don't think I will until I see him face to face. I want him to admit that he has a kid. I want him to pay his share, even though you're helping me. I . . ." Her lips twisted into a frown. "I still want a lot out of him. I just don't feel right about it the way that it is."

Meg swallowed hard.

"I'm sorry." Amber's blue eyes filled with worry. "I don't want to hurt your feelings. I couldn't be more grateful to you—"

"I know. It's okay. I get where you're coming from." Meg looked toward Jayden, who now wore a chocolate goatee.

After Stephen's departure from her life, Meg had never—not ever ever ever—wanted to set eyes on him again. But apparently, Amber needed face-to-face closure.

Oh, Lord, she beseeched. Just the thought of involving herself in a search for Stephen, of having to hear and think about him, made her want to cover her ears and hide in a closet. At the same time, the tenderhearted part of her, that big blasted nougaty center of the chocolate truffle, couldn't bear to respond to Amber's need in any way other than with an offer of help. Especially because she believed herself partly responsible for what Stephen had done to Amber. Her pride, fear, and silence had allowed him to continue his destructive behavior in the years since he'd left her.

Up until this point, she'd assisted Amber in ways that had cost herself little.

But the truth? That was expensive.

Her stomach tightened into a burning ball, making Meg regret everything she'd eaten for lunch. "Before I ask Brimm to help you, I'd like to talk to you about Stephen."

"Sounds good."

"One night soon, after Jayden's down?"

"Deal."

She'd tell Amber about her own experiences with Stephen. If, after that, Amber still wanted to find him, then so be it.

Meg returned to Whispering Creek, changed clothes, then rattled around the guesthouse alone, growing more anxious by the minute. Thoughts of Stephen dogged her, twining together with the job stress she carried around constantly. She grew so unsettled that she couldn't bring herself to read, take a bubble bath, or work on sudoku.

At last, desperate, she dashed to her car and drove to the horse farm. She *really* wanted to see Bo. She knew, however, that he wouldn't be working on Easter Sunday. Maybe a good thing, since his absence would prevent her from caving on her decision to keep her distance.

Her best hope? That the horses and scenery held some power to relax her, even without him.

She parked at the broodmare barn, then walked to the same spot at the same paddock she'd visited the last time. Blessedly—one of God's small mercies—she found several mothers and babies within.

She wrapped her hands around the top plank of the fence, watched the darling little foals, and tried to absorb the quiet of the setting. *Breathe in for a count of six, Meg, hold for six, breathe out for a count of seven.*

Minutes slid past, one into the next. A chocolate brown foal nudged its mother with its nose. Another mother/baby pair meandered along the rail, stopped to observe her, then moved on. They all looked so enviably content and serene.

Gradually, the burning orange ball of the sun lowered behind the treetops. Meg slid her glasses on, sending the horizon into focus. The sun was going. Going. Almost gone. Gone.

In its wake, the enormous Texas sky blazed with swaths of pale orange, white, and pink. An arrow formation of birds winged their way past, their bodies dark against the backdrop of the sunset. *Look at the birds of the air*, it said in the Bible, *they do not sow or reap or store away in barns, and yet your heavenly Father feeds them. Are you not much more valuable than they? Who of you by worrying can add a single hour to his life?*

"Amen," she whispered. If He could manage the horses, the birds, and the nature that surrounded her, then He could manage her life.

God, she prayed, *I honestly believe that you're on your throne at this very moment. I'm handing over this whole situation with Amber and Stephen to you. Help me to do the right thing and to be brave. Help me, also, to find my place at Cole Oil.* In her heart, she knew she wasn't cut out for the profession set before her. It was all wrong. A terrible fit. And yet duty didn't ask you your opinion, did it? *Show me what I can do there, Lord, that might bring you glory. Show me how to manage my father's fortune, this house, and the people that work here. Most of all, please, Lord . . . please help me manage my anxiety. It's eating at me again—*

A twig crunched behind her.

She jerked around to see Bo striding toward her. Instead of his usual cowboy clothing, he wore track pants and a black hooded sweatshirt zipped up the front over a white T-shirt.

Her body—traitor!—reacted the way it had reacted to cute boys when she'd been fifteen years old. Her heart tripped over itself, and her skin flushed with excitement.

His attention honed on her as he approached. "One of the grooms called me and told me you were here."

"Oh."

"I was just finishing up at the gym so I thought I'd swing by."

"You shouldn't have bothered to drive all the way out here on my behalf. It's Easter."

"It is." He stopped beside her at the fence and looked into her face with a combination of serious intensity and warmth. "Happy Easter, Meg."

"Happy Easter."

He smiled a little, which sent a dimple into his cheek. He had a face that would have suited an old-time Texas Ranger—firm features, determined jawline, placid eyes. A rugged, capable face. Just looking at that face caused the knots of stress in her stomach to loosen. "I don't want you to feel like you have to hang out with me whenever I'm at the farm. Especially not on your day off." *The lady doth protest too much.*

He hefted a muscled shoulder. "I wanted to come. I was worried you'd be out here crying over the foals. Who else was going to bring you tissues if not me?"

Ah, those pesky tissues! She experienced a sudden sentimental and wayward rush of gratitude toward him. She'd been out here alone, trying not to hyperventilate, needing a friend, and he had—very simply—come. There'd be time to worry about her attraction to him later.

"Need any?" he asked. "Tissues?"

"Not at the moment." Her lips curved.

"Just let me know." He rested his elbows on the fence. "How was your day?"

"Good. Yours?"

"Good."

"How'd you spend it?"

"I started off at church."

"Does your family go to church every Easter?"

"We go every Sunday, year round."

"You're a Christian."

"I'm from a small town in Texas." Self-mocking humor settled into the squint lines near his eyes. "Can't think what else I'd be."

"You mean other than a gun-toting hick with a backward view of the world?"

His head drew back. He gazed at her, arrested, then burst out laughing.

She laughed with him.

"I'm probably guilty of that, too," he said. "The gun-toting backwards part."

"No, I was just kidding. I'm glad to hear you're a Christian, though. I thought as much."

"Why's that?"

"I could just recognize it in you." In fact, she often felt like she could identify other believers without being told . . . as if the Holy Spirit in her sensed the Holy Spirit in them. Like attracting like.

"What about you?" he asked. "Did you grow up only going to church on Easter?"

"My father only went with me on Easter and Christmas Eve. Luckily, Sadie Jo took me the rest of the year. I'm from the same small town in Texas that you are, after all."

"We've covered this ground before. You're not from Holley."

"Yes I am."

"No. You're from the same zip code. But a person who's never eaten at our DQ wasn't raised in Holley."

She grinned. "Okay. Point taken."

They traded stories about their respective Easter meals, the foods they'd liked and the ones they'd avoided, the quirks of the extended family members they'd spent their afternoons with. The exterior barn lights flicked on and full darkness descended. She told him about Jayden hunting eggs. He told her about his concerns for his brother Jake, the crazy thing his little sister Dru had said to shock the relatives, and how his family had talked to his brother Ty on speakerphone because Ty was away touring with something called the Bull Riders' Professional Circuit.

Bo's presence, the hushed beauty of the animals, and their easy conversation sank into Meg like a balm. Culture touted solitary rest as the cure for anxiety. But for her, "the Bo effect" worked far better. His nearness comforted her more than aloneness ever could have. In her twenty-eight years she'd already had enough aloneness to last five lifetimes.

When a groom came to escort the horses into the barn, Bo walked Meg to her car and held her door for her. "I'll bet you're the only person in this county," he said, "driving around in a Mercedes convertible from the '80s."

"I'm sure you're right." She settled into the driver's seat and patted the wheel. "This was my mother's car." In a sentimental move uncharacteristic of him, her father had held on to the car long after her mother's death. So long, that Meg had asked if she could have it once she'd received her license. She'd been driving it and taking scrupulous care of it ever since. Sitting where her mother had sat, driving the classy little white car her mother had driven, helped her feel connected to a woman she otherwise knew only through photos and the stories of relatives.

"I kind of figured that," Bo said. "I like it."

"Thanks. So do I."

"G'night." He shut her door.

As she drove down the lane toward the big house with him

following in his truck, she glanced at his headlights in her rear-view mirror again and again.

She'd recently attempted to classify him as either someone who was trying to manipulate her, someone who wasn't interested in her romantically, or someone who was interested, but would never act on it. After their time together this evening, she thought that he *might* fall into the latter category.

If he'd come out tonight and made a pass at her, she'd have bolted in terror. But he'd done nothing of the kind. Everything about her time with him just now assured her that while he might be interested in her as a woman, he respected the line between them too much to cross it. She didn't need to put space between them, because Bo himself would see to that. Because of their work relationship, she could count on him to keep things between them honorable and friendly. He had old-fashioned values. He was actually . . . ethical.

She wanted to believe, maybe already did believe, that she could trust him. And if she could trust him, then an internal pang of desire here or there couldn't hurt her *that* much. Could it?

Hanging out with Bo was like peering at a mouth-watering slice of cheesecake at the Cheesecake Factory. The slice was beautiful. Intriguing. It filled you with tempting urges. But it was also very bad for you.

So, ultimately, you were glad for the glass case separating you from the cheesecake. The glass kept you from bingeing. The glass kept you safe.

Chapter Eight

*I*n the mood for Oreos and milk?" Meg asked Amber the next evening. Silly question. Because who wasn't—at any time—in the mood for Oreos and milk?

"Sure." Amber plugged her baby monitor into an outlet on the kitchen countertop and fiddled with the dials.

Meg poured two tall glasses of milk and set them on the granite-topped island in the center of the big house's kitchen. Like Jayden, the kitchen had been put to bed at this hour. Meg had always liked the tidy quiet of it at nighttime, the soft under-cabinet lighting that gave a person the sense that the room was resting after a busy day's effort.

Once she and Amber had settled on the bar stools that lined the island, Meg doled out napkins, then peeled back the flap on a brand-new package of Oreos. The scent of the dark chocolate wafers and soft vanilla centers wafted into the air. She scooted the package toward Amber.

Amber took three, so Meg took three. Better not to let Amber know that she could easily eat six or more at a sitting until they were closer friends. Also, she was working out now. Better for her weight-loss goals, not to mention her acid reflux, if she just ate three.

"I haven't had Oreos and milk since I was a kid," Amber said.

"Really? I haven't stopped eating them since I was a kid."

"Should I dunk?"

"Strictly a matter of personal taste."

Amber dunked.

Meg ate hers regular-style. First bite, second bite, chased with a sip of milk.

"You know . . ." Amber dunked her half-eaten cookie again, causing crumbs to frost the surface of her milk. "We don't have to talk about Stephen if you don't want to, Meg. I mean, thank you for offering, but it's okay."

"I do want to talk to you about him." Meg sighed. "It's just hard."

Amber regarded her sympathetically, then went back to her Oreos.

Amber looked vulnerably young to Meg tonight, in her faded skinny jeans and yellow hoodie. She'd tucked her feet into fuzzy turquoise slippers that had silver crowns stitched onto their tops and pulled her brown-streaked-with-blond hair into another of her messy ponytails.

Since Amber had moved in, the two of them had spent a good deal of time together. Meg suspected that Amber had once been brash and independent, had gone out into the world full of herself, and then been smacked down hard by the realities of life. Her bad decisions had left her without money, without education, and without a father for her child.

Unfortunately, as much as Meg wished it weren't true, everyone—including Amber and herself—had to pay the price of their free will. The two of them had both chosen poorly and paid highly. They'd both come out of their hardships with battered bravery.

"I guess I'll begin at the beginning." Meg picked up microscopic bits of Oreo with her fingertip. "I met Stephen when I was in college. I thought he was charming."

"He was."

"And handsome."

"*So* handsome, the big jerk."

"He came from a normal background, which I liked. I'd always wanted to be more like everyone else." Reminder to self, Meg thought, to beware of charming, good-looking, normal guys. Of which Bo was check, check, check—all three.

"What'd your dad think of him?" Amber asked.

"He had a lot of concerns. As soon as we got engaged, he hired a firm to investigate him."

"Seriously?"

"The firm couldn't verify everything that Stephen had told me about his past, which made my father suspicious. I wish it had made me suspicious, too, but it didn't. At the time I didn't want to hear or believe anything except that Stephen was perfect. We were married the summer after I graduated. I was twenty-two."

Amber watched Meg with utter stillness.

Meg released a painful exhale. "It started with one little lie. I didn't think much of it. Then I caught him in more little lies and a few bigger ones. I began to check up on him, and I found out that he was lying to me about his job. Our finances. Where he was at night. Everything." Meg caught herself nervously spinning her earring back and dropped her hand. "Whenever I tried to confront him about the lies, he'd get angry. Actually, if I stepped out of line in any way, he'd get angry. I'd never, not once, seen him lose his temper when we were dating. But after we were married, it got so bad that the smallest thing would set him off. And he'd just become furious. Horribly furious."

"I've seen him lose it, too."

"As the months went by, I realized that all the charm and all the sweetness he'd shown me when we were dating had been an act. The truth was that he didn't actually *feel* any of it. He didn't love me. It had all been a big con to get what he wanted. I've spent hours talking to therapists about him, and based on some of those conversations, I think . . . well, I think he's a sociopath."

Dead seriousness resounded like a gong through the room. Rightly so. The mind of a sociopath *ought* to terrify. Meg was painfully aware, as Amber must be at this moment, that Amber had had a child with this person. Meg could easily have been in the same predicament. She remembered the dreams she'd once dreamed, back when she'd been in love with Stephen. The hope she'd had that one day they'd have children together. "Basically a sociopath is someone who's completely self-centered and who doesn't feel any guilt or remorse. They have no conscience."

Amber swallowed audibly. "'One thing you can't hide is when you're crippled inside.' John Lennon."

"You didn't know Stephen as long as I did," Meg said carefully. "But I'd recommend that you do some research on the characteristics of sociopaths, then think back on your time with Stephen. Think whether or not he showed you some of those characteristics. After we were married, Stephen and I lived together for a year. By the time he left, he'd shown me nearly every trait on the list."

Meg's gaze passed over the glasses of milk with beads of condensation on the outside, across the orderly countertops, and out the window to the gardens aglow with professional lighting. But her heart didn't remain in the cozy kitchen. It traveled back to the crushing despair Stephen had put her through five years ago. "I can't tell you how much I wish that I'd been smarter, how much I regret that I fell for his act in the first place. But I did, all the way."

"That's not your fault, Meg."

It came as a surprising relief to hear Amber say those words, to have someone to relate to after all this time. Meg reached over and gave Amber's hand a squeeze.

Amber returned the pressure. "I fell for it, too. He's like, a really good actor."

After a moment, they dropped the link of their hands but not the link of their shared empathy.

"Wanna go back to eating cookies?" Amber asked hopefully. "How about we try to put Stephen out of our minds?"

"I'd like to, but I have one more thing I need to tell you." Meg took a moment to gather up her courage, because this next part was the hardest thing of all for her to admit and something she'd never told anyone else in the world.

"Oh?"

"When I graduated from college, my father gave me two million dollars as a gift." She knew she simultaneously sounded like the world's worst spoiled little rich girl and an unforgivable braggart.

Amber whistled low, her blue eyes rounding.

"I think it was his way of trying to provide for me, even though I'd already turned down a trust fund. I wanted to live on what Stephen and I made and nothing more."

Amber's nose wrinkled. "Why?"

"I needed to prove to myself that I could stand on my own two feet."

"I mean, I needed to prove the same thing to myself when I left home. But I'm not sure I could have turned my back on"—she indicated their surroundings—"all this."

"Yes, you could have. If all this had left you as empty as it left me."

"So what happened?"

"I didn't touch the two million dollars. I put it away in a private, separate account just in case of an emergency."

"Uh-oh," Amber whispered. "I'm afraid I know where this is going."

"Stephen stole it all from me. Every dollar."

The two women looked at each other for a long moment, their expressions stark. "He must have been going through my things, because I'd never told him about that account. Never."

"I'm *so* sorry. You found out about the money after he left?"

"Yes. About a week after he disappeared, I remembered the account. It gave me a sick feeling in my stomach because I knew what I'd find before I even called the bank."

Amber shook her head, her expression turning angry. "I can't *believe* he took your money."

"Once I confirmed it, I knew that he was gone for good. And I knew for sure why he'd pretended to like me in the first place. His relationship with me was never about anything except my father's money."

"I hate his guts. When I see him I'm going to bean him with my knuckles right here." Amber indicated the middle of her throat. "Did you send the police after him?"

"I couldn't file criminal charges against him because Texas is a community property state. But I could have brought a civil case against him."

"Did you?"

"I thought about it. But in the end I didn't because I was too afraid that the media would get ahold of the story. I didn't want everyone knowing what he'd done to me, so I kept silent. I didn't tell my father or anybody else about the money."

"I'm the first?"

"You're the first." Meg fiddled with the edge of her napkin. "I can't stand that I let him go free with my money. If I'd held him liable, I'd have slowed him down at least, pushed him off course. He might not have been able to do what he did to you. I apologize, Amber."

"You don't need to! After all you've done for me, how can I ever be anything but thankful? I don't blame you a bit."

"If you'd been in the same situation, I bet you'd have prosecuted him. You'd have been braver than I was."

"No way."

Moisture fogged Meg's vision. Amber's forgiveness and reassurance poured over her like warm rain. "Thank you for being so gracious."

Amber rolled her eyes. "Are you kidding me? I'm the one that should be thanking you. Here." She passed Meg a fresh napkin and Meg used it to stem the flow of tears. "So what did you tell people," Amber asked, "back when Stephen left?"

"I simply told them that Stephen and I had separated. And then, a year to the day after he left, I filed for divorce."

"Why'd you wait a year?"

"Because I filed on the grounds of abandonment, and to do that in Texas, you have to wait that long. It was a hard year." Growing up she'd been shy and sensitive, but mentally stable. After Stephen, soul-deep betrayal, desolation, and panic attacks had descended on her like vultures. She'd barely managed to hold herself together. "I was still living in Houston, carrying around his last name, having to answer all kinds of questions from friends and family. Once I got the divorce, I took back my old name and moved to Tulsa for a new job and just . . . just started over."

"Well, good for you."

Meg lifted a shoulder. "I wanted to tell you all this so that you'll know everything I know when you decide whether or not you want to find Stephen."

"Can I think a little longer about what I want to do next?"

"Sure."

"I say we finish our Oreos."

"Agreed."

Amber got busy dunking, and Meg got busy chewing. What do you know? Food tasted better after you'd cleared your conscience by dumping all your revelations.

"I can actually eat more than three Oreos," Amber confided.

"You know what?" Meg smiled. "So can I."

It took Amber two days to make up her mind about Stephen.

"So," Amber said to Meg on Wednesday evening over the phone, "I've been thinking a lot, trying to decide what to do about Stephen. I'm pretty sure I've made up my mind."

When her cell phone rang, Meg had been treating herself to a bath brimming with rose-scented bubbles. "Hold on a sec," Meg said, leaning out of the water, afraid of dropping the phone and electrocuting herself. She closed her eyes, cupped her forehead with her free hand, and braced herself for bad news. "Okay. Go ahead."

"I just have to find him."

Stephen. Meg's mind reeled at the thought of searching him out. It made her feel like a person taking part in a plan to walk up to a sleeping beehive and split it open with a carving knife. At least she could find comfort in knowing that she'd shared her secrets with Amber. Amber had been given all the information she needed to make an educated decision about whether or not to hunt out the beehive with the carving knife.

"I keep trying to talk myself out of it," Amber continued. "But I don't think I'll be able to relax until I finish things with Stephen for good."

"I understand."

"You do?"

"I do. And what's more? I'll help you. I'll help you find him."

After Amber's call, Meg slept poorly, chased by dreams of Stephen. Dreams in which she stood rooted to the spot, frozen, and trying but unable to move as he came rushing furiously forward to hurt her.

The moment she opened her eyes the next morning, anxiousness pounced on her. It stayed with her while she got ready for work, drove into the city, and went through the motions of her job.

She kept asking for God's help, kept telling herself to keep calm and breathe. But like a swimmer trapped in a tank, the waters of inexplicable, suffocating worry continued to mount. Up to her chin. Over her head, stealing all her air.

"So you'll oversee the team?" Uncle Michael asked her.

"Yes." He'd been talking for ages about some team he'd formed to create some report for some oil and gas exploration proposal for some company. Her mounting alarm hadn't been helped by him, his relentless expectations, and his overinflated assessment of her potential at Cole Oil.

When was he going to leave? They were surrounded by the rich confines of Meg's father's office, sitting in shiny leather chairs in the seating area, with folders full of numbers on their laps and silver pens in their hands. She really, *really* didn't want to come unglued in front of him.

"I'd like to have the team's report on my desk by Friday morning," he said.

"I'll work on it. If that's all," she pushed shakily to her feet, "I have some calls I'd better return."

His attention flicked over her. "Certainly." He rose, as smooth and elegant as always, and strode to the door. "I'll talk to you later."

Once he'd left, Meg counted to ten, then threw the lock on the door and exhaled a half-sobbing breath. *I'm crazy*, she thought. *Nuts. If Uncle Michael had any idea, he'd lock me up—*

No, Meg. Quit it. You're okay. You're just upset today. Overwhelmed by everything.

She crossed hurriedly to the desk, located her sudoku, and toed off her heels. "God, come," she whispered. "Help me." With quivering fingers, she smoothed open the book in front of her. Hardly any blank puzzles remained. She'd need to buy another because she'd certainly have enough psychosis left to fill it.

Her eyes screwed shut. *Please help me, Lord. Please please please. Help me to calm down.*

She believed in the Holy Spirit. Not just His closeness, but that He actually lived within her. **Trust me, Meg**, that Spirit seemed to whisper.

I'm still trying to. Wanting to. Is . . . is this job your will for me? It doesn't feel like it, but I can't see any other path before me. Will you show me your plan?

No plan burst full-blown and clear into her head. In fact, the only thing she sensed God saying?

Wait on me. Not very reassuring! Her sanity was teetering on a knife's edge, and she craved clear direction. How much longer could she battle this particular attack? How much longer could she live like this?

She opened her eyes, gripped her pencil like a lifeline, and tried to focus her thoughts on filling empty squares with numbers. Her mind skittered through the options. 1? 7? What about here? 5? Checking the columns up and down, up and down, to see what might fit.

She hovered on the brink of submerging in her own heart-pounding panic for endless minutes. Finally, the waters began to lower, giving her just enough air in the top of the tank to breathe.

When her phone rang, she felt confident that God was reaching out to her in the way that He often did, offering her support and comfort through one of His people. Since Stephen's desertion, He'd proven himself faithful a thousand times. She'd learned that she could count on Him in the same way that she could count on there being sixty minutes in an hour, or twenty-four hours in a day.

She pulled her phone from her purse, expecting to see Sadie Jo's or Lynn's name on the screen. Instead, the incoming call came from an unfamiliar number.

She pressed a button to answer. "Hello?"

"Meg?"

She recognized the voice instantly. A shiver raced down her spine and all the way along the rear of her legs, tingling against the backs of her knees. "Bo?"

"Hey. Sorry to bother you at work. I just . . ." He hesitated. "Are you okay?"

God had tapped *Bo Porter* as His ambassador? God had assigned *Bo Porter* to the task of assisting her? Oh my goodness . . . "I'm okay. It's been a rough morning at work."

"I'm sorry." She could hear the concern in his voice. "Anything I can do?"

"No, but thanks for asking." She rolled her lips inward and clamped them with her teeth in an effort to control her rickety emotions, to sound at least remotely together.

"Listen," he said, "I was calling because I meant to tell you when I saw you at the farm the other night that Amber and Jayden are welcome to come by and ride the horses anytime."

"They'd probably enjoy that."

"I was thinking Jayden might like horses."

"Sure. I'll tell them."

"Just have Amber call or text me to let me know when they'd like to come out. I'll have one of the grooms meet them."

"Great." A pause followed. Meg didn't want the conversation to end. She wanted to go on clinging to his words, to the steady, reliable calm of them . . . of *him* . . . for just a little longer.

"Want to tell me about what's been going on today?" he asked.

She rose and walked to the windows that overlooked downtown Dallas. Intentionally, she skipped over the news flash that she'd now be actively helping Amber find Stephen. "I'm just overwhelmed by my job. I'm in over my head, and it stresses me out." She told him about Cole Oil, and he patiently listened. She asked him questions about his work, the farm, the horses. When they eventually said good-bye and she disconnected, she remained standing at the windows. Outside, the pale blue sky reached into the distance.

Her emotions and thoughts had, for the most part, returned to normal. The terrified clamor of her body had stilled. Without a doubt, talking with Bo had soothed her.

Could it really be that God had spurred him to call her just now? The timing had been so exactly like God. Precisely his usual MO with her when she was struggling.

But . . . Bo? Was she supposed to believe that God had added his name to the roster of people He used to comfort her? The one man in five years that she had a little tiny crush on? Her employee.

Him?

Suddenly, the uncanny effect Bo had on her—that rush of peace she experienced when near him—made perfect sense. The inner serenity his nearness brought her didn't actually come from Bo, a man every bit as human and frail in and of himself as she was. It came from God, passed to her through Bo's words, Bo's compassionate eyes, Bo's trustworthy presence, the Holy Spirit within him. God was using Bo as His hands and His feet.

"Oh." An exhale seeped from her lungs.

Only, it wouldn't do to get too carried away. She should be careful not to convince herself of things that weren't true, simply because she hoped and wished that they were.

Bo's call might have been a coincidence.

Except.

Except she didn't really believe in coincidences. Not nearly, anyway, as much as she believed in God.

Stephen considered himself an expert at the game of black-jack. He'd put his mind to it, and what he put his mind to, he mastered.

Over the last few years he'd earned thousands of dollars at blackjack tables just like this one, in casinos just like this one—with their purified air, windowless walls, and background noise of voices and ringing slot machines.

He fully expected to win this hand.

The dealer drew her next card, and was then bound by the rules to draw again. And again.

She's going to bust, Stephen thought, satisfaction lifting sharp inside him.

Instead, she turned over a three, which gave her nineteen. Her nineteen trumped his eighteen.

Completely expressionless, the female dealer pulled his stack of chips toward her. And with that, she took the last of the five thousand he'd been playing with tonight.

Stephen allowed himself to show no reaction except a good-natured shake of his head. Inside, his temper exploded like fiery lava from a volcano.

The middle-aged blonde with the low-cut top sitting next to him crooned in sympathy.

"Not my night," he said to her and gave her a what's-a-guy-going-to-do smile.

"It could still get better from here," she said, her expression flirtatious.

As if. She was way too old for his tastes, a fact that he might have compromised if she'd had big money. But based on her purse, clothes, jewelry, and conversation, she didn't. "Sweetheart," he answered, "even though I lost money, I got to sit with you for a good, long time. What could be worth more than that?"

She turned misty-eyed and pliable, which allowed him to make a smooth getaway. He moved through the casino toward the parking garage, checking his watch as he went. Two thirty in the morning. And five thousand gone. Five thousand!

He gripped the key chain in his pocket so hard that the sharp edges of his keys bit into his palm. Inside his head he cussed the last dealer he'd had. He wouldn't be a bit surprised to learn that she'd been cheating him since the moment she'd arrived at the table.

Disgusting casino. They promised you on billboards, online,

and in TV commercials that they were giving away millions, but every fool knew they were the ones making those millions. They only cared about money. About themselves.

He took the elevator and exited at P2. A smattering of cars sat in their spaces, silent and devoid of people. With no one to see, he gripped the grimy lip of a nearby metal trash can, and stared at it for a long moment while his breath grew labored and his rage overwhelmed him. He kicked the trash can, kneed it, kicked it more, and then threw it as far as he could heave it. It landed on its side with a tremendous metallic clang that eased his emotions not at all.

It had been an unlucky night and an unlucky month. Even though a good portion of the money he'd played with tonight he'd scammed off Kelsie—one of the Phoenix girls he'd been sleeping with—a good portion of it had been his own money, too.

A few million dollars no longer lasted as long as it once had. Certainly not for someone like him. He wasn't like most American men, herd of dumb cows that they were: content with a desk job, a recliner, football on TV, and king ranch chicken for dinner. He had excellent taste and the smarts to appreciate fine things.

Soon, he'd need more money.

He didn't doubt his ability to secure it for himself.

The only question?

How.

Chapter Nine

Over the next two weeks, one sunny Texas day stirred by gentle breezes rolled into the next, punctuated here and there with a spring storm just ominous enough to toss the local weathermen into a frenzy. The final days of April passed the baton to the early days of May.

After much careful thought, Meg deemed her visits to the horse farm unthreatening enough and beneficial enough to continue. Three or four times a week she made her way to the paddock rail. Each and every time, no matter the hour or the temperature, no matter that she never summoned him, Bo would appear.

The two of them talked and talked, sometimes laughing gently, sometimes admiring the horses in a lull of quiet. They discussed their childhoods, the Marines, theology, her previous jobs, Tulsa, Kentucky, horses. He told her she worked too much. She told him the same.

Bo's friendship and the camaraderie they shared helped Meg. In those spaces of relaxation, standing at the fence beside him encircled by nature, her spirit started to recuperate.

Thanks to Bo, Sadie Jo, Lynn, Meg's frequent sessions on the elliptical machine, and most of all thanks to God's grace, Meg began to find her way back to herself and to her right mind. The spikes of panic she'd been struggling against since her father's death gradually started to ebb away.

Whenever she was with Bo, Meg continued to sense a cord of mutual attraction between them. And yet they both, as if they'd written out a pact and signed it in front of a notary, were careful not to say or do anything even close to inappropriate. They never stood too near. They never touched.

Meg no longer worried—or at least no longer worried *very often*—that Bo might be acting. She hadn't completely forgotten that he had, potentially, a lot to gain from her affection and thus might be using her. But every time she entertained the possibility, it seemed more and more farfetched.

So long as she protected her heart and didn't go getting all silly over him. So long as they preserved that respectful space between them. So long as they remained friends and nothing more. . . .

So long as those boundaries held firm, she judged her relationship with Bo a blessing from God and nothing that could cause her harm.

Over those same two weeks, Bo came to view his relationship with Meg as something that could cause him the worst harm imaginable. And yet, just as surely, as something he couldn't let go of.

One night after visiting with her at the farm, he parked his truck in the carport attached to his house, grabbed his two sacks of food, and let himself in through the side door. He didn't like grocery shopping, so he always waited to hit Brookshire's until the situation grew urgent, which happened every time he ran out of Dr. Pepper.

He flipped on the kitchen lights and set the sacks on the Formica countertop. After fishing his smartphone from his jacket pocket, he stuck it in its dock and set it to play "Tomorrow" by Chris Young.

He began putting away the food while mentally going over every detail of the conversation he'd had with Meg. How she'd held herself, the things she'd said, the way she'd looked at him with those light brown eyes of hers. He held tight to their time together whenever she came to the farm and spent every minute of the days she didn't come wishing she would.

When he finished putting away the groceries, he leaned against the counter, his hands on his hips, and frowned at nothing.

It was and would always be rich female boss, regular country boy employee between the two of them. On that understanding, they'd built a friendship that was only guaranteed to last as long as the farm continued to operate and not a minute longer. One month had passed since she'd told him she'd close his farm. Only five remained, and he'd drawn only slightly closer to earning back the farm's remaining balance. He hadn't made near enough progress.

When he was with Meg he worked hard to keep it polite and low-key between them. Not only did Meg employ him, but she'd been wounded somehow and was still trying to find her feet. Bo knew good and well that she depended on him to treat her in a gentlemanly, platonic way. She'd be terrified if she knew the depth of his feelings for her.

Even tonight, after he'd just seen and spent time with her, he felt physically compelled—the way he felt compelled to eat or sleep—to see her again.

William Cole would roll over in his grave if he knew.

He swore aloud. He still couldn't make sense of the effect

Meg had on him. Didn't understand his feelings for her. Over the years he'd dated plenty, and he'd sincerely liked each of his girlfriends. Ultimately, though, when it had come time to take them or leave them, he'd left them all without a problem.

With Meg, though? Just the thought of not seeing her again caused his heart to pound. His reaction to her was crazy, powerful, dangerous, and nothing he could *ever* act upon.

Amber Richardson had made a lot of F-minus decisions in her life. That short haircut in the seventh grade, for one. Her ninth-grade boyfriend, Justin. Her tenth-grade boyfriend, Robbie. The choice to try out for cheerleading, even though she had no coordination. Her eleventh-grade boyfriend, Chris S. All the times she'd gotten drunk at parties and let even drunker friends drive her home. Her twelfth-grade boyfriend, Cody. The times she'd mouthed off to her father, even though she'd known he'd mouth off back at her louder and angrier and longer. The choice to chase Cody to Lubbock instead of staying home and concentrating on school. Sex outside marriage. Her decision to move in with a group of party-girl roommates in Lubbock. Her romance with Stephen. Her sloppy use of birth control.

All bad. Bad, bad, bad choices.

The last two years of her life, especially, had been a long, hard marathon. A ton of times she'd worried that she and Jayden might not make it, that she might not be strong enough. But right now, at this moment, it looked like the two of them would maybe, somehow, survive. Because she'd *finally* gotten one stinking decision right. The decision to move in with Meg and turn her life around had been A-plus, one hundred percent, gold-star correct.

Amber was sitting on top of a big black horse with Jayden in front of her on the saddle, trotting around one of the pastures at Whispering Creek Horses. Jayden had never been on a horse before, but that hadn't mattered a bit. He'd been laughing ever since they'd started moving, and the sound of her little boy laughing was just about the sweetest sound Amber'd ever heard. She hugged her baby against her front and directed the horse to circle around the field again.

A redheaded high school kid named Zach rode next to them. He worked at the ranch and had saddled the horses. "How you doing?" he asked.

"Doing fine." Amber had never owned a horse herself, but she'd grown up riding plenty of friends' horses.

"You look like a natural, and your son there sure seems to be enjoying himself."

"He sure does."

On this afternoon the clouds above looked fluffy, like white icing God had whipped with a hand mixer. The air smelled like grass and new beginnings.

The motion of the horse lifted her hair off her back and brought it down over and over again. For the first time in ages, she didn't have to stress about all the things she couldn't handle.

She liked her new job at the law office, and she really liked the nanny that she'd hired this past week. With Meg, Lynn, and Sadie Jo's help, she'd decided on a lady in her mid-fifties who had gentle eyes and an outgoing personality, and called everyone *sweetie pie*.

Jayden let out a happy squeal.

Amber smiled. "You like horses, Jay?"

He patted his hands excitedly against the horse's mane.

When Meg had mentioned a while back that Bo Porter had

invited them out to the ranch, Amber had wanted to bring Jayden right away. But she'd been too busy to drive out here until today. Now she wished she'd come sooner.

They rounded the far curve of the pasture, which turned them back in the direction of the barn.

"Looks like Ms. Cole is here," Zach said.

Amber squinted. Sure enough, she could see Meg and a man walking side by side up to the white wooden fence. "Let's go say hi."

"Yes, ma'am."

Their horses crossed the length of the pasture. As Amber drew near, she could see that Meg had come straight from work. She had on a suit, her makeup looked like someone from the MAC counter had done it, and she'd clearly used a straight iron on her hair. If Meg hadn't been so nice, she could seriously have had her own reality show on Bravo.

Meg tilted her head to gaze up at them. "You guys look impressive."

"Thanks," Amber answered. "Jayden really loves riding. He's having a great time."

"I'm so glad. Hello again, Zach."

"Hello, Ms. Cole."

"Amber, do you remember my cousin Brimm Westfall?"

"Oh, sure." Now that she'd come close, Amber recognized the man next to Meg. She'd met him on Easter. He was the math and computer genius. "Nice to see you again."

"You too."

With his medium height and lean body, Brimm looked like a college kid more than a college professor. He wore a hip pair of glasses, a retro faded green T-shirt, jeans, and black-and-white Adidas soccer shoes with flat tan soles.

"I've explained everything to him," Meg said, "and he's agreed to help you with your—" she glanced at Zach— "uh . . . search."

"Really?" Amber stared at Brimm. "That's awesome. Wow. Thank you."

He shrugged. "Sure."

"Did you . . . were you wanting to start now?" Amber asked. Jayden grunted to let her know that he didn't like stopping, then started pointing toward the pasture. "I mean, we could get down."

"No," Brimm answered. "It's cool. Go ahead and finish." His straight brown hair fell forward over a pointy, but still cute, face.

"Would you guys like to ride with us?" Amber asked.

"Not me," Meg said quickly.

"Um." Brimm squinched his lips to one side, thinking about it.

"Can you ride?" Amber asked him.

"I'm decent."

"Then c'mon!"

"You can ride Huck here," Zach offered. He slid off and brought the reins over the horse's head.

"These aren't Thoroughbreds that are part of the breeding and racing business?" Brimm asked Zach.

"No, sir. Mr. Cole kept these horses for him and his friends to ride. Huck's real gentle. Would you like to give him a try?"

"Well, why not?"

"Because you could break every bone in your body," Meg whispered.

Brimm shot Meg a fast smile, let himself through the gate into the pasture, and mounted up. Zach excused himself to go and get another horse from the barn.

"Ready?" Amber asked Brimm.

He nodded, and they started off together at a walk.

Meg watched Amber, Jayden, and Brimm head off on the horses. Jayden screeched with pleasure and kicked his chubby baby legs, which caused Meg to smile.

This was a different barn than the broodmare barn Meg usually visited, yet the building itself and the arrangement of paddocks and pasture outside were almost identical.

She slipped on her glasses so that she could better enjoy the view, then relaxed into her familiar and comfortable post at the rail. Thankfully, she'd made it to another Friday afternoon, which meant she could enjoy two whole days before having to go back to Cole Oil.

Zach returned on a fresh horse and joined the others. Before the group had made even one loop around the enclosure, Meg heard footfalls approaching.

She knew who it was even before she turned because her tummy lifted and tightened with excitement. She glanced behind her, and sure enough.

Bo.

He walked toward her wearing his straw Stetson, jeans, ropers, and a white T-shirt under a beige corduroy jacket with a sheepskin collar. He smiled at her as he neared.

"Hi," Meg said.

"Hi," he answered, then came to an abrupt stop. "Are you cold? I'll just go and take a look in the barn. I can probably find you something—"

"It's all right."

"It'll just take a sec." He turned, then disappeared into the barn.

She whistled low under her breath. Why did he have to *look* like that all the time? Like an award-winning Marlborough ad?

Aunt Pamela had called Meg earlier in the day to talk about Tara's upcoming engagement party. She'd reminded Meg—again—to bring a date. If Meg had to ask someone to go with her to the party, which clearly she did, she wanted to ask Bo. For one thing, he looked like a Marlborough ad. Secondly, he'd make the evening bearable for her. Thirdly, her back-up plan was Mr. Son.

Unfortunately, though, she didn't know how to ask Bo to go out with her on something that sounded like a date without giving him the wrong idea completely.

He returned and handed over an orange cotton sweat shirt that said *HOOK 'EM HORNS* on the front. "This ought to help."

"Thank you." The sweat shirt would ruin her outfit, but she wasn't about to argue with him over it, so she put it on.

"I'm guessing you're not here for a horseback riding lesson."

"Just so you know, I haven't forgotten about our horseback riding lessons. I'll let you know when I've worked up enough courage."

"You do that. I'll be ready."

The group of riders drew up to them and exchanged greetings with Bo.

"It looks like you're taking good care of these people," Bo said to Zach.

"Yes, sir, Mr. Porter," the kid responded with clear respect.

"We're having an awesome time," Amber said to Bo. "Thanks so much for inviting us to come out and ride."

"Anytime."

"Brimm and I have just been talking about tomorrow night." Amber shifted Jayden on her lap. "Sadie Jo wants to baby-sit for me, but I'm not sure what to do around Holley on my big night out."

"What do you like to do?" Bo asked.

"Well, I haven't been in a while, but I love country and western dancing. Is there anything like that around here?"

"Yeah, there's a place called Deep in the Heart on the edge of town."

Amber's attention moved to Meg. "Would you like to go with me, Meg? Of course, you probably already have plans. . . ."

For the past five years Meg's weekend plans had mostly included Cashew, a bath, and a book. "I'm afraid I've only been country and western dancing a couple of times." All during her college years, and always because a group of friends had talked her into it. Deep in the Heart sounded like the last place in Holley she'd voluntarily choose to go.

"It's okay that you've only been a few times," Amber assured her. "How about it?"

"Um . . ."

"Please? It'll be fun."

She couldn't stand to leave Amber's invitation hanging, nor did she want Amber visiting Deep in the Heart alone. "I guess I could go."

"What about you guys?" Amber looked to Bo and Brimm. "If you come along, Meg and I won't have to rustle up local boys to dance with."

Meg had no intention, none, of *ever* "rustling up local boys to dance with."

"I'll be there," Bo said.

Thank God, Meg thought.

Everyone looked at Brimm. Meg fully expected him to decline. He had no rhythm.

Brimm lifted a shoulder. "Well, why not?"

"Because you could break every bone in your body," Meg answered.

On Saturday, Meg sequestered herself in the guesthouse and drudged her way through Cole Oil computer files. In the late afternoon, she reached a stopping point and made her way to her father's home gym, determined to sweat off as much water weight as possible. She wasn't positive what the term *water weight* meant. Nor did she know how much of it a person her size might be carrying around.

Hopefully lots, she thought darkly, because sweating it off was her sole hope of fitting into her tightest pair of jeans for tonight's outing to Deep in the Heart.

She stepped onto the elliptical and went to work. Her cardio sessions hadn't gotten any easier, even though she'd stuck to a regular schedule. They continued to kick her bootie every single time. She pumped her legs, wheezing air, fighting through the protests of her heart and muscles.

This is why people give up too early. Hang in there, Meg. It's good for you. She plowed on, determined. *It's helping with the anxiety. And eventually you'll get better at it.*

She'd decided that for the first time today, she'd finish her cardio, then try her hand at lifting weights. She'd surfed around online and found a weight-lifting workout for women, printed it off, and brought it with her.

Once she'd completed her time on the elliptical, she staggered over to the mini-fridge, toweled off, and guzzled a bottled water. She reread the weight-lifting instructions, picked up the recommended amount of weight for a beginner, lay down on a bench and, with a powerful case of doubt, attempted something called a chest press.

Was she doing this right? She shoved the weights upward toward the ceiling. Recalling the online photos of the move, she did her best to imitate the model's form.

After eight chest presses her muscles started to burn. She imagined her jeans and used the visualization to motivate herself. With a puffing exhale, she heaved the weights upward again.

Once she'd finished the set, she sat up and blew a piece of hair out of her eyes.

Thank goodness that Bo had agreed to join Amber and her this evening. Meg had never been comfortable around strangers, but with Bo nearby, she'd be all right. His company had the power to turn a potential nightmare outing into something that might even prove to be . . . enjoyable?

She consulted her instructions, then started to lower into and out of squats.

It wasn't fair, of course, to pin all her expectations on Bo. For one thing, he'd probably know lots of people at Deep in the Heart and go off and leave her for long stretches. Only fair. For another, he'd likely dance with other women. Also only fair.

He might take a liking to Amber.

He might hit the alcohol too hard.

Or he might, she reminded herself, *be wonderful. And you'll have fun.*

Remember fun, Meg?

Chapter Ten

eg's plan to visit Deep in the Heart upset Bo. He'd been on edge over it all day, and now that he was here, waiting outside for her like they'd arranged, his concern had doubled.

He watched several cars pull into the dark parking lot, lit only occasionally with light posts. People drifted past him on their way inside, talking back and forth in quiet tones. He recognized most of them.

At last Meg's Mercedes pulled into the lot. His instincts honed in on the car, and he pushed away from where he'd been leaning against his truck.

When Meg stepped out into the night air, his mood nosedived. She reminded him of Sandy in the final scene of *Grease*. She had on a pair of jeans that should have been illegal, a black top under a black leather jacket that clung to her curves, and a fifteen-hundred-dollar pair of boots. He guessed she'd spent even more time than usual on her appearance because her eye makeup was darker. Hair bigger. She looked powerfully, almost painfully, beautiful and every man in the place would surely notice.

Amber and Meg approached him.

"Evening," he said.

"Hi, Bo." Amber took him in with wide, excited eyes. Clearly, it had been a while since she'd had a night off from the mom thing.

"You look nice," Meg said.

"Thanks," he answered. "So do you."

"I don't look like I'm wearing a Halloween costume?"

"No."

"Sure?"

"Sure."

"Brimm is on his way," Amber said. "He told us to go on in and that he'd meet us inside."

"Let's head in, then." Bo held the door for the women, followed them into the entry hall, paid the cover for the three of them, and escorted them inside. He'd been to Deep in the Heart countless times. The low ceiling, the dim lighting, the faint smell of smoke, the glowing neon signs behind the long bar—all familiar.

This dark emotion inside of him? Unfamiliar.

The cover band's version of "Beer for my Horses" poured over them. Bo raised his voice to be heard. "Would you like a drink?"

"Goodness, yes," Amber answered. "Diet Coke for me, please."

"And you?" he asked Meg.

"Bottled water?"

Her choice came as a relief.

The women followed Bo to the bar. While the bartender dug around for a bottled water, which was probably an unusual request, Bo could sense the interest of dozens of men zoning in on Meg. His blood pressure climbed.

The horde stayed back long enough for Bo to pay. He led the women over to a tall table in a shadowy corner.

Around them several people threw back their heads, lifted their drinks, and sang along with the song's chorus, "Whiskey for my men and beer for my horses!"

"Are you hungry?" he asked Meg.

"I might be in a little bit." She unscrewed the lid of her water. "Thanks for this and for paying to get us in."

"No problem." It was hard to talk over the music, so the three of them watched the dancers slide across the big hardwood dance floor.

Bo's stomach knotted with worry. It wasn't right, Meg being here. She was one of the richest women—maybe *the* richest, for all he knew—in the state of Texas, and she was standing defenseless right next to him.

He wasn't used to bringing someone as fine as Meg into a place like this. Over the weeks he'd known her, he'd gained a pretty good understanding of just how rare Meg was. She was worth far more than her father's money simply because of *who* she was. And also who she was . . . to him.

He might as well have brought a priceless one-of-a-kind diamond into the room and tossed it onto the stage.

He honestly didn't think it was safe for her to be here. None of these people, including him, were anywhere near good enough for her. No telling what someone might decide to do once they realized her identity. He cursed inwardly. Why didn't she travel with bodyguards?

Meg and Amber bent their heads together, saying things to each other he couldn't hear. His attention scanned the crowd.

Sean and Brady, two guys who'd gone through school with his brother Ty, caught his eye and headed over. Both were cocky good-for-nothings that the women in Holley loved to love anyway.

"Hey, Bo," Sean said. "How you doing?"

"Fine."

"Good to see you here tonight." His gaze traveled from Bo over to Amber and Meg.

Bo's entire body tensed with protectiveness.

"Who've you got with you?" Sean asked.

Bo introduced the women.

"Meg Cole?" Sean's eyebrows lifted high. "*The* Meg Cole?"

"I don't know about that," Meg said.

Bo set his teeth together.

"The *one and only* Meg Cole?" Sean asked.

"I'm sure there are lots of Meg Coles."

"Not in Holley, there's not," Sean said. "Around here there's only one."

Meg fiddled with the back of her earring, and Bo knew that meant Sean made her nervous. He leaned toward her. "You all right?"

"I . . ."

Brady escorted Amber toward the dance floor.

"Care to join them, Meg Cole?" Sean grinned persuasively and held out a hand to her.

Bo barely managed to restrain himself physically and verbally. He didn't have any right to make decisions for her. He was her employee.

Meg chewed the inside of her cheek. "Okay."

Bo stood frozen as Sean led Meg away and swept her onto the floor. Through a haze of mute black fury, he watched another man's fingers wrap around hers, another man's hand settle on her waist. He himself had never given her more than a handshake.

Meg managed the steps gracefully, her face turned slightly

down and to the side as Sean talked to her. The song drew out forever. Unbearable. Never going to end.

Bo remembered, all at once, the many times he'd ridden out to Whispering Creek with his dad when he'd been a teenager. John Porter bred quarter horses and raised rodeo stock. But he was also known across all of north Texas as an expert horse trainer. Long before William Cole had decided to found a Thoroughbred farm, he'd owned a stable of riding horses. He'd relied on Bo's dad's opinion whenever he considered buying a new horse or faced a training issue with one of his existing animals. Bo had accompanied his dad to Whispering Creek many times, and his dad had always given him the same lecture on the ride over.

"The Coles," his dad had said to Bo in his calm, slow-paced way, "deserve our utmost respect. You understand me, son? Mr. Cole's accomplished a great deal. A very great deal. Don't speak to him unless you're spoken to. And if Mr. Cole asks you a question, don't let me hear you answer with anything that's not followed by *Sir*."

Back then, Bo'd had no trouble accepting the way of things. William Cole had been a powerful businessman, a multi-millionaire, born into a family of oilmen. Of course he was better than Bo Porter from Holley, Texas, whose only accomplishments were his B average and his position as a safety on the Plano East football team.

After high school there'd been no money for college, so Bo and his brothers had all followed the path of the men in their family and gone into the service. He'd succeeded in the Marines, and his skills as a horseman had served him well since. To tell the truth, he'd rarely regretted his lack of higher education. He'd never seen much need for it. Hadn't had much cause to be ashamed over it.

Until now.

He'd never, in his whole life, felt his faults as clearly as he did at this moment, standing alone in a dark corner of Deep in the Heart, watching Meg dance. He was a lower-middle-class kid from a small town who had no knowledge except about war and horses. If he and Meg had lived five hundred years ago, she'd have been a countess, and he'd have been the guy that worked in the stable making horseshoes for her horses. Her servant.

That was the way of things. But unlike when he'd been a teenager, he no longer found the gulf between them easy to accept.

The song ended, and Sean edged close to Meg to say something. No doubt he was asking her for another dance.

Bo took a half step forward—

Meg shook her head and gestured toward where he stood.

Bo released his breath.

They made their way back. When they reached the table, Meg glanced up at him and then quickly away.

"I'm going to go get a drink," Sean said. "Need anything?"

"No thank you," Meg replied.

"Let me know if you change your mind about another dance."

She nodded, and he moved off.

Meg turned to Bo and lifted onto her tiptoes, bringing her mouth close to his ear. "I don't want to dance with anyone else I don't know. I'm just . . . not good at that sort of thing. If anyone else asks me would you mind if I told them I was with you? Just as an excuse?"

Thank God. He pulled back, met her embarrassed gaze. "I wouldn't mind a bit."

"I appreciate it."

Only a couple of songs passed before the next guy tried his luck. This one's father owned the hotel on the square.

"Thanks for asking," Meg answered. "But I'm here with him tonight." She angled her head toward Bo.

Gossip traveled fast in Holley. Meg Cole was their resident millionaire and also someone the locals hardly ever got a glimpse of. The news that she'd shown up at Deep in the Heart would be big enough. That she'd turned guys away because she was with Bo Porter? This information would probably reach his employees at the horse farm in under thirty minutes.

He was going to be up to his shoulders in manure because of it.

Even so, he'd deal with the controversy. He'd much rather that, than go insane watching Meg dance with one man after another all night long.

There was just something an extra notch special, Meg decided, about a man who'd gotten dressed up to go out on a Saturday night.

Unlike her, Bo looked effortlessly hot at all times. Hot in a plain white T-shirt. Hot while baby-sitting a toddler. Hot in workout clothes. Hot at the end of a long workday. And hot, it turned out, while escorting her and Amber to a country and western dance joint.

He wore a crisp white shirt, more formal than anything she'd seen him in before. It fit him perfectly, the side seams running close along his frame. The bright whiteness of the fabric made his skin appear more tan, his gray eyes startlingly light.

Each time she'd leaned over to talk to him, she'd smelled a hint of spicy cologne. The bracing scent made her long to mash her nose into the hollow between his collarbones.

Goodness, she was losing it! She was twenty-eight years old. She hadn't experienced a single moment's interest in any man in years. And now, suddenly, she'd been overtaken by the most overwhelmingly acute interest in Bo Porter. Ever since she'd walked up to him in the parking lot earlier, her senses had been helplessly, unswervingly attuned to him.

The band settled into a slower, softer song. Another man asked her to dance, and again, she blamed her negative answer on Bo.

She hadn't wanted to dance with the first cowboy who'd asked her, either, but her inner niceness had cringed at refusing him to his face. So, like a cream puff, she'd agreed and then regretted agreeing the whole time she'd been on the dance floor.

She'd always been introverted. Part of her discomfort around strangers stemmed from that. The other part stemmed from her experiences. Because of her father and his money, she'd learned long ago that people regarded her as an oddity. In a room full of duck, duck, ducks, she was the goose. She'd become overly sensitive about it in situations like this, concerned that people were looking at her, whispering, judging her appearance.

She needed to get over it. How much more self-centered could she be? Most likely *no one* here cared who she was or what she looked like.

"Are you having any fun?" Bo asked.

"I am. I'm enjoying the people watching." Young women wearing jeans, thin necklaces, rhinestone-studded belts, and low-cut tops moved through the space on the arms of cute cowboys in Stetsons and Ariat jeans. Middle-aged couples who looked like they'd been boot-scooting together for decades glided across the dance floor. And a few suburbanites, more hiply dressed than the country folks, had apparently made the trip over from Plano or Allen.

Out of the crush, Brimm emerged. Meg waved, and he crossed toward them, his hands in his pockets. He'd eschewed western wear and instead had on khakis and a yellow T-shirt with a graphic of Pac-Man on the front.

Meg gave him a quick hug. "Are you late because you got stuck solving an unsolvable math equation?"

"Meg." He gave her a mock-chiding look. "You know I only solve unsolvable math equations on the weekdays. I got stuck playing Xbox LIVE."

"Ah."

Brimm exchanged greetings and a handshake with Bo, then took in their surroundings. "Cool place. Where's Amber?"

"Out there." Meg pointed through the weaving dancers.

"I see her," Brimm said.

Amber spotted him, too. "Brimm!"

He saluted her with two fingers.

As soon as the song ended, Amber made her way to their table. She grinned at Brimm, slightly flushed, her hair mussed from all the movement and twirling. "Ready to dance?"

"Is anyone here planning to video me and send the clip to You-Tube so that everyone in America can laugh at me tomorrow?"

They shook their heads.

"Then I guess I'll dance. At least the hilarity will be reserved to the enormous crowd currently present."

Amber pulled him onto the dance floor.

Sure enough, when Brimm attempted to two-step in sync to the fast beat of Garth Brooks' "Callin' Baton Rouge," Meg couldn't help but laugh. He'd always been her favorite cousin: calm, loyal, smart, self-deprecating. But sadly, her favorite cousin had all the natural coordination of a baby giraffe.

"I thought he was a Texan," Bo murmured.

"And men from Texas should be able to ride horses, hunt, play football, and two-step."

"Well, yeah." He looked at her sidelong, humor flickering in his eyes.

"Brimm can't do any of those things. He went to a private boys' school in Dallas that had a lacrosse team."

Bo's eyebrows drew down with disgust. "Lacrosse?"

"He followed that up with several years at MIT. So you could say he's on an unusual track for a Texas boy."

"Do you have to be a bad dancer to get on that track?"

"Yes," Meg confirmed. "Very bad."

The song wound down, which left Brimm shrugging and Amber giggling and patting his arm consolingly.

"Uh-oh," Bo said.

Meg followed his line of vision to a remarkably beautiful teenage girl with long dark hair and pale blue eyes wearing black leather from head to toe. The girl walked straight up to them, considered first Bo, then Meg, then Bo again. "Do you have a new girlfriend you'd like to tell me about?"

Meg cringed.

"We're friends," Bo answered.

The girl lifted a skeptical eyebrow.

"Meg," Bo said, "this is my sister, Dru. Dru, this is Megan Cole."

"No kidding?" Dru's eyes lit. "Megan Cole? The one that owns Whispering Creek Horses?"

"Yes."

"Any interest in selling it to me cheap? I'd love to boss around my older brothers."

Meg released a surprised gasp of laughter.

"That's enough," Bo warned Dru. He took the beer bottle she held away from her and set it on the table. "You're underage. Who bought this for you?"

She rolled her eyes. "What does it matter? There's twenty guys over there who'd buy beer for me."

"Not while I'm here, they're not. Does Dad know you're here?"

She ignored the question and swiped the bottle off the table.

Bo took it away again, and this time kept a protective hold on it. "Tell me you didn't drive the motorcycle over here—"

"What else am I supposed to drive? I'm grounded from using my car."

"Good grief, Dru. Did you wear your helmet—"

"Well," Dru interrupted in a light tone, "this has been fun. I'm heading over to play pool. I'll catch you later." She gave Meg a wink, turned on her heel, and disappeared into the crowd.

"Your sister," Meg said. Dru Porter radiated the kind of towering, headstrong bravado most often seen in action movie characters played by Angelina Jolie.

"My sister."

"How old is she?"

"Eighteen, with a fifty-fifty shot of making it to nineteen."

"Must be fun to be her older brother."

"It's a nightmare. She gets herself into one scrape after another."

The band kicked off the sort of song that made a person want to sing along and tap their toes. Meg drummed her fingertips on the table in time to the music.

"You like this one?" Bo asked.

She nodded.

"You do know"—his expression turned mock-somber—"you may end up having to dance with me a couple of times."

She half-hid her pleasure behind a quick sip of water. "Why's that?"

"To make it look like you're telling the truth about being here with me."

"You really think that's what it's going to take to prove my story to these people?"

"I'm real sorry, but I'm afraid so."

"High price."

"Very high."

"Well, Joan of Arc made her sacrifice. I guess I'll have to make mine."

A grin dawned slow across his mouth. He placed a hand on the small of her back and led her to the dance floor. Once there, he pulled her into his arms with total ease, one strong hand clasped around hers, his other curved behind her waist. Meg's nose came up about as high as the clean sweep of his shoulder.

"Ready?" he asked.

It was all perfectly textbook and respectful, yet her heart reacted like cymbals clanging. "Ready."

He moved her into the dance smoothly, with the competence of someone who'd done this all his life. With every step she grew more and more intensely aware of him physically. To hold his hand, to move in such close proximity to his body, to feel the heat and power of him was all so breathtaking. She'd had no idea that this simple contact between them could contain such force.

She could sense Bo struggling to adjust to the shock of it, too. He'd tipped his face down to hers, but she didn't have the nerve to look up. If she did, not only would that bring their profiles just millimeters apart, but she worried he'd be able to read tenderness for him in her eyes.

When the song finished, Bo didn't even begin to lead her off the dance floor. "We may need to dance a few more." He shrugged apologetically.

"Because who am I kidding?" she replied. "One dance probably isn't enough to verify my story."

"Right."

"A few more dances are definitely necessary."

"That's what I figured."

"Torture," she said. Another song began, they set off together again, and a jolt of humming bliss shot through her. "Pure torture."

They maintained an easy flow of conversation while dancing the next several songs in a row. Then Meg, Bo, Brimm, and Amber shared an order of nachos before returning again to the dance floor.

Meg found it hard to squelch the goofy smiles that kept wanting to overtake her mouth. None of her worries about this night had come to fruition. Bo hadn't left her all night, not once, and certainly not to dance with other women. He treated Amber politely, but didn't exhibit any romantic interest in her. He hadn't had anything to drink, let alone too much of something.

When the band took a break, Meg made a quick trip to the bathroom. She emerged into the main room to find Bo waiting for her.

"Can I get you anything?" he asked.

"Another water would be great." Might as well live on the wild side.

At this time of night, a far larger crowd circled the bar than had surrounded it when they'd arrived. Bo would have to exert both patience and muscle to get close enough even to place her order.

While Bo waded into the mass, Meg hung back. She glanced around at the people nearby and accidentally locked gazes with Sean, her dance partner from earlier. Though she rapidly looked away, he crossed over to her. Two of his buddies trailed behind him.

"Hello again." Sean regarded her with bright, unfocused eyes. He'd clearly been overindulging in beer and the admiration of his friends since they'd last spoken.

"Hello."

"Interested in another dance?" he asked.

"No, thank you."

"C'mon, pretty lady." He swept his hands wide. "I don't bite."

Charming. She gave him a tight smile.

"Just one more," he coaxed.

"No really, thanks. I'm good." She looked toward Bo. His attention had been on the bartender, but his head came around sharply, as if he'd sensed that she needed him.

"She won't dance with me, boys," Sean said to his buddies. "What'm I to do?"

"Shoo-oot." Brady, the one who'd danced with Amber, re-positioned the wad of chew stuck under his bottom lip. "She probably thinks she's too good for us."

"I'm sure that's true." Sean's grin started on one side of his face and sort of traveled, out of his control, from there. "She probably does."

"I don't think anything of the sort." Where was Bo? There, thank goodness, shouldering his way back in her direction.

"Will you invite me out to Whispering Creek sometime, Meg Cole?" Sean asked. "Everybody talks about that mansion of yours, and I sure would like to see it for myself."

"Umm . . ."

Bo finally reached her side.

Sean glanced at Bo, then back to her. "So, if you're too good for me, then why're you slumming with him?"

Bo stiffened, and Meg's relief torqued into genuine dismay. "I'm not slum—"

"I mean, he's no better than the rest of us. You can slum with me instead, pretty lady. C'mon. Just one more dance." Sean wrapped his fingers around her elbow.

Bo knocked Sean's hand away. "Don't touch her."

"What?" Sean scowled at Bo. "You're the only country boy around here allowed to touch her?" Sean bit off an expletive and extended his hand toward Meg again. This time Bo pushed him back with a shove to the chest.

Meg sucked in a breath. Bo's attention—intimidating, and without an ounce of compassion—had leveled directly on Sean.

Sean recovered his balance. Anger began to burn in his eyes.

"It's all right," Meg said to Bo in the calmest voice she could muster. "Maybe we should—"

"She's hot, isn't she, Bo?" Sean sneered. "I mean, hot enough, considering all that money—"

Bo swung. His fist connected squarely with Sean's cheek. Sean's face whipped to the side and he reeled backward. Caught himself. Froze for a split second.

"Bo." Meg reached out, stunned and shaking inside, to pull Bo away before anything more could happen.

But Sean leapt into motion, rushing at Bo. Sean's fist arced toward Bo's face. Bo deflected it with a cross swipe and punched Sean in the gut.

Meg sensed more than saw the crowd around them gasping and moving back, like waves expanding from a stone that had been dropped into a pond. Shock rooted her to the spot. She couldn't move, didn't know how to help—

One of Sean's friends launched himself at Bo's back and managed to grab Bo's arms from behind.

Sean, blood trickling from his nose, took the opportunity to throw a punch that landed on the side of Bo's face with a sickening *crunch*.

Meg cried out, moved toward Bo—

Bo jerked forward, flipping the guy behind him over his back and onto the ground. Sean and Brady closed in on Bo simultaneously. Bo moved swiftly, striking one with his elbow and trading punches with the other.

Dru stormed into the fray, blistering the air with expletives and kicking the one on the ground.

"Dru, *don't*," Bo snarled. Sean leapt at him. Bo spun Sean with a powerful blow, then grabbed him around the throat. Before Meg could find breath to speak, Sean went limp and collapsed to the ground.

Brady ran at Bo.

With all the strength Meg had, she pushed Brady off course. Brady stumbled, then glared at her, infuriated.

Bo threw his arm in front of her and edged her backward, behind him. "Careful."

Brady threw a thunderous punch at Bo. Bo dodged to the side, but Brady's fist still managed to connect with Bo's shoulder. Bo struck back, and Brady answered. Bo landed more than he took until Brady sprang at Bo, trying to tackle him to the ground. Bo managed to stay upright and toss Brady to the side.

Dru got pulled to the ground by the man she'd been kicking, which brought bystanders into the mix. Men swarmed over the fighters, pulling them apart and restraining them.

Two men held Bo. He was breathing hard, his chest expanding and contracting forcefully. His lip had split open, and one eye had already started to swell.

The sight caused Meg's heart to drop with a dizzying lurch.

Bo paused for a few moments, eyeing Dru, then his opponents before his gaze cut through the crowd, stopping firmly on her. He'd told her he'd been a Marine. She could see now that he remained every inch a soldier, his body as fit and dangerous as it ever had been.

Bo spoke to the men that held him and shook himself free. He moved to her. "Are you all right?"

"I'm fine," she promised. "Are you?"

He nodded and guided her over to his sister. "You okay, Dru?"

The girl adjusted her leather cat suit, rolled her shoulders once. "Heck yeah." She had the audacity to beam at them, like she'd just stepped off an adrenaline roller coaster. "I got to be included in the fun for once." She looked at Meg. "I never get to be included in the fun."

Fun? *Fun?!* Bo's face looked like a boxer's, and Meg felt like she'd been pulverized. She might have to pass out.

"You did well," Dru said to Bo. "That was awesome."

A voice raised over the din of the music. "What in the *tarnation* is going on here?"

"The owner," Dru said to Meg.

A Kenny Rogers look-alike parted the crowd and strode toward them. He took in the scene with a quick, angry sweep of his head. "Bo?" he demanded.

"Sean insulted a lady," Bo said.

"So what'd you go and do to him?" The older man went and stood next to Sean's body. He toed him with his boot. No response.

"I choked him out," Bo answered. "That's all."

The owner regarded Bo with blazing eyes.

"He'll be all right." There wasn't a shred of apology in Bo's voice or face. "When he comes to."

"He better be."

"He will be."

"Go on, then." The owner jerked his head toward the front door. "Git."

Bo glanced at Meg. She nodded in response. "Dru?" he asked.

"Don't look at me. I just got here."

Bo asked the owner if he'd keep an eye on Dru until either Jake or their father came to claim her. When the man agreed, Bo escorted Meg in the direction of the exit. Men murmured compliments as they passed.

"Nice fight, man."

"Sweet left cross."

Brimm and Amber pushed their way into Meg's path, their faces full of concern. Meg grabbed Brimm's hand. "Bo was in a fight."

Brimm looked at Meg, then Bo, eyes round.

"I'm going to go with him," Meg continued. "Here are my car keys. I was thinking Amber could drive my car home and you could follow her to make sure she gets home safely."

"Sure. Anything else I can do?"

"No. Thank you, though."

"You're white as a sheet."

"I'm fine." But honestly, her muscles and emotions had all turned to jelly.

She led Bo from the building. Blessed quiet and cool darkness rushed over them when they stepped outside into the parking lot. Meg made her way to the nearest light post, where a pool of illumination fell in a hazy circle.

Meg found she couldn't quite meet Bo's gaze. She crossed her arms and used the toe of her boot to pry a piece of gravel free from a pothole.

"Meg," he said softly.

She looked up at him. Bo, with his shirt rumpled, his lip cracked, his eyes stark, his big body motionless. The sight seared straight to the center of her heart and left her helpless, foolish, unable to trust herself.

"I'm really sorry, Meg. About what Sean said about you."

"No, *I'm* really sorry. You're hurt." She gestured ineffectually toward his face. "I'm so sorry."

He lifted the back of his hand to his mouth, noticed that it came away bloody, and dabbed at his lip a few more times. "It's no big deal. I've taken a lot worse."

"You're going to have a black eye."

"Won't kill me."

"I could take you to a doctor."

"I don't need one. I'm good."

Meg inhaled a big breath, held on to it as if to gain strength, and let it out slowly. Bo seemed impossibly still. Their roles had gotten flipped somehow. He, who'd been hurt—placid. She, who'd not had a single hair on her head disturbed—a mess. "I really think I should take you to a doctor."

"All my face needs is some ice. I swear."

"In that case, the sooner the better, right?"

"Probably so."

"Then let's go."

They climbed into his truck, the two of them sitting side by side on the bench seat in the dark. He drove from the bumpy parking lot onto the smooth drone of the paved road. The radio played a country melody much more mellow than the din they'd left behind. The cab smelled like him, like clean sea wind.

"Does your face hurt?" she asked.

"No." But one side of his mouth curved up unevenly.

"Liar," she whispered.

He turned the truck, and she watched his hands grip the steering wheel. His knuckles had gotten scraped. "Are you, uh . . . accustomed to getting in fights?"

"I haven't been in one for a long time."

They coasted through the main intersection in Holley, the one Meg passed through twice every day coming and going to work. Hundreds of birds gathered there at dusk, squawking and chattering, standing in long rows on the power lines. When startled, they rushed into the air, a chaotic swarming mass. And then, within moments, they settled again on their electrical lines, having gone effectively nowhere.

As Bo drove toward Whispering Creek, Meg managed to keep up her end of a subdued conversation. The commotion inside her head, though, reminded her of those birds. Her thoughts kept flying around in a wild mass, then resetting.

"She's hot, isn't she, Bo? I mean, hot enough, considering all that money." Those were the words that had sent Bo over the edge. *Hot enough, considering all that money* was exactly how most men her age had always viewed her, Meg knew. Sean's opinion of her didn't upset her all that much.

That Bo had been injured over Sean's comment? *That* upset her. As did the fact that Bo had heard Sean accuse Meg of "slumming" because she'd been with him.

She winced, remembering. She feared that Sean's words, like an arrow zinging through the air, had connected with Bo's chest and sunk deep. She wished she could have kept him from having to hear them, almost felt like she should apologize to him. He'd gotten hit with that simply for agreeing to accompany the girl who usually read biographies with her cat on her lap on Saturday nights.

She chewed the inside of her cheek and watched the line of electrical poles zoom by. They passed the water tower that had *Holley, Texas, USA* painted on it in bold red letters.

She couldn't *believe* that Bo had actually put up his fists and fought those guys for her.

For. Her.

She'd had an important and wealthy father once. But she'd never had a champion. In all her life, there'd never been anyone willing to stand in front of her and get bruised and bloody to protect her feelings.

She glanced at Bo, her emotions welling with affection, tears filling her eyes. Before he could notice, she turned to stare determinedly out the passenger window until she had control of herself.

They pulled up at Whispering Creek's gate and the security guard walked out to greet them. Upon recognizing Meg, he quickly ushered them through.

Bo parked as close as possible to the guesthouse, then escorted her along the walkway in silence. When they reached the guesthouse, Meg continued up the two steps to the front door. Bo stayed below on the path, his hands in his pockets. Light from the porch fixture eased over him, making his eyes shine.

Meg dug her keys out of her purse. Would he say yes if she asked him inside? She *ached* to fuss over him. Wet washcloth, bag of ice, Advil, his feet up on her sofa pillows. The whole bit.

"I'd best be going," he said. "Good night—"

"Wait." She wanted to ask him in and across the respectful line between them. Except she knew her own weaknesses too well. She'd been lonely all her life. She'd been yearning, so long and so desperately, for someone to lean on. And on top of that, tonight's events had rendered her perilously weak toward him. In this moment, her impartiality? Intelligence? Absent from class.

If she followed her heart tonight, she might misstep and ruin whatever it was that they had . . . the friendship, the trust, the respectful boss-employee relationship. "I just wanted to say thank you. For defending me the way that you did. It meant a lot to me."

"I'd do any—" He stopped. His gaze met hers with such a troubled look of burning emotion that her skin pebbled with goose bumps.

"And again," she managed to whisper, "I'm very sorry about your eye and your lip."

"Not your fault."

She sighed inwardly because it was, of course, all her fault. "See you soon."

She waited for him to walk away. He didn't.

"I'm not leaving," he said, "until I know you're safe, so go ahead on in and lock the door behind you."

She nodded, slipped inside, and locked the door. For long moments, she stared at the dimly lit interior of the guesthouse. Cashew slid around and between her ankles.

A very high wall circled Whispering Creek's property. Cutting edge technology kept watch over its buildings. And an armed guard manned the gate. Most people would have considered her safe enough without insisting she lock the guesthouse door behind her.

But Bo Porter wasn't most people.

She didn't know . . . Her heart squeezed with longing. She didn't know what he was to her yet.

Chapter Eleven

B o had set his phone to "Silent" even before he'd met Meg at Deep in the Heart. After the fight, his phone had started vibrating, alerting him to incoming calls and text messages.

It vibrated a few more times as he navigated the dark streets between Whispering Creek and his house. He knew exactly why people were trying to get in touch with him, but in his current mood he didn't feel like answering, talking, or even thinking.

Near the outskirts of town Bo turned onto his quiet, rolling street. He and all his neighbors had big plots of land surrounding their houses. Like his father, he couldn't breathe unless he had at least ten acres around him.

When the street dipped low and curved right, he turned left onto his land. His beige brick house sat a good distance back from the road. He could just make out the glow from the kitchen light he always left on. As he drew near the house, his headlights illuminated his brother's truck parked out front. He could see Jake sitting behind the wheel in the dark, waiting for him.

"Great." Just what he needed.

He parked in his carport, then made his way back toward Jake's truck. The motion sensor light mounted on the front corner of his house clicked on as he crossed under it. Jake met him halfway, the brothers standing on the lawn facing each other, hunched against the cool night wind.

"I've been trying to call you," Jake said.

"No offense, but I haven't felt like talking."

"I heard about the fight."

Bo nodded.

Jake's gaze was hard to read beneath the shadow of his Stetson. But Bo knew, at the very least, that his brother would be sizing up the injuries on his face.

"Did you go to Deep in the Heart with Megan Cole tonight?" Jake asked.

"With her and a few other people."

"Were you two on a date?"

"Look, Jake, I'm tired. I don't really want to get into this with you right now." Bo turned and started toward the house.

"I heard," Jake said, "that you started the fight because of her. That true?"

Bo stopped. He wasn't surprised that Jake had already heard everything or that his brother might be worried or angry over what had happened. He'd have sought out Jake, too, if Jake had been the one choking guys at Deep in the Heart. Wearily, Bo faced Jake and measured his brother's resolve.

Jake held his body in an aggressive posture. The familiar scar across his face highlighted grim features. All the resolve in the world, apparently.

Bo's mind raced back over the many times that the shoe had been on the other foot, the times he'd worried himself sick over Jake, the times he'd been the one trying to pry information out of his brother. "What was your question?" Bo asked.

"Did you get in that fight tonight over Megan Cole?"

"Sean Sutter had a few too many. He wouldn't quit grabbing her, so I pushed him off. Then he insulted her."

"So you had a knock-down-drag-out with him and his buddies."

"Yeah. I did." Bo scrubbed his hands over his throbbing face, his skull. He looked up at the blanket of stars above him. A milky cloud sailed past, moving fast, covering a band of stars and then revealing them again. He glanced back at his brother.

Jake watched him, expression tight. Jake knew, of course, about Bo's history with women. He knew that Bo didn't ordinarily care that much one way or another about his girlfriends, that Bo had never before lost his head over one of them by going crazy protective in a bar.

"Good grief, Bo. What are you doing? You told me that nothing was going to happen between you two."

"Nothing has. Listen, you're not going to be able to tell me any reason to stay away from her that I haven't already told myself a hundred times."

"I'm going to give it a try."

Bo waited in silence, his gut churning, his sense of pride howling like a gale force wind. He knew he wasn't the one for Meg. He sure as anything didn't need to hear his brother list all the reasons why.

"Our farm has only a slim chance of surviving as it is. You strike up a romance with Meg Cole and then it ends badly? I'm afraid Whispering Creek Horses would be done for." Jake lifted and resettled his hat. "There's a lot at stake."

"I know that."

"When the employees hear about what happened tonight, they're going to think one of two things. Some are going to think you're seducing her in order to convince her to keep the farm open."

Jake's words landed like an insult. "I hope they know me better than that."

"The others are going to think you've rolled over. That you're so blinded by her that you don't care about them anymore."

Bo glared. "Of course I care about them. I hired them. That makes me responsible for their livelihoods. You think I take that lightly?"

"I'm just telling you that once they hear about this, some of them are going to worry that you're not going to stick up for them."

"Is that what the employees are worried about or is that what you're worried about, Jake?"

Jake burrowed his hands deep into his pockets. Silence arched between them. "Yeah, I'm worried. I'd like to keep my job."

"I've worked harder," Bo said harshly, "than anyone for the sake of the farm. Day in and day out for four years. That's how much I care about it. If you and the rest of them doubt that now, 'cause of this . . ." He shook his head and strode toward his front door.

He could hear Jake's footfalls close behind, keeping up with him. "Look, man," Jake said. "I'm sorry."

Bo reached his door, unlocked it.

"I want you to be happy," Jake said. "I do. I just don't see what good can come from you getting mixed up with a woman like that."

Bo looked across his shoulder at his brother. "A woman like what? She's the sweetest person in the world."

"You know what I mean. She's William Cole's daughter. It's not just the farm that's the problem. She's different from us, Bo. All that money. The way she was raised."

"Look at me, Jake." He lifted his palms, anger at the situation growing within him. "Anyone who sees me knows I'm not good enough for her. I know it most of all." He wished down to the core of him that he could do something to earn the right to be worthy of her.

"Maybe Meg Cole isn't good enough for you. She's divorced, for one thing. I don't want that for you."

Meg's past was a part of her, like her hair or eye color. Something she couldn't change. Did he like to think about her ex-husband? No. Did he like to think about her married to someone else? *No.* But he accepted it for what it was: an experience that had shaped her into the person she'd become. "Like I said. Nothing's happened yet."

Jake nodded.

"Now go on." Bo motioned with his chin. "Drive over to Deep in the Heart. Dru's there by herself."

Jake's brows knit. Bo didn't have to ask Jake to make sure Dru got home safely or to tell their parents where she'd been. That communication passed unsaid between them.

"I'm on it." Jake turned toward his truck.

Bo let himself inside his house. Usually he turned on some music as soon as he walked through the door, but he couldn't stomach it tonight. After filling a plastic bag with ice cubes, he made his way into his bedroom and stretched out on top of his bed. Carefully, he lowered the ice onto his bruised eye and cheekbone.

The cold hurt like the blazes.

What had happened to him?

All his life he'd known himself well. He was simple, after all. He'd only ever wanted two things: to serve his country and to work at a horse farm.

Before William Cole's death he'd been so sure of himself, his job, his goals. Then Meg had walked into his life, and everything he thought he knew had come undone because now he wanted a third thing. He wanted Meg. Desperately wanted, yet couldn't have.

He longed with instinctive force to protect her. So much so that it almost felt God-willed. As if the cells, muscles, and bones of his body had been made for her. As if he'd been wired from the start to feel just this way about just this woman. His whole life—the childhood scrapes and lessons, the tours of duty with the Marines, his adulthood with horses—had brought him to this. To her.

He wished it wasn't so, that he'd fallen for some country girl as simple as he was. But that's not the way it had gone down for him.

His idiot heart had settled on the golden, intelligent, beautiful, rich only daughter of William Cole—who deserved to marry a man equal to her.

He covered his good eye with his free hand, dug his fingers into his scalp, and prayed for strength. He didn't know how much longer he could keep himself in check when he was around her.

He might need to force himself to give her up.

Lunch with girlfriends held a considerable capacity for joy. Especially at a girly restaurant. Especially on the patio of a girly restaurant with springtime sunshine shimmering on your arms and a pair of big sunglasses shielding your eyes.

Meg, Lynn, and Sadie Jo were seated at a linen-covered table on the porch of Mrs. Tiggy-Winkle's. Inside, the establishment was half antique store, half restaurant, and wholly covered in potted ivy and framed Beatrix Potter artwork. Outside, a black wrought-iron fence enclosed eight tables, separated by a cobble-stone path leading to the shop's door.

Their waitress emerged and set before them plates artfully arranged with chicken salad wedged between nutty slices of bread, fruit, chips, and frothy greens drizzled with poppy seed dressing. The girl glanced at their glasses and assured them she'd be right back with more iced tea.

She and Sadie Jo had gone to church together this morning and still wore their dresses. Lynn had on leggings, Birkenstocks, and a faded T-shirt featuring the words *Cottonwood Art Festival*.

As Lynn and Sadie Jo discussed the plight of a mutual friend suffering from shingles, Meg chewed her chicken salad sandwich and admired her surroundings.

Mrs. Tiggy-Winkle's had found a comfortable spot, like an aging woman in her favorite chair, on the old town square right in the center of Holley. The buildings on the square dated back to the days of wagons and gunslingers and county stores selling bolts of gingham.

Despite its robust history, Holley had teetered on the edge of extinction a few decades ago. Like most small towns across America, Holley had faced its make-it-or-die phase. Meg could remember walking around this area back then, her kid hand warmly clasped in Sadie Jo's grown-up hand. At the time, these storefronts had held little but panes of cracked glass and tattered paint.

Meg, always the worrier, could recall fearing that Holley would waste away and that Sadie Jo would have to move out of her little house.

Looking back, she should have known better. There was no way her father would have allowed any town in his zip code to waste away. William Cole, with his towering confidence and determination, had formed a planning commission. He'd given out interest-free loans to bring businesses to the town center. He'd written massive checks toward the renovation of the Holley Hotel and the planting and maintenance of every inch of green space the city owned.

To this day, bowls of flowers hung from every streetlight in town. Meg pushed her sunglasses higher on her nose and glanced overhead. One hung just a few yards away, bright with pink, red, and white petunias.

Nowadays the visitors' office passed out a driving tour that took guests on a route through town featuring Victorian houses, parks brimming with native Texas trees and wildflowers, and private gardens blazing with azaleas, snapdragons, and daisies. Thanks to the cheerfully painted Victorians and the abundant flowers, Holley had become known as the "Color Capital of Texas."

At present, the town square flourished due to the occupancy of trendy restaurants, cute little shops filled with things you didn't really need but bought anyway because they charmed you, a bank, a museum, the courthouse, and the three-story-tall historic Holley Hotel. The blocks that stretched outward from the square in every direction boasted the oldest homes in the county. The aging structures were now mostly filled with upper-middle-class people who'd moved here recently and brought with them the money and fortitude required to painstakingly renovate them. These newcomers intermingled with the small-town born-and-bred residents of Holley who lived further from the town's center. People like Bo Porter.

Meg remembered just how he'd looked last night after the fight: his chest heaving, his eyes settling on her with fiery intensity. Rich warmth swirled through her at the image and made her wonder for the hundredth time how he was feeling today—

"Meg?"

She focused her attention on Sadie Jo and Lynn, both of whom were looking at her. "Sorry," she said. "Daydreaming."

"I just asked you how your job was going," Lynn said.

"It's going all right, I guess." *I loathe it.* "Everyone's been patient with me."

"Even Michael?" Lynn asked.

"Even Uncle Michael."

"But?" Sadie Jo prompted. Empathetic Sadie Jo could sense a misgiving from fifty paces. Meg's feelings about her job were, she knew, no test at all for Sadie Jo's skills. Helen Keller could have deduced that Meg hated working at Cole Oil.

"I don't have a lot of . . . personal enthusiasm for the oil business," Meg answered.

Sadie Jo and Lynn regarded her kindly as they ate their lunches. "Go on," Lynn prompted.

"The work comes with a lot of pressure. It's competitive and fast-paced. There are all kinds of controversial environmental issues associated with oil that upset me. It's not . . . well, it's not what I would have chosen for myself."

"You chose a job at an art museum, dear," Sadie Jo said.

"Yes. So you see . . ." Meg raised her right hand. "Assistant art museum administrator." She raised her left hand. "Majority shareholder of Cole Oil." She moved her hands toward one another and then apart. "Not a lot in common between the two."

"I'm sure you're doing a wonderful job at Cole Oil," Sadie Jo assured her. "You're going to be the best president the company has ever had."

Sadie Jo, God bless her, had filled Meg's ears with sentiments like this for as long as Meg could remember. She cherished Sadie Jo's staunch love and belief. But she was most definitely *not* going to be the best president Cole Oil had ever had. Mrs. Tiggy-Winkle the hedgehog was more likely to spring from one of the pieces of art and join them for dessert.

"It's the rare person," Lynn said, "who loves their job. Most people just do what they can to make an income and support their families."

Guilt nicked Meg deep. "You're right. I don't have any reason to complain." She'd never had to worry about feeding her family, making rent, paying the utility bills. If only that head knowledge could instruct sense into her heart. Her heart and her gut still wanted to revolt every single time she walked through the brass-and-glass doors with the words *Cole Oil* etched on them.

"You're having a hard time seeing your way forward," Sadie Jo said compassionately.

"That's true. I am having a hard time seeing my way forward. I inherited my job, just like my father and his father did. I only wish . . . I only wish it felt more right." She couldn't shake the sense that God had not destined her, not ever, not even from the very beginning, for Cole Oil.

"You're still in a time of transition, dear." Pale pink blush dusted Sadie Jo's super-soft wrinkled cheeks. "It's upsetting for any of us when we're not sure exactly how God's moving in our lives. I know I've been through times like that in my own life."

Sadie Jo had lost her husband in the Korean War when they were both very young and before they'd had any children. She'd never remarried. Instead, she'd supported herself through her own hard work all her life. "Have you been through times like that, Lynn?"

"Absolutely. It's the not knowing that's the hardest thing."

"The uncertainty," Sadie Jo agreed. She reached across the table and covered Meg's hand with her own. "I don't think the Lord lets any of us get through life without some seasons like that. Otherwise, how would He grow our faith?" She squeezed Meg's hand. "Faith is moving ahead in obedience, dear. Just moving ahead one step at a time, trusting Him, until He shows you what's next. He'll make it clear to you eventually. Sure as anything."

Meg kissed the top of Sadie Jo's hand. "Thank you."

"Just wait on Him and then do what He says. That's truly your only responsibility. He'll take care of everything else. Now eat more of those chips. You're practically skin and bones."

Meg laughed. "No I'm not."

"Yes you are. Here, take my extra chips, too." Sadie Jo grabbed a handful.

"You keep them," Meg insisted. "You love chips."

With a longsuffering sigh, Sadie Jo kept her chips.

Just then a middle-aged man pedaled a three-wheeled bike past where they were sitting. A pair of bright blue sunglasses shielded his eyes.

"Who's that?" Meg asked.

"Everybody calls him Three-Wheeler," Lynn said. "He's sort of become a town mascot."

"His name's Al." Sadie Jo smiled at his retreating form. "He has special needs. Sweet, sweet fellow."

"He works part time at Brookshire's, bagging groceries," Lynn said. "Lives with his mother."

"Where's he going?" The wire basket situated between the bike's two back wheels contained several odds and ends.

"I don't think he goes anywhere, exactly," Sadie Jo answered.

"He just rides," Lynn said.

Exactly like me, Meg thought, feeling a pang of kinship with Three-Wheeler. Long on exertion and pedaling. Short on destination.

A verse moved through Meg's mind. *Trust in the Lord with all your heart and lean not on your own understanding; in all your ways acknowledge him, and he will make your paths straight.*

When their waitress returned to the table, the three ladies conferred, then ordered a slice of pecan pie to share for dessert. Once the girl had cleared their plates and left, Sadie Jo leaned toward Meg. "I've been meaning to ask you about Bo Porter."

"Yes?" Meg did her absolute, valiant best to keep an unaffected expression on her face. Despite her efforts, she could feel a hot, double-crossing blush creeping across her cheeks. She looked down and rummaged through her purse, pretending absorption in finding her lip gloss and applying a few dabs.

"Isn't he handsome?" Sadie Jo asked. "Oh my. And such a nice young man."

Meg straightened, cleared her throat, and looked to Lynn. Lynn looked back at her directly, one brow lifted in amusement.

"Help me out here?" Meg asked her.

"You kidding? I'm fascinated to hear your reply."

"Traitor," Meg whispered, without any zing.

"I heard he beat up six guys last night because of you," Lynn said.

"What?" Sadie Jo exclaimed.

Meg's jaw fell open. "How in the world do you know about that?"

"Holley's a small town," Lynn answered. "At church this morning people were talking more about the fight than about Jesus."

Meg just blinked. "It wasn't six guys," she said at last.

Lynn smiled, clearly enjoying herself. "How many?"

"Three."

"What?" Sadie Jo gasped.

They peppered her with questions, and Meg did her best to explain what had happened at Deep in the Heart.

Sadie Jo's eyes rounded with excitement. "Meg, you're interested in him, aren't you?"

Meg didn't want to lie, but she didn't want to fuel false hopes, either. Sadie Jo earnestly longed for Meg to marry (again) and have babies (for the first time). "I find him attractive," Meg allowed. "Who wouldn't?"

"Yes, indeed!" Sadie Jo looked every bit as delighted as if she'd just happened upon a weekend marathon of *Murder She Wrote*. "Who wouldn't?"

"But he works for me. We're just friends."

Sadie Jo's face fell.

"Are you still planning to close down his horse farm?" Lynn asked.

"Hmm?" Sadie Jo's face fell even further. "You're going to close down his horse farm?"

"That's what I told Bo I'd do on the very first day we met. I gave him six months to settle his accounts."

Their pecan pie arrived, and Meg took a quick and desperate bite. "Almost as good as your pecan pie, Lynn. Can you remind me again how you make it?" It was an embarrassingly obvious tactic to change the subject, but effective, nonetheless. Lynn had never been able to resist an opportunity to share her expertise with recipes.

While Lynn answered Meg's question, Three-Wheeler zoomed past them again, this time in the opposite direction.

After lunch, Meg and Sadie Jo indulged in a pastime they'd shared since Meg's childhood: Neiman Marcus shopping therapy. Although, in their case, it could more accurately be called Neiman Marcus *admiring* therapy. They enjoyed their visits to the department store in the same way that a person might enjoy a visit to a museum. Lots of looking and little buying.

The whole time they chatted and browsed together, the question Lynn had raised over lunch, the one about closing down Bo's horse farm, circled at the back of Meg's thoughts.

When she returned to the guesthouse that evening, Meg made herself some tea, then poured her best lavender bath salt and foaming body wash into the tub as it filled. She lit as many candles as she could dredge up. And then, with a long sigh, she submerged herself in the hot and fragrant water.

She'd have loved to read her Monet biography, but every single night before bed lately she did Cole Oil homework instead. She picked up the company papers she'd set next to the bath and tried to concentrate on them.

Did she want to close Whispering Creek Horses?

No. Not really.

Why? Because she'd come to know and like Bo, and because she didn't want to be the reason that all those people in their carefully ironed WCH shirts lost their incomes.

So what to do?

This part became more convoluted.

She'd told Bo very clearly and with utter conviction that she would close him down after six months.

It would be awkward, but not impossible, to reverse her decision. But if she did, she—of all people—would be committing to own—of all things—a Thoroughbred racehorse farm.

Meg set aside her papers and submerged herself deeper into

the tub, so that only her nose, eyes, and forehead hovered above the water.

She had a crush on Bo. She did, undeniably.

But she didn't know how he felt about her in return. Was it really possible that he liked her as much as she thought he might?

Maybe, yes. He'd fought Sean and his buddies and proved with his fists that he felt something for her.

But then again, maybe no. Even after all this time, she still couldn't bring herself to completely discount the possibility that Bo might be doing a convincing job of *pretending* to care, exactly like Stephen had pretended to care. Bo had just as much motivation to manipulate her as Stephen had.

Her head urged caution with Bo. While her intuition continued, doggedly, to hope in his honesty.

Disgusted with herself, she swatted a mound of bubbles. Her intuition stunk! She couldn't hang her business decisions on intuition. Imagine if she kept the horse farm open only to have her friendship with Bo go belly up. Then, not only would she have to continue to support ninety horses and more than twenty employees, but—worse—she'd have to interact with Bo as he went on about his life. She'd have to meet with him in a professional capacity, hear about him eventually marrying someone else, learn about the births of his gray-eyed babies.

A stab of envy pierced her. *She* wanted to be the mother of his gray-eyed babies.

Meg sat up in the bath, sending water sloshing. She covered her cheeks with her sudsy hands. She couldn't let herself think like that. The fact that she'd so much as dared to consider gray-eyed babies filled her with fear. She was opening herself too much, leaving herself much too vulnerable.

The smart, impartial tactic? To leave her agreement with Bo unchanged, with the horse farm still slated to close. So that's exactly what she'd do.

Fool me once, Stephen, shame on you.

Fool me twice, Bo, shame on me.

She might be a softie. But she refused to be a softie and an idiot both.

Chapter Twelve

*O*ver the course of the next few days, Meg waited not so patiently to hear from Bo. Yes, she'd decided to go forward with her plan to close the horse farm. But she was still female. And after a meaningful evening with a man, all females required follow-up!

Her evening with Bo at Deep in the Heart had definitely been meaningful, so much so that after all that had gone down between them, she felt a little self-conscious about seeing him again and especially about being the one to initiate contact. Though they typically only saw each other at the paddock rail, she hoped for a phone call or a visit or *something* from him.

She checked her cell phone's battery, voice mail, and text message inbox repeatedly. She looked for him whenever she walked along the central halls of the big house. She took baths until her fingers and toes turned white and wrinkly. She tried to plan how she could ask him ever so casually to her cousin's engagement party. She worked out in the gym. She daydreamed about Bo during the long hours at work.

But . . . nothing.

No call. No sign of him.

She soldiered through Monday, Tuesday, and most of Wednesday. But when Meg still hadn't seen or heard from Bo by Wednesday evening, she hit her limit.

She left behind the mountain of work remaining on her desk and drove home. Ignoring the chilly temperature, she grabbed Amber and Jayden and towed them to the stables under the pretext of visiting the baby horses and feeding carrots to them and their mothers.

Sure enough, four carrots and ten minutes after their arrival at the paddocks, she heard the unmistakable crunch of footfalls. A lump of foolish nervousness wedged in her throat.

Amber greeted him first. "Hi, Bo."

"Hi."

"Oh my gosh," Amber breathed. "Your eye."

Meg turned and found Bo already looking directly at her. His lip had almost healed; only a slight puffiness remained. But his eye was stained with purple and yellow, underneath down to his cheekbone and around the outside near his temple. His bruises looked absolutely awful . . . and perfectly beautiful.

"Hey," he said to her.

"Hey. We brought Jayden out to see the horses." Even to her own ears, it sounded like a transparent excuse for coming.

"I'm glad. How are you?"

"I'm . . ." She cleared her throat. "Well."

"You've got a pretty bad black eye there," Amber commented. "Have you been putting ice on it?"

Bo pulled his attention from Meg to answer Amber's question. "Yeah, I have been."

Jayden squealed at Bo from his perch on Amber's hip.

"Hey, dude."

The toddler reached his chubby hands toward the horses.

"Yeah," Bo answered, "I see the horses."

Jayden grinned.

Bo continued to chat with Jayden and Amber, giving Meg an opportunity, while he wasn't looking, to drink him in. All six-plus feet dressed in his usual work clothes, his straw Stetson, and the beige corduroy jacket with the sheepskin collar.

As soon as Bo wrapped up the conversation, he met and held Meg's gaze. Quiet lengthened. Amber glanced back and forth between them while Jayden strained toward the paddock. Meg knew she ought to say something, but her words had gone on strike.

The way he was looking at her! A whole conversation passed back and forth between them. His concern for her, her concern for him, her assurance that she was holding up fine under the gossip, his assurance that his injuries were minor and healing. Both of them telling the other one that they'd missed them.

Heady, intoxicating pleasure filled Meg's chest. This is what she'd been needing, she realized. The comfort of seeing him in person, of knowing that whatever they had between them still existed. His proximity brought her the same inner sigh of relaxation that it always had, plus a feeling of plain old right-ness. A smile tugged at her lips.

"Uh, it's cool out tonight," Amber said uncomfortably.

"Would either of you like to ride?" Bo asked. "I can get Zach to saddle up some horses."

"Thanks, but Jayden and I can't tonight," Amber answered. "We just came out real quick. It's dinnertime, and I need to take him back to the house. Some other time?"

"'Course."

Jayden, who looked adorable in his tiny coat with the hood pulled up to encircle his face, seemed to understand that his mother's answer didn't match his own desires. He started kicking his legs and wailing openmouthed. Amber countered by walking him along the fence and bouncing him to get him under control.

"What about you?" Bo asked. "Ready for your first riding lesson?"

"You know very well I'm not." She indicated her suit and heels. "*Big* bummer."

"How long are you going to use your work clothes as an excuse?"

"Has my grace period for that run out?"

"Officially, yes."

"Time for me to pay up?"

"Time to pay up," he confirmed, not unkindly. "A deal's a deal."

"And you've been more than patient."

"More than." He gave a lazy half smile.

In response, her body flushed with heat. "What are you proposing I do, ride sidesaddle?"

"Go home, change, and come back."

"Tonight?"

"Tonight." Bo's eyes held a distinct challenge. "There's still a few hours of daylight left."

She pointed to the low and overcast sky, which threatened to spit rain.

"It'll hold off."

Meg chewed the inside of her cheek, trying to decide if she was willing to brave death by horse in order to spend more time with him. "Okay."

"Good. Meet me at your father's horse barn, the one where Amber and Brimm rode that day, in twenty minutes."

A queasy rush of apprehension hit her when she spotted Bo and a brown horse waiting for her in the pasture outside her father's stable. The sensation had nothing to do with Bo and everything to do with the fact that he expected her to RIDE THE BIG UNPREDICTABLE ANIMAL.

Bo spent a long time talking to her about the horse he'd picked for her (a female named Banjo), the bridle thing and how it worked, the saddle and how it worked. Patiently, and in simple terms, he explained how to steer with the reins and how to get the horse to go and to stop. Meg found it hard to concentrate, though, because her brain was thinking *yikes yikes yikes* the whole time.

She should have taken riding lessons from anyone but Bo. Then she wouldn't have cared if she acted like a colossal baby in front of her teacher. With Bo, she did care, so she pretended courage.

Finally, it came time to get on top of Banjo. She surveyed the horse's head, trying to judge whether she had evil intentions in her eyes and also to make sure her ears weren't flattened back. She'd heard somewhere that was a bad sign.

The horse looked completely calm. Ears in the upright position.

"Meg," Bo said gently. He pointed to his own ear, and she realized she'd been spinning her earring back.

"Oh." She lowered her hand. "I'm ready."

"Look at me."

She looked.

"I'd never let anything happen to you." Clouds framed his face and dark birds took to the sky from distant treetops.

He said the words with such utter seriousness that tears sprang to Meg's eyes.

"Tissue?" He reached toward his pocket.

"No." She drew herself up, smiled gamely. "I really am ready."
Total fib.

He bent over and cupped his hands. She put her boot—the
only pair she owned and probably not at all correct for actual
riding—into his palms, and he hoisted her upward easily. She
swung a leg over Banjo's back and landed in the saddle.

In instant response, her throat tightened with fear and her
pulse thrummed fast in her ears. She remembered this from
childhood. This feeling of being at the horse's mercy.

The day she'd been thrown, the last time she'd sat in a saddle, the
horse had bucked, twisted, and veered underneath her. She could
remember scrabbling for control, terrified, before she'd fallen.

She thought back to when she and Bo had baby-sat Jayden
together. What had she been thinking? She should have changed
the two dirty diapers. Horseback riding stunk way worse than
toddler poop.

Bo kept up a steady stream of reassurance and teaching. He
positioned the reins correctly in her hands, fitted the stirrups
under her feet. "If it's okay with you, I'm just going to lead her
around at a walk."

Meg nodded tersely. She'd left the recommended amount of
slack in the reins, but that didn't stop her from gripping the
leather strips ferociously.

Bo had clipped a length of puffy rope to Banjo's bridle. He
didn't need to pull on it to make the horse follow him. As soon
as he started walking, the horse walked alongside.

Bo looked back repeatedly to measure the look on her face
while he kept on talking in that easy way, telling her about when
he'd learned to ride, and then about her father's favorite horses
and why they'd been his favorites.

His conversation helped. He didn't ask a lot of questions, which she appreciated, since all her concentration was tied up in staring at her horse's ears. She couldn't quite get accustomed to the elevation off the ground or the way the saddle tipped side to side with Banjo's gait.

They walked for what seemed like a long time, making two gradual circles around the pasture. Meg kept trying to make her muscles relax, but no luck. They'd tightened like piano wires.

Couldn't horses smell fear? Or was it that they could sense fear? It was one of those, she was pretty sure. Unfortunately, telling herself not to be afraid because the horse would know didn't help. It's hard to scare oneself into not being scared.

At one point, Banjo did a quick side step for some reason, and Meg barely managed not to yelp.

"It's all right," Bo whispered to her. "You're fine."

She nodded at him, because somehow *he* had the power to make it bearable. He'd said he wouldn't let anything happen to her, and she believed him.

Such a seductive idea, the idea of having someone assured and strong and knowledgeable to rely on. It almost tempted a person to think that if they had someone like that beside them, they could face anything. Even the death of a parent, panic attacks, and the demands that came with the role of majority shareholder.

Eventually, Bo brought them to a stop and helped her off. "You did really well."

When her boots landed on solid ground, relief spiraled through her. *Thank you, God.* "I was terrible."

"No you weren't. You're just new at it. That's all."

She tilted her face to regard him, standing there with his hand draped idly over Banjo's neck, his fingers playing with the horse's mane, his handsome face marked with bruises. She'd never have climbed onto a horse for anyone but him. She feared, in fact, that she'd do whatever crazy thing she could to make him happy, if he asked.

You can't, Meg. You can't afford to trust him so easily. No matter how good-looking, how seemingly honorable. "Well, I . . . I'd better be going. Thank you for the lesson."

"Am I going to be able to convince you to come back for another?"

"As you said earlier, a deal's a deal."

"So you'll come back one more time."

"Yes, but can I have a few days to recover first? At least until my next death wish?"

He smiled. "Sure. I'm going to be gone until next week anyway."

"Oh?" Her thoughts dipped at the prospect.

"Yeah, I've been wanting to tell you. I'm flying to Florida tomorrow."

"On business?"

He nodded. "There's this Thoroughbred Owners and Breeders seminar that I committed to attend months ago. Also, I've got a trainer who's been racing some of our horses down there that I need to check on."

"I see."

They walked to the mouth of the barn together, then hesitated. She'd be heading to her car from here; he'd be returning the horse to its stall. This was good-bye.

I'll really miss you, she thought. Everything she wanted to say bunched up in her mind. *I don't think I'll feel at peace again until you come home. A hundred books and a hundred baths aren't going to be enough. Would you be willing to come with me to my cousin's engagement party?* "Have a safe trip."

"I will."

"Let me know when you get back in town?"

"Sure."

She turned to go.

"You were brave today, Meg."

She paused, then looked back at him. "Thanks." She'd been a mammoth coward. But she didn't want to correct him, not when he was looking at her with admiration, as if she'd done something sterling. "By the way," she said, before she could lose her nerve.

"Yes?"

"No, ah, pressure or anything, but my cousin is having an engagement party next Friday night. I was wondering if you'd be willing to come with me. That is, if you're back from your trip in time."

"Absolutely."

"Really?" she asked, like a dummy.

"Yeah. I'll be back in time."

Meg wanted to launch herself into his arms and cover his battered face with grateful kisses.

"After all,"—his gray gaze sparkled—"I still have one good eye. Might as well blacken that one, too."

She laughed. "Yes, exactly. I've always appreciated symmetry." She gave him a parting wave and walked toward the parking lot.

She wanted one last peek at him.

No, she shouldn't—

She had to. Couldn't resist.

Meg glanced back and found him standing exactly where he had been, stock-still, watching her.

He tipped the front of his hat.

Oh, cowboy, she thought. *What in the world am I going to do with you?*

"Thanks for helping me with this," Amber told Brimm a few nights later. They'd just settled into chairs positioned behind the desk in Meg's father's home office.

"You bet," Brimm said.

Amber lifted one of the file folders she'd brought with her. "Meg was nice enough to get together all the papers and information and stuff that she still had from the time she was married to Stephen." Amber lifted the front cover and paged through a few, showing him. A photocopy of Stephen's social security card and driver's license. A wedding license. The rental agreement on their apartment. Bank statements, bills, tax returns. She handed the file to Brimm.

He nodded. "This should be helpful."

"And this is what I was able to get together for you." Amber opened her own, much smaller file. The only official document she had was Jayden's birth certificate, and didn't that just sum up everything that needed to be said about her romance with Stephen? She also had pages of notes that she'd written on spiral notebook paper. As soon as she'd realized that Stephen had left on purpose, she'd started writing down everything she could remember him saying about himself, his family, the places he'd lived. She'd been determined to find his sorry butt even then.

Brimm took it from her and went through it. Once finished, he set the files aside and studied her. "Are you sure you want to do this?"

"Find him?"

"Yes."

"I'm sure."

Brimm looked concerned. Maybe he thought she was like those low-class women on Jerry Springer who were always doing things like this, chasing down baby daddies and such.

"You don't still have . . . feelings for him, do you?"

"No." Not really true. She had *lots* of feelings toward Stephen, all bad.

"Good, because I wouldn't want to go to all this trouble just so you can hook up with a person whom I seriously dislike."

Amber raised her right hand. "I have no plans to hook up with Stephen."

"All right, then." Brimm spun to face the big Mac laptop he'd brought with him. "Let's get going."

"Let's do it. 'Action is the foundational key to all success.'"

"Mmm?"

"Pablo Picasso said that."

He angled his head toward her, one eyebrow cocked.

"I'd have been a genius, too," Amber said, "except I don't like geeky clothes."

He laughed. "It was the uniform of the genius that put you off?"

"That's right."

Still grinning, he returned his attention to his computer.

Amber had started reading quotes back in high school in an effort—that had bombed—to impress her boyfriend's mother. When she'd lost the guy she'd kept the quote book. Then added more books to her collection.

She still read and memorized a few quotes every single night before bed. She liked, when she switched off her light, to turn the ideas of famous and successful people around in her mind. She also liked that, thanks to the quotes, she knew at least one scholarly thing.

She hadn't made much of herself yet. But she *had* been able to memorize almost all the quotes in all her books, so she must be worth something. Right?

Brimm's fingers flew over his keyboard. She watched him pause, zoom the arrow around the screen, and type some more.

"I was expecting you to use Meg's dad's computer," Amber said.

"I brought mine because I'm used to it and because it has some extras that I've added. Uncle William's setup isn't too shabby, though. I'll use both computers here in a minute."

Both? Wow. She watched him for a few minutes. "What's our plan?"

"We're simply going to start with the search engines and see if we can find him based on the data in the files—his social security number, et cetera."

"Okay." She picked at her lime green nail polish and passed the time by checking out some framed pictures of Meg as a child. "I think there's something going on between Bo and Meg," she murmured while looking at a shot of baby Meg lying on a blanket and wearing a big bonnet.

"Like what?"

"Like a lot of *really* heavy interest."

He gazed at her. "Of the romantic variety?"

He was so nerdy that he was cute. She liked his funky T-shirts and the way his brown hair fell forward. "Yes, of the romantic variety. I went out to the horse farm with her the other night, and the two of them looked like they wanted to eat one another up with a spoon."

"Really?"

"Really."

He slowly raked his hair back with his fingers. "I was thinking Bo was more your type than hers."

"Country girl with the country boy?"

"Right."

"Isn't that a little *too* predictable?"

"I . . ." His look of confusion told her that in his world, his math world, the predictable answer equaled the right answer.

"I'm just teasing you. Bo's like, gorgeous, and I would be interested in him if he liked me. But he doesn't like me. He's into Meg."

"My family won't like it."

"Why?"

"They'll assume he's after her because of her inheritance."

Amber took offense on behalf of all poor people. "Not everyone is like that."

He lifted a skinny shoulder.

"I don't think Bo's like that. Do you?"

"No."

"Well, look at it this way," Amber said. "She can hardly do worse than Stephen."

Chapter Thirteen

Judy can pat the bunny,'" Sadie Jo read aloud to Jayden. "'Now you pat the bunny.'"

Jayden didn't make a move, so Sadie Jo took hold of his finger and used it to stroke the furry bunny inside the book.

Meg eased deeper into the patio sofa, content to watch the two of them together. Because Amber was working with Brimm tonight, Meg and Sadie Jo had volunteered to watch Jayden for her. They'd already fed and bathed him. The beautiful evening had convinced them to bring him outdoors for the remaining half hour before bedtime.

They'd chosen one of the weather-resistant sofas, tucked Jayden between them, and set a stack of books on the low coffee table. Even though the daylight had faded, the can lights in the overhang above them illuminated the books. The designer lighting scheme in the backyard lit up the trees.

"'Now you play peek-a-boo with Paul.'"

Sadie Jo had brought these books from her own private stash and had already reminded Meg twice that these were the very same ones she'd read to her when she was small.

Meg admired the moon, big and full tonight. The sight of

it made her wonder if Bo had looked up from wherever he was in Florida and noticed it, too.

It had come as a genuine and unwelcome surprise, how much she'd missed him these past few days. Whispering Creek didn't feel the same without him. She'd known that visiting him comforted her. But until he'd gone away, she hadn't realized that she'd also grown accustomed to the more subtle comfort of having him (at the very least) nearby. Somewhere on the property. Close. Working with his horses.

With Bo gone, Whispering Creek had turned lonely and empty. Without their long talks at the paddock rail to look forward to, her days had become bleak.

Mr. Son walked into view from the direction of his gardening room.

Jayden spotted him, jumped up, and ran to him like an entrant in the hundred-yard dash. Mr. Son didn't, as a rule, carry Jayden around. But he did greet him cordially with a handshake.

Jayden tugged Mr. Son over to the coffee table and spread out Sadie Jo's books. *Goodnight Moon. The Very Hungry Caterpillar. Green Eggs and Ham. Brown Bear, Brown Bear. Are You My Mother?*

"Evening, ladies." Mr. Son dipped his chin.

"Evening," they echoed.

Jayden picked *The Very Hungry Caterpillar* and thrust it into Mr. Son's hands.

"You want me to read this?" Mr. Son asked.

Jayden pushed it closer to him.

Mr. Son lowered himself into the nearest chair and positioned Jayden on his lap. With businesslike efficiency, he cleared his throat and began to read.

Jayden had been his usual whirlwind self for Sadie Jo and

Meg. But now that Mr. Son had arrived, Meg watched him morph into a perfect specimen of behavior. From what Amber had told Meg, this was always the case when Jayden visited Mr. Son for their thrice-weekly gardening lessons. In Jayden's world of women, it seemed as if the young boy recognized and cherished Mr. Son.

"'But he was still hungry,'" Mr. Son read. "'So he ate one slice of chocolate cake, one ice cream cone, one pickle . . .'" He grunted and lowered the book. "That's silly. Why would a caterpillar eat chocolate cake or a pickle?"

"It's fiction," Meg answered.

"Silly fiction."

"It's a children's book," Meg replied. "It's fun."

"Silly children's book."

"It's a classic!" Sadie Jo insisted.

"Not a classic of mine." He tossed it on the table.

Jayden peered at Mr. Son with fascination.

"Young man," Mr. Son said, "don't waste your time reading about a hungry caterpillar. Better to read books about the alphabet and numbers. More practical."

Meg laughed. "He's one and a half, Mr. Son. He doesn't have to be practical yet."

"That's the problem with you American people . . ."

Meg refrained from pointing out that Mr. Son was as American as the rest of them.

"All you ever think children should have is happy time, happy time."

"Well . . ." Meg scratched her temple. "I guess that does pretty much sum up my philosophy on toddlers."

"Hear, hear!" Sadie Jo smiled broadly.

Mr. Son shook his head over their hopelessness.

"Is anyone hungry?" Sadie Jo asked. "Meg? You hardly ate a bite at dinner. I have a bag of goldfish in my purse."

"No, thanks. I'm good." Meg checked her watch. "I believe it's Jayden's bedtime. I'd better take him upstairs and put him down."

They all rose to their feet, and Meg lifted Jayden into her arms. He stuck his hand in his mouth and began to fuss.

"Oh." Sadie Jo's face filled with distress. "Do you think he has a wet diaper?"

"I don't know," Meg answered. "We just put a new one on thirty minutes ago." Did babies wet their diapers every thirty minutes? And if so, did their mothers change them that often? "I'll check his diaper before I put him to bed. Okay?"

"All right." Sadie Jo clucked over Jayden, running her palm over his hair, gazing fondly into his eyes, and kissing him on the tip of his nose. Then she turned to Meg and reached out to cup Meg's cheek. "This is my baby," she said to Jayden.

His brows lowered comically. Clearly, he didn't understand what *baby* had to do with the grown woman holding him.

"My baby," Sadie Jo said again, smiling at Meg, patting her cheek.

Meg smiled back, feeling tears push against her throat and behind her eyes. Even though she was twenty-eight years old, it still felt good to be somebody's baby.

"Come, Ms. Greene," Mr. Son said. "You keep this up, and we'll be here all night. I'm ready to go home."

"Yes, of course."

"I'll walk you to your car."

Meg watched the pair move off together, then took Jayden to his bedroom. As she'd promised Sadie Jo, she dutifully un-snapped his pajamas and opened his diaper. Bone-dry. She didn't think she needed to change a bone-dry diaper. Unless diapers were like panties. In which case . . . once they'd touched your privates and been taken off, it was best to start over. Unsure of the protocol, she decided to put a new diaper on him, just in case.

She prepared his room for bedtime in all the instructed ways, then settled into the rocking chair with Jayden, his cup of milk, and his green frog. She launched into her mostly wrong version of "Hush, Little Baby."

Looking into Jayden's gleaming eyes in the dim light while she held him, rocked him, and sang to him was like gazing into the soul of God. There was timelessness there. And grace.

Just like the last time she'd done this, tenderness for the little fellow burrowed deep inside her chest. And exactly like the last time, Jayden returned her attention solemnly, almost unblinking.

Meg finished singing and switched to humming.

Thank God she'd invited Amber and Jayden inside that first night, more than a month ago now, when they'd shown up unexpectedly on her doorstep. The help she'd been privileged to extend to them had given her more satisfaction than anything else she'd done in years and years. For most of her adult life she'd had this deep, underlying sense that she was meant for more. More than working in a museum. More than the job of accumulating additional money for Cole Oil. But across all that time, she'd been unable—or maybe too selfish or maybe too unready—to figure out the calling God had placed on her life.

At long last, in helping a single mother and her son, Meg had finally found one small thing of true importance that she could do. To join with God in a pursuit that mattered felt like taking a deep breath, like a cool strong wind soaring through her.

She wished she could offer the same help to even more people, but—

Look after orphans and widows in their distress. The Bible verse sprang into Meg's mind as if God Himself had leaned over and said it softly into her ear.

Yes, Lord, Meg prayed, *I hear you.* Amber might not be a widow, but close. And Jayden had one firmly committed parent, but he'd been orphaned by the other.

Jayden finished his milk, and Meg set it aside. She watched the little boy bring his weathered frog up close to his cheek and stick his thumb into his mouth, sucking rhythmically, pausing, sucking again.

Meg could relate to Jayden's situation, because she'd been the same sort of orphan. . . .

Oh my goodness. Surprise reverberated though her. Why hadn't she noticed the similarity between Jayden and herself before now? No wonder she experienced such a strong pull of compassion toward him.

She'd *been* him once. She was *still* him, only older.

Goose bumps rose, then spread over her.

She'd look up the Bible verse about orphans and widows when she got to the guesthouse. It didn't say, she didn't think, "look after an orphan and a widow." It named both in the plural.

Orphans.

Widows.

Meg kept right on rocking and humming and watching Jayden's eyelids grow heavy. She'd taken on Amber and Jayden as a one-time deal. She hadn't thought until just now, tonight, about reaching out to others like them. But there must be lots of others. Many, many single parents in need of second chances.

Could she . . . ? Could she herself, one humble person, help many?

Her thoughts spun in several different directions. How would she find these people? What could she do for them? How? When would she do it, since she already worked more than full time? She wanted to drop-kick her Cole Oil job, but couldn't.

At length, Jayden's eyes closed all the way. His small, innocent face turned slack and peaceful with sleep.

Could it possibly be that the *more* she'd been meant for all along was the job of ministering to single parents and their children? Children just like this one? Children just like she'd once been?

She could see, all of a sudden, that she was uniquely suited for it, that God had used her past to prepare her for it. Her God most definitely had the power to redeem the pasts of His people.

Single mothers and their children—her ministry.

The idea clicked into place like a car key slotting into the ignition. A perfect fit. Meg quit humming but kept up the smooth movement of the rocking chair while tears of relief and gratitude rolled silently down her face in hot tracks. Finally. Finally! A perfect fit.

How was she going to do it? She didn't know. She had a hundred questions and just one answer. But the one answer she had trumped all the questions. That answer?

God.

If God worked through her, then yes, she—one humble person—could maybe, she thought, quite possibly, hopefully . . . help many.

Bo lay in his hotel bed in Florida, miles and miles from Texas, missing Meg down to the pit of his stomach. He'd stretched out on his back, the sheets low on his hips, his gaze focused into the gray darkness above him, his ears registering the drone of the air-conditioner.

His brain had refused sleep for the past two hours straight. In fact, his brain had been refusing sleep a lot lately, because it only wanted to obsess over the blonde who'd walked into his life, taken that life in her pretty hands, and broken it in half.

After the disaster at Deep in the Heart, he'd spent days wrestling with himself over whether or not he should cut off all contact with Meg. He'd told himself that Jake could be the one to meet with her if and when she returned to the farm.

Then the afternoon had come when Meg had indeed returned. His groom had called to report her arrival, exactly as Bo had requested. In response, Bo had remembered Meg standing outside the guesthouse the night he'd driven her home from Deep in the Heart. *"I just wanted to say thank you."* Moonlight had slid over her profile, her hair. *"For defending me the way that you did. It meant a lot to me."* There'd been trust in her eyes when she'd said those words.

And in the moment that followed, the moment when he'd had to make a decision about whether or not to go to her at the paddock, he'd been unable *not* to go because if he stayed away, he knew he'd betray her trust in him. No matter what it cost him, Meg needed someone in her life she could depend on, someone who'd put her needs above his own, someone who was willing to keep her safe.

He reached over to the nightstand, picked up his cell, and punched in her number. He stared at the ten digits. Let the pad of his thumb hover over the call button, even though he knew he wouldn't press it. Minutes passed. Finally, with a groan, he rested his wrist across his forehead and peered upward into the darkness again.

He used to enjoy industry conferences. But he'd gone through the motions of this one like a puppet, his body and voice doing the expected but his mind far away. Without the hope of seeing Meg, the days of this trip had no meaning. Everything he'd done had been empty, without a single stroke of color. He was on the verge of going out of his mind with loneliness for her.

At least, thank God, he'd fly home tomorrow. His return trip couldn't come one second too soon.

He and Meg were friends and co-workers who hadn't hugged, hadn't kissed. But if he had his way, he'd never travel this far from her again. Not for one day in the rest of his life. Not for any reason. He couldn't imagine a single place on the globe he wouldn't go to be with her. Or any place he cared to go without her.

What he was less sure about? How he was going to continue to keep a handle on himself when he was around her. He worried over it constantly, because if he ever did reveal himself to her, not only might he put the farm in more jeopardy, but he feared he'd terrify her. If he terrified her, she might end their friendship.

The engagement party for her cousin was coming up in a couple of days, which would present him with all kinds of temptations to say or do something he'd regret. Not only that, but he'd have to meet her family at the party. Sure as anything, they were going to recognize him for exactly who and what he was. They were—all of them—going to see him as a dumb hayseed not at all suited to Meg.

Meg, with her gentle heart, either hadn't noticed or didn't mind that he was far beneath her. But her family would. And he'd bet money that at some point during or after the party, at least one of them would feel duty-bound to point out the obvious to Meg.

It would probably be best for Meg to hear the truth from someone close to her. And yet he'd been hoping to God that she'd never hear the truth—that he wasn't worthy of her—from anyone at all.

The next day Meg straddled the seat of one of the machines in her father's home gym and started on her fifteen "rows." She scowled ferociously at the cables in front of her, watching as they raised and lowered the weight stack.

She'd made herself work out for two reasons today. One, Bo was away, and working out gave her something to do to attempt to keep her mind off of him. Two, she'd purchased a women's fitness magazine to motivate herself and read within its pages that muscles burned calories. Not just the act of building muscles. Of course that burned them. But the new, bigger muscles *themselves* burned calories all day and all night.

Say what?! She'd been floored by this revelation.

If she put on muscle, her body would burn calories while lying on the sofa! While eating Oreos! While sleeping!

Nine, ten, eleven.

She was—twelve, thirteen—going to do this. She was going to get herself into better shape, whether her body came along nicely or had to be dragged kicking and screaming—fourteen, fifteen.

Her phone chimed, letting her know she'd received a text.

From Bo? At last? Lord have mercy. She scurried over to her phone. The small screen told her she'd received a new message from Bo Porter.

In instant response, her outer body went still and her inner body went nuts with excitement.

She retrieved the text.

I'm back from my trip. Glad to be home. How are you?

For five straight minutes, Meg chewed the inside of her cheek and stared at her phone, trying to decide how to reply. Finally she settled on *Welcome home! I'm doing well.* She hit send.

The exclamation point communicated cheerfulness, and the mannerly tone of hers matched the mannerly tone of his. Still, her response struck her as horribly tepid. Well? She couldn't exactly reply to his simple friendly message with *You're back! You're back! I've missed you wildly, foolishly, embarrassingly. I'm so happy I could kiss you! Can I kiss you? I'd like to kiss you.*

She waited, but no reply came. Her text hadn't invited a reply. Even so, she tucked her phone into the waistband of her sweats so she'd have it close at hand.

She finished up the last few weight-lifting exercises on her list, then clicked on the History Channel and climbed onto the elliptical. Struggle, sweat, agony. Struggle, sweat, agony. Typically, she had nothing but the puny distraction of the TV to occupy her mind during cardio. This time, though, her mind was fully occupied, and then some, by the news that Bo had come home.

She hadn't seen him for six days.

It had felt, very sincerely, like six weeks.

Meg had procrastinated a trip to the grocery store too long. Lynn, in contrast, kept a perfectly stocked pantry at all times. So the next morning before work, Meg dashed into the big house kitchen to grab breakfast. She stuffed a granola bar that she would eat, a banana she probably wouldn't eat, and a bottled water into her purse, then poured coffee into a travel mug.

As she was leaving the kitchen, she glanced longingly down the main hallway in the direction of Bo's office. He might possibly be inside. Uncle Michael expected her downtown for one of his meetings soon, which meant she only had a few minutes to spare before she needed to start her commute. But it wouldn't hurt to walk past Bo's office. If the door was open, she'd indulge in a tiny peek inside.

The plush floor runner absorbed her footsteps. When she'd neared to within a couple yards of his doorway, Bo himself walked out. In the flesh. As if she'd called him into being by the force of her hope.

Meg came to an immediate halt and so did he. The shock and delight of seeing him again after days and distance broke over her like a riotous ocean wave.

A slow grin tugged up the edges of his lips.

Meg smiled back, purse over her arm, coffee in her hand, heart in her throat.

"Hi," he said.

"Hello." Her senses drank him in hungrily. The just-out-of-the-shower smell, the masculine face and extra short hair, those light gray eyes. All of it familiar and cherished. Every detail combined into a charisma so powerful that it all but bowled her over. "About time you came back," she managed.

"Yeah. I thought so, too."

"Did you have a good trip?"

"I did." He took in her outfit and her coffee. "On your way to work?"

"Yes, but I've got a little bit of time. I'd like to hear about your trip." *I'd like to stare at you longer.*

"It can wait if you're in a hurry."

"I'm not in *that* big of a hurry." Uncle Michael held a lot of meetings. I mean, seriously. She didn't need to be on time for every single one. "C'mon." She led him into the great room, where she settled into a spot on the sofa under the antler chandelier. He took a chair.

While they talked about his conference and his Florida horses and trainers, while she answered his questions about her week at home, she continued to revel in the reality of him: clothes, hands, the scratches on his boots, the line of his jaw.

There had been a magnetic pull between them for a long time, and it had grown mightier than ever. But something new made itself known during their reunion. A kind of joy. She could see it in his expression. Feel it within her, answering.

"How's your job going?" he asked. "Is it still overwhelming you?"

"Yes. It's monopolizing. I bring work home at night and on the weekends, and I still can't catch up."

"You've got to rest sometime, Meg. You work too hard."

"Tell that to my uncle." She wished to goodness that she could stay with Bo for the entire day. Maybe trail after him, mooning over him while he worked. But, alas, she had to go.

Bo escorted her to the garage.

"You haven't forgotten about the party Friday night, have you?" she asked, walking alongside him.

"I haven't forgotten."

"Still willing to go?"

"You bet."

"I don't know if I mentioned this before, but it's going to be held at the Crescent Hotel in downtown Dallas, and it's cocktail attire."

"What does that mean?"

"For me, a dress and heels. For you, a suit and tie." She worried, suddenly, that he didn't own a suit. Why hadn't she thought of this sooner? "Is that all right?"

"Sure." He glanced at her. "You might be surprised to learn that I do own a suit and tie."

"No." She did her best to hide her relief. "Not surprised. I—"

"It's all right if you are surprised. I only own one because your father insisted. He had his tailor make one for me."

"I should have known." She remembered now. Her father had always made sure that his employees looked impressive enough to represent him well.

"What time would you like me to pick you up?" he asked.

"Six thirty."

"I think I might have found Stephen," Brimm said to Amber late that night.

"What!" His words snapped Amber to attention. "You found him?"

"I believe I did."

They'd met here, in the big house's office, earlier in the evening for their fourth computer session together. Brimm had been working on both his Mac and William Cole's computer for three hours since. Amber had mostly been keeping him company, daydreaming, and giving herself a manicure. She quickly screwed the brush back into her nail polish and set it aside.

Brimm swiveled his chair so that he faced her. "Okay, so we spent hours looking for him through Web sites and search engines."

"Right." She stared at him with wide eyes. "No luck."

"Last night I decided to go back through your handwritten notes. In them, you mentioned that Stephen participated in a hacking forum online."

"I only know about that because he bragged about it to me one time. He'd been the first to figure out some kind of challenge that one of the other members had, like, posted." She frowned. "I can't even remember the name of the forum now."

"Hackers Anon. You wrote it in the notes."

"So . . . you went there? To the forum? And you found him?"

"Just between you and me, I already had a . . ." Brimm pushed his glasses up his nose, "small, legal, very benign familiarity with that forum."

"Oh."

"Everyone there uses aliases. But since I know that Stephen likes challenges, I decided to put one together. Then I ran a competition to see who could crack it first."

"You used it like bait. To bring Stephen out."

"Exactly. The virus is actually a kind of Trojan horse. Once it's downloaded into a person's computer and they start tinkering with it, then I can infiltrate their computer and take a look around."

"Whoa."

He gave her a quick, proud smile. "Yeah. So far ten people have taken up my challenge. In each case, as soon as I gained access to their computers I went straight to their photos." He rolled his chair to William's computer and wiggled the mouse to wake it. The monitor filled with an image. "This guy look familiar?"

"Yes." A cold shiver ran between Amber's shoulder blades as she stared at the picture. Stephen and a brunette sitting together at an expensive-looking restaurant with drinks in their hands. Stephen still had the same hairstyle as when they'd been together, same taste in clothing, same smile. But now Amber could see that his smile didn't reach his dead, cold eyes. He was as fake as a celebrity cardboard cutout in a movie theater.

"He's going by the name Stephen McKenzie, and he's living in Phoenix."

"Phoenix?"

"Yes. I checked his email inbox and found all his contact information on a receipt that he received for something he bought online." Brimm brought up a different screen, then scribbled the information from it onto a notepad. He ripped off the top sheet and handed it to her.

"Wow." She took it from him with numb shock. "Thank you." She'd been looking for Stephen for two years. And now, as suddenly as that, Brimm had found him. Amber looked down at the letters and numbers on the piece of paper he'd handed her.

"I'm going to get out of his computer." Brimm's fingers went to work on the keyboard.

Oh. My. Gosh. She'd found Stephen.

A slideshow of memories raced through her mind. The morning she'd given birth to Jayden with only a girlfriend there to hold her hand. Walking the carpet of her apartment in the middle of the night, trying to get Jayden to sleep. The ugly way her tummy had looked for months after he'd been born. The times she'd had to leave Jayden in a day care she didn't love so she could earn money for him. The moments when she'd broken down because she'd been so tired and overwhelmed.

She'd done it *all* alone.

Now she held Stephen's address and phone number. So why did she feel sick to her stomach? How come the last thing in the world she wanted to do was pick up a phone?

"Are you going to call him?" Brimm asked.

"Not right now." She met his gaze. "I will. But I might have to, you know, psych myself up first."

"Sure."

"Thank you, Brimm. I'm really impressed. Seriously."

"You're welcome."

She extended her hand to him. He took it in a handshake.

"Mission accomplished," she said.

"Mission accomplished."

Stephen much preferred not to sleep in the homes of the women he bedded. If the situation and the personality were agreeable, he always left early and returned to the privacy of his own place. The situation and the personality had been agreeable tonight.

Once he arrived home, he showered, then settled at his kitchen table to toy with the virus a compatriot of his had posted earlier. He'd fiddled with it a few hours ago, hit a wall, and needed to take a break. But his brain had been working on it the whole time since, and he thought he might know the tactic to take in order to crack the thing.

He brought up the program and went to work—

Wait. He paused, scowling. Something was wrong. The program wasn't performing the way that it should.

He typed. Waited. Typed. Tried to understand. His gaze traveled over the lines of information.

Someone had hacked into him.

The realization hit him like ice water. The person who'd posted the challenge on the forum had used the program to *hack into him*. It looked as if that had been their intent all along.

He pulled up his advanced and custom anti-spyware, anti-malware program. It hadn't detected the attack, which meant the program must be new and uncirculated.

Frozen and furious, he stared at the screen. Who? Why? Had they been searching for him in particular?

After all the laws he'd broken, Stephen lived cautiously and protected his privacy zealously. He needed to know—as immediately as possible—who'd found him out.

He went to work decompiling the code.

Hours later, Stephen finally tracked the trail of the virus backward through cyberspace to the ISP where it had originated. At last, near sunrise, he hacked into the ISP and traced it straight to its source. He rested his hands in his lap and leaned back in his chair, gazing at the address on the screen.

411 Farm Road 721. Holley. Texas.

His brow knit, because he recognized this particular address. It belonged to Whispering Creek Ranch, a place he'd visited many times when he'd been dating and married to Meg.

He knew, of course, that William Cole had died. He knew when he'd died, why, and approximately how much money he'd left behind. Meg would be the one living at Whispering Creek now. Meg, in control of a fortune that ranged into the hundreds of millions of dollars.

It was a twist of fate that made him want to spit venom each and every time he thought about it. He'd believed when he'd left Meg that he'd played her well. But a father who'd died young, time, and hindsight had revealed that he'd played her out too early and far too cheaply. If he'd had patience, he'd now be the one in command of William Cole's money.

The address on-screen burned into his brain. *Meg?* Meg had hired computer dogs to sniff him out?

He'd never in all these years considered weak, trusting Meg to be a threat to him. But maybe the power that came with the Cole family fortune had changed her. Made her vengeful. It appeared that all of a sudden, years after he'd walked out of her life, she'd decided to make him pay for what he'd done to her.

He'd committed a string of crimes across three states. If she tipped off the police to his whereabouts, he'd find himself in extremely hot water.

Rapidly, he shut down his computer and zipped it into its carrying case. Then he went into his bedroom and began to pack.

He was nothing, *nothing*, if not skilled at protecting his own hide. He'd been an expert at it since childhood. Instead of waiting for fate to find and punish him, he always took fate into his own hands.

His computer had been compromised, which meant he could assume that Meg now knew his current last name, his location, his phone number. He had to leave Phoenix. He'd ditch his phone and buy another. Switch cars, even.

Then he'd go to Holley. He could assess the situation better from there, and strategize his next move.

Chapter Fourteen

The night of the engagement party, Meg answered the knock on the guesthouse door to find Bo on the threshold. He'd dressed in an immaculate dark gray suit, a white shirt, a silver tie, and a pair of black wingtips. "Wow." It took her a moment to adjust to the sight of him dressed like an elegant businessman. "You clean up well."

"Not half as well as you." His glittering gaze took in her outfit, then returned to meet her eyes. "You trying to give me a stroke, countess? Because you've just about done it."

She laughed. "Did you just call me *countess*?"

"You are one, right?"

"I don't believe we have any countesses here in America."

"Sure about that?"

"Pretty sure."

"Well, if we had any, you'd be one. You look beautiful."

His compliment poured over her like a sunbeam. "Thank you. So do you."

"I don't look like I'm wearing a Halloween costume?"

She remembered that she'd asked him the very same thing when she'd met him at Deep in the Heart. "Not at all." The narrow cut of the suit fit him perfectly, flattering his height and build.

She grabbed up her beaded purse and let herself out. They walked in the direction of the driveway, the breeze lifting a few of the ruffles on her skirt.

Bo thought her beautiful! He'd said *beautiful*—used that exact word—and called her *countess*, which was a very cute nickname.

She'd spent every lunch break of the past week shopping for the perfect dress and finally settled on this pale pink confection—strapless and tight down to her hips, then frothy with diagonal chiffon ruffles down to a few inches above her knees. To complement it, she'd purchased pale pink shoes with very high thin heels and ruched ribbons on the front.

Today, she'd gone out for a mani/pedi and a massage, then hovered over every detail of her bath, shaving, and skincare regimen. She'd even attempted a masque. She'd hired someone Lynn had recommended to handle her makeup and hair via house call.

Suddenly all the fuss, every detail of it, seemed worthwhile. He'd called her beautiful.

Why were there so many glasses? Bo wondered. And so many forks?

Over the years, he'd attended dinners at fancy restaurants with Thoroughbred owners and buyers. But this engagement party dinner for Meg's cousin beat them all. So far, he'd survived the meal by carefully watching what Meg did and then doing exactly the same. He didn't think that he'd embarrassed her . . . yet. At least he prayed he hadn't.

A waiter set the meal's fifth course in front of him. Dessert. A puffy chocolate thing in a round white dish. Bo hoped this was the last course, but couldn't be sure. He wouldn't put anything past these people.

Meg didn't reach for her spoon. Instead, she waited for a separate waiter carrying a silver pitcher.

Bo waited, too.

The man with the pitcher asked each of them if they wanted warm chocolate hazelnut sauce. Bo passed, but for those who accepted, the man used a spoon to pop open the top of their dessert. Then he poured liquid chocolate inside.

"I'm so full," Meg whispered to him. "But I'm going to eat at least a little of this." She picked up her spoon and took a bite. "It's delicious. Try."

He tried some.

"Does it compare to the chocolate milk shake from Dairy Queen?" She glanced at him, humor in her expression.

He lifted an eyebrow. "You want my honest answer?"

Meg smiled.

The man sitting on the other side of her, one of her male cousins, asked her a question, and she turned to answer.

Meg had explained that tonight's party was for one of her mother's sister's daughters. However, he and Meg were seated at a round table with the only people here from the other side of her family, the Cole side.

Meg's uncle Michael sat directly across from Bo. He'd been eyeing Bo with suspicion all night and had made it pretty clear that he hated Bo's guts. Michael's wife, Della, had shiny light gray hair and a friendly personality. Their two adult sons seemed like decent guys: smart but laid back, willing to talk horses with him. Both men had brought along dates who were shallow and filthy rich.

Every one of them seemed completely at home in the luxurious ballroom.

Not him.

The place pressed in on Bo—heavy. The tables covered with cloth, flowers, and china. The drapes at the windows. The sconces mounted on the walls. The beige and blue rug that had to be five inches tall. The food.

It made him itchy. It made him feel like a regular man dressed up in rich boy's clothing trying to pretend to be someone he wasn't. It reminded him why the wealthy men in the room were much better suited to Meg than he was, a fact that filled him with black frustration.

He didn't like this party. Not at all.

But for Meg's sake, he'd volunteer to sit through a thousand more engagement parties just like this one.

Meg leaned toward him. "Do you think that my uncle Michael looks like my father?"

"Yeah, I do."

"I do, too."

Bo watched Michael reach over and clap his hand affectionately onto the shoulder of his older son. "Is your uncle like your father in personality, too?"

"Well, they both had lots of self-confidence and intelligence and ambition. But Uncle Michael's kind, in his own way. He has a heart."

"And your father didn't?"

"No." She pushed her dessert plate away.

Bo waited, watching her, hoping she trusted him enough to tell him more. She looked painfully gorgeous. So much so that his chest ached in response. Diamond earrings fell from her ears, and a diamond bracelet circled one wrist. She'd worn her blond hair down, every curl shiny and perfectly behaved.

He wanted to pull her into a closet, push his hands into that hair, and kiss her for an hour straight. He wanted to say things, do things—

He took a swig of his water, which had thin sharp pieces of ice floating inside it. Carefully, he set the long-stemmed glass back in its place and tried to take a deep breath. His body and its physical desires had turned on him lately, becoming scary hard to control.

Michael's wife threw back her head and laughed at something her husband had said.

Meg motioned to the couple. "See? Uncle Michael has always had Aunt Della. She and their boys mean the world to him. I think they're what saved him from becoming what my father became when my mother died."

"Which was?"

"Cold."

He angled his chair more toward hers. "I only knew your father as a businessman. He was tough, but fair. One of the most demanding men I've ever met."

She nodded.

"I've wondered what it must have been like for you to be raised by him."

He watched old, very old, hurt enter her light brown eyes. "I wasn't raised by him, Bo. He wasn't around enough. Sadie Jo raised me."

His gut tightened like a fist because it upset him to see her upset. He wished, uselessly, that he could fix the past for her.

"Were your parents around a lot?" she asked.

"All the time. My mom stayed home with us and my dad worked hard, but he worked on our property. Why was your dad gone so much?"

"Work. Trips." She lifted a shoulder. "Hobbies. I wouldn't see him for days at a time, and then when I did it was really uncomfortable. I don't think he knew what to say or what to do with me. I'm so completely different than him. I always felt like he was . . ."

"Always felt like he was what?"

Meg looked at him as if trying to decide whether or not she should say more.

"I'd like to know," he said.

"I always felt like my father was disappointed in me."

"Meg." He could see uncertainty in her face. "If he was ever disappointed in you, then he was a fool." Bo wished he could take William Cole out back and whoop his hide. "There's not one single thing about you that isn't perfect."

Her brows rose. "That's not true."

"Yes it is." He was going too far and saying too much. But this ballroom, his emotions, and her unhappiness had made him reckless. He couldn't remember at the moment why he shouldn't tell her exactly how he felt about her. Why he shouldn't tell her—

That he loved her.

That's what this emotion was, God help him. Fierce, single-minded love. He'd hadn't wanted it, but it had barreled through him anyway, unstoppable. This was the thing people wrote books about, sang songs about, died for. His cynicism toward his friends who'd landed themselves in this predicament had come back to bite him.

He loved Meg, and it felt like painful joy. Joyful pain. Chaos inside. Violent loyalty.

Meg blew out a long, shaking breath. "Oh, Bo. I can't believe I'm talking to you about this. I never talk about this."

"I guess you were due, then."

"I guess I was."

Just then, the engaged couple stood, tapped a microphone, and started talking. Meg slipped on her black glasses, and he groaned inwardly because they always made her look like a hot schoolteacher. *Lord, have mercy.*

He and Meg clapped their way through lots of champagne toasts and the giving of gifts from the bride and groom to their parents and wedding party. When it finally ended, all the guests rose from their tables.

Bo's main plan was to stay near Meg. Even here, where no one probably carried anything more dangerous than a gold pen, Bo's instincts warned him that she needed him as her bodyguard.

Meg introduced him to her grandmother Lake, an elderly lady sporting a mask of makeup and big blue jewels surrounded by diamonds, as well as a fourth husband who looked like Boss Hogg. Bo met a stream of aunts, uncles, and cousins, including the soon-to-be bride. Then a middle-aged couple who owned Thoroughbreds found him, trapped him, and started asking him questions about the horse business.

Meg excused herself, and he was stuck. While talking with the horse people, he watched Meg make her way through the crowd. He noticed other men watching her, too. Men who'd come from the same world as she did, who had fancy educations and seemed comfortable wearing stupidly expensive suits. Each time she spoke with one of them, Bo stiffened.

Some of the guests, like Brimm, she very clearly liked. But with most of them he could see, even from across the room, the way her expression turned polite, almost too careful.

The horse people introduced him to two divorced cougars who smiled at him over the rims of their wine glasses.

His attention followed Meg, who approached the bride's

mother, her aunt. The two women bent their heads together. At one point, Meg's aunt looked toward him with concern, then continued talking to Meg.

He'd known that coming here tonight would cause one of her family members to point out his flaws to Meg, and he'd been right.

Meg left her aunt, her features tight. She searched the room for him, and when their gazes met he felt the force of it physically. She headed back in his direction and, when she reached their group, took in the cougars with a long, cool look. The cougars and Meg all put on fake niceness, which didn't come close to the real thing.

When Meg at last asked him if he was ready to leave, it took some effort not to look too eager.

On the ride home, silence surrounded her. Bo kept glancing across the dark cab of his truck, trying to measure her mood. He could plainly see that she was troubled. He only wished he could figure out as plainly how to make it better.

"Want to tell me what's the matter?" he asked.

She took a good while to answer. They drove north on 75, the office buildings and stores that lined the freeway whipping past. "You know how there are some people in your life that build you up?" she asked. "And some people that drain you?"

"Yes."

"Several of my family members drain me. I wish it wasn't so, but it is."

"Anything I can do?"

"No. Thank you, though."

"Would fast food make it better?"

"Goodness, no." But she shot him a tiny smile.

"You sure? There goes Whataburger."

The smile grew.

"I could take you horseback riding."

"Possibly one of the only things more stressful than dealing with my family."

"I could tell you a corny joke."

"Hmm."

"I could prank call your family."

She chuckled. "What helps is having you around. That's enough."

He hadn't known, before her, that tenderness could hurt. But it did. The sweetness of her words burned him.

She shifted to face him. "Thank you for coming with me tonight. I know it wasn't exactly your type of thing."

"What do you mean? I love the Crescendo Hotel."

"The Crescent."

"Oh. Right."

They grinned at one another. The rest of the way home, they talked more easily while the local country radio station played.

Once they'd reached Whispering Creek, he walked her to her door. Right at the moment when he expected her to disappear into her little guesthouse, she turned to him, rose onto her tiptoes, and gave him a hug.

"Thank you," she whispered against his neck near his ear.

He stilled, stunned. He only had time to soak in the impression of softness and the smell of roses before she let go and vanished. The door closed behind her.

He stood outside in the dark, holding himself motionless. That simple contact had thrown his body—which had been on edge for days—into howling chaos.

Aunt Pamela had always had a spooky knack for reading minds. Something she proved by calling Meg less than a minute after Meg parted from Bo.

She was unstrapping her heels when her cell phone started ringing. She pulled it from her purse and read Aunt Pamela's name illuminated across the screen. Her daily portion of tolerance for Aunt Pamela had already been spent. She pondered ignoring the call, but knew from past experience that doing so would only make it worse. "Hello?"

"Meg, it's Aunt Pamela."

"Hello." She lowered herself onto her wingback chair. Cashew jumped into her lap.

"Listen, I'm sorry if I offended you earlier with what I said about your date."

As soon as her aunt had discovered that Bo managed Whispering Creek Horses, she'd wrinkled her nose and said, "Does he have two nickels to rub together?" Then she'd attempted to question Meg about his finances.

"You're the one," Meg pointed out, "who insisted I bring a date."

"Of course! But I thought you'd bring someone . . . more like yourself."

What? Riddled with panic attacks?

"I'm concerned about you," Aunt Pamela continued. "That's all. And you know why."

"No. I don't know why."

"Because now you have more reason to be careful than you've ever had before."

"You mean now that my father's gone."

"Exactly. Now that your father's gone and you've inherited an *incredibly* large fortune. You are not an ordinary girl."

Funny, when she often felt very ordinary on the inside. Goodness, her family wearied her. If only she could throw her phone into the pool, drag Bo inside her guesthouse, and shut out everyone in the world but him. He had at least one tattoo she *really* wanted to check out.

"It's certainly fine to be friends with men like this Bo Porter, to bring them to events like Tara's party, to date them, even. But take my advice and make double sure that the fun ends there. All right?"

"Aunt Pamela—"

"There are a lot of fortune hunters out there."

"I don't think Bo is one."

"Yes, but you can't be certain, can you? I've been around awhile and I've gained some wisdom. The only way to be certain that a man isn't marrying you for your money is to marry someone who's already wealthy."

Meg's bottom lip plopped open. She'd had no idea her aunt would ever speak to her so bluntly or stoop so low.

"A wealthy man will understand you better, Meg. It's important to have your upbringing in common, to share similar interests."

"Like what?" Meg asked. "Yachting?"

"Meg," her aunt scolded.

"I've known lots of rich men and frankly . . ." *I'd rather take my chances with Bo any day of the week.* "I find them to be some of the greediest people alive. How can I be sure that a rich man isn't going to marry me just to get his hands on more money?"

"Two syllables. Pre. Nup."

Charged silence filled the phone like static. Meg's anger spiked, and she knew she needed to disconnect before she said something regrettable. "I'd . . . ah, better let you go. I need to go take care of Cashew." Her cat remained on her lap, already halfway into a coma.

"All right, then. We'll talk more about this later."

"Bye." Meg ended the call and flicked the phone aside. Carrying Cashew, she went to stand at the window that overlooked Mr. Son's artistry and the shimmery, satin-like surface of the pool.

Every single good thing about her evening had come to her because of Bo. His words, his smile, the searing thrill of her attraction to him, the deep reassurance of his friendship. Those things and those alone had salvaged the party for her. When she looked back on this night, those were the only gems of memory she'd savor.

Aunt Pamela didn't give Meg's judgment much credit. And to be sure, Meg had never given her own judgment much credit, either. But sometimes a person just knew, sensed, recognized the difference between a safe haven and a toxic harbor. Even though Meg was related to Aunt Pamela and had known her since childhood, Aunt Pamela was the toxic harbor.

And Bo was the safe haven.

Meg herself had been uncertain about Bo's motives in the past. But tonight—after the careful way he'd treated her, after the possessiveness that had overtaken her when she'd seen those two women salivating over him—she'd grown more certain of Bo than ever.

It might be time to put the last of her uncertainties away.

As was his habit, Bo worked most of the following day, Saturday. Finally satisfied with the state of things at the farm, he left Whispering Creek, pulled into the gas station, stopped at

Brookshire's for Dr. Pepper and groceries, then headed home. Ordinary.

As he drove up to his house, he spotted a gleaming black Porsche parked at the end of the drive. Not ordinary.

His grip on the steering wheel tightened because he didn't need to see the face of the man sitting inside the car to know who'd come to pay him a visit, and why. This was just like the other night all over again, when he'd arrived home and found his brother waiting. Same situation. Same reason. Different man.

Feeling much older than his years, he parked and crossed to the Porsche.

Meg's Uncle Michael climbed out of his car.

"Sir," Bo said when he reached him.

"Bo." They shook hands.

Bo stuffed his hands in the front pockets of his jeans and waited, grinding his back teeth so hard that pain shot along his jaw. He'd always taken pride in his land and his house, but he understood how plain and simple they must look to Meg's uncle.

"Sorry to interrupt your weekend," Michael said.

Bo lowered his chin in acknowledgment.

"I came to talk to you. About Meg."

Chapter Fifteen

his'll be fun," Amber said.

"Mmm-hmm," Meg answered, though she wasn't so sure. She pulled her Mercedes into a spot in front of All the Time Fitness and looked dubiously at the medium-sized gym, located at the end of a strip mall. All the Time was the first nationwide chain of gyms to have ventured into Holley. It offered the local residents something they'd never had access to before: the boon of exercise at midnight, or four a.m., or dawn.

Personally, Meg preferred to exercise during regular human hours in the privacy of her father's home gym. She'd tried to tell Amber that she needed to tackle her Cole Oil homework, but Amber had been dying to try out All the Time Fitness and had convinced Meg to accompany her. Pair that with Sadie Jo's insistence that she needed a Jayden fix this Sunday afternoon, and here they were. They walked together toward the gym's entrance, dressed in workout gear and carrying water bottles and hand towels.

"It's just so much better," Amber said, "to work out with other people around, you know? I bet there'll be some cute guys in here."

"We're going to a step class. I'm pretty sure that cute guys don't flock to step classes."

"Not *in* our class, Meg! The cute ones will be lifting weights or running on treadmills. We can check them out as we pass by."

"Oh."

While Amber stopped at the desk to secure guest passes, Meg surveyed the interior. Amber's prediction had come true. Two cute guys were lifting weights. In fact, one of them looked a lot like Bo. Tingles and hope flowed over her and she took a few steps toward him, but when he turned, the tingles fizzled. Not Bo.

Her attention skirted past a smattering of people on the cardio machines before catching on a middle-aged guy on the mats in front of the mirrors. He was doing calisthenics, violent stretches, jumping, and martial arts moves. While Meg watched, he leaned over and executed a headstand.

Maybe there was something to be said for public gyms after all.

They made their way into the room used for group classes. Four other ladies and one not-cute guy were in the process of setting up their step benches by adding risers underneath. Amber and Meg went to work doing the same.

"Did you notice those guys by the weights?" Amber whispered to Meg.

"I did."

"See? I told you!"

"Did you notice the guy doing the headstand?"

"What? No! How could I have missed it?"

A woman no younger than seventy years of age strode into the room wearing bright pink lipstick, a black T-shirt with a jeweled fleur-de-lis on the front, black shorts over spandex leggings, and jazz shoes. Her short, matte black hair looked like it might have been aided by bald-spot spray—the stuff that had the consistency of the fake snow they sprayed on Christmas trees.

"Hello, everyone!" she called. "Let's get ready to rock out!"

"Is this our teacher?" Meg asked Amber under her breath.

"I don't know. I . . ." Amber, who'd been so confident about coming, suddenly looked doubt-riddled.

The woman slid a CD into the stereo.

"I guess she is," Amber said.

Maybe they'd accidentally happened into a class for senior adults. If so, this class would be way too easy, since Meg had been hitting the elliptical and the weights with such regularity. She glanced at their fellow participants, all decades younger than the teacher. Couldn't be a class for seniors.

"SexyBack" poured from the wall-mounted speakers. "Come on!" their pink-lipped teacher called out. "Let's do it!"

Before Meg knew it, she was following the woman's sprightly steps through a warm-up. Their teacher had no risers under her bench. It just sat, flat on the floor. And it didn't take Meg long to realize that the two risers she'd stuck under each end of her bench may have been a little ambitious. She rallied the inner cheerleader she'd never been, and determined to do her best.

"'Get your sexy on,'" their teacher chanted in time to the lyrics. "'Get your sexy on.'"

Pink Lips would demonstrate the steps with her bandy little legs and then, once they were all in the rhythm of the pattern, leave her bench to walk around the room tossing out cheerful encouragements. When satisfied that the group had killed themselves enough with one set of steps, she'd show them a new set, then walk around again.

"How're you liking this?" She stopped in front of Meg as Meg bounced up and down. "Getting a good workout?"

"Yep." She didn't have enough breath to heap further reassurances on the woman.

Had she actually worried for a split second that this class would be too easy? My word! She spared a look at Amber, who appeared to be weathering the class better than Meg. Apparently, the job of chasing a toddler all day rendered a person admirably fit.

"'I'm bringing sexy back!'" their teacher sung.

Way back, in Pink Lips' case.

Meg's face flushed a light, bright red. Her lungs pumped heavily. Sweat stung her eyes and dropped off her chin. At one point, she thought she might have to throw up. Her body screamed at her to stop, that she couldn't do it.

But something stubborn inside of her disagreed. She *could* do it. It hurt, but it wouldn't last forever. These muscles and bones of hers had to answer to her will. Her heart could seize with a heart attack if it wanted, but she *wasn't* going to stop. She clenched her teeth and gutted it through.

When a new song began, and the steps changed to something marginally easier, a surge of energy mounted inside her, strong and heady. She'd heard the term "runner's high." Goodness knows, she wasn't a runner. Her chest was too big, for one thing. And then there was the fact that she, well, hated running. But maybe this was her version of a runner's high.

She glanced at herself in the mirrors. A curvy blonde of medium height and medium attractiveness. Short tufts of hair had escaped her ponytail. Perspiration had caused her eye makeup to smear. Her skin had turned blotchy with exertion.

Despite all that, she liked the Megan Cole in the mirror because this Megan Cole was no weakling. This woman wasn't frozen with fear, self-doubt, or panic attacks.

She didn't know if exercise had made her thinner, or gotten her heart into shape, or added muscles that burned calories. What had it done for her? Tested her determination. Every time she'd faced it and bested it, she'd grown in strength. Working out had put her in touch with something she'd lost her grip on years ago and wanted back: her God-given power.

"Lookin' good!" Pink Lips hollered. "Work it hard, ladies and gentleman. C'mon!" She did a couple of big overhead claps. "Let's do it!"

Meg swiped sweat from her forehead. God had been patient with her for a long time now. She'd all but buried herself five years ago. Yet somehow, in His incredible strength, God had pulled her through the heartbreak, betrayal, divorce, and crushing anxiety.

Jesus had been buried once, too, after all. But He hadn't stayed that way. He'd risen, alive and victorious. He'd overcome. All along the way He'd whispered to Meg that He could do the same for her, that in Him, she, too, could overcome.

She'd trusted Him, and He'd been faithful. He'd helped her when she couldn't help herself. And gradually, she'd begun to leave the devastation behind. Thanks only to Him, she'd grown in strength until, for the first time in years, she thought she might be ready to stand tall and handle the demands of her life.

With her recovery came His call to help others just as He'd helped her. Full circle.

I'm willing, she told him. *Let's move forward together—you and me. I'm ready. Just show me the way.*

On the way back to Whispering Creek, Meg and Amber pulled into Sonic. They didn't dare order anything calorie-laden after the workout they'd just endured, so they opted for half-price happy hour iced teas sweetened with Splenda. They settled across from one another at an outdoor table, covered in cooling sweat and the satisfaction of cardio survived.

"Remember how Brimm and I were working on the search a few nights ago?" Amber asked.

"Yes."

"Well . . . we found Stephen."

Meg stared.

Amber fiddled with her straw.

"You did?" Meg kept her face and voice carefully neutral.

"Yeah. He's in Phoenix, going by a different last name. Brimm was able to give me his telephone number and address and everything. Brimm's amazing."

"Yes, he is."

"Anyway, it was strange because as much as I've wanted to find Stephen, once I had his number, it made me kind of sick to think about actually calling him. You know?"

Meg nodded. Just thinking about Stephen had the same effect on her.

"I finally dialed his number yesterday. One of those recorded messages from the operator came on, saying that the number had been disconnected."

"Oh."

"I guess I should have been disappointed. But I was sort of . . . glad. I mean, I did what I wanted to do: I found him. And I had the guts to dial his number. But when that recording came on, I took it as a sign. I think I oughta put him behind me like you have."

"Oh, Amber." Relieved tears sprang to Meg's eyes.

"Living at Whispering Creek, being around all of you nice

people, has helped me. I don't feel so empty and furious any-more. I feel . . . you know, peaceful. I have a good thing going. I don't need to find Stephen like I did before."

"You know I was ready to support you no matter what, but I'm glad to hear that. Come here." Meg hugged the younger woman, then kept hold of one of her hands when she released her. "I think you're right."

"You do?"

"Yes. I think you're doing the right thing for both you and Jayden."

"Leave him in the rearview mirror, right?"

"Leave him in the rearview mirror," Meg agreed.

"That doesn't mean I won't still tell him off if I get the chance though, Meg. If I ever seem him again, believe me—I'll tell him off good."

Later that afternoon, Meg drove along Whispering Creek's narrow back lanes. She hadn't seen Bo since the party Friday night and she missed him.

She checked her lip gloss, even though she'd spent twenty minutes primping before she'd left the guesthouse. It looked the same as it had the last time she'd checked it—ten seconds ago. "You've officially lost it over him," she said to the empty interior of her car. "Officially. You realize this?"

As usual when she arrived at the farm, she spotted a groom in-side the stable and exchanged greetings with him before making her way outside to the paddock. She took up her usual position at the fence and waited, not very patiently, for Bo.

The little foals had grown taller and bulkier over the past month and a half since she'd started coming. She'd given them all names. Tonight, little Fifi and Bartholomew were outdoors with their mothers. While she looked on, they took off on a game of chase, running with their long legs stretching, their bushy tails extended high. When they stopped, they reared a few times facing one another, then kicked up their back heels, then launched into what looked like baby equine wrestling.

Meg smiled. She might not like riding horses, but she sure did enjoy viewing them from firm land at a safe distance.

At length, she checked her watch. Strange. Every other time she'd come to the farm, Bo had arrived sooner than this. It was Sunday, but that had never stopped him before. Was it possible that something was the matter with him . . . or between them? She scanned the parking lot and the roads beyond for a sign of Bo's truck. Nothing.

She thought back over their evening at the party. She couldn't think of anything he'd said or done to indicate that their friendship had changed in any way. On the contrary, he'd been incredibly kind to her during the car ride home.

Surely that quick hug she'd given him at the end of the night hadn't thrown him. Had it? Surely not. She was overreacting. Hadn't she herself told Bo, several times, that he didn't need to meet her out here? He was probably just taking a nap or busy with his family. She caught herself spinning her earring back and let go of it.

For slow and grating minutes, she continued to wait. With every tick of her watch hand her uneasiness increased.

After a full hour, Meg returned to her car. She felt like a citizen of Gotham City who'd aimed the bat light into the sky, waited expectantly, and then finally realized that Batman wasn't coming. Bo had broken their pattern. He'd left her signal unanswered.

All evening long, while she pored over a report for Cole Oil, she continued to try to talk herself out of her concern over Bo's absence, to be rational and objective.

But her gut wasn't buying it.

Her gut told her that something had gone wrong.

The next morning Meg stood at the windows that ran along the wall of her father's office. Her bare toes curled into the carpet while she wound and unwound a lock of hair around her finger. Her mind traveled miles to the north and east, to a horse farm, and to worries about a very particular cowboy.

"Ms. Cole?" The voice of her male assistant came through the intercom. "You're expected in Mr. Cole's office in two minutes."

"Thanks." Grudgingly, she located her heels hiding under her desk, slipped them back on, and let herself into the hallway.

Her doglike assistants swung their heads in her direction. "Oh," her female assistant said, as if the sight of Meg had jogged her memory. "I've been meaning to ask you. Was Mr. Cole able to get in touch with Mr. Porter over the weekend?"

Meg surveyed the woman, trying to understand her question. "The two men saw each other on Friday night. Is that what you're asking?"

The woman's forehead wrinkled. "No, I . . ."

Meg waited.

"Mr. Cole called me on Saturday."

"Saturday?" Foreboding twisted inside Meg. "What for?"

"I'm sorry. Perhaps . . . perhaps I shouldn't have said anything."

"No, I'm glad you said something. Would you mind telling me what happened?"

The woman cut an uncertain glance toward Uncle Michael's

office. "Mr. Cole called me on my cell phone on Saturday and asked me to locate Mr. Porter's address. He said that the three of you had some—some business you needed to attend to together. Maybe I misunderstood that part."

Meg sincerely doubted it. "Were you able to find Mr. Porter's address?"

She nodded. "I logged on to my work computer remotely and ran a search for Mr. Porter's employment records."

"I see." What in the world had Uncle Michael done? Meg thanked her assistant, then walked toward her uncle's office, her brain spinning. Uncle Michael couldn't have wanted Bo's address for any reason except that he planned to visit Bo at home. *But why?* What had her uncle said to him? Did his visit have anything to do with Bo's absence at the paddock last night?

Her heart started to pound. *Oh my goodness.* Bo didn't deserve hostility from her uncle. Bo'd been nothing but kind to her, nothing but good.

Meg knocked on her uncle's door, waited for his muffled "Come on in," and let herself inside.

He didn't look up from his computer. "Have a seat. Almost done with this." His fingertips hunted and pecked at the keys.

She waited, her emotions rising, her hands starting to shake.

He finished and turned his full attention to her.

"Did you call my assistant on Saturday and ask for Bo Porter's address?"

Never one to exhibit surprise, Uncle Michael simply leaned back in his office chair. The chair bobbed while he considered her. "I did."

"Why?"

"Care to have a seat?"

"No. I'll stand."

She read no apology in him, only the forbearance of a powerful man accustomed to confrontation. "I wanted Bo's address because I'd decided to drive out to his house and speak with him."

"What—" The word came out unsteady. She blinked back tears by sheer force of will. "What did you say to him?"

"I told him why I don't like the idea of a romantic relationship between the two of you."

"You did what?" she choked.

"It was a perfectly reasonable conversation. For what it's worth, he seemed to agree with the fact that you're not right for each other."

Her cheeks flamed with embarrassment and anger. How dare he! She could barely stand to think about how her uncle might have made Bo feel, or that Bo'd apparently agreed with her uncle's assessment that they weren't right for each other. No wonder he'd not come to see her at the paddock last night. "Bo and I are friends."

His look turned chiding. "Come on, Meg. I sat across from the two of you all night on Friday. I'm not blind."

"You had absolutely no right to talk to Bo about his relationship with me. That's private."

"Yes and no. Any man you date is a man you might marry. And any man you marry will have a half share of everything my brother spent a lifetime building. That *is* my business."

"No it isn't."

"Sure it is."

"*No*, it isn't."

He tilted his elegant head, eyes challenging.

With a frustrated groan, she paced away from him and tried with every step to think straight, to calm herself. Not easy. He and Aunt Pamela had both *ridiculously* overreacted to one simple date!

She came back to face him, drawing herself up to her full height. "Like it or not, you're going to have to accept that my father's money is mine now. To be honest with you, I don't even like that fact most of the time. But it is what it is. The money is mine to worry about. Only mine. And whom I marry—that choice?—that's only mine, too." She'd never had enough courage to speak to her uncle this way before. She almost couldn't believe she was doing it now. She *wouldn't* be doing it now, except that he'd had the audacity to bring Bo into this. The protectiveness pounding through her bloodstream made her brave.

"You shouldn't be dating Bo Porter, Meg. For one thing, he's your employee."

Her uncle had just hit on the argument that she'd been hanging on to all this time in an attempt to guard herself from losing her head and her heart to Bo.

At this moment, though, standing here defending him to her uncle, it seemed stupid in the extreme that she'd kept Bo at a distance for any reason. The strength of her reaction to her uncle confirmed—for good—the depth of her feelings for Bo. She had so few true and trustworthy people in her life.

He was true and trustworthy. He was kind, funny, and genuine. And she suspected that he cared about her. All of which made him more rare and precious to her than all the money in her bank accounts. "It's not against the law to date an employee. Men do it all the time, do they not?"

"It's not against the law, but it is inappropriate."

"Then I'm willing to act inappropriately in this case."

Her uncle sighed and pushed to standing. Smoothly, he came around to the front of his desk. "Won't you take a seat?"

"No. Thank you."

He pursed his lips and sat on the edge of his desk. "I don't trust his motives, Meg."

"I take Bo to one family party. Just one! And you and Aunt Pamela both immediately jump to the conclusion that he's after me for my money."

"I don't think it's wise to underestimate how strong a lure your inheritance can be to a man like Bo Porter. Neither of us were raised without money, Meg. We can't really understand what going without money can do to people, how much others can desire money, what they'll do to get it."

A scream built at the base of her throat, circling to explode.

"Since your father died, I feel responsible for you, Meg. You know that. He's not here anymore, so it falls to me to protect you now."

"I don't need protecting."

"I disagree. You've always been . . . gentle. I'm just trying to make certain that no one takes advantage of you." He laid his hand on his chest. "I have your best interests at heart."

"In the future, if your 'best interests' cause you to have concerns about my relationships, then come directly to me. Please don't ever go over my head again. Are we agreed?"

A hesitation, then, "We're agreed."

"I'm taking the rest of the day off."

"Where are you going?"

"To talk to Bo. I've got to try to fix the mess you made." Halfway out the office door, she paused to look back at him. "One more thing."

"Yes?"

"I'm not *that* gentle. Not anymore."

Chapter Sixteen

eg passed the remainder of the day in a serious
state of fret.

At first she'd determined that she'd go see
Bo straightaway, at the horse farm. But she'd reconsidered, because she didn't relish holding this conversation in the vicinity
of his staff or his brother.

Then she decided that she'd call him. But she really didn't
want to talk over the phone, either.

So she'd finally resolved to wait until evening, then drive to
his house and speak with him there. She didn't love the idea of
arriving at Bo's home as an uninvited and unexpected guest,
but she could accept that fate better than the other options.

Unlike her uncle, she'd managed to find Bo's address herself.
It had been neatly filed in her father's home office amid all the
records for Whispering Creek Horses.

A little past eight o'clock, she arrived at what she guessed to
be the entrance road leading off the street to Bo's house. She
double-checked the directions and GPS map on her phone and
pulled in. The small dinner she'd forced herself to eat before
she'd left home had hardened like marbles in her stomach.

When she reached the end of the driveway, she killed the

engine of the Mercedes. He lived in a small brick house, accented with a dark brown wooden door that matched the square porch posts. Trimmed hedges lined the front. No pots or flowers.

It struck her as a place secure in what it was: a Texas house on Texas land. Unpretentious and unapologetic about it, masculine, and surrounded by bare nature.

Some interior lights were glowing, and she could see Bo's truck parked in the carport next to the house. He was definitely at home, which meant he'd likely spot her sitting out here, staring. That unwelcome thought motivated her to grab the package of Oreos she'd brought and walk to the door. Her jeweled sandals slapped against her heels and the marbles in her stomach knocked together.

The sun had almost disappeared, and the air had thickened with hazy twilight. She'd wanted to give Bo plenty of time to return home from work and eat before descending on him. Maybe she should have come earlier? Maybe she should have worn her green top instead of this pale blue one with the short sleeves that ended in little cinched ties? Maybe she should just blurt out "My uncle is an ogre!" as soon as he opened the door.

She took a huge breath and knocked. Almost at once, she could hear rustling inside. She chewed the inside of her cheek and waited.

He answered the door wearing a simple black T-shirt, low-slung jeans, and bare feet.

Oh-God-help-me-help-me-help-me. She briefly considered fainting.

"Meg." His brows lowered. Gone was the warmth and affection that usually flowed between them. It had been replaced, at least on his side, by guardedness.

Her uncle—several *very* bad words came to mind to describe

him—had done every bit as much damage as she'd feared. "Hi." She tested a please-don't-be-mad-at-me smile. "I apologize for showing up unexpectedly like this. I wanted to talk with you. I hope you don't mind."

"I don't mind."

He led her into a living room simply furnished with leather pieces and a wooden coffee table that held a couple of hardcover books and a *Sports Illustrated*. A baseball game played on a wall-mounted flat screen. He must have muted it, because instead of commentators' voices, she heard quiet country music. His computer sat, the monitor illuminated, on a desk against the back wall of the space. A desk chair stood in front of it, askew.

"Were you working on the computer?" she asked.

"I was."

"Sorry to interrupt."

"It's okay." After hesitating near the living room couch, he continued over to a square table that straddled the space between the living area and the open kitchen. "Is this all right?"

"Sure, thanks." She sat and carefully placed the Oreos on the table.

Still standing, he stuck his hands in his back pockets. "Can I get you something to drink?"

"No. Thank you, though."

"To eat?"

"No, I'm good."

"Sure?"

"Yes, thank you."

After a beat, he took the chair next to hers. He dwarfed both the table and her with his size.

"These are for you." Meg slid the Oreos in his direction.

"Thanks."

When she'd been back at home, bringing Oreos had seemed like a decent peace offering. Now it just seemed lame, because clearly she hadn't driven all the way out here to bring him something he could buy at any grocery store himself for less than four dollars. "They're my favorite dessert."

"I'd have thought your favorite dessert would be something more fancy."

"What, like crème brulée?"

"I've no idea what you just said."

"Crème brulée," she reiterated.

"Nope, never heard of it."

"It's a sort of custard with a hard, caramelized topping."

"Then no wonder you like Oreos better."

"Right. No wonder." She'd dug herself a neck-deep hole of awkwardness, coming here and then talking to him inanely about dessert.

He studied her with those gray eyes of his, so piercing, so serious tonight, so able to penetrate straight to her soul.

Where had all her bravery gone? She'd been brave with her uncle, but it had fled like a cowardly deserter in the face of battle. "Bo, I . . . I wanted to say that I'm sorry."

He frowned. "Why are you sorry?"

"About my uncle. I know he came out here on Saturday and spoke with you."

Instead of clearing with understanding, his expression only turned more troubled.

"I didn't know about it until I found out at work today," she continued. "I'm really so sorry. He had no right to do that. I'm embarrassed and—and angry because I'm sure that he offended you."

"It's not your fault, Meg. You don't have to apologize."

"He's my uncle."

Bo folded his hands together on the surface of the table and stared down at them. She could see the muscles of his jaw harden with strain. More than that, though, she could sense his inner turmoil.

She couldn't stand for him to feel bad because of her. Instead of jumping out of her skin or bursting into tears, she leaned over on impulse and gave him a quick kiss on the cheek—there and gone—and returned quickly to her seat.

Bo had been still before, but now he froze completely. He looked like a man bracing against a tempest, his only movement the tense rise and fall of his chest.

What had she just done? Kissed him? She'd kissed him. She opened her lips to apologize anew—

He shot to his feet, sending his chair crashing onto the floor. He looped his hands under her arms and lifted her until she was standing before him, just a breath apart. He stared down into her face for a burning moment, and then he kissed her.

A combination of shock and mind-spinning sensation submerged Meg. Bo. Her Bo. Bo Porter—her crush, her friend, her employee, her calm—was kissing her. And *oh my*. What a kiss. The most perfect kiss that heaven had ever dreamt up. Tender and passionate. Full of endless longing and eternal promises.

His hands burrowed into her hair. Her own hands reached up in answer. She couldn't believe she was touching him—his chest, his neck—weaving her hands behind his head to draw him closer. Cold chills sizzled against the backs of her knees in glaring contrast to the hot and demanding heat pulling at her from the inside.

When Bo finally lifted his head, his expression was stark, honest, intense. His color high.

"I love you," he said.

Plainly, just like that.

She gawked at him.

"I love you. I do. And I want to marry you."

A sound like the final, joyful, exultant note of a choir anthem filled Meg's head. "Bo," she breathed. It was the best she could do. He'd stunned the voice straight out of her.

"I can't do many things," he said fiercely, "but I can love you, Meg. I can love you every hour of every day for the rest of my life. I swear to you I can. I want to earn the right to try." The pad of his thumb rubbed her cheek. "I love you so much I can hardly see straight. I can't concentrate. I can't sleep. I can't make myself care about anything on earth except for you. I'm useless."

"No you're not."

"I'm a mess."

"No."

"I am." He insisted. "About you, I am."

Her gaze traveled over his familiar features with wonder. He loved her! Until now she'd only been able to guess at his feelings, unsure. To hear his feelings confirmed with such force caused joy and amazement to lift in her heart, violently sweet, almost uncontainable. She reached onto her tiptoes and kissed him on the lips, then the side of his neck, then she wrapped her arms around him and hugged him. In response, his powerful arms enclosed her against him in an I'll-protect-you-forever kind of embrace that spoke louder than a thousand words ever could. They stayed that way for long moments, heartbeat to heartbeat.

When he finally spoke, his words emerged ragged against her hair. "I wish . . . ."

She waited, but he didn't finish. "What do you wish?"

"I wish you could be mine."

That didn't sound promising. She pulled back enough to look at him.

His mouth twisted with bitterness. "I don't like your uncle—"

"No, neither do I at this moment."

"—but at least he had the guts to tell me to my face to leave you alone. I couldn't argue with him about it." He let go of her and strode away. "From the first day I met you, I've known that's exactly what I should do, but I couldn't make myself stay away. I've been kidding myself. Hoping, even though I knew better. . . . So stupid."

"Bo, my uncle was completely wrong—"

"No, hearing him say it the other day hit home for me just how right he is. You deserve way better than me, Meg."

"What?"

"You should be with someone who has framed degrees on his wall. Who's sophisticated. Rich." He threw up his hands. "Look at me! I'm none of those things."

"You think I care about those things? Really? Your heart is right, Bo, and that's what I care about. That counts for way more with me than everything else combined."

"I drive a ten-year-old truck. I live in this small house. I grew up in Holley. I'm simple. I'm just this normal guy, and then . . . there's you. You're everything that's beautiful. I'm not good enough for you, and it kills me, because I want to be."

Tears filled her eyes, blurring her view of him. "Of course you're good enough for me, Bo. Of course you are. I don't want to hear you say that you're not ever again."

He came to her at once. "Countess," he whispered, taking gentle hold of her face. She closed her eyes, and he mopped up all traces of tears with his fingertips. "I'm so sorry. Don't cry."

"You are good enough."

"Shh. Please don't cry. I'm so sorry. Here."

She opened her eyes to see him pull a tissue from his jeans. He handed it to her and she used it to press away her tears.

He carried tissues around in his pockets for her, even on nights when he had no expectation of seeing her. Despite his attempts to convince her otherwise, he was one of the best, most worthy, most deserving men she'd ever met.

She drew him over to sit in the leather chair. She perched on the coffee table facing him, his face higher than hers, his knees bracketing hers on the outside. She made one last attempt to sweep away runaway mascara.

Bo watched her, his expression drawn with concern.

"Okay." She took both of his big hands in hers. "I'm the one that's a mess. For the last five years, but especially since my father died, I've been weak and scared and unsure of myself."

"Meg," he protested.

"It's true." She squeezed his hands. "You, Bo. You, on the other hand, have it all together. You're solid and strong and full of integrity. There's no logical reason for you to consider yourself not good enough for me, unless this has to do with my money."

He scowled. He had pride, she knew. He was the oldest son, the caretaker of his siblings. He'd no doubt been born and bred to provide for his future wife and future children. He probably *wanted* it that way. It must go against his grain to be with a woman like her when their wealth was so unequal. He'd be teased for it by some. Others would always regard him with suspicion, would believe the worst of him, would whisper behind his back that he was with her for her fortune. There were advantages to wealth, but there were difficulties, too. Difficulties that she couldn't change or shelter him from.

"I want to tell you a few things about my money," she said. "First of all, I know I'm very, very lucky to have all that I do. I didn't earn it. I was just born into it. Whispering Creek, good schools, and all the rest of it." He'd said that he loved her. She could see it now, a deep softness in his gaze, as he looked at her. "I want you to know, though, that those advantages haven't come free. My family's fortune cost me my father, which in turn cost me a lot of my self-confidence." Her throat threatened to close with emotion, but she managed to keep talking through it. "My money cost me my first marriage. And it's cost me most of my ability to trust men ever since. So, between you and me, I'm done—*really done*—with letting my money cost me things. I'm not in the mood to let it cost me you."

"Meg," he groaned, his eyes turning shiny with moisture. "I only want what's best for you."

"What would be best for me is for you to try to see me completely apart from my last name and everything that comes with it. Okay? Just see *me*."

He still looked torn.

"You think God views us any differently, Bo? He doesn't. He doesn't care one bit about all the outward things. To Him we're equal. We're both loved the same, valued the same. We both need to find our worth in God's view of us. To look for it anywhere else is a big mistake."

"Meg . . ."

"It's a big mistake, Bo."

Taut silence traveled between them. She could sense him hovering on the edge of decision. The first day she'd met him, in her father's office, she'd hovered on the edge of a decision also: to let him stay or make him go. It had been a turning-point moment, just as this was. She couldn't bear to let him fall away from her reach. She had to persuade him.

"I'd really like to give this thing between us a chance." She pressed one kiss, two, three, into his hands. Then she looked up at him with a smile that felt wobbly. "How about we just date? Isn't that what everyone else does? Let's just date."

"I work for you."

"You know what? I'm ready to let that worry go."

"A lot of people won't like it."

"I've spent a lifetime caring about what other people said about me, and I've never been able to please them no matter how hard I tried. I can't let myself care about what other people say about me anymore."

"I care a lot about what they say about you, Meg."

"You're going to have to get over it."

He looked skeptical.

"C'mon. Let's just take it slow, date each other, and see where it goes. There's no real harm in that, is there?"

"No real harm? I'm already half dead over you."

"Any chance the half-alive part is willing to give it a try?"

He looked upward, sighed deeply, then returned his full attention to her for long moments. "Yes, God help you."

Triumph and hope pierced her. "Really?"

"Yes."

"You won't change your mind?"

"No."

Grinning, she launched herself into his lap. He clasped her to him, nuzzled his face against her neck, and pressed kisses against the tender skin below her ear. "I hope to God this is what's right for you," he whispered. "I'll do anything for you. Anything you ask. Anything to make you happy."

"You make me happy. You don't have to do anything."

He lifted his head, eyes alight with fire. "Meg." Then he claimed her lips with a kiss—territorial, demanding, adoring—that communicated his feelings with unmistakable certainty.

Chapter Seventeen

They talked for hours that night. Bo pulled sofa pillows onto the floor, and they stretched out on the living room carpet facing each other, their heads and shoulders propped up on the pillows. They ate Oreos. Kissed. Drank Dr. Pepper. Laughed. He toyed with her fingers, occasionally kissing their tips.

Bo felt like he was living wide awake inside the best dream he'd ever dreamed. He was almost too scared to believe it was real, because he wanted this—wanted her—so much. Worries kept trying to enter his head, and he kept shoving them aside.

In the wee hours of the morning, he climbed into his truck so that he could follow her car back to Whispering Creek. She'd tried to convince him it wasn't necessary to trail her home, but he wasn't buying. All the drunks swerved down the roads at this time of night.

As it turned out, between his house and hers, Bo spotted one green Honda, and nothing else. That didn't stop him from following her all the way to Whispering Creek, then watching as the security guard greeted her and waved her through.

There goes my heart, he thought. *My everything.*

When her car disappeared, he pulled away and drove through the pitch darkness back in the direction of his house.

He hoped he'd done the right thing tonight.

With every piece of him, he hoped so.

But he didn't feel sure. Alone in the quiet, the worries were harder to shove away.

When he'd caved and told her how he felt about her, had he done what was best for her? Or had he simply done what was best for himself? Was there any chance that his actions tonight might hurt her in the end? Might hurt the farm?

Too late now. He'd have to trust God to protect Meg. He'd have to trust Meg's judgment and kindness to do right by the farm and its employees. What had happened between them couldn't be undone. He'd told her to her face that he wouldn't change his mind. More than that, he *didn't want* to change his mind. He'd rather cut off his arm than change a single thing that had happened between them.

He pulled onto the shoulder of the road, his headlights drilling into the darkness in front of him, shadowy trees swaying above him. He stacked his hands on top of the steering wheel and laid his forehead on top of them. *Oh, God. Don't let anything bad happen to her. Not ever, and certainly not because of me.*

Concern hummed low in his gut, shapeless, hard to pin down. When he'd been in the Marines, he'd had this same intuition of danger sometimes, right before his squad had come upon hidden enemies.

Why this premonition of a threat against Meg now? Was it because of the turn their relationship had taken tonight? Was there someone out there who wanted to injure her? Or was it because he didn't want people thinking badly of her because of him?

The first person he didn't want thinking badly about her was Jake. Tomorrow morning, he'd call his brother and break the news.

God, please watch over her. Don't let me do anything out of selfishness. Keep my motives right. Show me how to protect her. I'm here, and I'm willing for you to use me. I'll do anything you ask to keep her safe.

Stephen McIntyre trained his binoculars on the intersection of Holley's main street and the road that led to Whispering Creek's gated entrance.

Still nothing. No sign of Bo Porter's truck returning from Meg's house.

He lowered the binoculars. He'd parked in an alley. Commercial buildings on either side shielded his position. The interior of the dark green Honda smelled like cigarette smoke and ground-in dirt. It had pained him to put his M5 in storage, but he'd done it because the M5 could be traced to him. He'd purchased this piece of junk with cash from a used car lot near the Texas–New Mexico border.

He rubbed a smudge off the front of one of the lenses. For several days now he'd been watching Meg and had familiarized himself with her routine. On weekdays she drove to work and parked her car in a garage belonging to Cole Oil, staffed by security guards. After work, she drove straight home.

On Saturday she'd left Whispering Creek to meet with her old nanny and to visit some of the shops in town. On Sunday, she'd attended church. While her car had been parked in the church parking lot, he'd placed a GPS tracking device under her wheel well. The device had freed him up considerably, because it meant he no longer had to trail her physically. He could trail her electronically.

He raised the binoculars back to his eyes. Earlier tonight, from his room at the Garden Inn, the tracking app on his smartphone had shown Meg exiting Whispering Creek.

She hadn't left home on a weekday evening since he'd been following her, so he'd driven to the location specified on the GPS: a small brick house in Holley situated on several acres of land. He'd parked at a distance and approached the house on foot. Though he'd been unable to see anything within, he'd recorded the house's address and the license plate number of the truck in the carport.

When Meg had been slow in leaving, he'd gone to the fore-closed, remote, and empty house that he'd been using as a base separate from his hotel. He'd pulled out his laptop and searched online until he discovered the identity of the person who owned the house and truck.

A man named Bo Porter, who apparently worked for Meg at Whispering Creek Horses.

About a half an hour ago, when his app had shown Meg on the move again, he'd followed her. He'd expected to find her driving home to Whispering Creek alone. Instead, Bo Porter's truck had been right on her bumper, so Stephen had taken a quick turn onto a side street and let them drive on together.

His GPS told him that Meg had returned to Whispering Creek. He didn't know where Bo Porter had gone, but he ex-pected the man to return to his home any minute now. Unless he was staying the night with Meg at her place. The Meg Stephen had known had been a terrific prude about sex before marriage, but people changed.

Through the binoculars, a truck came into view. Porter's truck.

Looked like Meg hadn't changed much after all.

The truck turned onto the main street and drove the few hundred yards towards Stephen's position, then zoomed past. Stephen watched the vehicle until it vanished from sight. Thoughtfully, he slid the binoculars back into their case and set them aside.

Bo Porter was someone to Meg. Probably a boyfriend. Maybe merely a friend. Either way, Stephen didn't like the potential complication the man presented. Didn't like to think that Bo Porter could influence Meg. She'd been—was—Stephen's to control.

Watching her these past days had caused bitterness to eat at him. Why should she have so much? Meg? She had no strength, no backbone, no merit, no skill for leadership.

He'd invested a few years of his life in her the last time. But two million dollars was a drop in the bucket compared to the kind of wealth she'd come into now. He had something much quicker in mind for her this time. And a score much larger.

Meg had suggested to Bo, the night of their first kiss, that they take their relationship slow. But truthfully, neither of them could stand to. Over the following days they spent every possible minute together.

The day after their first kiss, Meg texted Bo as soon as she returned home from work, around 8:30. Her hours at Cole Oil had left her frazzled, but as soon as he arrived on her doorstep and she got a good look at him in the flesh—poof. Her exhaustion evaporated. He made her spaghetti for dinner. She explained to him how her uncle had come to her and apologized for confronting him. Bo explained to her how Michael had called him and done the same over the phone.

The next two nights in a row Meg left work as early as possible, yet still well after dark. Both nights Bo postponed his own meal until she arrived, and they ate take-out Mexican together at his place. He asked her, repeatedly, sweetly, not to work so hard. He told her he worried about her.

The day after that she went shopping during her lunch break and bought a cookbook titled *Meals He'll Love*, then tested recipes for baked chicken and chocolate cake on him that evening.

When at work, Meg thought of almost nothing but him. Her mind constantly replayed memories of him—the things he'd said to her, how he'd looked, the shirt he'd worn, the way he'd stroked her face when he'd kissed her. Her daydreams rendered her even more useless to Cole Oil than she'd been before.

Saturday arrived like a gift on her doorstep. She ignored the work she could have and should have been doing. Instead, she and Bo worked out in her father's home gym, headed to their respective houses for showers, then met up again for BLTs (which he supplied) and a matinee of *When Harry Met Sally* (which she supplied) at his house. That afternoon, they returned to Whispering Creek and walked together across the hills and woods of the property hand in hand.

Bo had aspirations—delusions—of fishing with her, so they finally stopped at the largest pond on the property to share a picnic dinner and to try their luck at fishing. After two straight hours of talking, casting, and teasing, they put away the poles and moved to higher ground to watch the sun set.

Meg lay on her back on the blanket next to Bo, his bicep cushioning her head, her feet resting on one of his boots. Breeze tinged with the smell of jasmine brushed across her. Palest tangerine and darkest orange blazed across the enormous expanse of Texas sky. The underbellies of the clouds shone bright and opaque white.

Meg glanced at him. The mellow bronze light played over his features and his shorn hair. As he turned to grin at her, it caught and glittered in his eyes.

She grinned back. Neither one of them needed to say a thing.

Joy suffused every cell of her body as she shifted her attention back to the sunset. Each hour with him had been like this—golden. Impossibly perfect.

"If you and I were to share a house one day," he said, "where do you think we ought to live?"

"Hmm," Meg answered.

He hadn't said "I love you" or "I want to marry you" again since that first night at his house. He chose his words carefully, in an effort, she guessed, not to rush or frighten her. She appreciated his caution. It suited her because she didn't want to label her own feelings for him yet. She'd been mentally skirting around an I-love-Bo-Porter moment because to love Bo—to *really* love him—she'd have to trust him fully with her heart and also with the possibility of heartbreak if he let her down. After what she'd been through before, that level of vulnerability terrified her.

So, while they avoided formal declarations, they did occasionally discuss funny hypotheticals about their future together, like the one he'd just brought up. Things like: What would you name our sixth son? What breed of dog would you buy me for my birthday? If we wanted to vacation in January would you choose the ski slopes or the beach?

"We could live in a cardboard box," Meg said.

"Sounds windy."

"It would be good enough for me if you were there."

A pleased smile tugged at his lips. "No kidding?"

"Well. I am kidding, just a little."

He chuckled. "I can't say as I'd allow you to live in a cardboard box, anyhow. Not enough security."

"Your house, then?"

"Still not enough security."

"Really?"

"'Fraid not."

"I'll have you know that no kidnapper or extortionist has ever given me a moment's trouble."

"All the same, I like the big wall and the cameras and the guards."

She groaned. "You want me to spend my life in the big house?"

"Not if you don't like it."

"I don't like it."

"The guesthouse, then?"

"It's all right for me by myself, but not for a married couple."

"How about a new house? Right here on this very spot?"

"Now you're talking." The circle of the sun had sunk halfway below the horizon.

"What kind of house would you like?" he asked.

"Something charming. Something that looks like a cottage out of a fairy tale."

"A Texas fairy tale?"

"Yes, exactly. We could build it out of Texas stone—"

"That, I like."

"—and some of those big wooden timbers. High ceilings. White wainscoting. Distressed wooden floors."

"Why do new houses these days always have to have old-looking floors?"

"Because it adds character."

"How many stories?"

"One. With a rambling floor plan."

"Lots of windows," he added.

"Yes, and soft comfy furniture."

"Will the soft comfy furniture have pink on it?"

"Of course."

He made a dissatisfied sound.

"What's the matter with pink?"

"I'm a man. That's what's the matter."

Her lips curved. "Perhaps I could make some concessions."

"Generous of you."

"How about if I limit pink to the master bedroom only?"

"Definitely no pink in the master bedroom."

"No?"

"A man shouldn't sleep under pink covers."

She laughed, but her mind caught on the mental image of him with her under any-colored covers. Her skin flushed. "Well, then how about a pink guest room? Whenever I need a fix, I'll just go in there and breathe in the pink."

"I'll agree to that."

Their imaginary house sounded heavenly to her. She could almost envision how it would be, the two of them sharing a home, a life.

"Tell me about all the places where you've lived," he said.

She snuggled closer to him. "Let's see. You're already familiar with the big house. After that I lived in a dorm at Rice." She told him about her dorm room freshman year, and the apartment close to campus she'd shared with friends the following three years. Then her words trailed off.

"And?" he prompted. "What came next?"

"I . . ." Should she tell him what had come next or just gloss over it? They'd shared countless conversations this week, but they hadn't talked about this. She hadn't wanted to haul this ugliness into their beautiful bubble.

"Go ahead," he said. The sun vanished, leaving behind a streak of yellow at the horizon. "You can tell me."

She released a painful breath. "After college, I got married and my husband and I rented a house in The Village in Houston."

"I heard it didn't last very long between you two."

"No, it didn't."

"You want to tell me about it?"

"Yes and no."

"Okay." He simply lay there, his body relaxed alongside hers.

She sensed that it really would be okay with him either way— if she told him or if she didn't. His patience encouraged her to talk.

While the sky darkened to dusky purple above them, she told him about Stephen. Haltingly at first, and then with more assurance. She explained how they'd met, how he'd acted toward her while they dated, her father's reservations. She told him about the way Stephen had changed after their marriage: his lies, explosive anger, lack of remorse, and finally about the money he'd stolen from her when he left.

At that news, Bo pushed himself to sitting. He stewed in silence, the sawing noise of crickets loud.

She placed her hand on his back.

"No offense, Meg, but your ex-husband sounds like a world-class—" He set his jaw, holding in whatever violent word he'd been about to say.

Nonetheless, she understood him perfectly. "Yeah. He was."

He looked back at her on the blanket. His eyes, gleaming in what had become mostly moonlight, told her volumes more about his emotions. He extended his hand. She took it, and he pulled her up to sit next to him. "Did you get your money back from him?"

"No. I should have gone after Stephen and tried to get it back, but I didn't. I'm sorry now that I didn't."

"How old were you back then?"

"Twenty-three."

She didn't realize she was fiddling with the back of her earring until he took hold of her hand and pressed a kiss into her palm. Without a word, he pulled her into his lap, surrounded her with the two flaps of his corduroy jacket, and hugged her against him.

"If I'd gone after him," Meg murmured against his throat, "I might have been able to protect people like Amber from him."

"Is that why you took her in when she came to you for help?"

"In part. But also, I couldn't stand to turn her away. She needed a place to stay, and a job, and help finding Stephen."

"Help finding Stephen?"

"She wanted him to pay child support."

"I . . ." He paused for a long moment. "I didn't realize she was looking for him. Did she find him?"

"No. She got close but then changed her mind and decided to stop looking."

"What about you? Did you ever try to find him?"

"No. I never want to see him again as long as I live."

He set his chin on the top of her head and they stayed that way, intertwined so closely that she could feel his pulse.

"I wish," Meg whispered, "that my past was different. That I was new and shiny. That I'd never been married and divorced."

"I've done all kinds of things I regret, made all kinds of lousy choices."

"You didn't marry the wrong person."

"No, but I did other things that can't be undone." He slid his hands behind her neck, angling her head so that she was looking directly into his darkened face. "I'm sorry about what you've been through, but I can't be sorry about the person it made you into."

"I'd have been better without it."

"But you wouldn't be the same. And you wouldn't be as strong." She swallowed hard.

"God's forgiven you, Meg. Now you're going to have to forgive yourself."

She had no words.

"You hear me?"

"Yes."

He pressed her back into her spot against his chest. His embrace spoke to her of acceptance, of her and her past. And perhaps for the first time since her divorce, Meg felt as if she could fully receive God's complete and total grace, move on, and leave it all behind at the foot of the cross.

"What did you do after Stephen left?" he asked.

"My father and I had agreed a long time ago that I'd come to work at Cole Oil ten years after I graduated from college. But after what happened with Stephen, my father tried to talk me into coming home and working for him. I turned him down."

"Why?"

"For one thing, I'm not a fan of the oil business. Until those ten years were up, I wanted to choose my own career."

"And?"

"I knew that if I was living on nothing but a normal salary, then no one would have any reason to manipulate me or pretend to like me the way Stephen had. It just . . . it felt safer."

"It probably was safer."

"I ended up taking a job in Tulsa because it was far away from Houston." She told him about the condo she'd rented during her Tulsa years.

"And that ends the list of places you've lived."

"That ends it."

"So here's what I'm wondering."

"Mmm?"

"In which one of those places were you living when you decided that you had to look perfect all the time?"

"What do you mean?"

"Every time I've ever seen you, even when you're about to go to the gym, you look like you're ready to pose for a magazine."

"I . . ." Was he criticizing her? Pointing out her vanity? Her insecurity? "I was living in the big house, I guess, when I started looking this way." He couldn't know what it had been like to grow up as William Cole's daughter. "As a kid I was always aware that people were sizing me up. So, to some degree I've always tried to look presentable so I wouldn't let my father down. I was . . . Well"—she frowned—"probably more anxious about that than most kids."

"And after Stephen left?"

She groped for a reply.

"You made sure that you always looked extra perfect," he said gently, "so that no one could say or think anything bad about you."

His words struck her like a two-by-four. She froze in his arms, trying to absorb the blow. Difficult, because she knew at once, with piercing certainty, that he was right. She'd never consciously made that decision. *I'm going to be as pretty as I possibly can be so that no one can blame me for the fact that my husband abandoned me.* But that's exactly what she'd been trying to do and why. "Bo Porter," she whispered, "you shouldn't say things like that unless you have a doctorate in psychology."

"I'm sorry, Meg. I have no business talking like that. I shouldn't have said anything. I'm probably dead wrong."

"I wish I could say you were."

"Please forgive me. I'm such a jerk. I only said it because I want you to know how beautiful you are to me. You might doubt a lot of things about this world, but I never want you to doubt that." His voice had turned severe. "You'd be just as beautiful with no makeup and messy hair and—and old clothes that don't fit."

Tears rushed to her eyes, an inner pressure. "You're going to make me cry."

"Then cry. You know I have tissues."

Tears began to slip over her lashes.

"For me, you're perfect just the way you are, and nothing you do or don't do is ever going to change that."

"Oh, Bo. I'm just so-so looking, and I'm too curvy."

"Excuse me!" He glared down at her with the most insulted expression she'd ever seen on his face. "You're crazy if you think so. You're going to make me mad, talking like that."

He looked so outraged that she laughed.

"I'm serious!"

Meg smiled. "I know."

"You're gorgeous. In my eyes you're the most gorgeous woman that ever lived." He dug into his pocket and pulled out some tissues. "Now here."

"Thank you."

But she ended up not needing the tissues because he kissed away her tears, then just plain kissed her.

"Our house here on this hill," he said against her lips, their breath intertwining.

"Our Texas fairy-tale house?"

"Our Texas fairy-tale house will be the best place of all the places you've lived, countess."

She squeezed him around the middle.

"I promise you."

Much later they set off in the direction of the guesthouse. Bo insisted on carrying the tackle box, his pole, the picnic basket, and the blanket draped across his shoulders. That left Meg with only her fishing pole and the flashlight she was using to illuminate their path through the trees.

"My family eats lunch together at my parents' place on Sundays after church," Bo said. "My brother Ty's in town this weekend, and I'd like for you to come with me tomorrow."

So far they'd sheltered their relationship by keeping it secret from everyone except Jake. They hadn't been anywhere public together. Meeting his family? Very public. "I . . ."

"We don't have to make a big deal out of it or say anything to them about us."

His tone held a touch of defensiveness. Meg came to an immediate stop and pointed the flashlight down between their feet. "I hope you don't think I hesitated just now because I'm embarrassed to be dating you. I hesitated because I'm tempted to keep this relationship private longer so that I can protect it."

"From?"

She gestured with the pole. "Outside people. Would you want to go to lunch with my family tomorrow?"

"No." He gave her a sheepish, crooked smile.

"That's what I thought." They started walking again.

"So your plan is to stick your head in the sand?" he asked.

"Yes."

"Not gonna work. Holley's a small town, and the truth is going to come out sooner rather than later."

"How about we let the truth come out next weekend or next month or next year?"

"How about you go with me to lunch tomorrow?"

She sighed.

"I won't tell them we're dating, okay? They won't be any the wiser."

She snorted.

"Meg?"

"Yes?"

"Will you please come eat lunch with my family?"

His request, phrased so politely, rendered her physically, mentally, and emotionally incapable of saying no. "Yes, Bo, I'll come eat lunch with your family."

"Thank you."

"If I were Catholic I'd do the sign of the cross."

Chapter Eighteen

I've got two quick warnings for you," Bo said to Meg as they walked up to his parents' house for Sunday lunch.

"Warnings?" She was already nervous about making a good impression, worried that she'd overdressed, and second-guessing the bouquet she'd brought as a thank-you for Bo's mom.

"My mother's never met a stranger," he said.

"All right." That didn't sound too bad.

"So I apologize in advance for anything she might say."

"Second warning?"

"Don't you dare take a shine to my brother Ty." Bo mock glared at her from beneath the brim of his straw Stetson.

Such unbridled chemistry flowed between the two of them that simply looking at him full in the face—just that, just *looking* at him—made Meg's head swim and her body ache with desire. "Uh, I think I've got my hands full with you at the moment."

"Good. Hang on to that thought when you meet him."

"He's smooth with the ladies, huh?"

"Women have always found him irresistible. It's disgusting."

Bo pushed open the front door and ushered her into the house he'd grown up in.

Similar to Bo's own house, the front door emptied right into the den. At the back of that space, half walls revealed a dining room on the left side and a kitchen on the right.

A woman turned from the kitchen sink. "There y'all are!" She hurried over, grinning widely.

"Mom, this is Meg Cole."

"I'm Nancy. Nice to meet you, Meg."

"Nice to meet you, too."

Nancy greeted her son by rising on tiptoes and planting a smack on his cheek.

Bo's mom was a robust-looking woman, a few inches taller than Meg, with a tan face that didn't need makeup. Her brown hair, cut just below her shoulders, boasted a wide streak of gray that swooped upward from her forehead, then ran to the tips.

Meg handed her the bouquet of gerbera daisies, climbing roses, and dianthus. "These are for you."

"They're so pretty! You didn't have to do that."

"I wanted to."

"Thank you."

"Thank *you* for having me."

"It's our treat! Come on in."

It appeared that Nancy subscribed to the more-is-more style of decorating. Wall-to-wall tan carpet supported a den packed full of antique furniture accented here and there with faded blue and yellow pillows in a French Provincial print. Woven baskets and decorative iron pieces hung from the walls alongside framed posters—one of a church next to a field of lavender, the other of an aged French storefront with a bicycle leaning against it.

The Porters' whole house could have fit into the garage at Whispering Creek. Meg could already tell, though, that this home possessed something better than square footage: It had a kind of homey appeal that spoke to a person. That made them comfortable when they were within the walls, and made them want to return when they left.

Meg followed Nancy toward the kitchen, where the provincial theme continued with a ruffly yellow valance over the kitchen sink window, a blue table runner with roosters on it, and an entire hutch filled with pottery. Meg paused to admire the extensive collection. She liked the sunny background hue of the dishware, and the trios of navy dots and white swirls that accented the rims. "These are beautiful."

"That's my French pottery. I'm just *in love* with Provence." Nancy pronounced it like *pro-vonce* with her thick Texas accent. "Aren't I, Bo?"

"Yes."

She extracted a vase from one of her cupboards and ran water into it. "I'm convinced I was born in the wrong place. The Lord intended me to be a little French girl, I just know it." Her gray eyes, so like her son's, brimmed with humor. "He's got some explainin' to do to me when I get up there, because I was born in Farmersville, Texas, instead."

"I think He intended me to be a middle-class girl from the suburbs, so He's got some explaining to do to me, too."

Nancy threw back her head and laughed. "I knew you'd be funny, and I *knew* you'd like those dishes there. I told John that we ought to serve lunch today off them or even the china. It's not every day we have someone from the Cole family over—"

"Mom," Bo warned.

"Well, it's not," Nancy insisted. Her expression turned woeful. "But the boys wanted barbequed hamburgers, of course. And they were determined to eat them off paper plates just like we always do, so you'll have to excuse us. We're not ordinarily very formal around here."

"It's fine," Meg assured her.

Nancy nodded toward the pottery while she positioned the flowers in the vase. "I bought all that over at the first Monday swap meet in Canton. You ever been?"

"No, I haven't."

"Are you kiddin' me? There wouldn't be a stick of furniture in this house if it wasn't for Canton. I'll take you with me the next time I go." She spoke the statement with ease, as if accustomed to toting around strangers. "All right?"

"All right."

Nancy thrust a platter piled with hamburger fixings into Bo's hands. "Would you mind taking this out there for me?"

Bo tilted his head. "Are you going to mind your manners?"

"'Course! We'll be right behind you. Now shoo!" Nancy gave Bo a swat and sent him packing out the back door. "Want to know a secret?" she asked Meg as soon as he was gone.

"Sure."

"He's my favorite. Don't tell the others."

Meg smiled. "I won't."

"I can't help it. He's just so *good*. He's always been like that. So calm and responsible. And he can make me laugh, land sakes. You two are dating, right?"

Bo! So much for his *they won't be any the wiser* prediction. She and Bo hadn't said a single word to one another in his mother's presence, yet it had only taken her five minutes to arrive unswervingly at the truth. "W-we . . ."

"It's all right. You don't have to say a thing. I know you're dating." Nancy gave Meg a conspirational hug with one of her stout arms. If the occasion arose, Nancy would slaughter Meg in an arm-wrestling contest. "I'm pleased as punch about it," Nancy said. "That's all."

"I . . ."

"Now come on outside, and let me introduce you to the others."

Meg trailed the older woman out the back door to a small cement area that held a few lawn chairs, a grill, and a wooden ice cream maker, softly droning and packed with salted ice.

A short distance out into the Texas landscape, a long metal patio table and chairs waited under the shade of a gnarled tree. The remaining Porter family members, some sitting, some standing, turned en masse at Meg's approach. The sight of them there, all together and so forcefully attractive, seared into Meg's memory like a frame of a movie paused at the perfect moment. The Porter family: confident, red-blooded, and one hundred percent Made In Texas.

She'd definitely overdressed. What had possessed her to think that her church outfit, a pale lavender dress with a chunky necklace of glass beads and strappy silver heels, would suit this situation? Between her last name and her clothing, it was no surprise that Nancy thought she should be serving her off the wedding china.

The rich smell of hamburgers cooking wafted through the air as Bo met her halfway and walked with her to the table. He went through the introductions quickly. She'd already met two of his siblings. Jake, with the chiseled features and the wicked scar, worked at the horse farm. He regarded her warily from beneath the shade cast across his face by his black Stetson. And Dru, the dark-haired, blue-eyed teenager. She had on a jean mini, a black shirt emblazoned with tattered silver angel wings, and cowboy boots.

"It's about time we got some class around here," Ty said when he shook her hand. His persuasive smile flat-out begged a girl to smile back. "Goodness knows we've been needing some."

"Bo tells me that you're a professional . . ." Bull rider? Suddenly Meg doubted if she had the term right.

"Professional pain in the butt?" Ty supplied. "I'm afraid that's true."

Meg laughed. With his golden brown hair, snug gray Nascar T-shirt, and lazy charm, Meg could see why the ladies found this Porter brother irresistible. Female-attracting pheromones rolled off of him like sheets of water off a roof.

Bo cleared his throat and gave her a knowing glance.

"Do you follow bull riding at all, Meg?" Nancy asked.

"I'm afraid I don't."

"Ty was world champion a few years ago."

"Wow," Meg said. "That sounds impressive."

Ty shrugged a shoulder. "I ride bulls for a living because the hours are good. Can you believe they pay me to work for just eight seconds at a time?"

"That's if he makes it eight seconds," Bo said. "We'll have to go watch him sometime. It's pretty entertaining to see him get thrown on his head."

"True," Dru agreed.

"Well, listen," Ty murmured to Meg. "I've got to let the bulls buck me off sometimes, right? Otherwise they'd get demoralized."

"Ty!" Dru scowled at him incredulously. "Turn that off."

"What?"

"That thing you do with women."

"Dru," Ty said fondly, "isn't there a Disney show you should be watching?"

"You know Disney's too old for me," Dru shot back. "I'm only allowed to watch Teletubbies." She popped some chips into her mouth and grinned.

"Try not to mind them," John said to Meg. "We don't."

"It's fun for me to be here," Meg said. "And to meet all of you."

"The pleasure is ours," John said. Bo's father stood at a normal height for a man, which put him several inches shorter than all three of his towering sons. He had a wiry frame, and a haircut as tidy as his cowboy-style clothing. She knew from Bo that his mix of gentleness, integrity, and old-school discipline had earned him the deep respect of his children. "Did Bo tell you that I knew your father?"

"Yes, sir, he did."

"You can call me John. I was very sorry to hear about his passing."

"Thank you."

"He was a good man to work with. He was always fair, and he cared a lot about his horses." Meg couldn't help but be drawn to his thoughtful, soft-spoken demeanor and kind eyes.

"Speaking of William Cole's horses." Dru turned to Meg. "Have you given any more thought to selling me the horse farm?"

"Quiet, Dru," Bo cautioned.

"Cheap, remember?" she teased.

"That's enough," Bo said.

Meg tried to smile at Dru, but it felt tight. No one could broach a more awkward subject in front of her, Bo, and Jake than the future of the horse farm. She and Bo, for goodness' sake, hadn't said a word about it to each other yet.

Dru glanced at Bo. "Well, I for one would like to know what she's going to do with the farm."

"That's none of your business," Bo said.

"Maybe not, but I can still ask her, can't I?"

"No."

"You guys only have four months left now before her deadline." Dru returned her attention to Meg. "Are you going to close down the farm like you planned?"

Discomfort fell over the gathering.

Bo actually growled.

Meg didn't glance toward Jake, but she could feel the burning weight of his stare. She thought about the horse farm's fate frequently. A thread of indecision, growing thinner every day, still prevented her from reversing her initial decision. She kept telling herself she had time.

"Please excuse Dru," Nancy said. "She came ten years after her brothers and by then, I have to confess, John and I were tired."

Ty chuckled. "Meg, I've tried beating Dru over the head with a club, but it hasn't turned out to be all that effective. She's got a hard head."

"Maybe we should try the cat-o'-nine-tails on her," Jake suggested.

"Perhaps a mace?" John offered.

"Bring it on, boys," Dru replied. "You know how good I am with a gun."

"Welcome to lunch with my family," Bo said, pulling out a chair for her.

Animosity forgiven, they all held hands as John blessed the food. At the end of the prayer the entire family said, "Amen."

Nancy added a vigorous, "Bon appetit!" and then plunked a little orange jar that said *Herbes de Provence* onto the table. "In case anyone else wants to use this as seasoning."

They ate grilled burgers with melted cheddar on Mrs. Baird's buns that John toasted over the flame. Barbecue Lay's. Potato salad. The three brothers put away huge portions of the food and of Dr. Pepper.

The whole time discussion flowed, easy and lively, between the Porters. They talked at length about upcoming Thoroughbred races, particular horses, and noteworthy owners. They talked rodeo. They asked Meg questions, she asked them some, but mostly, she just enjoyed their banter.

Once they'd dumped the remains of lunch into a black trash bag, they served up the most delectable homemade vanilla ice cream Meg had ever put in her mouth. She scooped up and savored each bite, trying not to look like a victim of gluttony.

The family's plot of land could be classified as open prairie, broken only by horses, occasional trees, and functional buildings. Mr. Son would have disdained the few spare bushes that passed as landscaping across the back of the house. The adjoining garage was so overtaxed sheltering an old metal fishing boat, four wheelers, and storage boxes, that the Porters parked their cars on the driveway. Beyond the garage stood a barn and multiple paddocks that looked old but orderly, clean, and painstakingly kept up.

The Porters might live in plainer surroundings than she, but they were richer. They were loved. They were grounded. And they were accustomed to life within the context of a large family.

Nancy cracked a joke and everyone laughed. Meg looked at Bo and found him gazing steadily back at her, tenderness in his eyes.

You doing okay? he asked her with that look.

She gave an infinitesimal nod, and he nodded back.

Electricity snapped between them, and she very much wished

that she could wrap her arms around him and hold on to him with all her might.

Oh dear, she thought as she looked at him. *I just might have to . . .*

Love you.

It might not be negotiable.

The notion caused her ribs to tighten with sudden fear. While Ty told the family a story about a fellow bull rider, Meg set her ice cream bowl on the table and made a production out of folding her napkin alongside it.

Bo and I are just dating, she assured herself. *No pressure, no promises. I haven't fallen in love with him yet. I haven't risked everything for a man.*

It brought Bo deep, deep pleasure to see Meg here, in the surroundings he'd grown up in. To watch her with his parents, brothers, sister. She'd been hesitant to come today, but she'd done very well with his family.

While he watched her, she let go fussing with her napkin and turned to answer a question put to her by his father. In that purple dress with circular diamonds in her ears, she looked lovely beyond words.

"You think God views us any differently, Bo?" Her words had been coming back to him a lot lately. *"He doesn't care one bit about all the outward things. To Him we're equal. We're both loved the same, valued the same. We both need to find our worth in God's view of us."*

He was trying. And doing better at keeping that perspective.

He eased his shoulder blades lower into his chair, stretched out his long legs, and crossed them at the ankles. He could remember that his life had seemed full to him, before her. He'd had his career, relationships, activities he liked to do on his days off.

It came as a dull surprise to think that his world could have ever seemed complete without Meg in it. It could never be complete without her again. His heart beat because of her. His love for her was so powerful that in some mysterious way it caused him to experience everything more deeply—a deeper bond toward his family, a deeper appreciation of God.

When Bo looked at Meg he saw, felt, and heard God's blessing. Every day, every minute they were together. For the first time, he was beginning to grasp the size of the grace God had extended to him. In turn, Bo found that he wanted nothing for himself so much as he wanted to serve out God's purpose for him.

He believed that a big part of that purpose was to take care of Meg. God had been preparing him all his life for her, he was certain of it. So put a stake in it. Frame it. Draw a line in the sand. He'd lay down his life before he'd lay down the responsibility of protecting her.

Semper Fi.

Again. Meg had left Whispering Creek to spend time with Bo Porter—again. Stephen released a huff of annoyance. This afternoon, she was sitting around an outdoor table with Porter and a group of people who Stephen assumed to be Porter's family.

Clasping his binoculars at his side, Stephen walked back toward his car. His strides slashed with impatience.

He'd grown sick of his crummy hotel room, of this armpit town, of the long, boring length of his days. He wanted to get to Meg and get out. But as long as she spent every moment outside Cole Oil and Whispering Creek with Bo Porter, he couldn't.

He'd researched Porter's background, and he didn't like what he'd found. Six years in the Marines. Tours of duty in Iraq and Afghanistan.

Porter was a big, strong, dumb country boy with a military background. He probably kept a gun in his truck and a stocked gun closet at home. He probably liked to throw down and fight just for the fun of it.

Stephen didn't want to grow old and gray following Meg around, which meant he needed to orchestrate events to suit his goals.

First he'd separate Meg from Porter. Cleanly and surely.

Then he and Meg would have themselves a little face-to-face.

Chapter Nineteen

Meg stood at the pasture rail next to Sadie Jo, far happier to watch other people riding horses than to ride one herself. Did that make her an impossible wuss? Or merely wise?

It was the first Friday in June, and Meg and Bo would soon be arriving at their two-week anniversary. Because of him, Meg slept, ate, worked, and relaxed in a bliss-filled, walking-on-clouds daze. She'd hardly noticed the long hours of this past workweek come and go.

"You must be hungry." Sadie Jo pulled a lunch-box-sized bag of Cheetos from her purse and extended it to Meg. "I brought along a snack for you, dear."

"Thank you, Sadie Jo. That's sweet of you, but I'm fine."

"You need to eat something. It's almost dinnertime."

"It's only 4:45."

"You'll waste away!"

"Not a chance."

Sadie Jo sighed, and Meg returned the Cheetos to her purse for her. "Don't they look great?" Meg tipped her head toward the riders.

"Just wonderful. Wonderful."

Brimm, Amber, and Jayden were preparing to leave for a ride along Whispering Creek's trails. Zach, the redheaded teenager who worked for Bo, had been leading them around the pasture, giving out instructions for the past fifteen minutes.

Meg smiled at the sight of Jayden sitting on the saddle in front of Amber. Her tiny houseguest was a born cowboy. He gripped the saddle horn, grinned, and flapped his legs out to the side. When Amber lifted him momentarily to adjust her seat, he let out a screech of displeasure.

"Oh dear," Sadie Jo said. "Do you think he has a wet diaper?"

"Sadie Jo."

"Yes?"

"I'm forced to conclude that you have wet diaper OCD."

Sadie Jo used a hand to shade her eyes as she regarded Meg. "What does that mean?"

"Obsessive compulsive disorder?"

"Hmm?"

"It means that I must have had the driest diapers of any baby in the country."

"Oh my, yes. That's true enough. We went through diapers like water."

Meg motioned toward Jayden. "See there, he's content again. Even without a diaper change."

"I tell you, it does my heart so much good to see him and Amber like this."

"Mine too."

"I wish we had a bushel more just like Jayden. I could easily love them all."

"I know."

Well? a voice within her asked. *What's stopping you? Why can't you have more here just like Jayden?* The question struck her like a lightning bolt.

A chill enveloped Meg's body, followed by a cascade of tingling goose bumps. She could see, suddenly, her path forward. Like a curtain swept back to reveal a brightly lit stage, characters, action. She'd prayed for God to show her how she could move forward with the calling He'd placed on her heart, and He'd just in this moment—with Sadie Jo's innocuous words—answered that prayer.

A few months ago inheriting her father's empire had seemed to Meg like a tremendous burden and a challenge that she wasn't, and never would be, equal to. But recently God had been whispering a simple, quiet truth into her heart. He'd reminded her that none of it was actually *hers*. Not the bank accounts, the properties, the staff, the possessions, nor the controlling interest in the company.

All of it belonged to Him. And that new certainty liberated her the way unlocked chains liberated a prisoner.

God had entrusted her with the sacred job of stewardship, yes. But in order to steward what she'd been given, Meg didn't have to make a zillion dollars for Cole Oil, or strive to be worthy of the role of chairman of the board. Her role was far simpler.

All she had to do?

One thing: what God told her to do.

And God had just told her what to do with Whispering Creek Ranch. She and Sadie Jo *could* have more little ones like Jayden here. The big house had ten bedrooms, and Meg could fill every single one of them with parents and children in need of help.

She didn't personally care for the "I can kill deer!" decorating style of the big house, but that didn't mean other people wouldn't love it. In fact, visitors always ate up the whole lavish lodge thing. The home that her father had built decades ago provided the perfect—absolutely perfect!—place for families to come and get back on their feet. Whispering Creek was big, safe, empty, staffed with capable people, full of nature, and full of horses.

Horses.

If Amber and Jayden were any indication, her guests might actually come to regard the horses as the most beloved of Whispering Creek's assets.

The horses! The notion struck her as so new and astonishing that Meg could hardly get her mind around it. Her gaze tracked Brimm, Amber, and Jayden as they rode. They were smiling and talking, their hair combed by the breeze, sun shining on their shoulders. Horseback riding was like therapy for them, a chance to set aside their troubles, a treat, an activity that they didn't usually have easy or free access to.

But here, they did. Because she, Meg Cole, owned a dude ranch.

She released a stunned laugh. Dude Ranch Owner. The most unlikely job description she'd ever imagined for herself. Yet God, it seemed, had a way of making the unlikely certain and the surprising possible. She couldn't believe that she hadn't recognized the hand-in-glove fit of it before now. Kids and horses. Horses and Whispering Creek. Whispering Creek and the work she was meant to do. God had been planning exactly this for her all along. She could look back and see it now, everything that He'd put into place and prepared.

She'd been wavering over the decision to keep the horse farm open, but God had just answered that unequivocally for her. Bo's horse farm had a role in the future of her ministry.

She envisioned it all in a tumbling sweep that unfurled into the future. Bo could keep his Thoroughbreds and also expand the number of horses suitable for kids and beginners. Perhaps she might even be able to convince him to purchase some ponies.

She already had staff in place at the big house and could hire more. More cooks, more housekeepers. She could find a teacher who specialized in early childhood education and set up curriculum for the toddlers and preschoolers. She could bring in more nannies to assist. Older kids could attend the local public schools.

She could help the parents enroll in college courses if they were trying to attain a degree. Or, if they had their degree, she could help them with their job searches. Once they'd achieved the goals they'd set out to accomplish, she could find them safe places to live outside Whispering Creek's walls because her objective would be to bring each parent to a place where they could support their family independently.

So many details to research! She might need to establish a foundation and get civic approval to use the big house in such a way. She'd need to put an application process in place, to form guidelines for the people who came so that they'd understand what she'd be offering and what they'd need to adhere to in return.

She had a lot to learn, and yet it felt as if a towering fountain of determination inside of her had finally found the source of water that it had been seeking. The fountain flared to life, powerful, shooting streams of water high within her. This was her life's purpose. She knew it, and she knew how she could do it. She had the ability to offer families a new start and a shot at a stable future. Her! Unsure, vulnerable, tentative her.

As had always been the case, tears accompanied Meg's deep emotion. Through water-filled eyes she looked over at Sadie Jo, who was wholly unaware of the monumental things that had been transpiring inside of her. "I love you, Sadie Jo."

Sadie Jo took one look at Meg and started clucking and crooning. "What's this? Oh, my dear heart. Don't cry. Come here." She beckoned Meg into a hug that smelled like pink Dove soap. "I love you, too."

After soaking in a long dose of comfort, Meg pulled back and held Sadie Jo by the shoulders. "I'm so grateful for you. After my mother died, I only had my father left and I needed you. You were there. And you've made a huge difference in my life."

"I'm the lucky one." Never one to let a person cry solo, answering tears clouded Sadie Jo's eyes. "I needed you, too. God saw that I didn't have children or grandchildren and gave me you. I'm so blessed. So fortunate."

"I want to help children, like you helped me."

"You already are, honey. You're helping Jayden."

"I want a bushel more, exactly like you said a minute ago."

Sadie Jo's eyes widened with hope. "Do you think we can?"

"I know we can."

"Oh, Meg. That would be . . . that would be glorious beyond words."

She squeezed Sadie Jo's shoulders. "Do you know how often God has used you to talk to me? You've called so many times when I needed it, or visited me when I was struggling, or said something to me that I knew came straight from Him."

Sadie Jo laid a soft and wrinkly hand against Meg's cheek. "I suppose I did know about it, in a way. He's been my rock for a long time now. A person can hardly live with Him that long without understanding that He has a hand in everything."

The sound of horses approaching from behind them, from the barn, drew Meg's attention. She let go of Sadie Jo and turned to see Bo walking toward them, leading Banjo and two other horses, all saddled.

"Ladies." He took in the scene, his face softening into a what-are-they-crying-about-now? expression. "Anyone need tissues?"

Both women swept away their tears with their fingertips. "Thank you for offering, dear, but Meg and I only need tissues when we're having a good hard cry," Sadie Jo explained. "This was only a little sniffle."

"Ah." His gaze searched Meg's face.

It always took Meg a few moments to adjust to the reality of Bo after they'd been apart because the effect of him in the flesh tended to bring on heart palpitations and breathlessness.

"I'm sure you ladies are wondering," he said, "how I can possibly get any work done when I'm out here hanging around you so often. All I can say is that the person who signs my checks is way too lenient."

"The person who signs your checks," Meg replied, "is wondering why you brought out three horses."

Bo pointed at himself, then Sadie Jo, then her.

Meg pulled a face. "A few moments ago I was thinking how content I was *not* to be riding."

"But you owe me one more lesson, so you don't have a choice."

Meg mock scowled at him.

In response, he raised an implacable eyebrow. "You, on the other hand," he said, turning his attention to Sadie Jo, "do have a choice. I was thinking that you might like to join the rest of us on the trail ride. What do you say?"

"How old do you think I am, Bo Porter?"

"Fifty-five?"

Sadie Jo glowed.

"Come along with us," Bo said to her. "It'll be fun."

Mmm-hmm, Meg thought darkly. *Loads of fun.*

"I did love to ride when I was a girl. . . ."

"Since we'll be with Meg," Bo assured her, "we won't be going any faster than a very slow walk."

"Hilarious," Meg said.

"I might . . . well, I fancy I might like to give it one more try," Sadie Jo decided, "if you'll keep an eye out for me, Bo."

"Yes, ma'am. There's no way I'm going to let anything happen to either of you." He looked toward Zach, out in the pasture. "We're going to join you," he called to the teenager. "Give us a few minutes."

"Yes, sir," Zach answered.

Bo helped both Meg and Sadie Jo onto their horses, adjusted the length of their stirrups, then swung onto his own horse effortlessly. Meg sat on top of Banjo, tense as a jackrabbit, but trying to look as normal and cool about riding as everyone else.

Zach led their procession out of the pasture, followed by Brimm, Amber with Jayden, and Sadie Jo. Bo came next, leading Meg's last-place horse with a rope.

"It's a little embarrassing," Meg said to him under her breath, "that Sadie Jo is riding independently, but that I'm being led along by you."

"What? This?" Bo lifted the rope. "I only did this so that I could keep you next to me. Maybe we can make out when no one's looking."

Meg would have laughed, except that she didn't want to risk spooking Banjo.

She expected to loathe every minute of the ride and simply white-knuckle it through. Except that over the course of the next hour Bo's company, the scenery, and the slow gait of her horse combined to work a little bit of magic on her.

During the last stretch, she could even begin to glimpse why her father had been so fanatical about it. Horseback riding was never going to be her thing, personally—

Hold that thought. Bo controlled his horse with a masculine ease and level of expertise that she found extremely sexy. He wore his Stetson. His rugged hands held his reins, his thumb occasionally rubbing against the leather. If she could always ride with him and could admire him the whole time, then, well . . . she should never say never.

After the ride, Bo and Meg drove to his house and ordered pizza. He kept telling her how well she'd done with Banjo, and she kept wanting to tell him about her plans for Whispering Creek and his horse farm.

Ultimately, though, prudence kept her quiet. Before she could move ahead with any of her ideas, she had to figure out what to do about her full-time job and the duty, heritage, and responsibility that came with it. *Lord? What would you have me do with Cole Oil?*

By the next evening Meg had thought herself through circles and circles of excitement over her plans for the big house, but she'd gotten no closer to a conclusion about her day job. When she tucked herself into bed and attempted sleep, it didn't take long to deduce that sleep would be a no-go. She pulled her white robe over her pj's, brewed some Sleepytime, and took her mug for a nighttime stroll through the backyard.

She'd stopped halfway up the patio steps to peer at the stars when she heard rustling from the direction of Lynn's private wing.

"Can't sleep?" Lynn approached out of the darkness.

"No. You?"

"No." Lynn had on a shirt with the Salvation Army crest on the front, her leggings, and Birkenstocks.

"How come I'm the only one wearing pajamas?" Meg asked.

"What do you mean? These are my pajamas."

Oh. Lynn's night and day wardrobes appeared to be inter-changeable.

The two women stood shoulder to shoulder and watched the trees move lazily with the wind. Meg drank tea, offered some to Lynn, who declined, and enjoyed the comfort of Lynn's companionship.

"I remember," Lynn said, "how your father used to check on you every night before he went to bed."

"He did?"

"Every single night. I heard him walking down the hallway to your bedroom just this past Christmas. Still checking on you."

Meg gawked at Lynn. "I had no idea."

"Oh yes. I worked for your father for decades, lived right here in this house with him. He had his good qualities, and he had his faults, just like we all do. But I do believe, hon, that in his way he loved you."

She was no longer a child. She was an adult woman whose father's death had taken from her any final chance to rectify their relationship. So why did Lynn's words flow over her like life-giving heat? So dearly needed? "Thank you for telling me."

Time had brought her to a place where she wanted to re-member the good qualities Lynn had just mentioned, let go of the faults, and simply forgive her father for all the hurts. Meg wanted to accept that he had indeed cared for her as much as he'd been able. She wanted to let their relationship rest in peace.

"I've noticed, you know, the work you've been doing at night,"

Lynn said. "I've seen you through the guesthouse windows studying all those books about oil. All those binders and papers."

"I've been trying to educate myself. I'm not sure I've made much progress."

"Enjoying it any more than you did two months ago when you started?"

"If anything, I've become more sure that God has something else for me entirely."

"You know what? You've given Cole Oil a good shot. I hoped you would, and I'm glad you did. Your father always wanted you to succeed him."

"That's true, he did."

"Part of it had to do with his ego and part of it with tradition. I think, though, that he imagined you'd thrive off the work the same way that he did. He expected you to enjoy it."

Meg smiled ruefully. "The accuracy of his expectations for me were never his strong suit."

"No," Lynn agreed. She trained an unblinking look on Meg. "Do you know exactly what your obligations are toward Cole Oil? I mean, legally?"

"I . . ." Her father had raised her to think of Cole Oil as her unavoidable birthright. It was. Wasn't it? "I'm not sure."

"Huh."

Her thoughts spun. The world as she'd known it tilted.

"I don't think that the father who checked on his sleeping daughter every night would want that girl to spend her life doing a job she didn't like. Even if that job was the job he chose for her."

Oh my goodness.

First thing Monday morning, she'd ask her assistants to search out a well-respected, uber-expensive, unbiased attorney. Someone experienced in these matters. Then she'd find out from that person precisely how much of her life she was—or wasn't—required to give to Cole Oil.

The well-respected, uber-expensive and unbiased attorney turned out to be a heavyset woman who'd accented her suit with a fabulously colorful Hermès scarf. The attorney's chic office enfolded Meg in quiet while Meg explained her family's history and showed the woman several documents.

When Meg finished, the attorney regarded her levelly. "Ms. Cole, you may do anything you like with your fifty-one-percent share in Cole Oil."

Meg stared at her, silent with disbelief.

"You may give some of your shares away, or all. You may sell some of your shares, or all. The choice is absolutely yours."

"My—" Meg licked her lips. "My great-great-grandfather determined that the controlling interest in the company would pass to the oldest child of each generation, who would subsequently pass it along to their oldest child."

"Yes. From all you've told me and all that I've read here, the controlling interest in the company appears to have descended through the generations of your family in just that manner."

"None of the firstborn children who came before me gave away a single share."

"That's because the men who came before you all chose to follow Jedidiah Cole's wish for a line of succession that, frankly, reminds me of a monarchy." Her expression told Meg just how little esteem she held for *that* brand of primogeniture. "While Jedidiah's wishes might hold the weight of tradition, let me assure you that they are not, and never have been, legally binding in any way."

"I see," Meg said weakly.

"Your father, grandfather, and great-grandfather were never bound by Jedidiah's wishes, and neither are you, Ms. Cole. If you don't want to retain controlling interest, you don't have to. You're free to do anything you like with your shares. They belong to you and no one else."

Meg had always believed exactly and only what her father had wanted her to believe about her role at Cole Oil. Until last night, she'd never considered that she might have the freedom to slip out from under the mandate of history, to buck her great-great-grandfather's plans, and chart a different course for herself.

"Here's what you should consider," the woman said.

"Yes?"

"If you divest yourself of the shares, then they're most likely gone forever."

"I understand." If she chose to part with her shares, her choice couldn't be undone. Her branch of the family would likely never again control Cole Oil.

"If you have children one day, you'll be unable to pass the controlling interest along to them."

On one hand, it was possible that she could give away control of Cole Oil now, and then, years in the future, have a dark-haired, gray-eyed son or daughter or grandson or granddaughter that looked like Bo (purely as a hypothetical) and loved the oil business. Meg's decision would have forever obliterated that son's or that granddaughter's chance to run one of the world's foremost companies.

On the other hand, it was possible that she'd keep control of Cole Oil only to find that her son or daughter or grandson or granddaughter wanted to choose one of a thousand other futures for themselves. Just as she herself had always wanted to do.

The control of a powerful company versus the freedom to choose one's own path. That's what it came down to.

If she'd only had herself to consider, the decision would have been a no-brainer. But she had her descendants and also her ancestors to think of.

Her father, grandfather, great-grandfather, and great-great-grandfather. She'd known two of them in life and seen pictures of the others. She could almost envision those old ghosts, gray with translucency, sitting and standing around this office at this very moment, dressed in their stately clothes, looking at her with hawkish expectancy.

Did she have the nerve to turn from her father's plans for her? Did she have the courage to snub her nose at demanding old Jedidiah Cole? The codger had probably had the foresight to imagine a great many things. But she wasn't certain he could possibly have imagined her.

"You should take some time to think about it," the attorney suggested.

"I'll do that," Meg answered. But in actuality she knew that thinking wasn't really what she needed. Her own thoughts could take her down paths that led to destruction.

What she needed was to pray. Then listen hard for God's marching orders.

For the rest of the day, Meg did exactly that.

Prayed. Listened.

When evening came, she still didn't feel done. She required more time and privacy. Since her father had appointed his office as comfortably as any luxury hotel room, she decided to sequester herself there for the night.

Her assistants, grateful for activity, brought in blankets and pillows, placed a dinner order, held all calls and visitors. They drove to Holley to fetch the overnight bag that Meg asked Lynn to pack.

Meg dialed Bo. Not seeing him tonight would be the costliest part of her retreat.

"Countess," he said by way of greeting. She could hear the smile in his voice.

"Cowboy." Warm butterflies took flight within her.

"You home?"

"No. I'm going to stay in Dallas tonight."

A few beats passed. "For work?"

"Yeah. I have a decision to make about my job that's so . . . so big and important that I need to take time praying over it and considering it. Does that make sense?"

"'Course it does. You want to tell me about it?"

"Not yet. As soon as I make the decision, I will."

"How about I drive down and bring you something to eat?"

She wanted to say yes. If he came, though, she'd go all mushy and muddled. She wouldn't be able to find a coherent thought with a flashlight. "My assistants are going to have dinner delivered. Thank you, though, for offering. It means a lot to me."

"I'm not going to see you until tomorrow?" he asked doubtfully.

"We can talk now, though. Tell me about your day and your sad and lonely plans for an evening without me."

They talked for forty-five minutes straight.

Their conversation done, Meg turned to a new passage in her Bible. She ate. Journaled. Read her little book of verses. When it grew late, she went up to the rooftop garden and sat on a lounge chair wrapped in a blanket and surrounded by stars, enjoying God's company. She slept soundly that night on one of the plush office sofas and got up the next morning to do more praying and listening.

It turned out that God couldn't be swayed by the arguments of ancestors or birthrights. News flash! He didn't care about worldly human issues. God used Meg's self-imposed isolation to confirm to her the path that He'd already, unmistakably, shown her. She didn't need more time.

Meg scheduled an appointment with her Uncle Michael for that afternoon, then took time getting herself ready in her office's attached bathroom. Lynn had chosen Meg's clothes wisely. A dark gray tailored jacket, matching pencil skirt, and a pair of red Louboutins. Meg dressed, then contemplated her reflection in the mirror.

As a kid, she'd owned dozens of Barbie dolls. She could remember one in particular named Hawaiian Fun Barbie who'd come in a patterned swimsuit. Meg had been able to dress Hawaiian Fun Barbie like an accountant, but that hadn't changed who she was underneath. Hawaiian Fun Barbie had been made for the beach.

For weeks now, Meg had been dressing herself up as an oil executive, but it hadn't changed who she was underneath. Her Creator hadn't made her for Cole Oil.

When she arrived at her uncle's office, he came around from behind his desk and waved her toward the sitting area. She opted for the couch, a piece of furniture so deep that if she pushed her bottom all the way to the back of it, she knew from experience that her legs and feet would protrude straight out in front of her hips. Not exactly the professional image she had in mind, so she perched on its front edge. She set the folder she'd brought facedown beside her.

Uncle Michael settled into a suede chair. "What can I do for you, Meg?"

She cleared her throat. Unaccountably, her heart rate picked up speed. This was it. She'd thought about what she wanted to say to him, and now she simply needed to say it. "I . . . wanted to thank you. You've taught me a lot about this business."

"You don't have to thank me. It's been my pleasure."

"I wanted to anyway. Thank you."

"Don't mention it." He waited for her to explain why she'd called the meeting.

She couldn't find her voice.

"Is that all, Meg? I have some work I need to get to—"

"I'm not quite done."

He stilled, his eyes trained on her, his clothing flawless, his hair precise, his features so reminiscent of her father's. A rush of tenderness overtook her. Uncle Michael could be highhanded at times, like he'd been with Bo. But she recognized his good heart.

"Despite my father's best efforts," Meg said, "and despite your best efforts, Uncle Michael, it turns out that I don't like the oil business." She spoke calmly, but the words still managed to land with resounding force.

"What?" he barked. "Meg—"

"I don't like the oil business," she repeated. "I'm not cut out for it. I never have been, and I never will be."

"That's not true. You'll get there. You'll become more knowledgeable and more confident. Just give it time."

"I've given it two months of my time already, and you know what? I don't want to give it any more. Not a single hour."

He leaned forward and opened his mouth, but she halted him from speaking by raising a hand. "What I *do* want to give is controlling interest in this company. To you."

He stared at her with blank shock, unblinking.

Certainty flowed through her. No one on earth was more qualified or more deserving of the responsibility that came with the role of majority shareholder of Cole Oil. "Before today you owned twenty percent. I'm giving you thirty-one percent more so that you now own fifty-one."

"No."

"Oh yes," she assured him. "Congratulations, Uncle Michael. You're now the majority shareholder. You're going to be president of this company and chairman of its board. You've earned it."

He rushed to his feet. "No," he said loudly, confusion and distress in his expression.

Meg followed his lead and rose. In the past, a show of temper from Uncle Michael would have rattled her to her molars. Today, nothing could rattle her sense of peace.

"This isn't how it's done in our family," he said.

"No, but it's close. I'm interpreting Jedidiah's intentions. He didn't want the shares fractured, because he feared doing so would weaken the company. I've decided to respect his opinion. Instead of splitting my shares among many people, I'm passing them along, in bulk, to you."

"Meg, your father wanted you to be president."

"But it's not what I want for myself. And I'm not going to spend my whole life trying to please a man who passed away last January."

His gaze measured her face and her resolve. "Be reasonable. You and I, we need to spend a tremendous amount of time discussing this possibility. Months. Years, even."

Meg laughed. "No thanks." She handed him the folder, which contained papers she'd had her attorney draw up. "I'm going to retain twenty percent. That'll give me a seat at the table for board meetings and a say in the direction of Cole Oil, which is something I find I'd like to have."

"Meg—"

"I'll have my eye on you, Uncle Michael." She hugged him, then pulled back to smile at him. "So make me proud. Lead this company as honestly and as well as I know you can."

"Listen, this is ridiculous—"

"I've made up my mind. If you don't want the shares, then I'll give them to someone else. But I'm not keeping them."

"You've lost your sanity."

"Actually, it's the opposite. I've just lately found it."

Michael stood, stunned and troubled, framed by the luxurious interior of his office. The papers he held gave him something his birth order never had.

"You can thank me later," Meg said.

Chapter Twenty

*A*n hour after her meeting with Uncle Michael, Meg stuck her head into the warm room of the yearling barn. One of Bo's employees had told her where to find him, and sure enough, Bo sat alone at the room's table, poring over papers spread out next to his laptop.

When he looked up and saw her, he pushed immediately to his feet, crossed to her in two strides, clasped her face in his hands, backed her up against the nearest wall, and kissed her.

Her hands circled around to his back, where she could feel ridges of muscle running along both sides of his spine. Had she last seen him just the day before yesterday? It felt like she'd spent a month crossing a desert to make her way back to him.

When they finally pulled apart, they were both breathing hard.

"Hi," Bo said.

"Hi."

"I missed you like crazy."

"Missed you more."

"Not possible. How long has it been since I've seen you? A month?"

Her lips curved upward. "That's just what I was thinking. It feels like a month, but it's only been two days."

He swept a lock of hair back from her temple and looked her dead in the eyes. "Thank God you're home."

Her insides did a slow and delicious flip. *Home*, she wanted to say to him, *isn't a place for me anymore. It's you.* She pressed a kiss into the spot where his jaw met his throat and drew in a breath that smelled like him, like clean ocean wind.

He clasped her to him in one of his tight, nothing-bad-will-ever-happen-to-you hugs that filled every inch of her with a sense of belonging. The two of them had almost nothing in common except for the fact that they were each perfect for the other.

"I can't stand," he said, "to be apart from you that long. Honest. I almost couldn't do it. I've been staring at these papers for hours, not doing anything."

"Worthless, huh?"

"Worthless."

"Can I make it up to you by feeding you dinner?" She disentangled herself and lifted the cup and paper sack she'd set down in the hallway before peeking in on him. "Hamburgers and tator tots from Sonic."

"Now, that's just too good to believe."

"Believe it. I even got you the Route 44." She passed a cup as big as his head to him. "Despite the fact that no human can or should consume that much Dr. Pepper."

"Mighty generous of you. Thanks."

"I splurged."

"You splurged?"

"Anything for you, Bo," she said grandly.

Humor sent a dimple into his cheek. "Sure this dinner here isn't going to break the bank?"

"Pretty sure. I'll need to check with my accountants."

He laughed.

They sat down together and went to work on the food. Meg made it halfway through her burger and tots before eater's remorse struck her. "How long do you think I'll need to ride the elliptical machine to work off what I just ate?"

"About five hours."

"Hmm."

"'Course, your body's perfect, remember? So as far as I'm concerned, that thing you do with the elliptical machine is strictly for your cardiovascular health."

"Bo."

"What?" he said lazily, his eyes daring her to chastise him. If she did, he'd only insist on his truthfulness.

They'd been dating a short time, but Bo's dependable, unceasing, rock-solid approval of her had already begun to sink into Meg. His acceptance of her made her feel safe and dared her to view herself as he did—as good enough. Already, her driving need to look her best had begun to fade. Each day, she spent less and less time fussing with her hair and makeup.

She asked Bo about his day and found he'd not been nearly as worthless as he'd claimed. Today alone he'd settled on a course of treatment for a horse that had something called epiphysitis, fine-tuned the diet and supplement balance for some of his broodmares, been out to the racetrack to consult with his brother about their racers, and then worked for hours on payroll and tax issues.

"Is that all?" she asked.

"Yep, that's all."

"Slacker."

Meg had come to understand that Bo, as farm manager, worked as an overseer of employees, horse doctor, horse trainer, horse nutritionist, accountant, advisor, breeder, bloodlines expert, salesman, buyer, and mental health expert to both equines and the humans who worked for him.

"What're you thinking about?" he asked.

She hesitated.

"I can see that you've got something on your mind. What is it?"

"I was just thinking of all that you do for this place and wondering why you've never asked me to keep it open."

He paused, neither moving nor answering. She understood. She'd just broached the one subject they'd both carefully avoided all this time.

Slowly, he used the backs of his fingers to push his drink away. "Once I began to feel the way that I do about you, the idea of talking to you about the farm didn't sit well with me."

"Why?"

"Well . . . What would you have thought? If I'd asked you, say today when you walked in, not to close the farm? Wouldn't you have thought that I was trying to capitalize on our relationship? I decided a while back that I'd rather you shut this place down than think that about me."

She leaned over and kissed him. Their foreheads remained touching. "It would have been easier, wouldn't it, if we'd met in some ordinary way?" She pulled back so she could look fully into his face. "If neither of us had been tied to Whispering Creek Horses?"

"Easier, yes. But the fact is, I'm exactly who I am, and you're exactly who you are." His thumb skated along the edge of her jaw. "I'd change all kinds of things about myself if I could, but I wouldn't change one thing about you."

"Bo," Meg said, her voice hushed. "You love this farm."

He nodded gravely. "But when you close it down, I'll still feel the same way about you that I do right now."

"What about if I keep it open? Will you still feel the same way about me then?"

His features went blank with surprise. He inclined his head toward her. "What was that?"

She laughed. "You can keep your beloved horse farm open, Bo Porter."

He whooped and swept her off her feet. "Really?"

"Yes, really."

He spun her around a few times, then set her back on the floor. "No kidding?"

"No."

"You're not going to close down the farm?"

She shook her head.

He beamed down at her.

This is joy, she thought. To give him something that made him happy. She'd received jewelry every Christmas and gift cards to Neiman Marcus every birthday from her father. But opening those presents had brought her a raindrop of pleasure compared to the river of pleasure tumbling through her now.

Meg drew him down to the chairs so that they sat, knees touching, while she explained about giving her shares of Cole Oil to her uncle.

"Is that why you stayed in Dallas last night? To pray over that decision?"

"Yes and there's more." She told him about her ministry idea for Whispering Creek and the component of that plan that had to do with Whispering Creek's horses.

He listened intently.

"What do you think?" she asked.

He squeezed her hands. "I think it's perfect."

"What about providing horses for the kids and adults to

ride? Do you think that'll work? Do you think they'll like that?"

"Yes."

"And you'll help me?"

"Not just with the horses, but with any part of it."

A knock sounded on the door. "Bo?" A groom stuck his head inside. "I need to ask you about— Oh." He caught sight of Meg. "Excuse me."

"I'll talk with you as soon as I'm able, Mike." Bo showed zero embarrassment at having been caught holding hands with the owner of Whispering Creek, even though they'd yet to make any public declarations about their romance.

"You bet." The door shut behind the man.

Bo returned his full attention to her. "To do what you're describing, you'll only need one barn and a small number of horses and employees."

"I'm keeping the Thoroughbreds, too. I see them differently than I did when I first came. They've become a part of this place. How many hours have I spent at the paddock, watching them?"

"Lots."

"So I should know. Also, once the farm has paid back its initial investment—which it should do after the yearling sales, right?"

"Yes."

"Then the Thoroughbreds will, in theory, earn their keep from here on out."

"And then some."

"Most of all . . ." Sentimentality rose, and it took her a moment to gather herself. "The Thoroughbreds meant a lot to my father. The more I'm around them, the more I understand why. I'm not going to do what he wanted me to do with my career, but I can still honor him by keeping his farm going. He'd have loved to see his horses succeed."

"There's one horse in particular that I think might make him proud. Can I . . . would you mind if I introduced you to him? He's here in this barn."

Meg nodded, and Bo led her into the corridor. She spotted Mike further down, cleaning out a stall.

"Can I tell him the good news?" Bo asked her.

"Sure."

"She's decided not to shut down the farm," Bo called to him.

"What!" Mike threw his ball cap into the air, then hurried over to shake Meg's hand, smiling widely. "Thank you, Ms. Cole."

"You're very welcome."

"You won't be sorry, ma'am."

No, Meg thought. *I don't think I will be.*

"Can I send out an email to the others?" Mike asked Bo. "Letting them know?"

"And steal my thunder? No way." Bo grinned as he clapped Mike on the shoulder. "I'll do it in just a minute."

Mike tipped his chin to Meg, then returned to work, face glowing.

Bo drew Meg over to one of the stalls. The horse within stood tall and regal, sleekly muscled, his coat a watercolor mix of dark gray and light gray, his mane and tail white.

"You're not going to make me ride him, are you?" Meg asked.

Laugh lines deepened around Bo's eyes. "Not this guy, no. Meg, meet Silver Leaf. Silver Leaf, Meg."

"He's gorgeous," she whispered.

"Yes, he is."

Silver Leaf's dark liquid eyes regarded her calmly, as if he could read her mind. On her end Meg mostly said, *I'm blown away by how beautiful and placid and wise you are.* And he mostly said, *I have benevolence on you, small human.*

"He's descended from royalty," Bo said. "His grandfather was Seattle Slew, and his great-grandfather was Secretariat."

She'd seen a lot of Whispering Creek's horses, but this one possessed a unique blend of dignity, outright beauty, and something unfathomable that she couldn't begin to put her finger on.

"Your father was crazy about him. Jake and I both think he's full of promise."

"I can see why."

Silver Leaf approached her, and Meg rested her fingers on his silky-soft nose. In response, he blew his hot, sweet breath over her hand. In that instant they formed a connection, woman and horse. Meg couldn't help but feel that Silver Leaf might one day give her the opportunity to see her father's dreams come true.

Meg turned to look up at Bo.

He stood close by, his hands deep in his pockets, watching her. "Thank you for giving Whispering Creek Horses a future."

"I can honestly say that it's my pleasure. And now . . . " She stepped to him and took hold of the fabric on the front of his shirt. His arms came around her. His face angled down, hers up. "There's something that's been on my mind for weeks and weeks. I'm dying to know more about it. Dying, you understand? But I've been too embarrassed to ask you about it."

"You can ask me anything."

"Good." She cleared her throat. Smiled. "It's about your tattoo."

" . . . and that's my plan for the big house here at Whispering Creek," Meg finished.

Yesterday she'd told Uncle Michael and Bo about her life-changing decisions. And now she'd explained everything to the remainder of her staff. Lynn, Mr. Son, the rest of the big house workers, Jayden's nanny, Jayden, and Sadie Jo had all gathered in the kitchen for their customary noon lunch. In response to her long monologue, every face surrounding the large table regarded her silently.

Uh-oh. Maybe they were all thinking that their nutty heiress had taken another wrong turn toward crazy town.

But then the table erupted in a chorus of enthusiasm, and Meg released a pent-up breath of relief.

"What a wonderful idea."

"I'm behind it one hundred percent."

"I love it!"

Jayden celebrated by throwing cut-up squares of sandwich over the side of his high chair.

"Well done," Lynn said to her, with clear approval.

Sadie Jo's eyes had gone shiny and her face trembly with joy. "This is what you were talking about, the other day out by the horses, when you said you wanted to help children."

"This is it," Meg confirmed.

"Oh, Meg. It's perfect. Perfect!"

Meg turned to the lone adult male at the table. "Mr. Son?"

"I'm hungry," he said.

Meg laughed. "Yes, but what do you think about the future of Whispering Creek?"

"I like it. Fine plan. Can we all go back to eating now?"

"Yes, of course. Please do, everyone."

Lynn had made grilled cheese sandwiches and salad to complement their bowls of homemade tomato soup.

"I know this will affect all of you," Meg said to the group. "So I'd really like to hear your thoughts."

While they ate, Meg's staff peppered her with questions and ideas.

Despite the low clouds and the spitting drizzle beyond the windows, cheerfulness encircled the kitchen table in the same way that it always did at big house lunches. Perhaps even more so now that Jayden had joined their number.

The toddler sat at the far end of the table, concertedly picking his nose. His nanny flanked him on one side, which left his other side open to Sadie Jo, who gazed at him adoringly, stroked his hair, and continually coaxed him to eat more than he wanted.

Meg was answering a question about how she'd come upon the plan of turning Whispering Creek into a temporary home for single parents when her cell phone vibrated inside her pocket. She ignored it.

Someone else asked her how the horse farm fit into her vision.

While Meg explained, her cell phone vibrated a second time. She ignored it again.

But just a few minutes later, it vibrated a third time. Two calls close together? Somewhat normal. But three? Three translated to an emergency.

Bo, she thought, with a jolt of fear. Had something happened to Bo? Had he been hurt? "I'm sorry, I think someone's trying to get ahold of me." She pulled her phone out of her pocket and saw that it wasn't Bo, but Brimm calling. "Please excuse me. I'd better take this." She rose and headed from the room.

"You didn't finish your soup!" Sadie Jo called as Meg rounded the corner and made her way in the direction of the den.

Meg answered the call. "Brimm?"

"Meg."

"Is everything okay?"

"Listen . . . I'm on my way over there. Can I meet you at the guesthouse?"

"Oh no." The tension in her cousin's voice communicated *bad news* louder than words. Her stomach dropped. "Has something happened to Grandmother? Or someone else in the family?"

"No, it's nothing like that. All the Lakes are fine. I just need to sit down and talk with you about something."

"About what?"

"I'll be there in ten minutes."

Meg let herself into her guesthouse and turned on her lamps and chandeliers. With nothing else to do, she made herself sit on her sofa. Cashew climbed into her lap. What could Brimm possibly need to talk to her about that was so grave he'd drive out here during the middle of his workday? She couldn't imagine. A suffocating weight of foreboding lowered over her, and she jumped back up to escape it. She lit her gardenia-scented candle. Returned to the sofa. Cashew stepped back onto her lap. Meg popped up again and went to unload clean dishes from her dishwasher.

As if a well-lit, nice-smelling, tidy house could do anything at all to avert impending doom.

When a knock sounded, she hurried to the door. Brimm stood on the threshold in his professor getup: a button-down shirt, blazer, and brown pants. They exchanged greetings, she drew him over to the table, and they both settled into chairs.

"What's going on?" Meg asked.

He rested a briefcase on the surface of the table, toyed with its clasps, then seemed to think better of opening it. He faced her fully. "Do you remember that your father brought me in a few times as a consultant for Cole Oil's computer security?"

"Yes."

"In the past two years I've spent several days with the IT team at Cole. I've worked with them on fortifying firewalls and anti-hacking, both for the company's system and also for your father's private accounts."

"Are you here because of a computer security issue?"

"Exactly."

Thank God! Some of the rigidity eased from Meg's muscles. Brimm might view a computer breech as a crisis, but she sure didn't. He'd scared her good.

"One of the IT guys called me today," he said, "and had me come over to the Cole building. A hacker has been testing the security of your personal accounts."

"Trying to steal money from me?"

"No, not yet. He's simply been trying to take a look into all your various investments and holdings. It seems like he's trolling for information. As if . . . well, as if he's wanting to know exactly what you're worth."

"A tabloid journalist, maybe?"

"Actually, we've discovered his identity."

"Oh?"

Brimm scrubbed his fingertips through his hair and looked away from her. When he finally looked back, apology shone in his eyes. "It's Bo, Meg."

Shock—awful, sickening shock—thudded directly into her. She stayed still. But inside, her brain scrambled and flailed and tried to catch onto something firm. "Bo?"

"Bo's the hacker who's been fishing for information about your finances."

"No way."

"I'm afraid so."

"He wouldn't do something like that." Not in a million years!

"For what it's worth, I wouldn't have thought so either, Meg."

"He's not a hacker. He knows about as much as I do about computers."

"That's what he wanted you to believe, anyway."

"He just—just uses computers for work, and that's it."

"I wish that were the case, but it's not. He's been using his home computer to investigate the scope of your inheritance."

Bo loved her. He didn't care about her financial portfolio.

"I'm so sorry," Brimm said. "The IT guys have been working on it for days and they were finally able to triangulate the hacker's location. It's Bo's home computer, Meg. Bo's address."

"No."

"The evidence is certain. I've spent the last two hours checking it out myself. I wouldn't have come to you with this unless I was sure."

A howling refusal coursed through her in deafening circles.

"I can explain, if you'd like, how they were able to pinpoint the particular computer involved," Brimm said. "I even brought documents."

She wanted to beg him to take his evidence and his documents and his intelligence and leave. Instead, she watched him open his briefcase and lay papers in front of her. He spoke about the high-tech methods involved in catching hackers as he gestured to one page and then the next and the next. His words fell around her without penetrating. The only thing that did penetrate? Printed in black ink on white paper at the bottom of the final page: Bo's name, address, and his computer's specific ID number.

At the end of Brimm's speech, quiet widened between them.

"I feel so bad about this." He pushed his glasses up his nose. "I know you care about him. I could tell, just watching you guys together."

She had no words.

"Listen, we can share what we have with the police. They can go after him—"

"I can't deal with that thought right now."

"You sure?"

"Yes."

"I understand. Well, we can go that route later if you want. Are you okay?"

She nodded, but within herself she could see and feel entire skylines of hope crashing down in clouds of debris and ash.

"You want me to stick around?" he asked. "We can hang out. I can keep you company."

"Thank you, but I'd like to be alone for a little bit." She walked him to the door. He gave her one of his stiff side hugs, hesitated, and then left.

Meg closed the front door. Went into her bathroom and closed that door, too. She leaned her back against the inside of the door and slid down it onto the floor, her legs bending up. She covered her face with her hands and rested it forward onto her knees.

Bo. Oh, goodness.

Bo.

What a rotten, worst possible, and wretched time to realize that she loved him.

She loved Bo. And not just a little. She really, deeply *loved him.* Maybe even more miraculous for her, she'd come to trust him.

He was honorable and true and decent in every way. Wasn't he? An hour ago she'd have sworn that he was. She'd have bet everything she owned on it. Staked her future on it.

But according to Brimm, Bo had been hacking into her finances to see how much . . . how had Brimm put it? To see how much *she was worth.*

A wave of nausea heaved up from her stomach.

Bo wanted her for her money?

It couldn't be true. *God*, she pleaded, *it can't be true.*

She remembered how Bo had looked standing in the parking lot with her that night at Deep in the Heart—his face bruised because he'd fought for her. All dressed up in a suit to take her to her cousin's engagement party. Opening the door to her the night she'd gone to his house with a package of Oreos.

She had an entire mental catalogue of the beautiful things he'd said to her—every intonation of every syllable—because she'd rewound and replayed his words in her head a million times. "*I love you. I want to marry you. I can't do many things but I can love you, Meg. I can love you every hour of every day for the rest of my life. I want you to know how beautiful you are to me.*"

She remembered the kisses they'd shared, the heat in his eyes, the need in his touch, and how his arms had felt around her—tight and fervent. He'd made her feel as if she was his most precious treasure.

Her. Not her money.

God? she asked. *God, please. God? Come.*

But in the chaos of her mind, she couldn't hear His voice, couldn't find His presence.

God, he loves me. Doesn't he? You know everything that's happened. I haven't been completely wrong about him. Let Brimm's discovery be a horrible mistake.

Except that Brimm had just finished showing her pages of proof. He'd said the team at Cole Oil had been working on it for days and that he'd checked it out himself, personally. He'd said the evidence was certain.

No! She squeezed her head with her hands. She didn't want

to know about proof. What she wanted, so much she could hardly bear it, was for Bo to love her.

Once, many years ago, her father had confronted her with his concerns about Stephen. There had been some troubling evidence that time, too. Meg hadn't wanted to believe it then, either. So she'd gone her own headstrong way. She'd insisted on Stephen's goodness, on giving her heart to him, on marrying him.

And what an epic disaster that had been.

She'd ended up paying horribly for her mistake. Her experience with Stephen had made her the not-so-proud owner of a very, very expensive lesson: A woman should never ignore the facts to follow her own instincts about a man.

Instincts could lie. Instincts were biased by desire and emotion. But facts were immutable. To ignore them was as stupid as driving down a road marked with signs that said *DANGER— Impending Cliff*, refusing to read those signs, and then reacting with surprise when your car sailed into thin air and nose-dived into the canyon below.

The whole time she'd been falling for Bo, she'd known that she had no skill at judging a man's sincerity. Maybe because Sadie Jo had raised her to be trusting and to believe the best of everyone. Maybe because she'd been born into money and so had a hard time predicting the awful things others would do to gain it. Her aunt and uncle had both warned her. And she'd . . . she'd defended Bo.

She'd tried so hard to be careful with Bo. To be smart and protective of her heart. Yet, ultimately, she'd been unable to resist him. In a thousand ways, she'd been unable to resist him.

So she found herself here.

Again.

Confronted with evidence that warned her away.

What she wanted to do? Trash Brimm's revelations and wrap herself in denial.

What she was going to make herself do? Cut Bo out of her life.

Air seemed to be sucked out of the room, and suddenly she couldn't quite gasp enough into her lungs.

You have to get rid of him, Meg. He only cares about you because of the money.

Her heart raced so fast she grew dizzy. Terror descended on her like a great black bird, shrieking and sending freezing wind rushing over her with every flap of its dark wings.

A panic attack.

By willpower alone, she pushed herself to standing. She'd gone weeks without having an attack and she flat-out *wasn't* going to have one now. If her heart wanted to pound, then she'd give it a reason to pound.

She pulled on exercise clothes and went to the gym in the big house. Without bothering to turn on the TV, she climbed onto the elliptical machine and pedaled the thing so hard it rocked.

She pushed herself brutally—thoughts churning, gut twisting. She kept going even when sweat rolled down her body, even when her thighs burned and her chest ached, even when giant sobs overtook her.

She'd been racked with indecision for days about whether or not to close the horse farm. What a joke. He'd probably known all along, from their very first meeting, that she was so weak and gullible that he could easily convince her to keep the farm open—so he'd set his sights higher. He'd been angling for marriage, which would entitle him to half of it all.

For endless minutes, tears flowed unceasingly from the cavernous well of her grief.

Just twenty-four hours ago Bo had said, *"I wouldn't change one thing about you."* The memory turned like a knife in her belly. Likewise, just twenty-four hours ago, she'd assured him that he'd be keeping his job.

He most certainly would not be keeping it now.

How *could* he do this to her? How dare he manipulate her, deceive her, betray her like this?

How dare he?

Bo stood outside the broodmare stable, frowning down at his cell phone. Since they'd been dating, he and Meg had been exchanging several texts and often a call or two every workday. By 5:30 p.m., they'd always decided how and where they'd spend their evening together.

But since before lunchtime today, Bo hadn't heard from Meg. He'd sent her three texts, called once, and left a voice mail. Everything had gone unanswered, which worried him.

The time on his cell phone read 5:48.

He typed in *Everything okay?* and sent the message.

While he waited, he paced.

Within a minute, his phone beeped to let him know he'd received a reply. From Meg, thank goodness.

Can you come by my father's office in the big house? she'd written. *I'd like to ask you about something.*

Sure, he replied. *I'll be there in 5. I've missed you today.* He scooped up his keys, his sunglasses, and his corduroy jacket, and made his way to his truck.

He didn't know what she wanted to ask him about, but he hoped it'd be something like, "When would you like to get married?"

Answer: this evening.

Or, "How long do you think kisses should last?"

Answer: twelve straight hours.

Or, "Are you mine, Bo?"

Answer: yes. I always have been, am, and always will be undeniably yours.

Chapter Twenty-one

B o entered the hallway that led to Meg's father's office and immediately spotted a security guard standing outside the office's doorway.

His steps slowed.

A security guard inside the house? The concern for Meg that had been gnawing at him earlier came rushing back, double force. Had there been some kind of emergency? A security issue? Maybe that's why he hadn't heard from her all afternoon.

He didn't know this particular guard, but a patch on the sleeve of the man's uniform told Bo that he'd come from the same agency as the familiar faces that worked the front gate. Bo nodded to the guard, and the man nodded back.

Bo let himself into the office. The moment he saw Meg standing on the far side of the desk, he knew that something had gone wrong. She'd dressed in a white suit and had on big diamond earrings. Her perfect hair and makeup couldn't hide the redness of her eyes or the puffiness of her face.

Had someone done something to her? Hurt her? Fear overtook him hard. "What's happened?"

She swallowed with difficulty.

He moved toward her, intending to comfort.

She raised a hand. "That's close enough."

He stopped at once. "Why is there a security guard outside?"

"Because of you, Bo."

"Because of me?"

"Yes," she answered, her voice flat.

What did a security guard have to do with him? Why would—

"I know about everything. Brimm found out about what you've been doing."

"What I've been doing?"

Her lips thinned.

Bo struggled to remain calm, to understand through his confusion. She'd been crying because of . . . *him?* Called a security guard to protect her from *him?* Because of something Brimm had told her? His hands began to shake. "What did Brimm tell you I've been doing?"

"Computer hacking."

"Excuse me?"

"You've been checking into all my investments and my accounts. Trying to verify my net worth."

"What?" He felt like he'd been slammed in the head with a metal pipe. "Brimm told you that *I've* been doing this?"

"Because you have been."

"No I haven't." Where had this accusation come from? He couldn't make sense of it, couldn't think straight when Meg looked so devastated.

She crossed her arms.

"Look me in the face, Meg. I don't know what you're talking about. I've never once looked up anything about you on a computer. Never. And I definitely haven't hacked into your financial stuff. For one thing, I'd never do that to you. For another, I wouldn't know how."

"At this point, Bo, I'd really appreciate it if you'd just tell me the truth."

"I am."

She motioned to a few sheets of paper stacked on her father's desk. "These say otherwise."

"Then they're dead wrong." His pulse drummed, hurtling blood through his veins as he fought to piece together the situation. Brimm had come to her with these papers. These papers somehow incriminated him. Which could only mean one of two things. Brimm—or someone else—had framed him. Or this whole thing was a nightmare of a mistake.

It didn't look like Meg was willing to consider either of those possibilities, though. Her posture, her tone, and the accusation in her beautiful eyes all showed him, clear as day, that she actually thought he was guilty.

She thought he was guilty. The realization filled him with agony.

Last night she'd liked—maybe even loved—and trusted him. And now she believed him to be a liar who wanted her for her money.

His fingers curled into his palms. He couldn't bear for her to think that of him. He couldn't bear it. Desperation rose sharp inside him.

Meg realized that her decision to confront Bo in person had been a mistake. A big mistake. Because looking into his face, so familiar and starkly handsome, was unraveling her resolve and making her want to turn traitor and believe in his innocence, even now.

Her anger had demanded that she tell him in person that she'd found him out. She'd longed to watch his reaction and hear him admit his guilt. She'd even had some crazy notion that he might apologize or show remorse.

None of it would have helped much, in the face of the heartbreak crushing down on her, but it would have been *something*. Something to hang on to as she walked into the dismal days ahead. More than she'd ever gotten from Stephen.

It appeared, though, that Bo had no intention of giving her the truth or an apology. He was going to keep on denying everything right to the end.

He moved to her father's desk and looked down at Brimm's papers. "I don't understand what this says."

Meg raised an eyebrow.

"I don't. I'm not a computer expert. You can ask Jake, or anyone else in my family. Anyone I work with. Lynn, even. They'll tell you. There's no possible way I could hack into anything."

"It would have been easy for you to make everyone think that."

The small muscles along his jaw hardened, and his gray eyes glittered with pain.

She wanted him desperately. To be her husband, lover, best friend. She wanted, with a physical ache, a future with him. Marriage and children and the rest of their lives twined together into one, lived out side by side, inseparable.

But it wasn't going to be. None of it was going to be. "Can you be honest with me, Bo?" She hated the faint wobble in her voice. "Please? You owe me that much."

"I am being honest with you," he said raggedly. "I'd trust you with every single thing that matters to me. My family, my life, my reputation. I need you to trust me in this one thing. I didn't do these things you're saying I did."

"Of course you did."

"No. I love you, Meg." He fisted his hands in the front of his shirt and pressed the fabric against his chest. "I love you."

She reached out blindly to grip the top of her father's chair.

"I'm yours. Until I die, and even after that, I'm yours."

She shook her head as moisture rushed to her eyes.

"I didn't do the things you're saying I did. I don't know why you or Brimm think that I did them, but please believe me. Please. I would never, not for anything in the world, hurt you. Never. I swear it."

Her nails dug into the leather as she used the chair's bulk to keep her upright. "I think you'd better go."

He dropped his hands to his sides and moved closer to her.

"Stop," she pleaded.

He did.

She could not allow him one inch closer. Not an inch, or she'd crack.

"Can you trust me?" he asked.

"You don't deserve my trust."

He flinched as if she'd whipped him. His skin paled.

He was either telling the truth—which he couldn't be. Or he was a consummate actor—which he must be.

Had everything between them been fake? Or just some of it? Would it be worse or better if he'd actually liked her a little? Maybe there was a grain of reality in how he'd acted toward her and the things he'd said to her. Maybe he did find her attractive in some small way, and her money had made it possible for him to stomach kissing her—

All at once she felt like she was going to be violently ill. She moved to the nearest window and jerked it open. Air flushed in—heavy and moist after the earlier rain, devoid of relief. "I told you yesterday that I'd keep the horse farm open. And I will."

She focused on the grounds below the window. She'd decided to keep the farm running for many reasons she'd continue to stand behind. "But you'll no longer be a part of Whispering Creek Horses. Your employment here is over."

He made no sound.

She waited.

Nothing but more awful stillness.

She glanced at him and instantly regretted it. He looked stricken, and she didn't think it was because she'd just fired him. Sympathy welled inside her, and she battled down an urge to run to him and beg his forgiveness. *He should be begging you for your forgiveness, Meg.* She turned back toward the window. "I'd like you to leave now."

He continued to stand motionless.

"I mean it."

Bo's footfalls moved away from her. She looked around in time to see part of his back and shoulder disappear into the hallway beyond.

She rested a hand against the window frame and leaned into it, letting it steady her swaying weight.

She'd done the right thing just now. She'd broken their relationship, irrevocably. But doing so didn't make her feel better. All she felt? A black and roiling despair.

Because the hardest thing of all to take—harder even than Bo's deception or the realization that he'd never loved her—was the loss of him. She'd just lost someone irreplaceable. She'd just lost the one man she cherished more than any man on earth.

"You need to calm down," Jake said.

Bo had all but worn a track in his kitchen floor. His thoughts and emotions wouldn't allow his body to be still. He pushed his fingertips against his forehead, fought to keep himself from splintering into a hundred pieces.

He'd called Jake as soon as he'd left Whispering Creek. His brother had arrived at his house minutes later, and Bo had just finished explaining everything to him.

"Are you going to say I told you so," Bo asked, "about my relationship with Meg?"

"Listen, if I was right in any way, then I'm sorry I was. I've seen how happy you've been the last few weeks. I didn't want that to stop." Jake leaned against the kitchen counter, his hands in his pockets. "Hey, you think you can just *try* to calm down?"

"I can't stand to think that she's out there hating me."

"She might not hate you. She's mad because she thinks you pretended to like her because of her money."

"How's it possible she could think that?"

"You know why." Jake jerked his chin toward the papers Bo had brought home with him from Whispering Creek.

How was he supposed to defend himself against evidence he couldn't even understand? "I need to find someone who can read that and tell me what it says."

"There's some kid over in Wylie who's supposed to be a computer genius. Mom's friend's son. You remember Mom telling us about him?"

"Barely."

"I'll call her and get his number." Jake pulled out his cell phone and dialed.

The kid from Wylie showed up on Bo's doorstep an hour later. He wore a knit ski cap over curly hair, a hoodie, tight jeans, and a pair of black Converse high-tops. He couldn't have been older than sixteen or taller than five foot seven.

This was the person who was supposed to help Bo save his relationship with Meg? In this part of Texas, the shoes alone probably got the kid's butt kicked on a weekly basis. "Kyle?" Bo asked.

"What's up?"

Bo introduced himself and Jake, then took him into the kitchen to show him Meg's papers.

Kyle went through the sheets one by one while Bo waited, grinding his teeth. The seconds dragged into minutes, driving him insane with impatience.

"Yeah. Hmm." Kyle scratched his forehead with one skinny finger while he considered. "Can I look at your computer?"

Bo led him to the desk against the back wall. The kid sank onto the chair and took over the computer, making the cursor and screens fly. "This, uh, setup is seriously old and slow. You need an upgrade."

Bo scowled at Jake above Kyle's head.

Jake lifted a shoulder.

Bo wanted to take the kid by the shoulders, shake him, and growl at him to hurry.

At one point, Kyle tilted the hard drive tower so that he could read some information on the back of it. Then he turned to Bo. "What would you like to know?"

"What do the papers say?"

"They basically show how a group of investigators were able to find a hacker."

"Why do they think I'm him?"

"This your computer?"

"Yes."

"The hacking was done on this computer, that's why."

Bo paused, thinking. "How can they, or you, be sure it was done on this computer?"

"Because every computer has a unique ID . . . like a fingerprint, you know? The hacking had this computer's fingerprints all over it."

"I didn't do it."

"Well, somebody did. Using this machine."

"Could the hacker have done this whole thing through my computer remotely?" He'd been on calls with technical support before, when they'd taken over his computer right in front of him.

"No. In this case the hacker sat right here"—Kyle turned toward the monitor, hunched over the keyboard, and mimicked typing—"and did it all on this computer."

Someone had been in his house. Someone had framed him for certain.

Kyle looked back and forth between the brothers. "Anything else, you know, you need help with?"

"I think that's it," Jake answered.

Bo stood frozen while Jake thanked the kid and walked him out.

When Jake returned, Bo met his brother's gaze. "Do you believe I'm innocent?"

"Yes."

So he hadn't lost his mind. Regardless of the evidence, Jake had faith in his truthfulness.

"It's looking, though," Jake said, "like Meg thinks you're guilty for a good reason."

Bo's heart twisted. He nodded.

"She seems like she's pretty guarded to begin with," Jake said. "Like she'd be slow to trust anyone."

"She is."

"Probably in part because of her money."

"True."

"And who her father was."

"Yes."

"And her experience with her husband."

"Yeah."

"So she's already cautious. Then her cousin brings her this information about you—information that seems legit. I'm not saying it's right, Bo, but I guess if I put myself in her shoes, I can see why she kicked you out."

Bo wanted to break or punch or shoot something. To scream. How in the world was he ever going to get her back?

Unable to remain still, he strode into the kitchen, gripped the front of his sink, and stared hard out the window into the darkness. Jake had been right. Meg *was* careful. She'd been raised the rich daughter of a famous businessman, and yes, that had shaped her. But Bo knew that her relationship with Stephen had wounded her most. No way she'd risk letting a man play her like that a second time. Which was, at this very moment, exactly what she thought Bo had been trying to do to her.

Bo hated that he'd been accused of doing something he hadn't done. It filled him with fury on one hand and made him helpless on the other because he couldn't defend himself. Still, as bad as that part was, he could stomach it.

But Meg thinking he'd betrayed her like Stephen had?

That undid him.

Jake came to stand next to him. "How'd the hacker get in here?"

"I don't know."

"You keep your doors locked."

"Yes, but that's it." Living in Holley, he'd never thought much about security. Never had a house alarm. "Unless the hacker has a copy of my house key, he or she must have come in through a window."

"Let's see if we can find which one."

The brothers moved through the house, testing each window. Back when Bo had bought the place, he'd had new windows put in. They all slid easily open, but had latches to lock them in place when closed.

In his bedroom, Bo tugged on a pane that slid open in answer. "Here," he said to Jake.

They each took a close look. No scratches on the sill or smudges on the glass. No sign that anyone had forced the window open.

"When did you have this one open last?" Jake asked.

"Maybe a week and a half ago. It's possible that I forgot to latch it when I closed it."

"Or possible that it was jimmied open."

"It doesn't look like that, though, does it?"

"Think there's any chance the person left prints?" Jake asked.

"No. A person this smart would have worn gloves." Bo had no desire to call the police. Most likely, he'd alert them to the crime, then find that evidence pointed straight back at him.

"Why would someone do this to you, Bo?"

Bo shifted his attention from the window to his brother. "To get me away from Meg and away from Whispering Creek."

"Who'd want to do that?"

"Her family, for one. I know for sure her uncle doesn't want us together."

"You think he's capable of setting you up like this?"

"I wouldn't have thought so. But he can certainly afford to hire someone to do this kind of a job."

They grabbed flashlights and went outdoors to examine the window and the surrounding area from the exterior. They couldn't find a single indication that someone had used the window to enter and exit Bo's house. They searched and searched.

But found nothing.

For hours that night, Bo walked the back acres of his property.

A June storm full of thunder, lightning, and anger ate up the distance, closing, and then covering him. He let it come, let the cold and rain rush against his face and down the open neck of his shirt. Nature could do its worst and still not hurt him half so much as the pain clawing him on the inside.

Her voice. Her perfume. Her face. The things she'd said to him. Her tender heart. The way she'd gradually come to place her faith in him.

For days—weeks—an intuition of danger had been riding Bo. He'd been unable to shake his worry over Meg's safety. But maybe *this* was what his sixth sense had been picking up on. Perhaps she'd never been in physical danger. Maybe their relationship had been the target from the beginning.

If so, the disaster he'd been waiting for had come.

Someone had taken aim at his relationship with Meg. Then, with the precision of a sharpshooter, they'd pulled the trigger.

He'd hoped. He'd wanted . . .

He prayed prayers of desperation that didn't make sense. His eyes filled with tears, his steps echoed with hopelessness.

He loved her. Ferociously, he loved her.

He didn't want to live without her.

Chapter Twenty-two

As a child Meg had often taken herself, when heart-sick, to Mr. Son. She could remember bouts of sadness over all those Mother's Days without a mother, her father's indifference, friends who'd excluded her, boys who hadn't called.

Those minor hurts seemed laughable today. She'd passed a horrible night sleeping in snippets crawling with bad dreams, tossing from side to side, or curled into a ball fighting off panic attacks. Morning had taken a harrowing long time in coming.

Once she'd gotten herself dressed, she'd followed her old habit and gone in search of Mr. Son.

She found him on his knees next to Jayden, the two of them hard at work filling a backyard flower bed with yellow lantana.

Mr. Son peered up at Meg, studied her, then silently motioned her down beside him. When she knelt, her knees registered cool wetness, her nose the smell of dirt.

Jayden glanced at her. He had on pint-sized gardening gloves, rubber boots, a green apron over his play clothes, and a fisherman-style hat.

"Hi, Jayden," she said, dismayed that her voice sounded hoarse.

Jayden responded with an unintelligible string of syllables, then "ball," then a definitive nod. With a shrug, he returned to gardening, drilling his small spade into the dirt and flicking the clods upward.

Mr. Son handed Meg his own spade, then set about showing Jayden, probably for the five thousandth time, how to dig the appropriate-sized hole. "Like so," he said.

Meg dug a neat row of her own holes. Mr. Son freed the plants he'd raised himself in his greenhouse and handed them to her one at a time. She gently loosened their roots, placed them in the ground, and patted dirt around them.

Mr. Son didn't say much. Never had. But he was secure and reliable. He'd always believed her to be capable. So when she was near him, she believed herself to be capable, too, even if just for a moment. She dearly needed to feel capable today. Bo—

Don't think about him, Meg. She concentrated on the physical sensations of planting and nothing else.

"You're going to do a good thing," Mr. Son said. "Having parents come, kids come to Whispering Creek."

"I'm glad you like the idea."

"I'm proud of you." It was the most lavish praise he'd ever given her. "Now get back to work. We have many plants here."

She did as he asked, but his unexpected kindness had slipped past her sorry defenses and nicked her heart. The floodgates crashed down, and she started to cry. Oh dear. She might never stop.

She peeked at Mr. Son, who, she could tell, had already noticed the tears running down her face. He didn't censor or coddle, however.

She went on planting. Bo—

Don't think about him. But the more Meg tried to wrestle

him out of her head, the more clearly she could see him at the paddock rail, looking sideways at her with a slow smile.

How could you have done this to me, Bo? She gripped the spade with all the strength she had, tears streaming, rage and misery tangling within her. *I love you. I LOVE YOU! I'd have gladly given you anything in the world you wanted. I'd have shared everything I own with you. If only you'd loved me back—*

A whimper reached her ears. She jerked her gaze to the side and saw Jayden watching her. His eyes had rounded at the sight of her grief, and his little bottom lip trembled.

Mr. Son clapped his hands to distract Jayden. "Like so, young man. See here." He helped Jayden plant a flower. "Like so."

Meg turned away from Jayden, sniffed, and wiped at her eyes with her forearms, because her hands were caked with dirt. She couldn't bear to scare or upset Jayden. What had she been thinking? She should have known not to cry in front of a child.

She registered a soft touch on her shoulder and looked up to see Jayden standing next to her. He regarded her with his somber eyes. Then gently, he patted her cheek, bent forward, and rested his head against her collarbone. She hugged him to her.

This small boy, God bless him, hadn't been born into an easy situation or to a worthy earthly father. He'd experienced his own share of worry and upheaval, and so, somewhere within him, he already had a capacity for empathy.

Oh, my dear Lord. She took a shuddering breath and kissed the top of Jayden's head. She'd thought all this time that she was the one helping and blessing him and Amber.

She realized, her arms filled with the weight of him, that God's plan had been the opposite all along. Amber and Jayden were the ones helping *her*, blessing *her*. She'd heard God ask her to support them, and Meg had thought that He'd wanted something from her, for their sake. But it turned out that in asking her to care for them, He'd wanted something for her instead: the soul-deep assurance that came from following His will, even when everything else had been stripped away.

Jayden held on tight. He smelled like baby soap and clean clothes and gardening.

You are loved, God assured her through that embrace. **You are loved.**

I'm so thankful for you, God, Meg prayed. *No matter what, you are still on your throne. You're good, and mighty, and full of grace. My heart's broken, my body's wrung out, my mind's drained, but I have you and no one can take you away from me. I'm grateful for my blessings. I worship you with my whole heart. I trust you with my life.*

When upset, Bo typically threw himself into his job.

Since Meg and his job had both been jerked away from him at the same time, he didn't have that option. The only two options that remained? Go crazy or find something to do.

He'd seriously considered going crazy. But in the end, he hadn't been able to take the inactivity of it. So, driven by his restless body, he'd started working on his land. Every backbreaking, exhausting thing he'd dreamt up, he'd done. He trimmed trees, then cut and stacked the wood. Built the shed he'd always intended to build for his lawn equipment. Repaired the roof of the carport. Cleaned gutters. Weeded and pruned. Hauled away rotting logs.

For two days during the daylight hours when he worked and during the nighttime hours when he searched the Internet for information on how hackers operated and the tactics used in catching them, Meg filled his head. He racked his brain, trying to think of ways to prove his innocence to her, ways to convince her to give him another chance.

On Friday evening, he dragged himself indoors, so bleak and bone-tired that it took all the strength he had to stand upright in the shower. He let the spray pound his body until the hot water ran out. Then he pulled on a pair of jeans and eyed the bed, wondering if he could finally find sleep—

His cell phone rang.

He let the first ring go. But by the second ring, foolish hope had him picking up the phone and checking it, to see if it was Meg. It wasn't. Unfamiliar number. "Hello?"

"Bo, dear? How are you? It's Sadie Jo Greene."

He'd never before received a call from Sadie Jo. He stilled in the middle of his bedroom, his upper back still damp.

"Bo?"

"Yes, Ms. Greene. I'm here."

"It was so nice of you to take me out horseback riding the other day. I had a wonderful time. It had been years." She went on to compliment the horses, the stables, and the employees.

He made the expected responses. Had Meg told her what had happened between the two of them?

"I was especially pleased to see Meg up on a horse," she said. "Have you, by any chance, spoken with her in the last few days?"

"No, I haven't."

"Well, I have. She seems sad to me, and I'm . . . I'm concerned about her. I keep asking her if she wants to talk about it, but she doesn't."

"What can I do to help?"

"Meg and I like to go shopping together now and then. I

couldn't go today, because I'd promised to visit a friend at the convalescent home. But I suggested she go on her own because I thought it might lift her spirits. She didn't want to, but I eventually talked her into it."

Bo waited, on edge.

"She's been at the mall for an hour or more. I just called her, and she didn't sound any better." She made a sighing sound of regret. "Perhaps I shouldn't have sent her off alone like that."

Worrying about Meg had always come naturally to Bo. He didn't need much of a reason. Sadie Jo's concern more than did the trick. Unease tightened in his gut.

"When I hung up with Meg," Sadie Jo continued, "I got to thinking about you. I know the two of you are friends. Meg could probably use a friend right now."

Meg definitely hadn't told Sadie Jo about what had happened between them. "I'll drive over there and check on her."

"Oh, would you? Thank you. I'd so appreciate it. Maybe you can cheer her up."

Not a chance. But he *could* check on Meg, without her ever having to see or talk to him. "Where is she?"

"The Neiman Marcus at Willow Bend Mall."

"It'll take me twenty or thirty minutes to get there. Do you think she'll still be in the same store?"

"Oh yes. It's our favorite. We park in the Neiman Marcus parking garage right next to it and make our way through the store floor by floor."

"I'm on my way."

Meg had come to Neiman Marcus with honorable intentions. Over the past several years, she and Sadie Jo had perfected a "Neiman's on Twenty Dollars or Less" style of trip. They began on the bottom floor and went up from there, browsing and admiring. They took a break in the middle for a meal, coffee, or dessert at the NM Cafe. Occasionally they purchased a small gift here or the rare affordable item there.

Just such a visit had been her intention today when she'd let Sadie Jo talk her into this. But somewhere between Jewelry and Lady's Handbags, Meg had remembered that she was no longer on a budget. No, indeed.

She stopped to survey a Jimmy Choo tote bag. She could own it and any other item that caught her fancy.

Except that after the epiphanies she'd had over the past weeks about how her money was God's money, indulging in a million-dollar shopping spree would make her the biggest hypocrite alive. Not only that, but any pleasure would be fleeting, and she'd feel wretchedly guilty afterward.

Step away from the tote bag, Meg. Don't make any sudden movements. Just step away.

She turned herself in the direction of the escalator, held on to the strap of the purse she'd bought three years ago with one of her father's gift cards, and started walking.

Coming here had been a bad idea. She'd moved through the last few days—speaking, eating, bathing, reacting to the people around her—while thoughts like *I can't believe he deceived me, I miss him, It's over, I'm crushed, How could he?* had run through her consciousness like a train on a circular track. She was in the toilet emotionally, and women in emotional toilets should keep themselves far away from malls.

She made her way across the second floor, pushed through the exit doors, and took the outdoor walkway across to the parking garage. In contrast to the store's bright and noisy interior, the world outside wrapped her in the semidarkness between sunset and full night.

As she walked deeper into the parking garage, a car eased past her, then disappeared up a ramp. She could see one couple walking around a far corner away from her, but no one else.

Unsettled by her aloneness, she picked up her pace and dug her keys out of her purse. Almost to her car. She'd get herself home and medicate with a bubble bath, a biography, and prayer—

"Hello, Meg."

A chill of recognition raced down the back of her neck. The voice had come from right behind her, even though there'd been no one there a second ago. Her feet stumbled to a stop. She turned, and for the first time in five years, looked into the face of Stephen McIntyre. She remembered it all, like a fist to the stomach. The lines of his features. His neat blond hair. The businessman's clothes.

"Well?" He smiled, lifted his hands. "Aren't you going to say hello? It's been a long time."

Her pulse went into an uproar, clamoring. She was alone in a parking garage with Stephen. Was she in danger? Or could this meeting be a coincidence? He looked calm. His words had been benign.

"Fancy running into you like this, Meg. I'm glad. I've been wanting to talk to you. I'd like to apologize, if you'll let me."

She took a halting step back, scanning the space behind him, hoping to spot someone, anyone.

Empty.

He motioned to a nearby car. "How about we go somewhere and talk? I can buy you coffee or dinner."

"I'm not interested."

"No?"

She was in danger. His words still hadn't revealed it, but her instincts knew it. *Oh, God.* Should she run for her car? Or head back to the safety of the store? She could see the walkway leading back to Neiman's. She'd return to the store.

She passed by him.

He didn't respond.

She set off fast, sparing a glance back.

He was following. Gaining. Pulling a folded square of cloth from his jacket pocket as he reached for her.

Panic. She bolted into a run and drew in a breath to scream—

He clamped the cloth onto her mouth, then hauled her body against his.

She screamed with all the force she had, but the cloth swallowed the sound. She fought his hold, striking at his arms with her keys. In response, he wadded and stuffed the cloth deep into her mouth, then wrenched her hands behind her. Something tightened around her wrists. A plastic restraint? *My God,* she called out in the frenzy of her mind. She yanked to free her hands. Couldn't.

Stephen dragged her toward the row of cars. Meg writhed and gagged and worked to yell around the cloth. Not loud enough! Not loud enough to alert anyone.

He pulled her to a green sedan, and all the warnings she'd ever heard crushed down on her. *Don't let an assailant put you in a car,* the experts said. She thrashed with increasing alarm, scanning her surroundings, searching for someone to help her.

Still no one.

He forced her down into the passenger seat, then clicked the seat belt across her. Heavily, he leaned against her knees, and she felt another plastic restraint cinch her ankles together. When he closed her in and walked around to the driver's side, she tried to jerk her feet upward, but they wouldn't move. She could see that he'd fastened her ankle tie to a metal ring drilled down into the frame of his car.

He'd planned all of this. Her throat worked against the cloth. Air panted desperately through her nose. He'd planned all of this.

He started the engine.

She twisted in her seat, trying to free her hands and feet.

"Chill, Meg. I'm not going to hurt you." He spoke in a casual tone, as if nothing out of the ordinary had just happened. "You've always been a cooperative girl. If you sit there and relax, I'll let you stay awake. Otherwise, I'll have to give you a shot that'll make you fall asleep. What'll it be?"

His words cut through the clatter in her brain and caused her to still. She could not—NOT—afford to let him knock her out. There's no telling what he'd do to her unconscious and defenseless body.

"I hate being interrupted by cell phone calls. You?" He switched on a black rectangular device plugged into his cigarette lighter. "This will keep that from happening." He reversed out of the parking place and maneuvered the car toward the exit.

What did he want from her? Where was he taking her? He had no conscience, she knew that. Sociopath, she knew that. Terrible temper, she knew that. But he'd never physically harmed her before. Maybe he'd meant what he'd said and didn't plan to hurt her.

Then why had he just kidnapped her? Bound her hands and feet? Blocked her cell phone signal?

Fear plunged through her.

God, come, she begged. *God, come.*

He reached over and removed the cloth from her mouth. She gasped and screwed shut her eyes, sucking in air.

"There you are," he said companionably. "Better?"

Bo turned his truck into Neiman Marcus's parking garage and began to look for Meg's Mercedes. A black suburban passed him going the other way. Then a dark green Honda. He caught a flash of pale color from within the car as it swept past.

He refocused on the lane in front of him, searching for her car on either side. . . .

A trickle of recognition had him looking in his rearview mirror at the Honda. He'd seen that car. Where?

He braked and watched the Honda exit the garage.

The night he and Meg had kissed for the first time. He'd followed her home through Holley. It had been late, and he'd seen only one other car on the road. A dark green Honda like that one. Come to think of it, he thought he might have driven past a car like that in Holley a few other times.

He pulled into an empty parking space, backed out, and headed in the same direction as the Honda.

This was ridiculous. He hadn't been thinking straight since Meg had dumped him, and now he was so out-of-his-mind paranoid that he was suspecting . . . what? That this Honda and the one he'd seen in Holley were the same car? C'mon.

The Honda slid away from him, down the road that circled the mall, its red taillights burning into the gray haze of the coming night.

He'd told Sadie Jo that he'd check on Meg. He ought to find her car in the garage, then find Meg herself inside the store.

She'd be fine, and he'd feel like an idiot for worrying about some stranger's Honda.

Except his intuition wanted him to follow the car. When he'd driven past it a few moments ago he'd seen something inside it. Nothing much. A flash of pale color that might have been, could have been . . .

Meg's blond hair.

Go, the voice within him urged. *Go.*

Shaking his head, he turned onto the road. He'd pull up beside the car and take a look inside to prove to himself that he'd been mistaken. Then he'd return to the mall like a sane person.

The Honda took the on-ramp to the tollway heading south, then less than a mile later transferred onto the turnpike going east. Once on the turnpike, the Honda settled into a middle lane. Bo stayed to the right of it, hanging back, then gaining gradually. When he came even with it, his much taller truck hid the Honda's driver from view but gave Bo a shadowed look downward at the passenger.

It only took a fraction of a second to recognize her profile. Meg.

Meg was inside that car. Why in the world would she have left her car behind and gone off with this person? He didn't think she would have, voluntarily.

He swore and changed lanes until he could get a look at the driver. A light-haired man, about his age. No one he recognized. Both Meg and the driver stared straight ahead.

Bo eased off the gas and let his car fall back. If this person had abducted her, Bo was going to kill him. He was going to rip him apart, piece by piece. If the man hurt her in any way—

The coldest fear he'd ever known seized him. His breath sawed in and out. Between his fury, the darkness, and the light rain that had just begun to fall, he could hardly see the road in front of him.

He had to see, to think. Meg needed him. He switched on his windshield wipers and kept a close watch on the Honda, illuminated by his headlights.

What did he know?

He knew that this Honda must be the same one he'd seen in Holley the night he and Meg had first kissed. That night had been what . . . more than two weeks ago? So the driver had been following Meg at least that long if not longer. The man probably knew all her patterns by now, probably knew that in the past few weeks she'd hardly left her property except to go to work or spend time with him. Meg had been alone in an unprotected place tonight, maybe for the first time in days.

Could this man, her abductor, be the one who'd framed him? To get him out of the way? He didn't know the man's identity, his plan, his weapons, or where he was taking Meg.

His top priority? To tail the Honda until he could get help from the police. He needed to do it without causing the driver to suspect he was being followed. Bo let a few cars come between him and the Honda, grateful for the rain that blurred everything, glad that his truck had no remarkable features. It looked like every other truck on the road in north Texas.

He dug his phone out of his pocket, but paused just before hitting 9-1-1. He should attempt to reach Meg on her cell first. If he'd made a mistake and she hadn't been taken against her will, she could simply say so. Since Meg no longer answered his calls, he phoned Sadie Jo. Trying to sound normal, he told her he was having trouble locating Meg and asked if she'd mind getting in touch with her, then calling him right back. She agreed. He waited, tense, counting the seconds.

Bo had been in high-pressure, dangerous situations as a Marine. But not like this. Not with Meg involved, Meg the one in danger, Meg at some man's mercy.

When he got his hands on the driver of that car he was going to *tear his head off—*

His phone rang. Sadie Jo informed him that Meg hadn't picked up.

Bo thanked her, disconnected, and punched 9-1-1. When a female operator answered, he explained the situation. She asked him to describe their location, their direction, and Stephen's vehicle, then told him she'd send out a squad car.

Bo ended the call and prayed for the police to arrive quickly.

The Honda turned north on 75, backtracking the route that Bo himself had taken from Holley to the mall. It made sense that the man would be returning to a location near Holley. If he'd been watching Meg for as long as Bo suspected he had, he'd probably been staying near Whispering Creek.

Where were the cops?

When the Honda exited 75, Bo stayed five cars back. It went east, through a north Plano neighborhood.

Bo called 9-1-1 again. They put him through to the operator he'd first spoken with. He updated her on their location. "Where's the squad car?"

"Sir, there's a major freeway accident south of you that includes a chemical spill and fatalities. The squad car that was coming to intercept you has been delayed."

"Exactly how soon," he gritted out, "will it catch up to us?"

"I just don't know."

"Listen, a woman has been kidnapped and she's in danger. I need a policeman to pull over the car she's traveling in *right now.*"

"Sir—"

"I need you now!"

"Once again, sir, we'll be there as soon as we're able."

Bo hung up and released a string of curses. If he couldn't count on the police to arrive in time, Meg only had him.

Since he'd spotted Meg inside the Honda, his attention hadn't left the car for a second because so long as he hadn't lost the car, he hadn't lost Meg. The sight of its paint under the streetlights, its rear bumper, its back windshield had all drilled into his head.

But the farther they drove from the highway, the fewer the cars. If Meg's kidnapper noticed Bo tailing him, Bo feared the man would turn panicky. He likely had a knife or a gun with him in that car, and if he chose to use one of them on Meg while they were traveling, Bo would be too far away to protect her. But if he let the Honda pull out of his line of sight, he might lose the car.

He decided to do everything he could, as safely as possible, not to be noticed. He hung back. Changed lanes. Forced himself to turn onto side streets a few times, dying inside until he caught sight of the Honda again.

Like an accomplice, the rain continued, faithfully shielding him. The neighborhood thinned into more open country Bo recognized, about five miles south of Holley. He killed his truck's lights and called Jake. He willed his brother to answer as the phone rang, rang, and finally sent him to voice mail. He tried calling two more times. Still no answer. The recording asked him to leave a message.

"I need your help. Meg's been kidnapped and the police are trying to get here but haven't made it yet. I'm following the car she's in, and I think we're getting close to the destination. I'll call or text the location as soon as I know it."

The Honda took a right onto a farm road. When Bo reached

the intersection, he didn't dare turn in. He continued past a short distance. Then he stopped, counted to ten, and turned down the farm road the Honda had taken.

His vision strained as he searched the heavy darkness. He kept expecting at any moment to regain a visual on the other car, but he could see nothing but countryside.

Terror washed over him.

Where was it? He hunched forward, looking down each dirt road that broke away from the farm road. Barely breathing. Trying his hardest to locate the Honda—and Meg—again, to see where it had gone. His lips moved soundlessly as he prayed, begging God to protect Meg, to give him judgment.

He couldn't find it. *Couldn't find it.*

Sheer panic suffocated him.

Meg! Her name ripped from deep within.

Where are you?

Chapter Twenty-three

For almost the entire drive, Stephen said nothing to Meg. And she said even less to him.

The man she'd once loved and been married to, the one who'd crushed her so brutally with his lies and his theft, the one who'd been gone all these years, the one who'd fathered Jayden and walked out on Amber had come back. And he'd done *this* to her.

He was at the same time chillingly familiar and a total stranger.

Meg sat in the seat next to him, her muscles taut with fear, her mind laboring to comprehend that he'd restrained her and put her in his car. As far as she could tell, they'd almost arrived at their destination. He'd taken her deep into the country, into remote land where no one could possibly find her.

He must want money. She knew very well it was the only commodity Stephen cared about or understood. What could he be planning? To ransom her? To coerce her into giving him money? How? Through physical violence? The threat of rape?

Oh, heaven. Dread wrapped around her and squeezed, as real as the physical ties binding her hands and feet. Her teeth kept trying to chatter, so she bit down hard to keep her jaw steady.

Bo's face came to mind. The Bo she'd thought she'd known would have helped her. Her Bo would have fought for her. She ached for the man she'd believed him to be, for his strength and protection.

He's not coming. Not coming, Meg.

She saw other faces. Sadie Jo, Lynn, Mr. Son, Amber, Jayden. How would they learn about this? What would they think, feel?

Fear started to overtake her as surely as Stephen had inside the parking garage. She was going to lose it—

God, she prayed, concentrating hard, *fill me with your Spirit. I'm terrified, and I need you.*

A tiny warmth, as small as the fire at the end of a match, kindled to life inside of her. She waited, praying. The warmth grew, spreading through her trunk and limbs. Her body relaxed incrementally as she gave herself over. In response, His peace flowed into the empty shell of her weakness and frailty.

He wasn't just near her. Or watching over her. She felt certain that He was *within* her. *The one who is in you,* she'd once memorized, *is greater than the one who is in the world.*

Her human fear remained. But she believed God's power inside of her to be stronger.

I trust you, God. She'd said those words to Him hundreds of times over the past years, but they'd never been more true. All those times had been stairsteps. So that now, in this grave situation, she found that she could and did trust Him, with all of it.

Her life.

Her death.

"You look good, Meg. Better than you did when you were younger. Daddy's money must agree with you." Stephen glanced at her, then returned his attention forward. The light from the dashboard illuminated his neck and the underside of his chin.

"Of course, your daddy's money would agree with anyone, wouldn't it?"

His voice affected her like an insect crawling along the surface of her skin. She bit the inside of her cheek against a wave of revulsion.

"You want to tell me why you've been searching for me?" he asked.

"Searching for you?"

"A few weeks back someone infiltrated my computer. I followed the trail backward, and what do you know? It brought me to Whispering Creek."

He was talking about Amber's search for him, Meg realized. The one that Amber and Brimm had conducted. Stephen had discovered their investigation, somehow traced its origins to Whispering Creek, and assumed she was behind it.

"Meg? Why have you been looking for me?"

She kept her lips firmly sealed. The car bumped over uneven, hard-packed earth spiked with stones. Above, the clouds had cleared, taking the rain with them and giving her a glimpse of the stars.

"When I left you five years ago," Stephen said, "you let me go without a fight. But things have changed, haven't they?"

She didn't answer.

"Haven't they?" he repeated, louder and with an edge of menace.

"Yes."

"Now you can afford to hire hackers to find me and attorneys to advise you. Were you planning to let the police know where I was living? You interested in seeing me arrested, Meg?"

She couldn't reply because she refused to breathe a word about Amber or Jayden to him.

"You sought me out, Meg, and here I am. What do you say we skip over the police and the attorneys and settle this ourselves? Just you and me."

A small one-story clapboard house came into view.

Stephen parked, then extinguished the engine and the lights. They sat in the sudden silence while he waited, listening and watching. Both the sound of crickets and a sense of their isolation pressed in on Meg.

"You can scream all you like out here," he said.

"I don't think it would help."

"No," he agreed. "It wouldn't."

He came around the car and released her seat belt, then cut the tie that bound her ankles. After hauling her out of the car, he pushed her in front of him to the house.

Her hands were still cuffed behind her back. Even so, before he got her into that house, she knew she needed to attempt escape. She gathered her reserves, then bolted as fast as she could. His grip slipped away and she ran—

His hand latched on to her forearm, heaving her to a stop.

She turned to fight him, kicking at his shin, his knee.

The force of his palm slapping her face jerked her head to the side and sent her body spinning. Meg staggered and went down hard on her knees. She pulled in air, ears ringing, cheek throbbing, as she tried to recover from the stunning pain of the blow.

She should get up. Maybe she could still get away. She should—

He pulled her to her feet. His relaxed facade had stripped away, and only the harsh lines of his anger remained. "You're going to do this my way. It can go easy for you, or it can go hard." His fingers bit into her arms, and he shook her. "But you *are* going to do this my way. You try a stunt like that again, and I'll cut you." He dragged her toward the house.

354

She resisted, throwing herself in the opposite direction, but he used his greater weight and muscle to pull her past the wooden porch posts and rail, and through the doorway.

He forced her to the fireplace and switched on a camping lamp that sat on the mantel. Its light revealed an abandoned room, empty except for two folding chairs and a card table that held a laptop, a gun, and a knife.

He shoved her into one of the chairs, lowered himself into the remaining chair, and booted up the laptop. "You made a mistake when you decided to come after me," he said. "I'd have left you alone. Live and let live, right? But since you didn't see it that way, you've cost me a lot of time and effort. I'm going to let you pay me back for your mistake, and then we'll call it even."

Meg's attention riveted on the weapons.

"I'm familiar with your finances," he continued. "I know there are at least two accounts you can access right here with your online banking." His hands moved over his keyboard with ease. He'd always been skilled with computers, but by the looks of it he'd graduated to the level of a hacker. . . .

Meg's breath seeped from her lungs as understanding dawned. "You," she whispered. "You're the hacker. You're the one who's been investigating my financial information."

He ignored her and continued to work.

"You did it on Bo's computer. You set him up. You must've . . . Did you break into his house? Do it while he was at work?"

He didn't answer and didn't need to. She could see that she'd gotten it right. Using Bo's computer to check into her accounts had allowed him to kill two birds with one stone. He'd gained information about her money and simultaneously swung suspicion in Bo's direction.

She'd fallen for it. She'd ripped Bo out of her life, and in doing so she'd lost her closest ally. Her love. Her protector. The man who'd been as good as—better than—a bodyguard. Which had, in turn, given Stephen an opportunity to grab her.

Bo hadn't betrayed her. It had been Stephen.

Not Bo. Not Bo.

Tears sheened her vision. Bo *had* loved her. Just like he'd told her. He'd asked her to trust him and she'd . . . oh my goodness . . . she'd said those horrible things to him. Fired him.

Regret and shame pierced straight through her. She'd had no faith in him.

"We're going to move four million dollars into an account I've set up. It's ready and waiting." Stephen angled the laptop to face her. Her bank's Web site filled the screen. "What's your code?"

She met his gaze. "I'm not giving you any money."

"Yes you are."

Her determination intensified. She was *not* going to hand over four million dollars to Stephen McIntyre, a man who'd left a trail of destruction everywhere he went. "No."

"You used to be so accommodating."

"Not anymore."

"That so?" He picked up the knife and tested the blade with his thumb. "If we were still married, I'd have access to every bit of your money, by rights. In comparison, four million dollars is just a drop in the bucket—and you know it."

She glared at him.

"A reasonable bargain."

"Absolutely not."

"Let me put it to you this way, Meg. You're going to do something for me. You're going to transfer money. And afterward, I'm going to do something for you. I'm going to let you walk out of here alive."

"What guarantee do I have of that?" As soon as she transferred the money, he'd have no reason left to keep her alive.

"None. But then again, I don't think you're in a position to ask for guarantees right now."

"I'm the one that knows the code."

"I'm the one that has the knife."

"Use it, then."

"You doubt that I will?" Moving slowly, he placed a hand on her shoulder, then pressed her back against her chair. He trailed the knife's tip across her forehead, into her hair, along the length of one of the long strands.

Meg held still, her throat tight, her heart knocking.

"Where would you like me to cut you?" he asked. "Your face?"

She shook her head.

"No? You don't want me to cut you?"

"No," she rasped.

"In that case, I have an idea." He pulled back a few inches. "Maybe I can use my knife on your friend Amber instead? Or on her little boy . . . my little boy. What's his name again?"

All the blood rushed from Meg's head. Her brave intentions spiraled. Stephen knew about Amber and Jayden. Which meant that he . . . he'd trumped her. Because she'd give him every penny she had before she'd allow him to hurt them.

"You were difficult to get ahold of. But either one of them would be a piece of cake. As I said, Meg. Easy way or hard way."

Just then a faint *creak* sounded from the rear of the house.

Both Stephen and Meg jerked their heads in the direction of the sound. It had been subtle, the kind of noise an old house might make all on its own, or the kind of noise a floorboard might make when someone stepped on it.

"Help!" she cried. "We're in the front room. Help, please!"

Answering footsteps pounded toward them down the hallway. Someone was here! "He has a knife!"

Stephen snatched her in front of him, lifting his knife's blade to her throat.

Bo rounded the corner into the room. He stood framed in the rectangular opening, a gun in his hands and murder in his eyes. His eyes connected with hers for a fragment of a second before his attention and the muzzle of his gun moved to Stephen.

A sob born of gratitude and the joy of seeing him broke from Meg's throat. Bo. Here. She might not make it out of this alive, but at least he'd come, and she wasn't alone. She'd been given one more chance to see his face.

"Lower the knife," Bo ordered.

Meg could hear Stephen's fast, agitated breathing near her ear. "How did you find us?"

"I followed you."

"Are there more with you?"

"Not yet, but there will be." Bo made a downward motion with his chin. "Now lower the weapon, and I'll let you leave before they arrive."

Stephen held silent, probably listening for any reinforcements already on site.

"Be smart." Every line of Bo revealed his steely fury. "You haven't done anything unforgivable yet, but hurting her would be unforgivable. Release her and go now, while you still have the chance."

Stephen relaxed his grip on her slightly. Meg stepped to the side to see if she could get herself free, but instantly, he wrenched her back in front of him. The motion caused his knife to nick the skin of her neck.

"No!" Bo yelled, extending one hand.

Stephen paused, then adjusted his hold of her. "You don't like to see her hurt?"

Bo set his chin, but he'd paled. She winced inwardly, knowing Bo could see her bloodied knees, the swelling on one side of her face, and now the hot blood trickling down her neck.

"I only scratched her," Stephen said. "But trust me, I can do far worse." He began to move closer to the table and his handgun, using her as his shield.

Bo's aim followed Stephen. "You hurt her, and I'll kill you. Let her go."

"She's staying right here."

Bo stepped toward them.

"Stop!" Stephen's voice rose.

Bo stopped.

Stephen grabbed his gun and leveled it at Bo's chest.

"No," Meg breathed.

"Put your gun down," Stephen commanded.

Bo didn't so much as flinch.

"Put it down."

"No."

"Put it down, or I'll cut her throat. I swear I will!"

"Don't do it, Bo," Meg urged.

"Put it down!"

Bo began to lower his gun.

"No," Meg whispered, horror overwhelming her.

Carefully, Bo set his gun on the floor.

"Kneel," Stephen demanded.

Bo knelt, his hands up, his eyes burning with defiance. Defenseless. Because of her. Even after the way she'd treated him, he was willing to sacrifice himself for her sake. "Bo," she gasped. She couldn't believe he'd do this. Couldn't bear that he would.

Stephen's finger tightened around the trigger.

"Don't hurt him," she pleaded. "I'll give you the money. I'll give you anything you ask. Just—just don't hurt him."

The sound of a car reached them at that moment—motor roaring, tires crunching over stone, nearing the house at great speed.

Stephen's attention swung toward the front door.

Bo motioned to Meg, showing her how to thrust her head back into Stephen's face.

She did so, throwing herself into him as hard as she could, feeling her skull connect with his chin and nose. The shock of the blow caused his arms to jerk forward. Meg sprang from his grasp.

In the next instant Bo launched himself at Stephen, tackling him.

Stephen's gun went off, deafening, as they hit the floor.

Meg screamed. Had Bo been hit?

He rose on top of Stephen, uninjured. The two men wrestled, swung at each other, twisted. Bo disarmed Stephen of the gun and knife and Meg went after the weapons, sliding them into the corner of the room behind her. Bo landed a punishing blow across Stephen's jaw, and Stephen's head snapped to the side, his eyes rolling.

The door banged open, and Jake rushed in carrying a shotgun. He stopped when he saw Bo's position over Stephen.

Bo hit Stephen again. And then again, knocking him out. When Bo pulled back to strike again, Jake moved in and stayed Bo with a hand on his forearm. "Whoa. He's out. You got him."

Bo tried to shake Jake off.

"You got him," Jake repeated firmly. "He's out, Bo."

Still Bo didn't move. His breath pumped in and out, his attention fixed on Stephen. He raised his fist.

"Bo," Meg said.

Instantly, he dropped his arm. He turned his face to her, and his haunted expression skewered her heart. She waited. As he looked at her, the haze of bloodlust cleared from his eyes.

"It's over," she said.

He strode to her, then clasped her to him fiercely. "Are you all right?" he asked into her hair, near her ear. "His knife . . . He cut you."

"It's not deep. Can you release my hands?"

In answer, he turned her gently. The constricting pressure of the plastic tie released. She sighed with relief and brought her hands in front of her to rub her wrists.

Jake knelt over Stephen. "Can you toss that over here?"

Bo flicked the cuff to him, and Jake rolled Stephen to his stomach, then pulled Stephen's arms behind him and restrained his wrists. "Who is this guy?"

"Stephen McIntyre," Meg answered. "My ex-husband."

Jake nodded once. "I'm calling the cops."

Bo lifted Meg's hands and inspected the red welts on her wrists. Tears gathered in his eyes.

"I'm okay," she assured him. "You saved me."

He released her hands and moved back toward Stephen as if intent on finishing the job of killing him.

She cut in front of him.

Again, she watched his gaze return to her, refocus. "Let's go outside," she said.

He hesitated, then followed her onto the front porch. Away from the sight of Stephen, privacy and a dark and bracing wind swept over them.

Bo moved to the porch rail and stood with his back to her, trying to regain control of himself, she guessed, because she was trying to do the same. She took slow breaths and attempted to calm the shuddering deep within her. *He's safe. I'm safe.*

"That was an incredibly close call," he finally said, his back still to her. "He could have sliced your throat and killed you just now."

"But he didn't."

Bo turned, his expression still harrowed. "But he could have. And I can't even stand to think about it. I was terrified that he'd injure you. I've never been that scared of anything in my life."

"You didn't show it."

"I was trying to focus on him so that I could do what needed to be done. But inside, I was sort of folding in on myself. If he . . . if he'd hurt you any worse, I'd have gone crazy. Are you sure, positively sure, that you're fine?"

"I'm sure."

"You promise me?"

"I promise you."

Bo drew her to him. Carefully, he held her against his broad chest. "I'm sorry I couldn't get here sooner. I'm sorry that he scared you and hurt you."

He was apologizing to her? She placed her hands on the sides of his face. "I'm the one who needs to apologize."

"Meg."

"Please, let me." The words wobbled pitifully. "*I'm* sorry. I'm so sorry for not trusting you. For the things I said to you in my father's office."

"It's all right."

"No, it isn't." He was trying to make this easier for her, but she refused to let him. "I saw the evidence that Brimm brought to me, and I believed the worst of you when it was Stephen all along."

He smoothed a lock of hair off of her face.

"I feel terrible about the way I treated you. I thought for a moment in there that I might not ever have the chance to make it right, that he might kill me before I'd be able to beg your forgiveness, or that he might kill you and it would be all my fault." Tears cascaded down her cheeks. "Thank God that didn't happen."

He wiped away her tears with his thumbs.

"Bo?"

"Yes?"

"Can you forgive me?"

"Countess. I've spent the last few days praying you'd give me a second chance."

"And now it's my turn to ask for a second chance."

"I've already forgiven you, Meg."

"You shouldn't have . . ."

"I couldn't help myself."

She linked her hands behind the warm cords of his neck. "Do you think you can bring yourself to trust me again? I swear to you that I'll never lose faith in you again."

"Nor I you. I love you."

"I love you, too."

He stared at her as if she'd cleaved him with an axe.

"I do." She gave him a shaky smile and shrugged. "I love you." After all the despair of the preceding days and the terror of the preceding hours, this moment of amazing blessing struck her as one of the sweetest of her entire life. *The* sweetest.

He pressed his lips to hers in a soft, reverent kiss. A wordless conversation of humility and thankfulness.

Then she nestled into his chest, her ear against his heart, and soaked in his heat and solidity. As long as she lived, she'd never forget the sight of him setting down his gun and kneeling on the floor, giving himself over for her. Imagine it! For her. Too wonderful and astonishing to believe. Until now, in all her life no man had ever truly loved her. Not her father or Stephen or anyone before or since.

But on this night, she could say with certainty that Bo Porter loved her. He. Loved. Her. After what he'd done for her tonight she'd never again doubt that she could trust him completely with it *all*. Everything she had. Her heart, her money, her home, her whole future.

Stephen's plans for her tonight had been for evil. But miraculously, God had redeemed them for good. Through the events they'd just survived, He'd not only used Bo to protect her, but He'd shown her Bo's true character. In doing so, He'd given her a gift beyond price: a man, a husband, the father of her children.

"I thought you told me once," Bo murmured, "that kidnappers and extortionists never troubled you."

She lifted her head, her lips curving. "Tonight's events were a first."

"And a last. You know the expression 'white on rice'?"

She nodded.

"That's how closely I'll be sticking to you from now on every time you leave Whispering Creek."

"Yes, sir."

"Just warning you. I don't want to hear any complaints."

"No complaints." She ran a fingertip along his jaw and down the side of his neck.

Distant police sirens carried to her on the air. "How in the world did you find me tonight?"

He explained it all to her, from Sadie Jo's phone call to the moment when he'd been unable to locate the Honda on the farm road.

"So if you lost Stephen's car, how were you able to find this house?"

Bo motioned in the direction of the intersection between the farm road and the dirt driveway that led to where they were standing. "I was driving along that section there when a man waved me down. He was on foot."

"A man was out walking on the road?"

"Yes. He'd seen the green Honda and showed me where to turn. I asked him to wait and tell Jake where to go when Jake got here. Then I texted the directions to Jake as I drove."

The sirens grew louder.

Bo stepped over to the doorway. "Did that guy on the farm road tell you to come down this way?" he asked Jake.

"Sure did," she heard Jake answer. "I told him to go home and fetch a gun if he had one, then meet us up here."

"Then where is he?"

"Don't know."

"Strange."

Meg edged over next to Bo so she could see into the house. He took hold of her hand, interlacing their fingers. Stephen remained on his stomach, his hands secured behind his back. His eyes had opened, and he was staring at the wall, his features rigid.

Jake stood next to him, his shotgun over one shoulder.

"Where did you and your brother get your weapons from?" Meg asked Bo.

"Our cars."

"You drive around with handguns and shotguns in your cars?"

Bo slanted a look down at her, humor in his eyes. "We're hicks from a small town in Texas. 'Course we do."

She shook her head.

"Wait till you see the arsenal I'll be driving around with from now on."

Meg met Jake's gaze. "Thank you for coming to help. Your arrival made all the difference."

"You're welcome." For the first time since she'd met Jake Porter, Bo's brother regarded her with an expression of approval. "I'm just glad you're both safe."

"The police will be here any second," Bo said to Meg. "Is there anything you want to say to him," he motioned in Stephen's direction, "before they arrive?"

"I don't know. Is there anything you want to say?"

"I don't think I should even look in his direction. Every time I do I want to kill him."

Meg regarded Stephen's prostrate form. The last time he'd wronged her, she'd been too ashamed and broken to do anything about it. So she'd let him go and then spent years regretting her inaction.

God had handed her a do-over, and this time she was going to get it right. Even if prosecuting him brought the media down on her. Even if she had to personally admit to everyone in America that she'd married a sociopath. Even if it cost her stress, time, and money to pursue Stephen through the various stages of a trial.

"Stephen," she said, "I forgive you. I do. I'm sure you don't care one way or the other, but I want you to know that I forgive you for everything."

He gave no indication of having heard her.

"That doesn't mean that I won't try to see justice done, though. Because I will. You were wrong about a lot tonight, but you were right about one thing: I can now afford attorneys."

Police descended on the crime scene.

Bo asked someone for a first-aid kit, then sat Meg down on the porch and doctored her knees, wrists, and neck with antiseptic and Band-Aids. Treating her injuries tied his gut in a sick knot of anger and remorse, but she chatted and smiled through the process, even teasing him for looking so grim.

Together they watched the officers arrest Stephen for aggravated kidnapping, secure him in the back of a squad car, and drive him away.

A crime scene unit investigated the house, taking photos and notes. A detective arrived and asked Bo, Meg, and Jake questions.

Bo did his best to answer fully, but he found it hard to pay attention with his mind so completely focused on Meg. He was burningly aware of her sitting beside him, of her every movement.

The detective informed them they'd need to drive to the station and give formal statements.

Bo situated Meg in his truck. As they started down the bumpy driveway together, he took one last look at the house, a place where everything could have gone wrong. It would take him days, maybe weeks, to get over the stone-cold fear of Meg's kidnapping. She'd been so close to death this evening. Literally, there'd been no space between her neck and Stephen's knife.

The fact was, that as bad as things could have gone in those final moments after they'd heard Jake driving toward the house—everything had gone right instead. As Meg kept telling him, she really was all right. Sitting beside him, alive, breathing, her heart beating. Whole. *Thank you, God*, he prayed with everything in him.

He finally understood why God had placed that sense of danger inside of him. God had been preparing him for something only God had seen coming.

"After we finish up at the station," Meg said, "I'm not really looking forward to returning to the guesthouse."

"No?"

"To be honest, I'm a little freaked out. I'm not sure I'm going to want to be alone at any point in the next five years."

"If you don't want to be alone, then I'll make sure you're not."

When they reached the farm road, Bo shifted his truck into park. "You mind if I check something?"

"Not at all."

He pulled a flashlight from behind the seats. They climbed down and stood at the junction. "This is where I drove up to that man I was telling you about."

"Where was he?"

"Just here." Bo pointed to the side of the road. "I'm curious why he never arrived at the house."

"Are you suspicious of him for some reason?"

"No. I'd just like to thank him. Let's see which way he went."

He shone the beam of light down where the man had been standing, and they both leaned over, looking closely. Bo saw no sign that the man had been there at all, much less a clue that would tell him which direction he'd taken.

The moon came out from behind a cloud, rolling brighter light over the landscape. Apart from the house they'd just come from, there were no other structures. Nothing but empty land for miles.

Bo and Meg stared at each other.

"God was in all of this tonight," Meg whispered slowly. "Wasn't He? Starting with Sadie Jo. God's always used her like that in my life. She always calls right at the moment I need it."

Bo nodded.

"And then you arrived at the parking garage just as we were leaving. If you'd been a minute later, you'd have missed us."

"Yes."

"And if you hadn't followed your hunch and gone after that Honda—which even the detective said was a long shot—Stephen would have gotten away with me."

"I'm starting to think it wasn't a hunch."

"No, it was God talking to you. And then, when you'd lost Stephen's car and couldn't find me . . . There was a man here to show you the way. Walking along this road at night, out in the middle of nowhere, far from any other houses. Jake saw him and spoke with him, too."

"He did."

"Bo?" Meg asked.

"Yes?"

"Do you believe in angels?"

Chapter Twenty-four

Closure.

Amber was no psychologist. The furthest thing from it. She didn't even know what the term *closure* meant for sure. But she thought it had to do with finishing something the right way.

She'd decided all on her own to give up her search for Stephen, and she hadn't regretted her choice. She'd been good with the way it had stood. But suddenly, because of how things had gone down between Stephen, Meg, and Bo last night, it looked like she was about to get herself some closure, after all. Just as a bonus prize.

"Miss Richardson?" the deputy asked.

"Yes." She stood up from the waiting room chair at the county jail.

"Right this way."

She followed. When Bo had brought Meg home last night, Meg had told Lynn everything. Then when Amber had woken up this morning, Lynn had, in turn, told her everything.

"Just here, miss." The deputy showed her into a room that looked like the ones she'd seen in movies. Here, people talked to prisoners on phones, looking at them through Plexiglas. She sat down and waited.

It didn't take long.

A guard walked Stephen, wearing prison orange, to the seat opposite her. He sat.

For a long and rushing moment, Amber just gaped at him. Stephen, one of the meanest people alive, sitting right across from her. He'd hurt her and he'd hurt Meg and who knew how many others. Maybe she ought to feel angry, like she had for so long. Or maybe she ought to feel afraid.

But she didn't. Instead, satisfaction doubled, then tripled in size within her. She'd been *craving* this chance—and boy, oh boy, was she ever about to give him a piece of her mind. She'd been raised in a poor family by a father with a temper. She didn't know much. But she *did* know how to tan a person's hide.

He regarded her coldly.

She picked up her phone.

He picked up his.

Then she inhaled deeply and let him have it.

Meg awoke to the warmth of her bed cocooning her and a mind that hummed with pleasant peace. Welcome feelings . . . and totally unlike what had greeted her the past few mornings, when she'd awoken sad and exhausted.

Gradually the events of the night before filtered back, reminding her of the reason for her happiness. She cracked her lids and saw him.

Bo, sitting exactly where he'd been sitting when she'd fallen asleep last night, on the chair they'd dragged in for him from the living room. He had a pillow stuck behind the small of his back.

His feet were stretched out and crossed at the ankles, resting on a footstool. His hands interlaced across his lean stomach. He was watching her, looking right at her, tenderness on his face.

Attraction curled deliciously through her midsection, then went racing and sizzling across every inch of her skin. He was gorgeous. Those even features, the pale gray eyes, the calm strength of him. The evidence seemed to suggest that she hadn't made it through the drama with Stephen, but had died and gone straight to heaven.

She smiled, remembering how Bo had stayed at her side last night while they'd given their statements at the station. How he'd made her tea while she'd showered and changed into sweats. How she'd felt guilty about him sleeping in an uncomfortable chair and so had tried to convince him that he didn't have to stay. His polite, very sweet insistence that he was staying. How she'd fallen asleep holding his hand, in a state of acute bliss.

He'd been here when she'd closed her eyes. Hours and hours had passed. The bright light edging the curtains told her she'd slept late. Yet he was still here, just as he'd promised.

"Good morning," she said.

"Good morning."

"Do I look terrible?"

"You look beautiful." Bo pushed into a more upright position, planting his boots on the floor. "How'd you sleep?"

"Very well, which is more than you can say, I'm afraid."

"I slept better in this chair than I've slept the past few nights in my own bed. Having you nearby and safe and not hating me made a big difference."

"I definitely don't hate you."

"No?" He smiled, lazy and sexy.

"No. Quite the opposite."

He knelt beside the bed. She rose onto her elbow and reached out with her free hand to hold the side of his face.

They gazed at each other, hot intensity crackling between them.

"I love you," he whispered.

"I love you, too."

"As long as I live, Meg, I will love you."

And she believed him, the same way she'd believed him last night when he'd told her he'd stay. He was everything and far more than she'd ever dared to hope or dream she'd find.

He caught her hand and bowed his head to kiss it, the way a knight might have done in medieval times when swearing fealty to his lady.

"Bo."

He lifted his face.

"I took a gamble the first day I met you. Remember? When you bullied me—"

"Bullied?"

She laughed. "*Somewhat* bullied me into letting you keep the horse farm open."

"I remember."

"Well, I'm about to make another gamble, but this time the odds are strongly in my favor and I feel very, very good about my chances."

"What're you going to do, countess?"

"I'm going to place an all-in bet, Bo. On you."

Epilogue

ONE YEAR LATER

Based on your application," Meg said to the lovely African-American woman sitting across the desk from her, "I know it's been difficult for you to afford rent, groceries, and clothes for your kids."

The woman nodded. "I'm a single mother."

"You had to leave your apartment and move into a shelter."

"Yes, ma'am, I did."

"Well." Meg straightened the papers in front of her, then looked up and met the woman's gaze, her heart swelling with gladness. "It gives me great pleasure to tell you that your application has been accepted. I'd like to invite you and your sons to live here, at Whispering Creek, until you're ready to go back out on your own again."

The woman started to cry, and Meg's own eyes filled with tears. It humbled her deeply that God had entrusted her with this particular calling that brought her so much joy. "While you're here, the Cole Foundation will cover the costs of your food and clothing. I understand that you also have some medical bills."

"Yes, ma'am." The woman knuckled the moisture away from

her eyes, sniffling. She spoke haltingly. "My youngest son needed surgery. It . . . it ended up costing so much."

"The Cole Foundation is going to take care of those bills."

The woman's eyes rounded in shock. "What?"

"We're going to take care of all your medical bills. Every one." Meg could see the woman's tentative hope struggling to break through years of hardship and solitary struggle. She reached across the desk and clasped the woman's hand. They both gripped tightly.

"I read that you've been using the bus as transportation," Meg said.

"Yes."

"We're going to provide you with a car."

Fresh tears ran down the woman's cheeks. Relief, Meg knew. They all experienced such staggering relief when the foundation came alongside them and lifted the weight of their burdens.

"I read," Meg said, "that you'd like to take business courses to become an executive assistant."

"Yes. I . . . I believe I could be good at that."

"I believe it, too." Meg squeezed her hand. "As you know, we offer child care here so that you can work to earn income and also take courses toward a degree."

"Oh my. Oh my. Oh my. Thank the Lord!"

"Yes," Meg agreed. "Thank the Lord. We're going to get you and your family back on your feet. All right?"

"Thank you, ma'am. Oh, thank you."

"You're welcome. I know you're a believing lady, so you'll understand when I say that it's not me who's helping you. God's been good enough to let me take part in His work."

A knock sounded on the office door, and Bo looked in.

They'd been married for more than ten months. And still,

every time she saw him after they'd been apart, *every time*, her heart hitched in her chest with emotion.

"Sorry to interrupt," he said.

"Come on in. We were just finishing." They all stood, and Meg introduced him as her husband, then explained that he ran the Thoroughbred horse farm on the property. "We have an entire barn full of horses that are just for the use of the families who stay here. You're welcome to ride anytime."

"The boys would love it, but none of us know how."

"Doesn't matter a bit," Bo assured her. "We have instructors. We'll teach you."

The woman turned to Meg, arms outstretched, face streaked with moisture. Meg hugged her and both women continued to cry.

Bo took tissues out of his pocket and smiled affectionately at Meg as he handed them over. She took two, laughing and tearful at the same time, and gave one to their newest resident.

Lynn and Sadie Jo filled the doorway.

"These ladies are here," Meg said, "to show you where you'll be staying and answer all your questions."

"I can't wait to meet your boys!" Sadie Jo took hold of the woman's hand and patted it continuously. "How soon can you get them here so I can dote all over them?"

"They're an ornery bunch, ma'am. I'm still working on teaching them to mind."

"That won't stop me from adoring them," Sadie Jo answered. "Not at all, so don't you worry." The women left, Sadie Jo's chatter trailing behind.

Bo looked down at Meg. Eyes twinkling, he slowly lifted his hand. A key dangled from his index finger.

Meg gasped.

He grinned.

"The house?" she asked.

"They just finished it."

"You didn't take a look inside without me, did you?"

"'Course not."

"Then what are we waiting for?" She pulled him into the hallway. As they made their way outside, they passed two giggling eight-year-old girls who'd met when they'd both come to live at Whispering Creek and quickly become BFFs. "Hello, Mr. and Mrs. Porter."

"Hello, girls."

As they walked down the staircase, Meg could see Amber and Jayden in the backyard. Jayden kept trying to blow bubbles, and Amber kept taking the wand from him and demonstrating. From outside, Meg could hear the shriek of kids enjoying the pool.

When she'd come to Whispering Creek, both she and the house had been cold and empty. Not anymore. Now they both brimmed to overflowing with life.

Meg climbed into Bo's truck. As he drove them down the well-traveled new road to their building site, anticipation lifted within her. "I thought it was going to be another few days at least."

"They finished early."

"Since when does that happen with construction?"

"Never."

But then, miracles small and large happened to Meg these days. The biggest and most astounding was that she could love Bo the way that she did—head over heels, madly—and that he could love her back every bit as much. He kept trying to convince her that he loved her more, but she kept arguing that such a thing wasn't possible and violated the laws of physics.

They pulled up to the place where they'd once watched a sunset together and talked about the imaginary house they'd build to live in together. It wasn't imaginary anymore.

They got out and stood side by side to take it in, their arms laced around each other.

From this picturesque spot on a hill that overlooked a sweeping view of Texas land, they'd built a home for themselves out of stone and wooden beams and windows. The shutters and door shone with paint the color of coffee heavily doused with cream. Two chimneys reached for the sky. And Meg could see that Mr. Son had put in time here today, overseeing a crew of landscapers that had planted shrubs and small trees to border the front of the house and flowers to pour over the sides of the pots on the porch.

"What do you think?" Bo studied her, a thread of anxiousness in his expression. He wanted her to be happy, she knew.

"I love it. It looks like something from the pages of a picture book. It's quaint and charming and perfect."

"You'll be there. That's what makes it perfect for me."

She turned to face him, wrapping her hands around his neck. "We'll both be there. It's ours. Yours and mine."

His lids grew heavy as he looked at her.

"Our Texas fairy-tale house," she whispered.

"Our happy ending."

"Our happy beginning, you mean."

He chuckled and kissed her while their house looked on, ready and waiting for them to fill it with devoted love, years, and dreams.

"And we know that in all things
God works for the good of those who love him,
who have been called according to his purpose."

—Romans 8:28

Discussion Questions

1. While she's writing, Becky always boils the theme of her book down to a few words. In the case of *Undeniably Yours,* she got it down to two words. What do you think those two words might be?

2. All through the book we see God communicating to His people through other Christians. Has God ministered to you in this way? When? Have you been moved by Him to minister in this way to others?

3. Over the course of the book, what metaphors did Becky use for the changes happening within Meg? What metaphor did she use for Christ's sacrifice on the cross?

4. Which character in the book did you empathize with the most?

5. Meg's character was inspired by two Christian friends of Becky's who have endured divorce. Have any of you been through a divorce (either yourself, your parents, your child, your sibling)? Was it hard for you to claim God's grace through the situation?

6. If you fell in love with Bo right alongside Meg, why? What was it about him that stole your heart?

7. Which scenes made you laugh?

8. The importance of family is seen throughout this novel. How did family impact Bo and Meg, in both positive and negative ways? How has your own family influenced your decisions for good or bad?

9. According to some estimates, sociopaths account for as much as 3 percent of the male population. Do you think you've known any?

10. Did you guess ahead of time exactly what kind of trouble Stephen was planning to cause? If not, what did you think was going to happen?

11. In the end Meg decided to give up something valuable (controlling share in her father's company) in exchange for God's best for her. Becky likes to write about conflicts that are gray, instead of black or white. When has God asked you to give up something good for His best?

12. Which scenes in *Undeniably Yours* made you the most emotional? Why?

Becky Wade is a graduate of Baylor University. As a newlywed, she lived for three years in a home overlooking the turquoise waters of the Caribbean, as well as in Australia, before returning to the States. A mom of three young children, Becky and her family now live in Dallas, Texas. Visit *www.beckywade.com* to learn more about Becky, her writing, and a behind-the-scenes look at her novels.